HERMES UNVEILED

ROY NORVILL

Hermes Unveiled

ASHGROVE PRESS, BATH

First published in Great Britain by
ASHGROVE PRESS LIMITED
19 Circus Place, Bath, Avon BA1 2PW

First published 1986

British Library Cataloguing in Publication Data
Norvill, Roy
  Hermes unveiled.
  1. Bible – Gospel – Commentaries
  I. Title
  266'.06   BS2555.3

ISBN 0-906798-73-6 Pbk

Photoset in 10/11½pt Bembo
by Ann Buchan (Typesetters) Surrey
Printed and bound by Booksprint, Bristol

Contents

ACKNOWLEDGEMENTS

The author and publishers acknowledge with thanks permission to reproduce illustrations as follows:

Augustine Publishing Co for the First and Second Degree Tracing Boards of the Freemasons from *Darkness Visible* by Walton Hannah; C. W. Daniel Co for the Mutus Liber, Plate 1 from *Gold of a Thousand Mornings* by Armand Barbault; the Bibliotec Nacional, Rio de Janeiro for the page of text from the Relatorio; the Louvre for *Les Bergers d'Aracadie* by Poussin.

INTRODUCTION

At an undiscerned point in the past – estimates range from 30,000 to 100,000 years – the slow evolution of Man from his basic stages reached a critical phase and a significant step forward was taken. Homo Erectus acquired a larger brain case and became Homo Sapiens – Man of Wisdom.

The visible effects of that long ago change are now evident for all to ponder upon. Progressing from the humble beginning of a first creative cave drawing and the primitive bow and arrow, our inexorable technological advance has taken us through the invention of writing to world wide, electronic communication; to the Moon, and to the brink of annihilation here on Earth. Such are the outward, material results of the evolutionary shift – and if they constituted the sum total of progressive growth, the human race might be justified in questioning the true value of the change.

Thankfully, there is more. A shift of an infinitely more subtle nature took place all those years ago, an inward expansion of the mind that placed within reach the key to a higher evolutionary plane – a state beyond that at which most now exist.

Many centuries were to pass before the first few discovered that key, but when they did, it caused humanity to emerge into its present mode of existence as one or the other of two possible entities. The first lives and dies without ever suspecting that he is other than a human animal whose sole function is to survive until inevitable death overtakes him. The other – a minute fraction of every culture in every age – comes to realise that around him, unseen but intuitively perceived, are possibilities of a strange development giving access to a higher level of the universe at which the meaning and purpose of life is revealed, and at which the animal humanity is transcended once and for all.

Of this cognisant few, Nature has dictated that an even smaller percentage will actually turn the mental key in its lock and thereby achieve such a transition. Nevertheless, at regular intervals down through the centuries, the feat has been accomplished by an elite minority. Their efforts and experience has served to lay the foundations of a Science, the basic tenets of which are astoundingly simple, yet are presented to the world only in a heavily disguised manner.

The generic word by which this Science is known today is Hermeticism.

Traditionally elusive, the Hermetic Art proffers itself only in a multitude of ever changing guises, here deeply concealed in popular religious systems, there surviving as the basis of countless Orders and non-religious groups. It lies behind the caste system of the Hindu, and the Cult of Longevity in China's Taoism; it was presented as a superior order centred about the Mysteries of ancient Egypt, and as Alchemy in Arabia and Greece. More recently, in a Europe of the Middle Ages, it has been seen as the vague corpus round which the names Rosicrucian, Cathar and Templar have circulated.

For thousands of years, the prospectus for enrolement which it presents in every age has never been offered in plain language. Yet, despite this inherent secrecy, the first step across the Hermetic threshold requires nothing more than that the novice has come to suspect its existence.

As Hermeticism has played a major role in human history, there have been excellent reasons in the past for maintaining the strictest anonymity. But this was applicable to people and times which fell short of a particular level of evolution. That level has now been reached, and for the first time, it is both possible and permissible to reveal the method by which the knowledge was encoded and the inner meaning of the symbolism so extensively employed.

This book presents a complete exposition of the Hermetic Code, offering what to many may be seen as a revelation.

In recent years, one Hermetic Operation has been partly brought to light by a former BBC producer named Henry Lincoln. Intrigued by a strange legend and even stranger facts, he began to explore the astonishing consequences of some documents found in a little French church at Rennes le Chateau. His co-authored work, THE HOLY BLOOD AND THE HOLY GRAIL, a recent best-selling volume, gives a comprehensive analysis of both fact and legend. And yet, although his dogged and painstaking research uncovered a most incredible labyrinth of clues, his work remains, in the end, speculative and inconclusive. The true key to the mystery has eluded him.

In truth, Rennes le Chateau is an excellent example of the way in which Hermeticism can survive undetected, even when exposed to intense public scrutiny, and therefore we begin with the story Henry Lincoln has told so well. But by the end of the present work, Rennes le Chateau will be a mystery no longer – and the reader will be in a position to decode for himself even greater secrets.

And he said unto them Unto you it is given to know the mystery of the kingdom of God: but unto them that are without, all these things are done in parables. That seeing they may see, and not perceive; and hearing they may hear, and not understand; lest at any time they should be *converted,* and their sins should be forgiven them.

Mark 4; 11–12.

CHAPTER ONE

The Enigma of Rennes Le Chateau

The tiny village of Rennes le Chateau is perched precariously on one of the many rocky eminences which dot the countryside of southern Languedoc, in south eastern France. Its few weathered houses, served by a solitary steep street, command a view across a plateau that is wild and desolate, a scene of primitive beauty broken only by a small number of modest-sized vineyards. A little way to the north lies the town of Couiza, at the confluence of the rivers Aude and Sals, and if a traveller were to continue in this direction, tracing the course of the Aude for some thirty kilometres, he would arrive at the city of Carcassonne.

To the south, from Rennes le Chateau, the country becomes ever more rough and deserted as it rises steadily towards the great mass of the Pyrenees and the Spanish border. Even today, it remains a ruggedly beautiful but isolated region, and it must have been more so in 1885, when the bishop of Carcassonne had occasion to appoint a new priest to take charge of Rennes le Chateau's somewhat dilapidated centre of worship, the church of Sainte-Madelaine.

Francois-Berenger Sauniere, at the age of thirty-three, was a man of humble upbringing, with no foreseeable future other than his chosen vocation with the Church, and when he arrived at Rennes le Chateau, he had no reason to suppose that his existence there would be any more than frugal and obscure. He settled in and – as was the custom among the priesthood of his day – engaged a local girl, Marie Denarnaud, to reside with him and take care of the household chores.

Some five or six years after his appointment, Sauniere was gratified to discover that a predecessor had bequeathed a small legacy towards the upkeep of the church, and in 1892, drew on the money to carry out some badly needed restoration of the altar. The existing structure was considerably old, being little more than a solid stone slab, one end of which was cemented directly into the wall, while the other was supported on a single, carved stone column that had survived from the time of the Visigoths. In the course of the work, the altar slab was moved and the column was found to be hollow.

It contained three wooden cylinders, each tightly sealed with wax.

To those around him at the time, the priest's subsequent actions must have presented a profound and inexplicable mystery. The cylinders were found to contain four parchments written in archaic style and to which Sauniere devoted a considerable amount of time in study, the restoration work seemingly forgotten. Suddenly, early in 1893, he made a hurried journey to Carcassonne to see his bishop, Monseigneur Felix-Arsene Billard, and although there is no record of their conversation, it is known that Sauniere was provided with the necessary funds to travel to Paris.

During the three weeks that he remained in the capital, he placed the documents in the hands of the Abbé Bieil, the director of Saint-Sulpice, for examination by palaeographic experts. Sauniere himself spent much of his time in the Louvre, where he purchased reproductions of three paintings. But the most surprising aspect of the visit was that the penniless parish priest met and became firm friends with the beautiful Emma Calve, an operatic soprano then at the height of her career. It was a friendship that was to endure, for she later came to Rennes le Chateau on regular occasions that ended only when she married the tenor, Gasbarri, in 1914.

On his return from Paris, Sauniere engaged some young men from the village to help him move a second stone, this time a large slab set in the floor directly in front of the altar. When lifted, the underside was found to be carved into a pair of symbolic pictures of extremely ancient date. According to the testimony of one of the helpers, who was still alive in 1962, they dug down several feet, but at the very moment when they seemed to encounter something, the priest immediately halted the work, sent them home, and locked himself in the church alone.

Although a rumour persists that two skeletons were uncovered, along with a pot containing some bright objects which Sauniere dismissed as worthless medallions, the only certain fact is that a later excavation in the same spot brought to light a human skull with a ritual slot cut in the cranium. Whatever the truth, all restoration work ceased. Instead the priest took to wandering about the countryside with a sack on his back, accompanied only by his housekeeper, Marie. He returned each evening, the sack filled with stones, his explanation being that he had decided to build a stone grotto in the tiny garden in front of the church. And indeed, the remains of it can be seen today, although it has been virtually decimated by the hordes of souvenir hunters who thought it might hold a clue to the real reason for Sauniere's activities.

While controversy was averted by the priest's explanation for his daily forays, the activity in which he engaged at night gave rise to scandalised gossip. He set to work in the cemetery of the church and carefully transferred two memorial gravestones from one end to the other and then slowly chipped away at the stones until their inscriptions had been permanently erased.

For the next two years, he spent much of his time away from Rennes le Chateau. It has since been discovered that he travelled considerably, opening three bank accounts, one in each of the neighbouring cities of Perpignan and Toulouse, and a third in Paris. Recently, a fourth has been traced, as far away as Budapest. Throughout this period, Marie remained in the village to receive money orders from Germany, Switzerland, Spain and France – some apparently sent by religious communities.

In 1894, Sauniere ceased his wanderings and instead, devoted his time to a major refurbishment of Sainte-Madelaine – and the outcome of this is, perhaps, the most astounding of all.

Into the junction of the nave and the transept, a checkerboard floor was laid, of alternate black and white, square tiles, while at the entrance door, stood a garish, demonaical figure, the 'devil' of Persian and Hebrew tradition, Asmodeus, bearing on its head a holy water stoup. Above the figure, rose four winged angels, accompanied by the ancient Templar motto; 'in this sign shalt thou conquer'. A series of reliefs decorated the interior walls, unconventional interpretations of the Stations of the Cross, and above the confessional, a similarly unusual representation of Christ on the Mount. Sauniere himself painted one panel of the altar, a scene showing Mary Magdalene kneeling in a grotto, in front of her a skull, an open book, and a crude cross made out of an acacia bush. An addition to the church porch became a talking point, for directly over the centre of the arch were carved the words uttered by Jacob upon waking from his dream of the Ladder; 'how dreadful is this place'.

The priest's inexplicable activity was far from complete, however, for he next turned his attention to the church exterior. Purchasing land adjoining it on the western side, he built a semi-circular promenade which terminated at the southern end in a two storied tower called the Tour Magdala. Within the curve of the raised walk, he created a garden, and at the eastern end, separated from the church by a small courtyard, he erected a guest house which he named Bethania. When it was completed, he moved in, furnishing it with valuable antiques and equipping its larder with ample stocks of the finest wines and the richest food with which to entertain his many guests. Here, the once impoverished Sauniere lived extravagantly,

paying for everything out of his own pocket, until his death in
January 1917.

Afterwards, it was calculated that he had spent well over a million
francs d'or, a currency worth twenty times the value of the present
day franc. Marie Denarnaud lived on until 1953, but she wanted for
nothing – and to give some idea of her personal wealth, a letter
written by her in 1920 estimates it at 100,000 francs.

The Search for the Treasure

Later investigators leapt quite naturally to the conclusion that
Sauniere had stumbled on the key to a lost hoard of gold, and it must
be admitted that certain finds tend to support the idea. Recently, a
slab of gold made from a fused mass of antique coins was found near
Rennes, and in 1928, the remains of a large, gold statue was discovered in the ruins of a hut on the edge of a stream that flows below
the village. It had been mostly melted away, but the idol's feet were
clearly distinguishable.

It has been suggested that Saunier's two years of travel were
conducted in order to sell a small quantity of the hoard in each
locality, thereby avoiding the mistake of attracting too much attention – and the possibility must be conceded. But we must not forget
that upon the discovery of the parchments, the priest's first action
was to take them to his bishop in Carcassonne, who then provided
the money to send him on to Paris, where the authorities saw the
documents for themselves. It must be concluded that the Church
was fully aware of the nature of the discovery. Why, therefore, was
Sauniere allowed to behave in the spendthrift fashion that he subsequently did – and even more pertinent, why was he allowed to
make such controversial alterations to the church of Sainte-
Madelaine?.

The mystery deepened as further facts gradually came to light. Of
the four parchments, only two have been photographed and published. At first glance, they appear to be merely transcriptions of
passages selected from the New Testament, penned in a form of
archaic Latin. The first describes Jesus's visit to the house of Lazarus,
at Bethany. The second is the parable of the disciples plucking ears of
corn on the sabbath, but it has been constructed from three different
texts, those of Matt (12; 1 to 8), Mark (2; 23 to 28) and Luke (6; 1 to
5). The remaining two parchments have not come to the public eye
and do not seem likely to do so.

On careful examination, the two texts reveal some unexpected features, such as additional words as if in error; dots placed above certain letters; and enigmatic monograms. It did not take long to realise that the texts were ciphered.

When French writer and researcher, Gerard de Sede – determined to get to the bottom of the mystery – procured a copy of one of the parchments and submitted it to modern crypto-analysis, the experts were astonished at the complexity of the cipher. To uncover the deeply buried message, it was necessary to apply the standard technique known as the Vigenere system, but with additional, highly complicated variations. The final step required was the most extraordinary of all, for the meaningless jumble of letters had to be laid out on a chessboard. Then, having selected the correct starting point the experts made the only sequence of Knight moves that would cover the entire board, touching each square only once. In this bizarre manner the message at last emerged – and the most amazing confirmation of its validity was that it was a perfect anagram of the headstone text which provided the key phrases. The English translation reads:

SHEPHERDESS NO TEMPTATION FOR POUSSIN TENIERS HOLD THE KEY PAX DCLXXXI BY THE CROSS AND THIS HORSE OF GOD I REACH THIS DAEMON GUARDIAN AT MIDDAY BLUE APPLES.

To date, no one has been able to provide an interpretation of this enigmatic text. True, it holds certain apparent clues, but these have served only to make the mystery more obscure. It has been ascertained that the three paintings, of which Sauniere was so anxious to obtain copies while in Paris, were 'The Arcadian Shepherds', by Nicolas Poussin; 'The Temptation of St. Anthony', by Teniers; and a portrait of pope Celestine V by an unknown artist. In the first two, we can see a definite link with the first line of the message – but what 'key' is it that Poussin and Teniers hold?

Teniers' picture depicts a cave-like room with St Anthony shown kneeling before a rough stone altar on which rests a human skull. The saint is trying desperately to read a book which he is holding in front of him, but his attention is constantly diverted by the imps and goblins, bats and snakes which infest the room. It is a scene which could hardly be considered an easy guide to a buried hoard.

As for Poussin, there are two versions of his 'Shepherds of Arcadia', the first painted in 1629, and a second, slightly more elaborate canvas, thought to have been completed in the mid 1650's. It is the latter that so captured Sauniere's interest. Three shepherds and a shepherdess are shown in a craggy but beautiful setting. They are examining a strange, square-shaped tomb, and one of the men kneels to trace a finger over the Latin inscription carved on the front. It reads: 'Et in Arcadia Ego'.

Investigators who hoped to find some clue to the vast treasure reputed to have been located by Sauniere must have experienced a thrill of anticipation when they discovered that, less than ten kilometres from Rennes le Chateau, on a rocky mount beside the road, there exists a stone tomb identical to that in Poussin's canvas. The surrounding countryside bears more than a little comparison to the craggy grandeur of the artist's setting, featuring almost identical skyline prominences. But the real tomb, although its shape is unmistakable, has been covered with a thin layer of cement so that any inscription that might have been visible is now well and truly concealed. Obviously, Sauniere had gone to some lengths to ensure that no other would uncover the secret.

And yet fate decreed his nocturnal intrigues to be in vain, especially with regard to the defacement of the two gravestones. Unknown to the priest, antiquarians had visited Rennes le Chateau long before his appointment there and faithfully copied out the inscriptions that he later erased. Library researchers were delighted to discover these records, one in an antiquarians' journal, the other in a rare book devoted to grave markings.

It was found that both stones were once mounted over the grave of Marie de Negre d'Ables, the wife of Francis d'Hautpoul de Blanchefort, seigneur of Rennes in the late 1700's. The headstone, which has been lost since Sauniere's time, boasts an inscription which is notable for its errors, even for a period when monumental masons were notorious for their carelessness (see fig.1).

In the first line, the words 'here lies' have been written with a T instead of an I, while the last letter of 'noble' has been cut as a small round 'e'. Examinaton of the whole text will reveal similar errors, showing that eight letters have been given the same curious emphasis: four large, and four small. Of the large ones, T, M, R, O, only one word can be formed: MORT, meaning 'death'. The smaller letters can be put together in the same way to make e, p, e, e, 'epee', a sword.

'Mort Epee' was the first key phrase required to unlock the parchment cipher.

The second stone, which originally lay horizonatally along the length of the grave, can still be seen today as a cover for an ossuary in the north-west corner of the cemetery, and now shows nothing but a blank face. But previously, as the records plainly show, the phrase 'Et in Arcadia Ego' was carved in two lines down each side. The left

FIGURE 1.
The headstone on the grave of Marie de Negre d'Ables d'Hautpoul de Blanchefort.

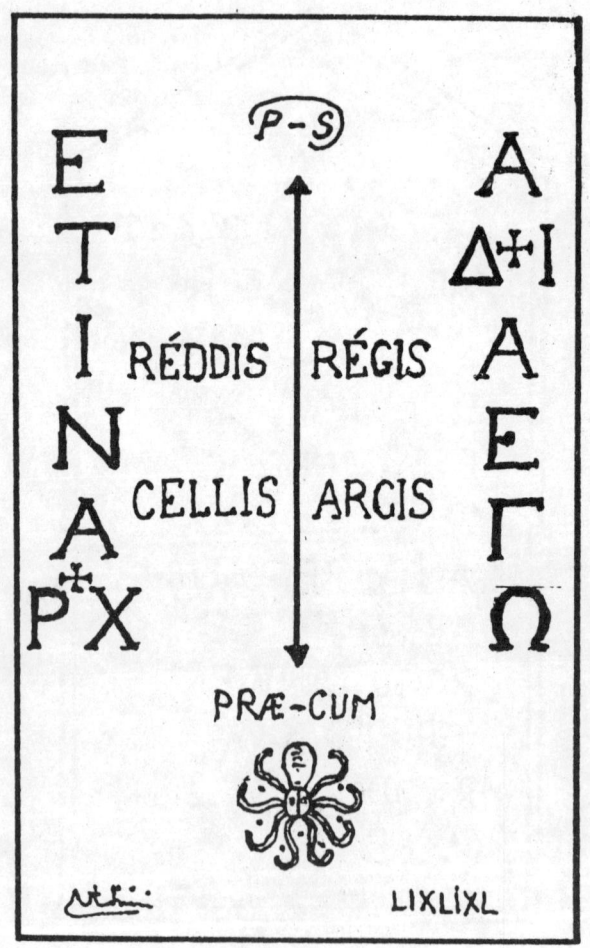

FIGURE 2.
The strangely carved stone which lay horizontally along the length
of Marie de Blanchefort's grave

hand line appears to be bad Latin, the right hand, Greek, but the phrase is unmistakable. And it proved to be the second key phrase necessary to decipher the texts (see fig.2).

If nothing else, the importance of this phrase as part of the parchment cipher implies that Poussin was in some way connected with Sauniere's secret. Art historians have always assumed the tomb and the landscape of the picture to be entirely imaginary, but if the painted scene is compared with the real location, the match is almost precise. Accurately reproduced in the centre of the horizon is the hill on top of which rest the ruins of the Chateau de Blanchefort, while on the right of the picture's skyline, there is a small rocky eminence. It is the hill of Rennes le Chateau. And as for the tomb, even the small round stone on which one shepherd rests a foot, actually exists.

Poussin and Teniers

Nicolas Poussin spent most of his life in Rome after arriving there at the age of thirty, in 1624. There are one or two significant facts about him which link with Rennes le Chateau in a less direct way than his 'Shepherds of Arcadia', but which nevertheless hold a certain importance. The first is that he often referred to the writings of Blaise de Vigenere, one of the foremost innovators of the cipher system, in order to find inspiration for his works – and the motifs that resulted from this consultation were blatantly alchemical. A second item of significance is to be found in the form of a letter received by Nicolas Fouquet, superintendent of Finance at the court of Louis XIV. It was written by the minister's younger brother, Louis, who had been urged to make contact with Poussin while on a visit to Rome. Louis did so, and shortly afterwards informed his brother of the outcome. The letter is in a rough, ungrammatical form, but here is a modern translation:

I delivered to Monsier Poussin the letter that you did him the honour to write, and he expressed his utmost joy. You would not believe, Monsier, either the pains that he takes in our service, the affection with which he carries them out, nor the worth and integrity that he brings to all things. He and I discussed a certain matter, which I shall easily be able to explain to you; something which, through Monsieur Poussin, will bring you tremendous advantages, and which even kings would have difficulty in drawing from him. According to him, this matter is such that no one in the world will uncover it, perhaps for centuries to come –

and yet it could be done without expense, and possibly great profit. Nothing on this earth could prove a better fortune, nor be its equal . . .

Finally, we may note that Poussin thought so highly of his second 'Shepherds of Arcadia' that he ordered a relief of it to be mounted over his tomb in Rome.

Convinced that Poussin was the key to the Rennes le Chateau enigma, researcher Henry Lincoln concentrated his attention on the canvas in question. Aware of the tricks of the art profession, he journeyed to the Louvre and requested that the original painting be X-rayed in the hope of discovering alterations that might be hiding a clue. The results were at first disappointing, for no underlying differences could be detected, but the investigation reaped benefits in an unexpected manner. It would have been presumed that the artist would build up his picture from the background to the foreground, painting first the landscape and then adding the figures. But the X-rays disclosed that Poussin deviated from the normal method. The line of a shepherd's staff was seen to be cut off by the line at the top of the tomb, a sure indication that the staff had been painted first – a fact which evoked some surprise from the experts. From this small clue, Lincoln subsequently discovered a vital detail contained within the canvas, for an analysis by Professor Cornford of the Royal College of Art showed that the painting had been constructed over the geometric figure of a pentagon. This revelation was surprising, for the system had been discarded centuries before Poussin's time, and there seemed little outward reason for him to revert to it. Even more remarkable was the fact that the pentagon was not contained within the canvas area, but governed its form from without, and this could only have been achieved by Poussin calculating a precise ratio of height to width of his canvas. But for what reason?

Unable to answer this question, Henry Lincoln considered the earlier version of the 'Arcadian Shepherds'. The original painting is part of a collection owned by the Duke of Devonshire, and which is held at Chatsworth House, Derbyshire. But Lincoln found a copy in the stately home of Shugborough Hall, in Staffordshire – and it was here that he unearthed a totally unexpected link with Rennes le Chateau. In the grounds, close by the banks of the river Sow, stands what is known as the Shepherd's Monument. No one seems to be able to explain its purpose, and indeed the edifice appears to be merely an over-decorative showcase for the classical relief placed in the central position.

History tells us that it might have been erected on the instructions of Thomas Anson, the elder brother of the famous, eighteenth century seaman, Admiral George Anson. Thomas succeeded to Shugborough Hall in 1720, and together with brother George, undertook a number of improvements to the house and grounds, at which time the monument presumably came into existence. However, the first documented reference to it does not occur until 1758.

It takes its name from the centrepiece, a fascimile of a marble relief by Peter Scheermaker – which happens to be the scene of the Arcadian Shepherds. The relief is mounted beneath a curved arch set between two pillars, a fact which has a significance that will be appreciated later on, but the noticable difference in the picture is that it is a complete mirror image of the original.

Immediately below the relief, a small plaque shows something that is instantly reminiscent of the Rennes le Chateau cipher, a series of letters which has never been satisfactorily explained.

O U O S V A V V
D   M

In the course of his research at Shugborough Hall, undertaken in the mid 'seventies, Henry Lincoln reported one other promising link with the French cipher. Apart from a copy of Poussin's early version of the 'Shepherds of Arcadia', he also came across a work by the Dutch artist, Teniers, depicting St Anthony and St Jerome. Those seeking the answer to the lines of the cipher had always concluded that it referred to the many versions by Teniers of the 'Temptation of St Anthony'. Yet the message reads 'no temptation'. Lincoln realised that he was staring at the only Teniers painting of the St Anthony theme in which the saint is not being tempted. And included in the picture is a shepherdess, just as there is in the Poussin canvas. Thus, he felt, he may have arrived at the inner meaning of the first segment of the cryptic message. If we insert the necessary punctuation, the meaning does become more clear:

SHEPHERDESS. NO TEMPTATION. POUSSIN AND TENIERS HOLD THE KEY.

Apparently something in the work of both artists will yield the answer to the Sauniere riddle: and as the first word of the ciphered message refers to the 'shepherdess', we must re-examine this particular element.

Professor Cornford, in his analysis of 'The Arcadian Shepherds', discovered that the exact centre of the pentagon on which the painting was built was occupied by the head of the shepherdess, and in searching for some significance to this, we must recall that the shape of the pentagon is also the centre of a much larger figure, the pentacle, or five pointed star. By simply adding five triangles of the correct shape, one to each face of the pentagon, a pentacle will result – and there are some references to the pentacle in the Rennes le Chateau parchments.

The Pentacle

The figure is constructed of overlapping triangles, the sides of which are 72 degrees by 72 degrees by 36 degrees – and in relation to this, astute observers have noticed that a similar angle presented itself in the layout of the Rennes le Chateau countryside. From Rennes le Chateau, two ancient Templar castles are visible. To the north east, lie the crumbling ruins of the Chateau de Blanchefort, while south east, barely four miles distant, stand the remains of the Chateau des Templiers. And the angle between the two bearings is exactly 36 degrees.

Following this unmistakable line of investigation, a pentacle was traced out on a map of the area, allowing the two remaining points of the figure to be determined. One, they found, was marked by a hill surmounted by two massive menhirs. The fifth point lacks any man-made mark, but there is a natural outcropping of white, convuluted rock, a landmark that is clearly visible from Rennes le Chateau (see fig. 3).

As the pentacle of Poussin's canvas has a centre conspicuously marked, so the larger figure has a centre – and it was here that yet another, even more exciting find was made. At this spot, there is a mound – small but nevertheless easily visible to an observer at Rennes le Chateau – which is known as the mount of Coume-Sourde. Here, in 1928, searchers unearthed another engraved stone tablet similar to the gravestones of Marie de Blanchefort (see fig. 4). At last, it seemed, a reliable guide to the discovery made by the spendthrift priest had been found, for the crude Latin inscription reads:

In the middle of the line where M cuts the lesser line.

The geometric figure is unmistakably an incomplete section of a pentacle, and thus it appeared to indicate a location connected with the five giant points laid out over the Rennes area. The Latin text suggests that the 'lesser line' may be the one drawn between the two points – and indeed, although the main text is in Latin, the 'sis' on the

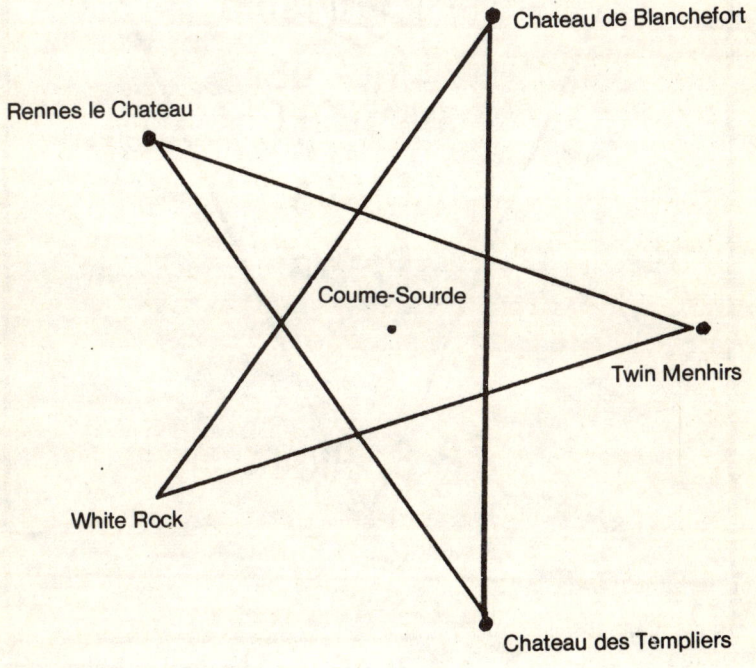

FIGURE 3.

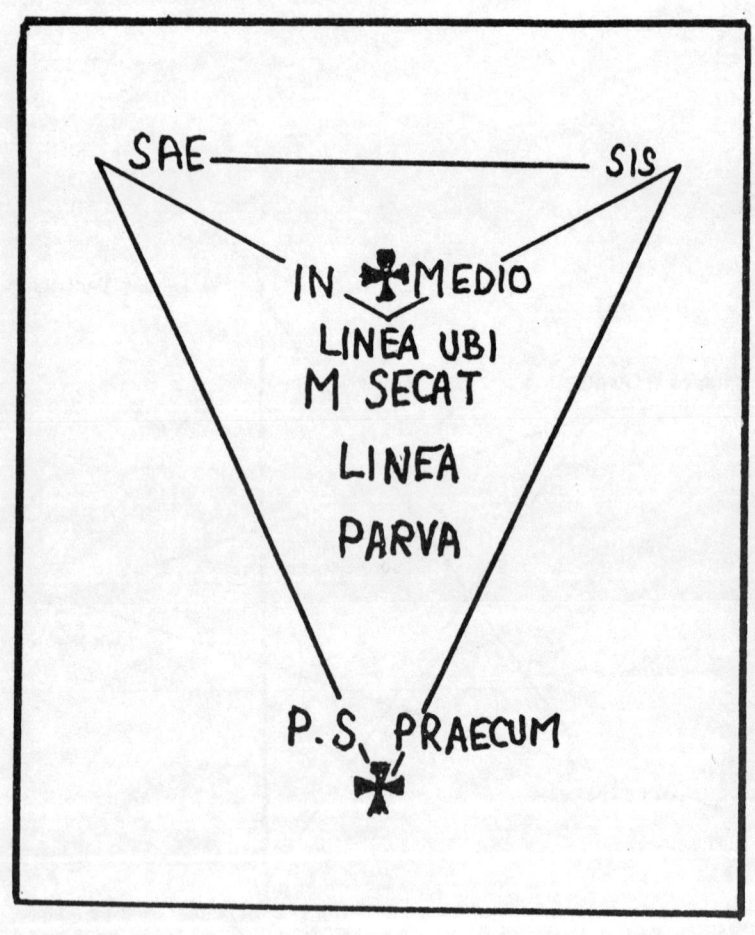

FIGURE 4.

right hand point is French for 'situated', while 'sae' is an ancient form of 'so', giving the complete statement:

So situated in the middle of the line where M cuts the lesser line.

The treasure hunters carefully picked their way over the terrain between every point of the great pentacle, finding four of the routes to be most difficult. Apart from the fact that the uneven contours of the countryside make it impossible to keep the bearing points in view, the thick undergrowth and craggy hills are at times virtually impassable. Only in one instance did they find a direct line of sight, and that from Rennes le Chateau southward to the great white rock, the one point that is marked by a natural feature of the landscape. On this line, exactly equidistant between the points, there exists a narrow slit in the ground, a cavern mouth in the rock which once gave ingress to a subterranean tunnel system.

To verify this, it is only necessary to superimpose the geometric figure on the carved slab over that of the great pentacle, and it will be found that the bottom point, marked with a Templar cross, indicates the hill on which stand the two menhirs. This hill lies just beyond a known landmark, a spring called La Source de la Madelaine. Thus, if the line is drawn from this point, passing through the centre of the pentacle and onwards until it cuts the imaginary line between Rennes le Chateau and the white rock, it will unerringly arrive at the mouth of the cave. Here, then, is where M cuts the lesser line (see fig. 5).

Today, it is not possible to penetrate very far into the cave for a deep layer of sand has raised the original floor level and progress is further barred by rock, either fallen, or deliberately placed in order to discourage too thorough an investigation. What Sauniere may have found must be left to conjecture at this point, but it is well to mention a legend attached to the area about a young shepherd boy named Ignace Paris. In 1645, so it is rumoured, he wandered into the ravine in search of strays and discovered the cave. On entering, he found some skeletons and many gold pieces, some of which he hastily stuffed into his pocket. When he returned to Rennes and excitedly began to display his new found wealth, the villagers would not believe his story. Accusing him of theft, they stoned him to death.

On a slightly firmer foundation, we find that historical records hint at the presence of precious metal within the great pentacle. In the 12th century, the Chateau de Blanchefort was the castle home of Bertrand de Blanchefort, Grand Master of the Knights Templar, and it is known that he imported labourers from Germany to dig gold from his mines. Certainly the area is rich in minerals: copper, lead,

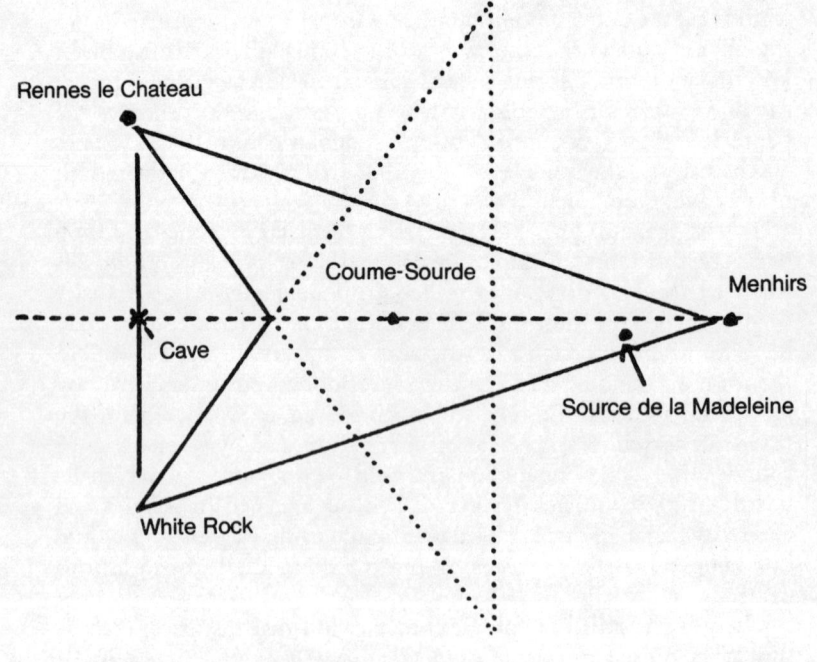

FIGURE 5.

silver and gold having been mined there since Roman times, but local tradition emphasises a different aspect of the story. According to the report of Cesare d'Arcone, an engineer who was sent to assess the region's mines in the 17th century, de Blanchefort's Germans were not miners, but goldsmiths. The same rumour is echoed in a letter dated 1880, by a local historian named Louis Fedie, when he wrote;

> The people of the Middle Ages believed that the precious metals extracted from the Blanchefort mine came, not from a vein in the rock, but from a store of gold and silver ingots, buried in the dungeons of the fortress by its first masters, the Visigothic kings.

This historic finger, pointed in the direction of the Visigoths, presented researchers with a fascinating possibility.

The Visigoths and the Templars

When the Romans sacked Jerusalem in 70 A.D., they removed many sacred objects from the great Temple and transported them to Rome, an event clearly depicted by the carved relief on the arch of Titus Flavius, in Rome. Legend has it that this collection of Jewish treasure was immense, but its ultimate fate is the subject of several conflicting stories, the first and the least believable being that Maxentius took it with him when he fled from Constantine in 312 A.D. As he crossed the Milvian bridge, it fell into the Tiber and was lost.

A second report describes Alaric the Visigoth carrying it off as booty when he sacked Rome in 410 A.D., while a third – this time attached to Gaiseric the Vandal who attacked the city in 455 A.D. – has the treasure transported to North Africa. It remained there for a century, until the Byzantine general, Belisarius recovered it and moved it to Constantinople. A short time thereafter, the emperor Justinian restored it to Jerusalem, where it was placed in a Christian shrine. But in 615 A.D., the Holy City was ravaged by the Persians, and since that time nothing more has been heard of the treasure.

Of all these stories, the most promising in conjunction with Rennes le Chateau, is that of Alaric the Visigoth. He died soon after his triumph over Rome, but was succeeded by Ataulphus, who led the Visigoths to settle in France and Spain. That they were possessors of considerable wealth is a well known historical fact, a large portion of it being known as the Old Treasure, consisting of booty pillaged during their war-like forays. In the seventh century, this was lodged at Carcassonne, having survived threat of capture by Clovis, king of the Franks, in 507 A.D. But continual harrassment impelled the Visigoths to remove the major part of their hoard to Toledo, their Spanish headquarters. It was an unfortunate decision, for in 711 A.D., the Moors overcame the city and seized most of the treasure. Those items which the Visigoths managed hastily to conceal, lay undiscovered until the nineteenth century, when they were unearthed at Guarrazar, not far from Toledo.

This much is known from the historical documents of those concerned, and it does leave the possibility that not all of the Visigothic hoard was removed from the Carcassonne area, but was dispersed among local hiding places, out of reach of the Franks.

An equally promising line of enquiry lies in the fact that Rennes le Chateau is Templar country. The Knights Templars were formed in 1120, under the leadership of Hugues de Paynes, inaugurating their first lodge in Jerusalem, which had been captured by the Crusaders a little more than a century before. Their subsequent history is well charted – a steady rise in strength and wealth until they became the most influential organisation in Europe. Fearing them to be a threat to their own supremacy, the Church engineered accusations of heresy against the Order, and with the reluctant aid of Philip IV of France, managed to have the Templars forcibly suppressed in 1307. At their height, the Templars governed large estates, with an established chain of treasure houses, and although their suppression was violent, the leaders being subject to torture and burning, much of the wealth escaped falling into the hands of their persecutors, remaining stored in secret vaults all over Europe.

There are a number of Templar fortresses in the Rennes le Chateau area, and for reasons which I will later clarify, it can be said with certainty that the elaborate and enigmatic clues to the Rennes treasure are partly of Templar origin. Thus, if Sauniere did unearth such a cache as investigators believe, there is every likelihood of it being a residue of Templar wealth.

Many have committed themselves to the idea of a Visigothic or Templar cache, with the result that the Rennes area has become overrun with determined hunters, armed with shovels, metal detectors – and even dynamite. But there is far more to the Rennes mystery than meets the eye. It is necessary to scrutinise the actions of Sauniere after he became blessed with such unexpected and by no means modest affluence. His refurbishment of the little church took a form that has since raised many an ecclesiastical eyebrow, especially in view of the figure of the Devil just inside the entrance. The interpretation of certain biblical themes is irreverent, and indeed, Sauniere appears to be quietly laughing to himself, as in the representation of Christ on the Mount. This large, wood and plaster relief shows a steep, flower-dotted little mount upon which Jesus stands to deliver his sermon to an adoring congregation. But the background landscape shows a great similarity to the countryside round Rennes – and dominating the immediate foreground is an object that is not mentioned in the Scriptures. It is a golden sack, its neck tied with rope.

Whatever construction may be placed on this, investigators have drawn attention to an obvious allusion to a local family line within the scene. The area of the mount directly in front of Jesus has been left conspicuously clear except for a number of flowers – 'fleurie' in French, a word that is phonetically similar to the name Fleury. The Marquis Paul-Francois-Vincent de Fleury de Blanchefort was the son-in-law of Marie de Negre d'Ables and Francis d'Hautpoul de Blanchefort.

Strange Clues

The Fleury name leads directly to a mystery surrounding the inherit-ance of the family Hautpoul. In 1644, Francois-Pierre d'Hautpoul, baron of Rennes, made his will and attached it to documents which laid claim to the family's title for over 600 years. But the documents vanished, remaining lost for 130 years before they were discovered among papers in an office of a local notary. The inheritor of 1774, Pierre d'Hautpoul, immediately asked to see them, but received a reply saying:

> . . . it would not be prudent on my part to make a will of such importance public . . .

Before any further action could be taken, the documents disappeared again. According to researcher Gerard de Sede, they were entrusted to the Abbé Bigou who, at the death of Marie, passed them to her unmarried daughter, Elizabeth. Throughout her life, Elizabeth refused to disclose their contents, claiming that it was

> necessary to decipher and determine what comprised the title of the family, and what did not.

The Blanchefort title, surprisingly enough, descended not to the elder sister of Marie, who was the wife of cousin Hautpoul-Felines, but to the youngest, Gabrielle, and through her to her husband, Paul de Fleury. And here we encounter a further minor mystery. There are two gravestones to mark the passing of Paul de Fleury, both in the little cemetery of Rennes le Chateau. One reads:

> Here lies Paul Urbain de Fleury
> Born 3 May 1776
> Here lies Paul Urbain de Fleury
> Died 7 August 1836

The other has a radically different text:

> He passed away doing good
> The transferred remains of
> Paul Urbain comte de Fleury
> Died 7 August 1856 aged 60 years

Quite apart from the confusion of dates, Paul Urbain was in fact born neither in 1776, or 1796, but in 1778. Thus it takes no feat of deduction to recognise that something important is contained within these deliberate errors and that it is connected with the Fleury estate.

The slab which covered the resting place of Marie holds even more conspicuous pointers (see fig. 2). The central phrase, 'Reddis Regis Cellis Arcis', is in crude Latin and so translation must be loose, but taking each word separately, we have the following:

> *Reddis* 'of Rennes', or of 'Rhedae' (Rhedae was the Visigothic name
>   Rennes).
> *Regis:* 'of the King'
> *Cellis:* 'in a concealed place, or shrine'.
> *Arcis:* 'enclosed', or 'in safe keeping'.

The King in question, indicated by the word 'Regis', may be the one mentioned in the first parchment cipher. Decoded, it reads:

> This treasure belongs to Dagobert II, King, and to Zion, and he is here dead.

Dagobert was one of the last kings of the Merovingian Dynasty of France and was assassinated in 679 A.D., but oddly enough, the message holds a religious reference in the word 'Zion', which is Jerusalem. It is this connection that led researchers to believe that the treasure was the famed Treasure of Jerusalem – or at least, part of it.

At the bottom centre of Marie's gravestone are carved the words 'prae-cum', beneath which is the unmistakable motif of a spider. 'Prae-cum' can be translated as 'with emphasis', and so could be considered as a device with which to warn observers that the inscriptions which accompany it should not be read at face value alone. The same phrase appears on the carved slab found at Coume-Sourde.

The spider holds a double meaning, the most obvious being appreciable by the use of phonetic equivalents. The French for spider is '*araignée*', which in the local dialect is pronounced 'arenn'. Thus, it sounds almost exactly the same as '*à Rennes*', meaning 'of,' or 'at Rennes.' The second meaning of the spider emblem requires a great deal of explanation and will be dealt with in due course, but some small hint of its importance may be given by drawing attention to a painting of the Descent from the Cross, to be seen in the church of Rennes les Bains, a small village close to the Chateau de Blanchefort. It was presented to the church by the old Marquis, Paul-Francois-Vincent de Fleury, and shows the crown of thorns upon the head of Jesus stylised as a gigantic spider. Sauniere, it appears, was not the only one to take unusual liberties with biblical themes.

In fact, we cannot help but notice that although this is supposed to be the history of a hidden cache of wealth, there exists an underlying religious tone – or rather, a parody of religion. Add to this the persistent rumour that Sauniere, on his death bed, made a confession that profoundly shocked the priest who heard it, and we must wonder if Sauniere had become a heretic – and if so, why?

The question is worthy of investigation, if only to find out what prompted him to place the statue of the Devil in such a prominent position. And here, the parchment texts provide a clue. As on the headstone of Marie, certain letters may be picked out by reason of their difference in size, and they spell out 'Rex Mundi', meaning 'king of the earth', an epithet generally applied to the Devil

The Cathars

Rex Mundi is an entity that stems from the religious system of the Cathars, or the Albigensians, as they are alternatively called, a 12th century sect who followed the ancient beliefs of Dualism. This pagan religion was prominent in Persia in the 3rd century, due to the teachings of the reformer, Mani. After five hundred years, it spread to northern Italy, and then slowly up into western Europe until it was suppressed in the 13th century. Cathars believed that there were two gods to rule over all, and that all physical matter was the work of one, Rex Mundi, the god of evil. Only the soul, the spiritual part of Man, was able to associate with God, the god of good. But God was not the omnipotent creator that other religions claimed him to be, for he was incapable of creating physical matter. This concept logically led to the idea that Christ, as the son of God, could never have been a physical person, and therefore could not have been crucified in the way related in the Gospels. So the Cathars accepted Christ as the son of Mary, but rejected his crucifixion.

A careful examination of historic documents tends to indicate a hidden knowledge within this sytem, for the Cathars were divided into believers and initiates. The latter taught that only by living a life of purity could a believer achieve one-ness with God and so progress to the status of an initiate. Hence the name 'Cathar', from the Greek for 'purified'.

The Catholic Church looked upon these beliefs as dangerous heresies and was the force behind the crusade that eventually suppressed the sect. During a bloody persecution lasting twenty years, the Cathars were slowly driven to take refuge in Languedoc, where sympathetic noblemen in Toulouse afforded them some measure of protection. But when the French crown successfully annexed the Toulouse lands, overthrowing the protectors, the sect was doomed. They retreated to their last stronghold, the fortress of Mont Segur, an almost sheer rock rising some five hundred feet out of the surrounding plain. In 1244, the Cathars surrendered, but chose to be burned at the stake rather than renounce their beliefs. Mont Segur is a mere thirty kilometres west of Rennes le Chateau.

The accusations levelled at the Cathars were that they denied Christ and trampled on the cross – exactly the same charges that were made against the Templars a century later, the only variation being that instead of Rex Mundi, the Templars worshipped an identical idol known as Baphomet. Comparison of the two Orders leads inevitably to the conclusion that their religious beliefs were the same, and it is beyond doubt that the ideas of Dualism have survived to be found within the Rennes le Chateau mystery. At Rennes les Bains, for example, there is a cross that was erected as late as 1856. Where an observer would expect to see the body of a crucified Christ, there is instead the Virgin and Child.

Historical documents exist which tend to show that the Cathars, like the Templars, were possessors of a considerable amount of treasure which their persecutors were never able to lay their hands on. This, investigators say, may be what Sauniere found. But even if this were true, it still fails to explain why Sauniere's artistic endeavours should show a leaning towards Catharism. Quite clearly, there is a depth to the whole intrigue that goes a long way beyond the discovery of ancient gold.

The Priory of Sion

Some inkling of this depth may be gained by examination of one final clue – in reality the central pivot upon which the whole mystery turns. Within one of the parchment texts we have noticed a reference to King Dagobert II, and to Zion. The latter appears elsewhere in the texts as 'Sion', in company with the enigmatic initials 'P.S.', also observed on the gravestone inscriptions.

During his extensive research into the history of Dagobert, Henry Lincoln went to the Bibliotheque Nationale in Paris, where he uncovered an obscure book containing detailed family trees which attempted to establish a line of descent from the 7th century Merovingian king. The list was of considerable interest, but the book was to yield a secret of far more importance in respect of the Rennes mystery, for on another page, Lincoln came across a most impressive list of names. Prominently, there was Nicolas Flamel, the most famous alchemist of the Middle Ages, but other equally remarkable names were present: Leonardo da Vinci; Isaac Newton; Victor Hugo; Claude Debussy; and Jean Cocteau. All these eminent personages were listed as Grand Masters of a little known Rosi-crucian Lodge whose motif is 'P.S.' – the Prieure de Sion (the Priory of Sion). As an integral part of the list, beneath a strange coat of arms is the Priory's motto:

Et in Arcadia Ego.

CHAPTER TWO

The Rosicrucians

No one could ever lay hands on the Rosicrucians, and notwithstanding the alleged discoveries of 'secret chambers', vellums called 'T', and of fossil knights with ever burning lamps, this ancient association and its true aims are to this day a mystery. Pretended Templars and sham Rose-Croix, with a few genuine kabalists, were occasionally burned, and some unlucky Theosophists and alchemists sought and put to the torture; delusive confessions even were wrung from them by the most ferocious means, but yet, the true Society remains today as it has ever been, unknown to all, especially to its cruelest enemy – the Church.

(Isis Unveiled – 1877 – Vol II)

A little over a hundred years ago, when the erudite Madame Blavatsky penned the above paragraph, none but a select few were in a position to appreciate the tremendous truth at which she hinted. The greater mass of her readers were, of course, fully acquainted with the Rosicrucians as an Order born of the great Furore of the early sixteen hundreds, when a startled Bohemia woke up one morning to read the first of the strange Manifestos of Christian Rosencreutz. But at the latter end of the nineteenth century, the Rosicrucian name merely signified the dying branches of an Order that had preceded the Society of Freemasons – the lodges of which, with the exception of the initiation ritual and passwords, were by no means secret or mysterious. Rather, both organisations were looked upon as no more than long established and fairly exclusive social clubs.

It is true that the Catholic Church held out no hand of friendship, either to the Freemasons or the Rosicrucians, but this is purely because the rites upon which the Orders were founded are remnants of ancient Egyptian and Greek Mysteries, and are therefore unforgivably pagan in the eyes of Rome – in spite of the well known fact that members paid lip service only to a ritual that most of them never fully understood.

It is also true that the Church of the past is the holder of an unenviable record of torture and murder by the most inhuman means, practised in the name of Jesus Christ upon all those whose religious beliefs were unorthodox enough to be condemned as

'heretical'. The history of such religious persecution stretches back
over many hundreds of years, and we are already well acquainted
with two of the chief victims, the Cathars and the Templars. But did
the original Rosicrucians fall into this category as Madame
Blavatsky suggests?

Looking back from the closing decades of the twentieth century,
there is a tendency to conclude that the founder of the Theosophical
Society was indulging in more than a little romanticism when she
asked her readers to envisage a gathering so exclusive and
mysterious that no outsider has ever penetrated to its inner sanctum
– a fraternity so at variance with Catholic Rome in its concept of
religion that it became the focal point of papal venom. One has the
feeling that such an assertion might have been more readily acceptable had the author confined her remarks solely to a sequence of
events that took place more than two centuries previously, but the
paragraph contains the unequivocable statement that this occult
lodge still existed at the time of writing – and, by inference, exists
even now!

Naturally, the idea is totally unacceptable to the average, no-
nonsense academic, and indeed, many have turned away with a
smile of scepticism to pursue what they have considered to be more
realistic objectives. And yet even a casual glance through historical
data would have revealed that Madame Blavatsky never for an
instant stood alone in her apparently fanciful claim. To quote a
single, corroborative source, we may invoke the illustrious name of
Sir Isaac Newton, a scientist whose prodigious mental prowess is
recognised the world over – and yet a man who confessed to the
belief in a chain of 'initiates' stretching back into the far past. Also, a
man whose name appears as a past Grand Master of the Priory of
Sion, a Rosicrucian lodge.

It seems a far cry from the theory of gravitation to an elaborate
cipher laid out across the French countryside, but the link presents
itself and so however tenuous, we must examine it further. In doing
so, we will be led unerringly back to the ever present question of the
Church, for Isaac Newton held religious ideas that were markedly at
variance with the dominant Catholic ideas of his time.

Newton the Initiate

The great scientist devoted certain periods of his life to an intense
study of Theology, eventually to arrive at a concept of religion so
different from that which he had been taught that he refused to be

ordained, for the ceremony required him to swear on the Trinity, which he despised. For the benefit of non-theologians, the Trinity is the recognition of God as three separate entities – the Father, the Son, and the Holy Ghost – a doctrine imposed as Church law after the Council of Nicea settled the Arius controversy in the fourth century.

Newton's stubborn refusal could have precipitated a crisis in his career, for ordination was necessary if he were to remain as a Fellow in Cambridge. Fortunately, intercession by no less a person than King James saved him. A draft of dispensation was hurriedly made official, the terms of which exempted Newton from taking Holy Orders unless he wanted to.

It is significant that Newton did not arrive at his revised religious concept by studying the Bible alone. In his late twenties, he began to take an interest in Alchemy, pondering deeply on the enigmatic tracts penned by ancient philosophers and soon gathering together a prolific library of Hermetic volumes. Later, when the scientist suddenly deviated from his normal studies in order to probe into Theology, his fellow academics were considerably amazed, but as you will see, it would have been no surprise to a Rosicrucian.

In directing his thoughts to the exact nature of God, Newton soon became convinced that a massive fraud, beginning in the 4th and 5th centuries, had perverted the legacy of the early religions. Central to this fraud were the Scriptures, the true message of which, Newton believed, had been distorted through ignorance and an obsessive effort to project the idea of the Trinity. He quoted a number of instances in which he considered the present Bible texts to be misleading, a small example of which is I Timothy, chapter 3; verse 16:

And without controversy great is the mystery of godliness; God was manifest in the flesh. . .

During his deep research into Theological history, the scientist found that the early versions did not contain the word 'God', which is essential to the concept of the Trinity, but read:

. . .great is the mystery of godliness which was manifested in the flesh. . .

The numerous commentators on Newton's life work find it all but impossible to reconcile his long and obsessive interest in Alchemy with his more scientific work on gravitation, concluding that one is entirely separate from the other – Alchemy belonging to a world of philosophic fantasy, while gravitation is a wholly material science. In fact, Newton's interests and conclusions in both subjects show that he knew them to be merely different aspects of the same thing. Certain passages in his correspondence show that he considered the force which keeps the planets in their orbits not to be purely mechanical, but stemming from Intelligence. To put his ideas in modern terms, he believed in the existence of a Universal Mind, that it was responsible for the creation of the Universe, and that the force we know as Gravity is merely one aspect of it that can be appreciated by the physical senses. However, there was no way in which he could express his conclusions, either in a manner that would be understood by a layman, or – more important – as a concept that would be acceptable to the ruling Catholic law. With regard to the latter statement, it must be remembered that the Church hierarchy of the scientist's day was still powerful enough to invoke a charge of heresy with disastrous results – even against a scholar of Newton's stature. Nevertheless, he managed to drop a few hints:

> 'There is yet another argument,' he wrote, 'for a Deity, which I take to be a very strong one. But 'til the principle on which 'tis grounded be better received, I think it more advisable to let it sleep.'

And in a letter to Richard Bentley, an aspiring Cleric who had set himself the task of mastering Newton's 'Principia' and was in constant correspondence with him, the scientist had this to say:

> Gravity must be caused by an agent acting constantly according to certain laws, but whether this agent be material, or immaterial, is a question I have left to my readers.

By 'immaterial', he was referring to that which we would today term 'paranormal'.

Forced to be content with hints like this, Newton made sure that his true ideas were never openly associated with his name. But he was appalled by the way in which the greater mass of people held blind faith in the Catholic ideal with never a question of its origin. He summed up his feelings about this when he wrote:

> But the world loves to be deceived; they will not understand; they never consider equally, but are wholly led by prejudice, interest, the praise of men, and authority of the Church they live in; as is plain because all parties keep close to the Religion they have been brought up in, and yet in all parties there are wise and learned as well as foolish and ignorant. There are but few that seek to understand the religion they profess, and those that study for understanding therein, do it rather for worldly ends, or that they

may defend it, than to examine it whither it be true with a resolution to choose and profess that religion which in their judgement appears the truest . . . Be not scandalised at the reproaches of the world, but rather look upon them as a mark of the true church.

(Yahuda MS)

It is plain that Newton's theological conceptions are centred around the classic, fourth century argument which resulted in the Trinity becoming Catholic law: Athanasius versus Arius.

Athanasius, a doctor of the church in Alexandria, became its bishop in 325 A.D., and is credited with the introduction of the Trinitarian doctrine later adopted by Rome. He is also noted as the bitter opponent of Arius, a Gnostic priest who steadfastly denied Christ to be of the same substance as God the Father. In the latter, we can instantly recognise one aspect of the Cathar and Templar beliefs – an aspect to which Newton obviously leaned, since he was so opposed to Trinitarianism. Thus we have another similarity between the ideas of the great scientist and the underlying religious theme of Rennes le Chateau.

In 1726, when Newton was preparing for death, two events occurred which are worth noting. First, in a direct re-affirmation of his true religious views, the scientist flatly refused to receive the last sacrament, even when he lay dying and – by all reports – in considerable pain. Compare this with the rumour concerning Sauniere's death! Secondly, according to the testimony of a fellow scholar, John Conduitt, Newton took the unprecedented step of burning a number of papers. As biographer Richard Westfall remarks, when one considers the abundance of papers he left behind, multiple drafts and scraps of annotation on every topic known to have interested him, it is difficult to imagine what he destroyed and why. One possible answer may be that it was written material that would have linked his name with the Rosicrucian Order, and which he did not wish the rest of the world to know about. The world may never have known had it not been for the sequence of events put in motion by Sauniere's discovery.

Thus a careful review of the foregoing Newtonian studies, along with the great man's conclusions, lead us to an unexpected relationship between three subjects hitherto regarded as entirely unconnected: Dualism, Alchemy and Rosicrucianism.

Dualism

This Old Religion has a surprisingly long history and even a superficial examination of records will trace it back to the time of
Zoroaster, the Persian prophet of the 7th century B.C. His concept
envisaged a world contest between the forces of good and evil, light
and darkness, two entities that were personified as Ormuzd and
Ahriman. It can readily be seen that this theme is identical to that of
the Cathars and the Templars. But in all cases we are confronted not
with a simple explanation of the entities. Instead, a profusion of
symbolism has amassed, a myriad of different emblems which when
traced to their root, will resolve in just the two entities. A less
cursory investigation will reveal that the same dualistic symbolism
was present as far back as the Egyptian and the Sumerian cultures of
3,000 B.C.

Similarly, the science of Alchemy has remained hidden behind an
impenetrable facade of symbolism that is totally incomprehensible
except to a fortunate few, but it has been noted that certain emblems
seem to relate in some strange way both to Religion and Rosicrucianism. We will examine Alchemy at the appropriate stage of the
book and it will be seen to be far more than just the pseudo-chemical
philosophy of a few Dark Age occultists.

The same, deliberately confusing mass of symbolism shrouds the
true activities of the Rosicrucians. As Madame Blavatsky has indicated, the real Brothers of the Rose Cross have never been fully
exposed to the eye of the general public, and what little is known is
no more than they have condescended to allow. A typical example of
the obscure emblems in which they deal may be glimpsed by
quoting from her volume, THE SECRET DOCTRINE. She gives
the following sign:

This, she says, is the union of the Rose and the Cross,

the great mystery of occult generation, from whence came the
name Rosicrucians.

Elsewhere in the volume, she relates another ancient Rose Cross
emblem:

It is that of the Pelican, tearing open its breast to feed its seven
little ones (with its own blood).

At first sight, such statements are incomprehensible, but as you will see, they have a rational and astonishingly simple foundation associated directly with Dualism.

The Rosicrucian Manifestos

It is thought that the death of Emperor Rudolph II of Bohemia in 1612 triggered the release of the first of the strange Manifestos that were to bring the Rosicrucians to the attention of an excited public. With the Emperor's demise, widespread and radical changes in the social structure of Europe were expected to take place, and it may be that those of the inner lodge deemed it an opportune time to arouse interest in their ancient ideals by promoting them under a new name. Hence,a short time after the nation had been acquainted with news of the royal death, there appeared a strange manuscript. At first, it made the rounds as a pamphlet, but as interest increased, someone decided that it warranted a more prominent presentation. Consequently, in 1614, the first printed edition of the FAMA FRATERNITATIS came off the presses at Cassel.

It opened with an observation that the world at large will doubt the existence of a great wisdom by which man might understand his own nobleness. If only all great men could be brought together, it urged, and made to forsake their erroneous doctrines for the Truth of Nature, this great wisdom would be made manifest to them. What was needed, it continued, was a reformation towards enlightenment. It just so happened that the founder of the Rosicrucian Order, a German named Christian Rosencreutz, had been labouring towards this goal for a long time. The Manifesto then related the life story of the movement's founder, informing readers that he died in 1484, at the ripe old age of one hundred and six.

In his early years, Rosencreutz had journeyed to Arabia, there meeting with many wise men who taught him

> what great wonders they wrought and how Nature was discovered to them.

After much travel and the gathering of considerable knowledge, Rosencreutz returned to Germany and there built himself a fine house in which to continue his studies. Later, he desired to share his accumulated wisdom for the betterment of Mankind, and to this end he gathered around him three other philosophers and formed the Order of the Rose Cross. Their first task was to write their combined knowledge into one large book:

which we yet daily use in God's praise and glory, and do find great wisdom therein.

By means of careful selection, the membership was soon increased to eight, and when all knowledge was correlated, they dispersed themselves throughout various European countries in order to teach the Rosicrucian doctrine for the rest of their lives.

In later years, the Manifesto went on, a young Rosicrucian brother, while making alterations to his building, discovered a brass plaque on one of the walls. Seeing that it was inscribed with the names of some of the original Rose Cross brothers, he decided to move it to a more fitting place, but there was a strong iron nail stuck in it, embedded so deeply that great force was needed to extract it. But the effort of removing the nail dislodged a big stone behind the plaque, and when this was removed, it revealed a hidden door. Agog with excitement, the brother opened it to find himself in a strange vault, constructed in three parts. In the centre was an altar, which when later removed, exposed a second brass plaque. When this was raised, the brother was astonished to find the perfectly preserved body of Christian Rosencreutz. In one dead hand was clasped a large book containing all the secrets of the great wisdom collected by the original brothers.

The FAMA went on to express the hope that this example would inspire others to search for the burial places of the other co-founders, in order that their great knowledge be brought to light.

Finally, the document stated, despite the fact that men of discretion hold the transmutation of metals to be the high point of philosophy, the real philosophers were of another mind, holding the making of gold in little esteem;

> 'Our building,' says the text, 'shall remain untouched, un-destroyed and hidden to the wicked world (although one hundred thousand people had very near seen and beheld the same).'

The appearance of this strange manuscript, with its romantic text and general air of mystery, generated intense speculation as to the reality of the secret Order. No one could say for certain that it did exist, for although many tried to make contact by publishing tracts of their own in reply, no person could be found who would admit to membership in the Order of the Rose Cross. The mystery deepened one year later, at the appearance of a second Manifesto, this time entitled THE CONFESSIO. Its contents seemed to be an attempt to explain the FAMA in more readily acceptable terms, but still no one could trace the authors.

The whole event developed into what later became known as the Rosicrucian Furore, for large numbers of people were attracted to the possibility of being acquainted with the superior power – comprehensively described in the CONFESSIO – of the Brothers. Many others were alarmed at the prospect of dangerous magical powers being made available to all and sundry. And inevitably, the Manifestos were misconstrued by certain factions who concluded them to be documents of political intent. But the Rosicrucians were never found, and thus earned themselves the title of the Invisibles.

The extent to which the idea gripped the public imagination may be appreciated by an experience said to have befallen the French philosopher, Descartes, when he returned to Paris in 1623, after a stay in Germany. According to a biography written by Adrian Baillet, LA VIE DE MONSIEUR DESCARTES (Paris 1691), the philosopher found it rumoured that he was a member of the Rosicrucian Order.

'He was surprised at this news,' wrote Baillet, 'since such a thing was not in keeping with his character, nor with the inclination which he had always had to think of the Rosicrucians as imposters and visionaries. In Paris, they were called the Invisibles, and it was proclaimed that of the thirty-six deputies which their head had sent throughout Europe, six had come to France in February and were lodged at the Marais in Paris; but that they could not communicate with people, or be communicated with, except by thought joined to the will, that is to say in a manner imperceptible to the senses. The chance of their arrival in Paris at the same time as Monsieur Descartes might have had an unfortunate effect on his reputation had he hidden himself, or lived in solitude in the town, as he had been accustomed to do on his travels. But he confounded those who wished to make use of this conjunction of events to establish their calumny. He made himself visible to all the world, and particularly to his friends who needed no other argument to convince them that he was not one of the Brotherhood of the Rosicrucians, or Invisibles.'

If we are to take this biographical note at face value, certain questions present themselves. After smiling at the gullibility of those who were happy to exonerate the philosopher purely on account of his visibility, we must wonder at Descartes' alleged opinion of the Brotherhood. If the Invisibles really were imposters and visionaries, is it likely that a scientist of Isaac Newton's stature would accept a position of Grand Master presiding over the Paris lodge? It must be quickly admitted that the Rose Cross movement has embraced a number of personages whose names would bring an immediate frown of suspicious scepticism to the brow of a modern scholar. Paracelsus, practitioner of unorthodox medicine, was a prominent Rosicrucian – as was Doctor John Dee. Later came another controversial figure of myth and mystery, the Comte de St. Germain, considered by most to be a charlatan. Yet just as many highly regarded personalities have enjoyed membership in the Order without attracting the slightest hint of notoriety. Isaac Newton was one – and another was Descartes himself. To rationalise the denial attributed to the philosopher, therefore, we have only to recall how unwise it was at that early period to admit to ideas that were so far removed from the Catholic view. Rosicrucian initiates had two choices: either to remain silent, or to strongly deny their affiliation. Descartes, endangered by rumour, chose the latter.

And what of the fanciful claim that the Rose Cross membership could only be communicated with by means of 'thought joined to will . . . in a manner imperceptible to the senses'? With so short an extract under examination, it would be unjust to dismiss Baillet's work as an historical outline unhappily marred by the inclusion of unproven rumour, as no doubt many an academic already has. However, the words are there, emanating not from Descartes, remember, but from Baillet himself. Was he gullible too, or was there a hint of truth behind the apparent fantasy? It is at this point that we arrive at the crux of the Rosicrucian 'secret' and take the first step towards discovering the real mystery of Rennes le Chateau.

The Secrets of the Rose Cross

True Rosicrucian affiliation did not consist merely of the usual proposal of membership and initiation ceremony, followed thereafter by regular assembly for the purposes of wining, dining and social or academic discourse. If such had been the case, the Order would never have been so constant in retention of the inviolate secrecy that it has enjoyed for centuries. No; the true Rosicrucian works alone, subjecting himself to a long period of self-analysis at the end of which, if he is one of the lucky few, he will discover a basic truth regarding the power of the human mind, a faculty which remains dormant in all others unless they follow the same difficult path of self-examination. There is never any need, therefore, for this elite to meet in general assembly.

Those who enter this highly exclusive circle move from the normal state of perception into an exalted mental sphere – one step higher in the level of cognition – and as such, constitute the chain of initiates hinted at by Newton. Having developed this third state of consciousness, the adept finds that it is one thing to attain it, but quite another to communicate the reality of it to less fortunate non-initiates. He discovers, however, that adepts of the past have applied a certain manipulation, a unique style of phraseology or pictorial design, to the fields of literature and art, thereby creating an allegorical code by which each can appraise the other of their mental accomplishment. It is also hoped that the non-initiate, with curiosity perhaps aroused by certain anomolies in such works, will be impelled to search for something deeper than the surface meaning, and in doing so, receive personal revelation of the key to the code.

Knowingly or not, Baillet's biography contains such contrived phrases which, if copied from works by Descartes, unfailingly inform the knowledgeable of the philosopher's initiateship – or if originated by Baillet himself, disclose the author's own heightened understanding.

As masters of such a code, initiates could not help but know that the doctrines taught by the Catholic Church were superficial only, with never a hint of the real truth regarding the basis of religion. Hence, it comes as no surprise to find that every true Rosicrucian held religious beliefs that were in stark contrast to the Catholic view. Dualism, the original religion, is strongly represented within the Rennes enigma, with the suggestion that it existed long before the Catholic concept of the Trinity was ever established. I can tell you that the symbolism of Rennes denotes knowledge – the real 'treasure' contained there, and it follows that if I am to substantiate the apparent fantasy of Rosicrucian powers, I must lay before you the key to the great mass of symbolism relevant to it, and perhaps also express a hint of the means by which such mental development may be realised.

CHAPTER THREE

The Reality of 'God'

Ancient theological traditions propound that the whole of the visible universe is contained in one, all-encompassing field of energy – an invisible power which is sentient. It is said to be the source of all intelligence in animals and men, the animating force within all physical bodies. It has been known by countless names. In ancient China, it was called the One; throughout Dynastic Egypt by such god names as Maau, Tmu, Ra and Osiris. The biblical Israelites knew it as Jehovah, while the near and far Asiatics employed the terms Allah, Mohammed, Buddha and Brahma. The Hermetic fraternity of the Middle Ages more correctly called it the Universal Mind – and Carl Jung touched on it in his concept of the Collective Consciousness. Today, under its Christian appelation, 'God', we acknowledge this force in a manner that becomes increasingly off-hand as each decade passes.

This apathy on our part stems mainly from the fact that, despite our high standard of technological expertise and electronic wizardry, we cannot adequately prove to ourselves that the energy field exists. And to a culture that has hoisted itself to a pinnacle of industrial endeavour under the auspices of the great god, Science – the maxim of this deity being 'if you can't measure it, it doesn't exist' – this fact alone leaves very little room for further discussion.

And yet, since the earliest days of his advent on this planet, Homo Sapiens has consistently acknowledged the presence of a supreme but invisible deity. Either consciously or intuitively, he gives recognition to a higher spiritual force. True, the basic idea has become vague, hidden as it is behind a multitude of conflicting names, but this is because the energy field is intangible to the physical senses and therefore a description that would be instantly recognisable to all has remained beyond the scope of mortal invention. As a poor substitute, Man resorts to symbolism, allowing the followers of the Christian faith, for example, to identify God only as 'Our Father who art in Heaven'.

In consideration of humanity's faith in this intangible force, unflagging through countless centuries, how can we possibly be content for it to remain as a mere intuitive abstraction in the mind?

And if the reply is that it has always been so, how do we account for the unequivocable statements of our supposedly less sophisticated ancestors? In the centuries old Chinese manuscript, T'AI I CHIN HUA TSUNG CHIH, for instance, there is to be found the following statement in relation to the Universal Mind:

> But even if man lives in the energy, he does not see the energy, just as fishes live in water but do not see the water.

And in the 16th century manuscript by the alchemist Paracelsus, his PHILOSOPHIA SAGAX, we read:

> The activity of the Universal Mind can only come to the consciousness of those whose spheres of mind are capable of receiving its impressions.

Ah, but of course, these two quotes are taken from texts on Alchemy, and therefore cannot be regarded with any great seriousness by a modern, sophisticated mind.

Perhaps this leads us to another explanation for the prevailing academic disdain, the fact that the concept of this intangible force is so often linked with tales of magic and fantasy, where at the touch of a wand, or the utterance of a word, miraculous wonders are performed. Even the Bible contains stories which place an intolerable strain on established credibility, such as the parting of the Red Sea, or the description of Jesus walking on water. In our ultramaterialistic conception of reality, it is well known that such illogical events could not possibly take place, no more than the ancient alchemist could make fine gold out of common lead. The laws of physics would not allow it.

Equally, it is established in the minds of men that there is no known method by which ordinary mortals may come into deliberate and controlled contact with God, the Universal Mind – a reluctant but inevitable conclusion which is reflected in the inexorable decline in the Church as the focal point to which we look for spiritual guidance.

In the preceding chapter I briefly outlined a concept which, to all but a few, seems to have been drawn from the pages of a fantasy fiction – the possibility of a higher level of consciousness. Even worse, I attributed the knowledge to those ancients of more than five thousand years in the past – an unthinkable proposition to those who firmly believe modern technology to be Man's greatest achievement. The idea is ludicrous – but what if I could show factual evidence, the disguised knowledge of the elite few who have consistently maintained that such a higher state is available to the ordinary mortal, and while declining to describe openly the process by which it may be achieved, have pointed out that the clues to its existence have been enciphered into some of the world's most respected and historically important texts?

There is, and there always has been, a method whereby the human subject can reach out and become associated with the energy field that we commonly call God, and while the actual process has not often been described, symbolic clues to its existence are manifold. According to a long standing code of practice, each man who is lucky enough to discover the process deems it his duty to pass on the knowledge to the rest of humanity. But he does so in the form of parable and fable, symbolism and allegory. Seldom does the initiate speak openly. Thus the great uninitiated mass is entirely unknowing of the visible signia and literature which contain the clues to the process, and which always lie within easy reach. Lacking the mental key that will unlock the true meaning, such material is assessed at face value only – and so the Great Secret has endured.

Yet it is not so much allegorical or symbolic encipherment that is paramount in holding the veil so tightly drawn over the Rosicrucian method, as the total lack of credence afforded it. As I have pointed out, modern Man has very fixed ideas regarding the limitations of his mental self, and his established laws of physics dictate very clearly just what is possible in the material world and what is not. But ask yourself this: by what method is knowledge attained? The simple answer is that by concentrating your mind in a single direction, to the exclusion of everything else, and by maintaining such focus for a long enough period, the knowledge you are seeking will present itself. Isaac Newton was renowned for the way he worked on his problems, becoming so absorbed that he forgot his meals, and even his sleep. When once asked how he discovered his laws of universal gravitation, he is said to have replied, 'by thinking on it continually'. The same principle governs the mental process of the Rosicrucians – but with one slight adjustment.

The mechanics of the process are by no means well advertised, it is true, but neither are they an inviolate secret, for material which explains it in detail is available today and can be obtained without great effort. But the one almost insurmountable barrier, ever present, to prevent widespread appreciation of this invaluable knowledge, is the total lack of belief in the outcome. This is a stumbling block which no persuasive speech or letters can overcome, it being entirely a matter for the individual. In the chapters that follow, I will offer a comprehensive survey and interpretation of the allegories which hide what has become known as the Great Secret, showing on the way that many traditional and fondly cherished beliefs have no real foundation in fact, but are based on erroneous readings of the texts. As we proceed, the reader will come to realise that because of the consistent failure to accept the reality of the hidden process, and due to the compound misinterpretations of the written word by those who have set themselves up as national and spiritual leaders, bloody religious wars have occurred, are still occurring, and will inevitably recur – all of which are totally unnecessary. It will be suddenly appreciated that certain historical incidents need to be seen in an entirely different light. And the minor enigma of Rennes le Chateau will be put into its proper perspective as just one of a long succession of carefully constructéd encipherments pertaining to the mental process. The evidence I provide may well be instrumental in eradicating the barrier of disbelief, but I won't count on it.

The Seat of the Power

The first step is to assume that such a thing as the Universal Mind does exist, just as Newton indicated, and then we may begin by asking ourselves how we can reach it. Religion supplies us with the answer. In fact, it is one of the few basic tenets upon which all religions are unanimous. God, they say, can be reached by prayer.

Exactly!

It will be instantly recognised by all that the act of prayer is an inner communing, a concentration of thought within one's mind. If conducted with the proper fervour, prayer is a mental appeal made with the conscious mind centred solely on a sphere beyond the range of physical senses. Instinctively, we know that God cannot be found in the outside, material world, but must be sought somewhere in the inner consciousness. Therefore it is to this inner centre that we must turn to institute our search. We call this inner centre the subconscious.

From the results of many a latterday experiment, we are aware that this mysterious, inner mind evinces inexplicable powers when conditions are favourable, none of which we fully understand. In the field of Hypnotherapy, for example, researchers have witnessed unprecedented abilities in their entranced subjects. Supernormal memory recall has been discovered and put to practical use in police investigations, while other hypnotised persons have displayed calculative abilities far beyond that of any normal brain. Some subjects have unexpectedly lapsed into languages from remote lands and ancient times, or what is more startling, complex languages of unique, personal invention, none of which are manifest in the waking state.

Most astounding of all is the discovery of a link between individual subconscious minds, a phenomenon that shows the inconclusive results of experiments in extrasensory perception to be not without valid foundation. There are many cases of supernormal abilities on record, and which need no repetition here, but I would like to quote just one, pertinent instance, as reported by Timothy Hall and Guy Grant, in their book, SUPERPSYCHE.

During a planned and carefully controlled experiment in Hypnotherapy, one subject in deep trance began to write in what was obviously a very complex form of code. But no matter how the experimenter tried, he was unable to make the subject explain what the coded message meant. Some time later, a woman subject taking part in the same series of experiments, was shown the message while she was still in her hypnotic state. Immediately, she launched into a long and complicated explanation of the code, after which she provided a full interpretation of what had been written. Shortly after this, the man who had written the code and who had never met the woman, was persuaded to give his own key. Researchers were flabbergasted to find that it matched the woman's in every respect. Yet, in the waking state, both subjects regarded the code as sheer gibberish.

In reviewing this sequence of events, it is instinctive to conclude that the whole performance was an elaborate hoax on the part of the two concerned – except that the researchers were completely confident that it was not, for they knew that neither subject had been acquainted with the other, not even while the experiment was taking place.

Comparing this episode with other baffling examples of communication at a subconscious level, and not forgetting the many instances of enhanced mental abilities, it is inevitable to conclude that if we were able to reach the subconscious area while still in our waking state, and then exercise control over it, each of us would be in possession of a supermind.

By a strange coincidence, this desirable facility is exactly what is promised in the Rosicrucian Manifestos of the seventeenth century – and almost a hundred years beforehand, Paracelsus was expounding the same impossible idea when he wrote:

A man may come into possession of creative power by identifying his own mind with the Universal Mind, and he who succeeds in doing so will be in possession of the highest possible wisdom.

Can it be true after all, that there is a glimmer of reality in the preposterous claims of the old traditions? You may be sure that there is. Merely substitute the modern word 'subconscious' for that of Universal Mind, and you will see what Paracelsus the Rosicrucian was hinting at.

What is it that prevents us reaching this subconscious power in the normal course of events?

Quite simply, it is the constant activity of our waking consciousness, with its incessant stream of outwardly directed thought. If we pause to evaluate the art of both hypnotist and psychic medium, it will be apparent that the only way in which the subject is able to make contact with the mysterious inner power is by suppressing the activity of the waking mind. The hypnotist does exactly that when he puts his patient 'under' – as does the medium who descends into a self-induced trance. Without resorting to this deadening process, it has not proved possible – except in rare and very exceptional circumstances – to reach the subconscious.

It becomes quite clear, therefore, that the two areas of consciousness are made up of radically differing ends of an energy spectrum, rather like radio waves of varying frequencies. By deadening, or damping, the frequencies of the waking consciousness, it becomes less opposed and a partial contact takes place, bringing with it the phenomena witnessed by experimenters. The more the outer mind is deadened, the more the subconscious power is made available, a fact which may explain why some hypnotic trances are fruitful, while others are not, and why rare few psychics are exceptional in their paranormal ability.

Thus, we are cognisant of a great power which lies just beyond our mental grasp, but have very little idea of how to reach it other than by barely touching it through hypnosis and mediumistic trance. The Hermetic process known to all Rosicrucians provides the solution to this problem.

Discerning readers may by now have guessed that the process I refer to is already well known in Asia and the Orient as the practice of the 'stilled' mind, and at this realisation there may be little inclination to afford the matter further thought, for this doctrine of mental mastery has come to be appreciated by the average Westerner as merely a method employed by fakirs in order to gain abnormal control over the functions of the physical body, while the wild claims of paranormal abilities have been adjudged to be nothing more than a fantasy, propagated in an attempt to attract an audience. But perhaps it has not been fully realised that the truth about the process is little known and invariably misinterpreted, bona fide

Adepts being as rare in the East as they are in the West, their presence effectively obscured by the ostentatiousness of the many charlatans.

Make no mistake. Real power is attainable. The would-be Adept, by long repetition of a simple process of daily meditation, endeavours to bring about the deadening of the conscious mind at will, but in a manner superior to that obtained by the hypnotist or the medium. He achieves it by gradually learning to suppress the constant flow of uncontrolled thoughts within the waking mind, for the subconscious part has *no movement* compared to the waking consciousness, and thus, if the outer thoughts can be stilled, the two will become harmonious. The end result of this long and very tedious process will be a transmission of personal consciousness from the waking mind alone into a shared existence with the subconscious – and through it, the Universal Mind.

In this classic difference between the waking mind and the subconscious, we arrive at last at the true foundaton of centuries of symbolism. The conscious mind, the movement of which prevents Man from reaching the great power of the subconscious, is regarded as *evil*. The subconscious, with its inlet to the all-encompassing knowledge of the Universal Mind, is regarded as *good*. And in this basic concept of good versus evil, we discover the true origin of the Old Religions: Zoroastrianism, Dualism, Catharism, Templarism and Rosicrucianism. This is the knowledge that Newton discovered but was obliged to keep to himself.

The main qualification to the foregoing, and one which needs to be stated without further delay, is that since the process involves fundamentals of the mind which are indeed 'imperceptible to the senses' and therefore well-nigh unexplainable in material terms until the requisite level of *understanding* has been acquired, the phrases 'transmission of consciousness' and 'stilling of the mind' have a rather more subtle meaning than appears on the surface. Such nebulous enhancement of the normal consciousness might favourably be compared to the common conception of the 'astral body' and the phenomenon of its 'travels', although again I emphasise that there is a deeper meaning intended, since 'astral travel', as it is usually depicted, requires the medium of that part of the conscious mind that normally lies dormant in order to allow the experience to manifest as it does. The true experience seeks to invoke powers of the mind which lurk beyond the recesses of the waking consciousness – intuition, conscience – elusive 'feelings' that are mere undercurrents to ordinary thought and emotion but which must necessarily be referred to in terms acceptable to the outer intelligence.

The whole operation of the process, the transmission of the

personal consciousness which allows it to be freed from the bonds of the physical environment, has been allegorised the world over in countless myths which centre about the theme of Death and Resurrection: the 'death' of the waking thoughts which allows the 'birth' of the so-called astral body. The most prominent of these is the story of the 'death' and 'resurrection' of Jesus as recounted in the Gospels.

Although the panorama of symbolism which conceals the meditational process is tremendously extensive – a lasting monument to the collective ingeniousness of the scribes who conceived it – there occur certain inescapable repetitions of clues which allow decipherment of the inner message. Some of these clues are present at Rennes le Chateau, but to appreciate their significance at all, it is necessary to trace the course of allegorical history from its inception many generations ago.

The Hidden Message

The first clue pertains to the division of the long period of meditation into three successive but distinct phases, each being represented by a colour. These are Black, White and Red, in that order, although it is as well to interject here that in truly ancient times, a fourth colour – Yellow – was utilised as an intermediatory between the White and the Red. In the main, however, just the three colours will be predominant. The triplicity of the phases, with their colour code, were as familiar with the initiates of pre-Dynastic Egypt as they were to the alchemists of the Middle Ages; or as they are to the modern Rosicrucian.

The colour Black is used to signify the gradual deadening of the conscious mind – the 'death' – and thus everywhere you will find the first stage symbolised by anything which is black, dead, or heavy (dead-weight). Alternatively, symbols may relate in an obscure way to the colour through a compound meaning, in the form of the double symbolism so loved by the ancient Egyptians, as in *Night* (the black of), or *North* (because the far North has less sunlight and consequently more *darkness*). The direction North, incidentally, is more often used to indicate that place to which the attention is turned during meditation: the inner mind. A comparable emblem is the *nether regions*.

To sum up, a sample range of signia to indicate the first stage would be:

A black bird; a skull; a scorpion (poisonous and therefore a bringer of death); an eclipse of the sun; the appearance of shadows; the coming of darkness; the mention of Saturn (the heaviest planet); the metal lead (the heaviest of metal) . . . etc.

There are, of course, countless variations on the theme, depending on the ingenuity of the originator.

The second stage of the process is symbolised by the colour White, because the conscious mind has been 'cleansed' of unwanted thought with which it is normally filled and over which we seem to have no control. Achievement of this is seen by the Hermeticists as a 'purification'. The conscious mind has been 'killed', or as the Bible would have it, the 'lamb' has been 'sacrificed'.

The final colour, Red, denotes the accomplished Adept, who has no need to continue with his daily meditation, for the transmission has been made and is permanent. From now on, he will live in a third state of consciousness, with mental powers at his command that cannot be credited by those who remain in the normal state. Yet his outward appearance will not change. This is why the Rosicrucians were dubbed 'the Invisibles'.

To carry out the process to its ultimate goal requires of the Neophyte the utmost mental stamina, to say nothing of an unfaltering faith in the final outcome, for a number of years may pass before success is achieved. There is no physical battle endured by Man that can compare to the struggle that will take place in his own mind but, as with the description of God, there are only physical experiences to relate with, so the whole of the mental task has been allegorised as a combat or feat of endurance, some examples of which are:

A long and dangerous journey, partly on water, partly on land; the ascent of a high mountain; a combat to the death with a monster; a wandering journey through a maze, or labyrinth; a task of Herculean proportions; or a voyage through uncharted waters, or to a lost island.

As before, these are a mere handful of analogies, the scope being limited only by the creative imagination of the writer.

The initial step of the practice requires the candidate to sit down quietly and disassociate his attention from the material things about him, directing his thoughts instead into the very centre of his mind. To do this with any degree of success, it is necessary to divert the *whole attention* inwards, cutting off all awareness of seeing, or hearing, until a state of reverie is attained.

This complete reversal of the normal application of the mind has been symbolised in a number of novel ways, and as an example, we may quote the quaint tradition that St Peter was crucified upside down (an unusual reversal of the normal procedure). You may be sure that such an unorthodox turn of events never actually took place, for the tradition was born at the inspiration of the initiates who wished to draw attention to their process. A comparable emblem is to be found in card number twelve of the Tarot pack: the Hanged Man, who is suspended upside down. Elsewhere, the act of reversal has been suggested by the picture of a *man turning round,* or by an animal, drawn so that it *looks back* over its own shoulder.

In the old Egyptian and Greek mythological schemes, the emblems used have been instruments of either natural, or artificial reflection, such as a *lake,* or a *mirror* worked into the theme. The most prominent symbol of reflection was, as you can guess, the Moon, and reference to the orb by way of god names will be found everywhere in classic texts, generally personified as a *woman.*

The ultimate accomplishment of the transmission allows the ordinary conscious mind to harmonise with the realm of the subconscious, an event which considerably enhances the life of the man lucky enough to succeed, and for this reason, the attainment of such a goal is symbolised by suitable expressions of feeling, as a place of wonder, or natural beauty, or as a mythical land where conditions are perfect:

Happiness; Nobleness; Purity; Good; a Forest, or Garden; a Divine Land; a Temple; a Holy City; Avalon; Shamballah; Eden; Punt; Atlantis.

It is with this list of clues in mind that apparently innocuous stories must be scrutinised in search of allegory, and as a small but practical example, may I recount a tale familiar to all. Afterwards, I will analyse the text and reveal the hidden message, but so as to prepare the way, I will emphasise the key words.

The Ugly Duckling

The little duckling is *unhappy* because he realises that he is *not as others are.* He is *black* and therefore *ugly.* In desperation at his plight, he *wanders off on his own,* determined to find a *new life.* Lost and *alone,* he chances upon a *lake* upon which are *three* beautiful *white* swans. Seeing how beautiful they are, compared to his own ugliness, the little duckling despairs and decides there and then to let the swans *kill* him. But just as he is about to enter the water, he catches sight of his own *reflection* and is astounded to see that he has been magically *transformed* into a lovely *white* swan, just like the others. Thus, he lives *happily* ever after.

Comparing the text of the story with the brief list of clues I have provided, it is obvious that there is a certain correspondence, and we may conclude that the originator of this popular nursery tale knew, and wished to perpetuate the Hermetic secret. We interpret the story like this.

The little duckling is unhappy because he realises that he is not as others are (the author of the tale somehow found out about the secret of the meditation and its result). He is black and therefore ugly ('ugly' is used by the initiates to describe the uninitiated mind, while 'black' indicates the first stage of the process). In desperation, he wanders off on his own (embarks upon the process), determined to find a new life (in order to invoke the astral body). Lost and alone (in the course of the process, which one can only undertake by oneself), he chances upon a lake (reflection and *water*, the initiates' code word for mental energy) upon which there are three beautiful white swans (the figure three indicates the stages of the process, the colour White, the second stage, and the word 'swan', the inner spirit). In despair, the duckling decides to let the swans kill him (he 'sacrifices' his conscious mind – that is, it is 'killed' by the process), but just as he is about to enter the water, he sees that he has been magically trans- formed (the transmission of consciousness has taken place) into a white swan like the others (like the other initiates). Thus, he lives happily (initiated) ever after.

As I will subsequently show, exactly the same message has been enciphered into other well-known nursery tales: Cinderella, Aladdin, Mother Goose and Puss in Boots. But now let us make a most unusual comparison by turning to a genuine 17th century, Hermetic text by the English mystic, Jane Leade.

Jane Leade

It is extremely rare to find an Hermetic manuscript accredited to the pen of a woman, but Jane left two descriptions of the process that are more than helpful to the investigator, for she did not resort wholly to allegory, preferring to write down her experiences in a manner that is only partly veiled. If we look at her text from the point of view that I have outlined – that she is discussing a long, meditational process – the contents are revealing, yet can still be favourably compared to the saga of the Ugly Duckling.

'GARTEN BRUNN' Published Amsterdam, 1697.

Jane is in deep meditation when she hears a voice which says;

Behold, I am God's everlasting handmaiden of wisdom, whom thou hast sought. I am here to unseal for thee the *treasure* of the deepest wisdom of God, and to be to thee even that which *Rebecca* was to her *Joseph*, namely a true, natural *mother*. For from my body and womb shalt thou be born, conceived and *reborn*.

Jane rejoices that the *morning star* on high has sought her and secludes herself during the following days to await developments, seeking in her spirit for the key that will open the entrance to the great secret within her. Her efforts to reach the *holy city* are great, but at first ineffectual. She *wanders* around the *city*, but finds no entrance and becomes apprehensive that, lacking the wonderful key she will 'grope all her days in darkness . . . never find the gate,'

"While I," she continues, "now overpowered with fear and horror at all this, was plunged into a deep *silence* and *stillness,* the word of wisdom was revealed to me and said

O deeply searching spirit, be not surprised that you have not realised your hopes for so long a time. So far you have been with many others caught in a great error, yet as you know and are sorry for your error, I will apprise you what sort of key it must be . . . And although this wonderful key of wisdom is a free gift, it will yet come to be of high value to you, O searching spirit, when you once obtain it

The voice went on to tell Jane that the most distinguished master work consists of keeping the spirit *disciplined* and learned, making it a skilled worker, or *artist,* to give it knowledge of what material, as well as in what number, weight and measure to make this pure key, which is 'the bright pure divinity in the number *three*.'

Several weeks later, Jane hears the voice again, saying:

Separate thyself and withdraw from thy animal, sensuous life, it is too coarse. I cannot appear until that is completely lost and vanished.

Later still she is told

God requires a *sacrifice* of thee. Understand me then, thou hast an earthly element that has spread and covered thee, and consequently has got the upper hand and mastery of thee; these thrones and powers must be overthrown and their place found no more. This is the first baptism that you must experience, but ah, how many have rushed into this too abruptly, because they have not given their earthly selfishness a single, mortal blow right to the heart. So I recommend to thee my *flaming sword*. Be courageous and let it achieve execution in the field of nature.

Jane finds these circumstances and conditions very hard: 'Especially,' she remarks 'Do I find myself dwelling in the offspring of a mortal shadow where whole millions of spirits tempt me and employ all their ability and strength to hinder and hold me back from high and noble exaltation.' 'You yourself must be the paschal *lamb* that shall be slain,' the voice replies. At this, Jane *submits her life*, and feels the *separation* taking place.

This narrative is far more explicit than that of the Ugly Duckling, yet a similarity can be detected. The number three is mentioned outright, and we are left in no doubt that the task is one of meditation, undertaken by Jane alone. It is far from easy, and Jane despairs, just as the Ugly Duckling did, until at last she 'sacrifices' herself (the conscious mind is deadened) and the separation of the astral body takes place. Other significant indications appear throughout the text, as for example the 'treasure' mentioned in the first words spoken by the inner voice. This should give you a hint as to the nature of the treasure supposedly hidden at Rennes le Chateau. You may also have noticed that certain emphasised words relate to biblical themes, a foretaste of what is to come.

The same correspondence of clues will be found hidden away within other, far more familiar and revered texts, demonstrating undeniably the great extent of the Rosicrucian tradition. At the pinnacle of this form of literary endeavour rests the story of the Crucifixion of Jesus, to which I shall now briefly turn as a third introductory example of the concealed wisdom.

The Crucifixion

An encapsulation of the Crucifixion and the Ascencion as reported in the Gospels will appear thus.

In spite of a prevision of his impending fate, Jesus enters Jerusalem and is condemned to be crucified, thus he *sacrifices himself* to a form of slow and painful *death* (just as the conscious mind 'dies' slowly and painfully). While on his way to the crucifixion, he is made to pass through

> . . . a place called Golgotha, that is to say, a place of the *skull*. (Matt. 27; 33)

Golgotha, as Bible readers will certainly know, is also called Calvary, a name derived from the Latin 'calvaria', meaning 'a bare skull'. Here, then, is a double reference to death, but concealed in the two names. No colours are mentioned outright in the English translation, for various reasons, but there is more than an adequate suggestion of the stages of the process, for Jesus is seen to be one of *three* victims; there were *three* Marys present; Jesus was crucified at *three* o'clock, and *died* after *three* hours of *darkness*. Then his body was taken to a *cave* in a *garden*, where it lay for *three* days before his *resurrection*.

There are, I must make it clear, a great many more obscure clues within the fabric of the story, but they will be interpreted at the appropriate place. Suffice for now to say that all three stories quoted have an identical theme running through them: that of a *self-inflicted death* followed by a magic *transformation* into something far superior. This, as you no doubt can plainly see, is exactly what happens in the meditational process that I have described to you.

The Superior Existence

The Hermetic theme is to be found in countless prominent texts – those which portray Man's desire to attain immortality – and to all except those with the knowledge of the truth behind the allegories such legends have been accepted as a reference to an abstract state which all hope to reach after the advent of physical death. But as none has ever returned from the grave either to deny or confirm such immortality, the stories require nothing less than blind faith in what a logical mind can only designate as wishful thinking of a better future, with never a hint of reality to support the idea. Uninformed Man's only recourse has been to seek psychological refuge in an earthbound doctrine, steadfastly closing his eyes to the stark truth that those who lead the faith are as uninformed as their followers. How many supposedly knowledgeable representatives of God can tell you that the 'cave' into which the body of Jesus was placed is merely an age old symbol of the inner mind? How many will carefully explain that the fire which consumed the burnt offerings, those biblical 'sacrifices', was never a physical heat, but the 'fire' of concentrated thought?

The churches of the West are not alone in their misinterpretation of 'sacred' books. In the Middle East, thousands pause every day to bow down to Mecca, an act of physical obeisance that is totally meaningless in terms of any beneficence. 'Mecca', their own sacred books tell them, is in the east and therefore the obeisance is towards the rising sun. But the sacred books have been misinterpreted, for the 'sun' therein mentioned is not the physical orb of Sol, but an emblem of the Universal Mind – the subconscious – the 'sun' within our own minds. Thus, the term *rising sun* is indicative of approaching harmony with the subconscious – the process is on the point of being completed.

Some modern schools of meditation in India have made utter fools of their pupils when they have urged them to sit cross-legged and attempt to levitate the physical body. The self-styled Gurus point out that the ancient Hindu manuscripts say it can be done, but what they fail to realise is that the text is deliberately analogous, referring really to a state of mind. And when a Buddha is depicted contemplating his navel, it does not mean that he sits with his eyes fixed on the end of his umbilical cord. The term 'navel' is used in the ancient texts to indicate the centre of the mind, and thus the *Buddha* (the initiate) should be seen as in the act of reversing his attention to the inner mind (meditation).

The production of the astral body – that is, the transmission of the personal consciousness into the Universal Mind – removes all doubts as to the reality of another, far superior existence, and this fact alone will account for the overwhelming profligacy of the Hermetic allegory that I am about to reveal. But the meditational process is obviously not one that can be carried out with ease, to be completed within the space of a week or two, or the whole world would already be acquainted with it. The basic procedure is simple enough; all that is required of you is the ability to redirect your consciousness, to bring under conscious control the incessant flow of random thoughts that constantly crowd the waking mind. Put like this, it sounds quite straightforward – but to actually accomplish it demands mental effort of a very special kind. However, it is an art that can be learned. Great patience will be necessary, for a considerable time may pass before any sign of the desired result begins to materialise, and it is true to say that the length of the process will depend wholly upon the individual and the quality of his meditation. Certainly, results will not be forthcoming in a few months. Perhaps the words of Paracelsus, a Rosicrucian, may offer some guidance;

> . . . the thing is not to be hastened, according to their opinions who suppose such work to be like unto that which is discerned in the production of corn, and of mankind; to wit, the bringing forth of one in the space of nine months, the other, ten or twelve months . . . For it is to be known that everything that is quickly or hastily made or born, doth soon perish.

(THE ARCHIDOXES MAGIC: Part II of the Secrets of Alchemy)

Or perhaps some clue may be gleaned from the words of the 16th century initiate, Jacob Boehme, who tells us that he meditated for twelve years before he wrote his 'Aurora'.

Further, anyone who embarks upon the process must be prepared to endure a radical psychological change, to say nothing of a coincidental upheaval in his personal circumstances. The period of the process brings about a mental change, induced by gradual disassociation from all that which has hitherto been accepted as the reality of the environment. Such psychological upheaval is symbolised in the Gospels as the 'suffering' that Jesus endured on the Cross. Elsewhere, it is stylised as the mortal combat between St Michael and the Dragon, between Horus and Typhon, or by Hercules cutting off the head of the Hydra.

At this juncture, I will refrain from elaborating further on the mechanics of the process, for the Hermetic science will appear much less a figment of the imagination were I first to offer an interpretation of the allegories pertaining to it. I therefore embark upon their disclosure as they appear within some of the most prominent texts available to us. With the tale of Ugly Duckling I provided a small and relatively insignificant example of the hidden message, but my inference that the same message lies within the story of Jesus is a lot less insignificant and will require a great deal of support. In the following chapters, I will endeavour to provide it, at the same time enhancing your interest by examining complex texts of myth and magic, so that you may realise the true meaning of them. I will adequately reveal the inner message of Rennes le Chateau in the final section which deals with similar caches of non-existent treasure.

So that the reader may check for himself – and it is sincerely to be hoped that the interest aroused will be sufficient to impel him to do so – I have deliberately remained with historical texts that are easily available to the casual book buyer. However, when browsing through these yourself, you will be required to break a habit of long standing. Seldom, when perusing an historic document, is there any urge to look further than the basic meaning given to the words. You must remember, though, that the Hermetic writer never failed to capitalise on that fact. Every single one of their texts is in the form of a code which you will have to break.

Let us take history in its correct chronological order and begin by stepping back into the dry as dust era of the long dead Egyptian Dynasties, for it is only here that we can uncover the foundations of the complicated word play so expertly used in the allegories of many subsequent generations. The visit will be as brief as possible, for I appreciate that the archaic names are likely to try the patience somewhat, but it is a necessary hurdle. Thereafter, the stories will remain on more familiar ground.

CHAPTER FOUR

Ancient Egypt

The religious system of the ancient Egyptians was based on the immortality of Man and his resurrection after death, and it was once conjectured that the science of embalming was conceived and perfected for the purpose of preserving the physical shell so that it would be ready for the spirit to re-enter at the appointed time. But when it was found that the old embalmers had a habit of disembowelling the corpse – a bit of surgical tidiness that would effectively preclude its return to life – it was more logically assumed that the final resurrection would take place in the 'after life', whatever that may be. Yet, logical though this assumption is, it somehow fails properly to account for the elaborately constructed, legendary picture left in the records of the Egyptians, depicting planes of existence supposed to lie beyond the realms of physical perception. Are we to conclude that the myriad of gods and goddesses, the strange underworlds, the long 'journeyings of millions of years' as portrayed in the surviving material, were brought into existence purely as a result of imaginative impulses – and then revered, copied, hoarded in secret temple archives through the passage of five thousand years or more?

The true answer is that the astral body and the means of producing it were known in Egypt exactly as they are in the Europe of today – accepted as true knowledge by a select number of initiates, while the rest were either ignorant of the phenomenon, or gave it no credence. The writings that remain to us, therefore, describe the 'resurrection' of the more noble part of Man – and just as in all Hermetic manuscripts, the message is deeply buried in code.

The social structure of ancient Egypt was one of great simplicity. At the top was the Pharaoh, with a select school of initiate priests to guide him. At the other end, the ordinary masses. The initiates were in possession of the highest skills – not, of course, the technology of our time, but none the less a high proficiency in mathematics, architecture, metallurgy, agriculture, geographic measurement and other allied arts and crafts – and these were open to all. The one science that was restricted to the Pharaoh and specially selected candidates was the Hermetic Art, the method by which the transmission of consciousness could be achieved. This secret constituted the innermost knowledge around which the famous Mysteries were centred.

The priest class, with their knowledge of hieroglyphics, enjoyed a special form of secret communication. One aspect of it materialised as the symbolic picture, an ostensibly innocuous scene in its superficial appearance, but composed of certain articles or actions which contained a hidden significance recognised only by the initiates. From this first pictorial code, a collection of special glyphs gradually evolved, far more sophisticated in their conception and which could be interpreted in three different ways; the literal (or face value); the collectively symbolic; and the individually symbolic. It was by use of these glyphs that an initiate of some thousand years or so before the Christian Era set down the text we know as the Pentateuch. Thus, it will come as no surprise to find that a number of analogous devices used in Genesis will have already appeared in earlier Egyptian and Sumerian texts.

The concept of the Universal Mind is plainly discernible. According to the renowned Egyptologist, M. Maspero, they reduced everything to one kind of primaeval matter which they believed contained everything in embryo, an idea which they symbolised as *Water*. In the opening verses of Genesis, in a story of Creation that comes directly from the Egyptian and Sumerian conception, we are told that in the beginning, the spirit of God moved on the face of the waters. The initiate knows that this passage does not refer to physical water, but expresses the idea of the birth of the Universe. The 'water' is primaeval matter, the prima materia of the Alchemists: energy vibrating at the speed of light and therefore not only formless, but timeless. The 'spirit of God' is the sentience of the Universal Mind, which gave birth to the physical universe by thought – a thought which 'crystalised' matter into the physical suns and planets that we observe from our earthly position.

One of the finest sources from which we can derive the Egyptian idea of the all-creative force are the writings of the classic Greek scholars. Plutarch, the great historian of the 1st century A.D., sets out at length the traditional story of the Egyptian deity, Osiris, in his DE ISIDE ET OSIRIS, but he makes a point of telling his readers that his account is a 'reflection of something real', and for this reason differs from that of other writers. What he meant to convey by that statement is the fact that he was an initiate and that his text concealed a deeper meaning. Briefly reviewed, his version of the story runs thus.

The Legend of Isis and Osiris

The central characters are Osiris, the King of Egypt, and his wife, Queen Isis. After detailing the birth and geneaology of Osiris, the account arrives at the point where he becomes king. Law and order are established and he reigns benignly with Isis by his side. Osiris, however, has one implacable enemy: his brother Set, who covets the throne and schemes to take over the kingdom. To this end, he comes to the palace and by devious means, obtains the exact measurements of Osiris's body, after which he constructs a coffin-shaped chest, richly fashioned and heavily be-jewelled. Knowing it will fit only the king, Set offers it as a priceless gift to any person whose body it fits exactly. When Osiris eventually lies down inside it to try it for size, the lid is slammed and locked, and the casket set adrift on the Nile.

While the distraught Isis searched in vain for her husband, the coffin was washed up on the shores of Byblos, the force of the waves tossing it high into the branches of a tamarisk bush. In time, the bush grew into a magnificent tree, enclosing the coffin within its trunk. It was such a remarkable specimen that it came to the attention of Melcarthus, the king of Byblos, who was so impressed with its height and beauty that he had it cut down and made into a pillar to support the roof of his palace.

Learning of the plight of Osiris, Isis hastened to Byblos where she approached the palace incognito and secured a position as nurse to one of the sons of Melcarthus. Every night, when the others had retired, Isis would pile great logs on the fire and then thrust the child among them, after which she would sit and mourn for her lost husband. News of this strange behaviour soon reached the ears of Queen Astarte, who concealed herself in the great hall to find out if the rumours were true. When night came, and Isis thrust the baby into the fire, the horrified Astarte rushed forward to snatch her son back – at which Isis reproved her sternly, declaring that by her action she had robbed the boy of immortality. Isis then revealed her true identity and explained about the plight of Osiris, begging that the tree be cut open so that she could take the coffin back to Egypt.

Melcarthus and Astarte complied, and the coffin was brought back and secretly concealed. Set, however, while out hunting by the light of the Moon, happened on the hiding place, and in a great rage, tore the body of Osiris into fourteen pieces and scattered them throughout the land. In the final stage of the drama, Isis sets out to recover the pieces, building a shrine to mark the spot at which each piece was found, until Osiris is whole once more.

In order to make the interpretation of this allegory quite clear, it is necessary briefly to consider the ancient Egyptian teaching regarding the transmigration of souls. It was believed that there existed on a plane not visible to human eyes, a Central Soul, and each time a babe was born, a small part of the Central Soul detached itself and became incarcerated in the infant's body as its personal soul, remaining there until the end of the subject's earthly life. At physical death, the soul would then be re-united with the parent Soul. All the time the small portion of the Central Soul was encased in the human body, its owner had no idea that the spirit inside him was connected to, or came from, the bigger Soul, because it was prevented from doing so by an evil force.

Careful appraisal of both allegory and tradition shows that the two relate to the same circumstances. The Central Soul (the Universal Mind) is represented by Osiris, who is cut up piecemeal and scattered throughout the land (many small parts of the Central Soul encased in human bodies). The incarceration of each soul-portion is allegorised by the body of Osiris in the casket, which in turn is trapped within the tree. As you read on, you will find that the 'tree' analogy is one that has endured for centuries. Set is, of course, the evil one, a personification of the constantly-moving conscious mind which prevents access to the subconscious power. Isis, the woman, symbolises that action of the waking mind which will make harmony with the subconscious possible, the power of inwardly directed reflection. Her strange rite, that of placing the infant on the fire each night, is intended to convey the method of the process, the 'fire' being the power of reflected thought, and 'night' indicative of the spot where such a process must take place – in the mind. That is why, when Astarte snatched back her child from the fire, Isis is made to say that the babe had been denied immortality (without the 'fire' of the process, the transmission of consciousness cannot be made).

The basic plot of the Egyptian legend, one of cruel death followed by a resurrection, is therefore an allegory of the initiate's process. Plutarch added his own little touches, it is true, but then as I have remarked, the scholar was an Adept.

Throughout this volume, I will be using the term 'initiate', or 'adept', quite frequently, and I am aware that it may infuriate some readers, but I must make the point that hitherto, the term will likely have been employed without an accompanying explanation of the precise meaning of such 'initiateship' – not the case here, so I hope to be excused.

The Origin of Mother Goose

The idea that a nursery tale character stems from Egyptian traditions may be hard to accept, but consider, for instance, the comparison between Cinderella's foot fitting the slipper where all others had failed, and the body of Osiris being the only one to fit the casket. The themes are identical. Similarly, certain other fairy tales have an ancestry far more ancient than is normally believed.

The Westcar Papyrus, translated from the Egyptian hieratic by A.Erman (Berlin 1890) contains a quaint fable that holds a message for us. According to the text, Herutataf, son of the Pharaoh Khufu (better known as Cheops, the builder of the Great Pyramid) brought his father news of a sage reputed to be 110 years old, who lived in the township of Tette-Senefru. It was rumoured widely that this wise old man was able to re-join to its body a head that had been completely cut off. It was also alleged that he had influence over the lion and was acquainted with the mysteries of Thoth.

By Khufu's command, Herutataf brought the sage to the King's court, whereupon Khufu gave the order for a convicted criminal's head to be cut off so that he could watch the sage put it back again. The wise man intervened, begging to be excused from using a human victim, so a goose was brought in instead. Its head was cut off and placed on one side of the room, while the body was laid on the other. The sage thereupon spoke certain words of power, at which the body of the goose struggled to its feet and began to waddle towards the head. The head, meanwhile, was seen to inch its way along the floor in the direction of the body. When the two met, they were immediately joined together again – and the goose stood up and cackled.

In assessing this tale, it is at once apparent that it is a fable of the nursery style, like the story of the Ugly Duckling, and therefore fiction. But as we now know the tales to be fictitious with a purpose, we must look for the hidden meaning. In this instance, the Hermetic process is conveyed not with the various clues that are so abundant in other texts, but by the main theme of Death and Resurrection. That the object of the 'resurrection' is a goose may give some idea of the hoary antiquity of the character Mother Goose, for the early Egyptians knew their most powerful god as the Great Cackler and stylised him/her as a goose.

The Great Cackler represented the power of reflected thought that would eventually produce the transmission of consciousness. Thus, when the narrative says – after the dead goose is alive again – that the 'goose stood up and cackled', it is a coded way of saying that the astral body has been born, the process accomplished. Virtually the same expression can be found in the Gospels when Peter is made to deny Christ, and the cock crows *three* times, it being merely an adaptation of the earlir theme.

The sage, it is said, had influence over the lion, a statement that has nothing whatever to do with the physical king of beasts, but must be deciphered by reference to the zodiacal sign of Leo. As you will be shown in the following chapter, each sign of the zodiac has some relation to the mental process, and that of the Lion holds the same symbolic meaning as *Gold,* or the *Sun,* referring not to the beast, the metal or the orb, but to the Universal Mind. Therefore, the statement in the fable telling readers that the sage was influential over the lion is an expression of his initiateship.

Perhaps it would be helpful at this point to pause and remind ourselves that the span of Egyptian history covers a considerable period, especially in respect of the texts we shall be examining. The time from just prior to the Christian Era back into that of the early Dynasties – some five thousand years or more – saw many generations who inevitably imposed their own individual revisions and additions to the existing range of symbolism. Thus, the whole Egyptian period will present a wide range of gods and goddesses, each one of which has been assumed to personify something entirely different, but which in reality have an identical foundation. This situation gave birth to double, or even compound symbolism – a wide choice of emblems that resolve to a single root – and so we find that the gods Maau; Nu; Tmu; Ra; and Osiris, all represent the Sun – which in turn represents the Universal Mind.

The power of reflected thought on the other hand, was symbolised by the names Nut; the Great Cackler; Ptar (or Ptah); Thoth; Isis and the rest, and when traced to their common source would be found to be emblematic of the Moon, the initiate's prime symbol of reflection.

This use of the sun and the moon to convey the Hermetic principle gives substance to the oft quoted maxim 'as above, so below', for as the moon is seen to reflect the light of the sun so the conscious mind reflects the *light* of the inner power. And in this basic expression of the mental practice, we once again find the elements of Dualism, the *Sun* being the Father, and the *Moon* the Mother.

Returning now to the sage in our fable, we can complete the explanation of the enigmatic announcement that he was acquainted with the mysteries of Thoth. Thoth was the god of the Moon, and so the remark means that the sage knew how to implement the power of inner reflection in pursuit of the Hermetic process. It is a reiteration of the statement that he was an Adept.

The fable of the sage and the goose offers one more slender clue inasmuch as the name Herutataf is linked with it, indicating that the prince was most certainly an initiate himself. And since no Egyptian prince was likely to be initiated into the great secret before his father, it follows that Khufu himself was in possession of all there was to know about the process – an assumption that is adequately supported by the fact that the Pharaoh built the Great Pyramid of Giza.

The Pyramid and the Sphinx

Egypt's astounding Pyramid Age commenced with the massive, but rather crude, stepped monument constructed in the time of the Pharoah, Zoser. Less than two hundred years later, during which a trial and error period of architectural evolution took place, the Great Pyramid of Khufu demonstrated that the art form had been perfected to the ultimate degree. Thereafter, the peak having been reached, Pyramidism declined as quickly as it had arisen. Nearly five thousand years later, the monuments remain – in their varying stages of dilapidation – to present researchers with a brow-furrowing mystery. What was the motivation behind such an impressive endeavour?

There has been much wild and often unfounded speculation as to the true purpose behind the Great Pyramid – whether it was a tomb, built on a grandiose scale merely to satisfy the ego of the monarch, or if it was designed as the legend says, to contain the wisdom of the whole world. It is certainly true that, with the aid of an unfettered imagination, the great stone edifice can be interpreted in a number of surprising ways, but the more rational explanation is that Khufu erected it as a monument to point the way to Man's highest possible goal whilst here on Earth: the completion of the Hermetic process.

Support for this lies in the appearance of a powerful religious centre in a city just a little way north of Memphis – an appearance that coincided with the advent of the Pyramid Age. The Egyptians knew the city as On, and it was so mentioned in Genesis, but the later Greeks called it Heliopolis, the City of the Sun, a title that must be identified with the symbolism explained in the fable of the sage and the goose. Those monuments which belong to the Pyramid Age were, in almost every instance, built on that section of the Nile's bank which stretches southward from Heliopolis, like a great serpent line of monuments with the City of the Sun at its very head. There is ample evidence to show that the priests of the Temple of On were initiates, and that the city was at that period the centre of Egypt's Hermetic fraternity. In the very beginning of the era, the main emblem of the initiate priest was either a pillar, or a mound with a pointed top, thought by some to symbolise the primaeval mound from which emerged the 'waters of creation'. It can now be appreciated that the Pharaohs, with their great resources of money and manpower, erected the pyramids as an extension of the symbol – for don't forget that the Pharaohs were initiates too.

We interpret the Great Pyramid in the same manner that the old priests interpreted their 'mound', beginning with the single point which shows the way in which the mind must be concentrated in order to achieve success. The Pyramid utilises four upward pointing triangles for its sides, and these denote the four, symbolic 'elements' which are always connected with the Universal Mind: Air; Earth; Fire and Water. The triangular shape has a meaning of its own, the upward pointing figure signifying the subconscious (the Universal Mind, or the Macrocosm), while the downward triangle represents the conscious mind (the Mother, the Microcosm). When the two are made to connect, or intertwine, as they must do if the process is to be successful, the two triangles become one figure, the six pointed star later known to the Jewish race as the Star of David.

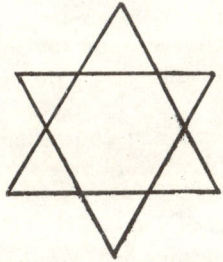

The inner chamber where the Pharaoh was supposed to be buried with his *treasure*, is in the *centre* of the great mass, a design meant to indicate the centre of the mind, the point upon which the inward meditation must be focussed. You may recall older texts which relate that the Pyramid was originally encased entirely in *white* stone, and that the entrance to the gallery was *hidden* and *had to be discovered*. And there exists a very old legend that the missing tip of the edifice was of solid *gold*.

There has been considerable archaeological discussion regarding the fact that the King's chamber was found to be empty, and it was wondered if grave robbers of earlier times had already found their way into the tomb to remove both mummy and treasure. But knowledge of the Hermetic symbolism tells us that there was never meant to be a body in Khufu's sarcophagus, and that the Pharaoh had his remains interred elsewhere. The empty scarcophagus has been placed there to indicate that the 'resurrection' has already taken place, and as it is Khufu's pyramid, it is his voice from the past telling us that he was an initiate. An almost identical expression of the same theme can be found written into the New Testament, when the *cave* which held the body of Jesus was found to be empty.

We are all cognisant of the enduring tradition connected with the Great Pyramid which hints at the existence of a secret chamber somewhere beneath it, and in which will be discovered all the knowledge of the ancients. Whether or not this story is a remnant of fact, or merely a long held myth has been hotly debated, but I feel that it has no basis in fact. Rather, it is a surviving part of the Hermetic tradition attached to the monument, for it indicates that if the symbolism of the Pyramid is interpreted correctly, then indeed the 'knowledge of the ancients' will be made available (initiation will reveal all).

I cannot move on from the Great Pyramid without mention of its companion symbol and guardian, the enigmatic Sphinx. This monument has always presented an impenetrable mystery to those seeking the reason for its shape and purpose, but to others versed in the Hermetic knowledge, there is no mystery, merely an admiration for the inspired architects who were able to combine such simplicity of expression with true grandeur.

In the Sphinx we see a lion with a human head. Some say the head is that of a *woman*, some say a man, but it hardly matters, for the meaning remains open to the same interpretation. Pliny once wrote that the Sphinx was

a wondrous object of *art* upon which *silence* has been observed.

I have emphasised two words in the sentence to show that Pliny himself was an initiate and that his manner of writing immediately connects the Sphinx to the 'art' of the Hermeticist. The Lion motif, as we have already seen is representative of the subconscious, while the human head is self-evident as the conscious mind. The fact that the two are joined together in the one body is a reiteration of the theme expressed by the Star of David, that the two must be so intertwined, or connected, for a successful conclusion to the meditational practice.

The Sphinx is positioned so that it faces east and is therefore looking towards the *rising sun*.

The historian, Alexander the Great, has written that the Sphinx was a follower of the goddess Latona, a deity who is symbolically identical to Isis, Thoth, the Great Cackler, and, in later times, Mary the Virgin, all emblems of the reflective power.

Corroboration of this interpretation can be obtained by the examination of hieroglyphics in the Temple of Edfu, in Upper Egypt, where a god can be seen changing himself into a lion with a human head in order to vanquish Set. The reason for the lion/human *transformation* is self evident now that we have discovered Set to be the Egyptian Satan, a personification of the unstilled conscious mind. When Set is defeated, it allows the birth of the astral body, symbolised in Egyptian lore by the god Horus.

Finally, I would like to add that one of the most important aspects of the symbolism rests in the fact that both the Great Pyramid and the Sphinx are constructed entirely of stone. This may seem irrelevant, seeing that there was very little choice of alternative materials, but in later times the term 'stone' became one of the leading emblems of the conscious mind, as in the New Testament where the symbol was interlinked with the name Peter.

The Origin of St. Peter

The name of Herutataf, Khufu's son, leads us to an old and exceedingly mysterious section in the compendium of funeral rites known as the *Egyptian Book of the Dead*. As it does so, we must bear in mind that Herutataf was a prominent initiate and therefore to find him linked with the text almost certainly indicates that Hermetic allegory will be present.

No scholar has been able to determine exactly how old the contents of the *Book of the Dead* really are, or when it was first compiled, but a copy of the hieratic text inscribed on the coffin of Queen Menthu-Hetep (11th Dynasty – about 2,500 B.C.) informs us that a certain chapter of it was discovered far earlier, in the reign of Hesep-Ti, the fifth king of the 1st Dynasty (about 4,266 B.C.). This particular chapter is so old that even the early Egyptians themselves looked upon it as an antique and were uncertain of its origins. The rubric on Queen Menthu-Hetep's coffin says:

> This chapter was found in the foundations beneath the hennu boat by the foreman of the builders in the time of the king of the north and south, Hesep-Ti, *triumphant*.

I have emphasised the word 'triumphant' for as you will shortly come to appreciate, it was the signature of an Adept, a sign of the process accomplished.

Of the same mysterious chapter, the Nebseni Papyrus says;

This chapter was found in the city of Khemennu (Hermopolis) on a block of ironstone, written in letters of lapis-lazuli, under the feet of the god.

The Turin Papyrus (26th Dynasty, or later) adds that the name of the finder was Herutataf, son of Khufu (about 3,733 B.C.), who was at the time making an inspection of the temples.

Thus, the real origin of the chapter is shrouded in myth and all that we can safely assume is that it is extremely ancient. Why, then, should it survive? The answer is in the fact that Herutataf's name is connected with it – and this, coupled with the fairy tale quality of the quote from the Nebseni Papyrus regarding the way in which it was found, plainly warns us that there is more to the text than just the literal message. Today, the translation of the chapter is easily available to the reader in the form of a paperback edition of the Papyrus of Ani, entitled THE EGYPTIAN BOOK OF THE DEAD, by A.E. Wallis Budge.

The Papyrus of Ani, all seventy eight feet of it and the longest known of its period, was found at Thebes in 1882, but now resides in the British Museum. The papyrus itself has darkened with age, but originally it was fairly light, almost white in colour. Most of the chapters therein are illustrated by a series of brightly coloured vignettes, whilst the text is in black with the introductory rubrics in red. At the top and bottom there is a border painted in yellow and red. No doubt casual observers would fail to notice any significance in the fact that the predominant colours are thus black, white, yellow and red – the four ancient Hermetic emblems.

As the reader who wishes to examine the whole text at first hand has only to go to the nearest bookseller, I will not unnecessarily lengthen this section by quoting the whole of the chapter in question – number seventeen in Budge's volume – but will suffice with a limited example of its style and form. I add that it will make little sense, for I give the original form from the hieroglyphics, not the transliteration into grammatical English. The phrases in large letters are those which are written in red and are therefore of significance.

(first quote from text)
THE BEGINNINGS OF THE PRAISINGS (AND) GLORI-
FICATIONS, OF COMING OUT AND GOING INTO
NETER-KHERT glorious in Amentet the beautiful. Of coming out by day in forms of existence (which) he pleaseth, of playing at

draughts (and) sitting in the hall, (and) of coming forth as a living soul. SAITH Osiris, Scribe Ani, AFTER HE HATH ARRIVED IN PORT, being glorious what hath been done on Earth, become words of all Tmu.

(second quote from text)
. . . WHAT, THEN, IS IT? The horizon it is of his father Tmu I have made an end of my failings, I have removed my defects. WHAT, THEN, IS IT? The cuttings off of the corruptible matter it is of Osiris the Scribe Ani, triumphant before gods all. Driven away are the defects all which belong to him. WHAT, THEN, IS IT? The purification it is on the day of his birth. I am purified in my double nest great exceedingly which is in Suten-hennen, (on) day that of offerings of the people to god that great who (is) in it. WHAT, THEN, IS IT? 'Millions of Years' (is) the name of the one. 'Green Lake' (is) the name of the other. . .

To make a comparison with information to be given in forth-coming chapters, I ask you to register the fact that the Scribe Ani seems to be celebrating his safe arrival in port, not from a journey on a material sea, but travel in a world beyond mortal ken, the sphere of the gods. He is now 'triumphant' and his name, whenever it is mentioned, is always linked with that of Osiris (the Universal Mind). Mentioned too, is the incongruous fact that he is sitting in the hall playing draughts.

In the second quote, the attention is drawn to a certain phrase which is repeated with monotonous regularity. In the Papyrus itself, the phrase has the added emphasis of being written in red, whilst the rest of the text remains in black. Throughout the length of the chapter, the same phrase is continually employed, and as translated by Budge, is 'pu tra eref su' (What, then, is it?) and 'peti tra eref su' (Who, then, is it?).

It must now be brought to mind that the hieratic text of Egypt, along with a similar text which emerged from ancient Sumeria, developed more or less from a common root, a script that employed only consonants, leaving the vowel sounds to be added at the reader's discretion. Such a loose arrangement left the way open for deliberate use of the wrong vowels, to be applied independent of the context of the subject matter, and which rapidly established a complicated system of phonetic equivalents by which the initiates concealed their Science. The repetitious phrases in the Papyrus of Ani are an example of this, and to detect the inner meaning to which our attention has been drawn, the phrases must be reduced to their

original, consonantal form. We find that they would have been
written thus

PTR RF S'

Upon seeing this, a non-initiate would naturally interpret it in
terms of the subject under discussion and would render the vowel
sounds that appear in the transcription: 'What, then, is it?'. But an
initiate would not fail to notice a glaring alternative, for out of
context, the letters PTR can be made to yield Ptar, a principal deity
of Hermetic symbolism. In the temple festival performances, those
who played the part of Ptar (or as the name is sometimes spelt, Ptah)
were always dressed in *white*, for the god was considered to be the
Regenerator, assisting in the birth of the 'white ones', or the
'purified'. As I have explained, the inner meaning of these statements
relates to the attainment of the transmission of consciousness.

The name Ptar was also said to mean 'Illuminator', and was
symbolised by the drawing of an open eye, an emblem which
parallels the Third Eye of the Hindus, and relates to the same thing.
As a solar god, Ptar was known in Egyptian manuscripts as the 'Disc
of Heaven who illuminateth the world by the fire in his eyes' – and
when this phrase is compared with the mechanics of the process as
discussed, for example, in the works of Plato, it will be recognised
that Ptar's connection to the Hermetic science is no figment of the
imagination.

Thus, every time the text of chapter seventeen querulously asks of
its reader 'what, then, is it?', it is secretly stating the name of one of
the chief gods of the mental process, a fact that would not be missed
by an initiate. The same device crops up in the second of the
Rosicrucian Manifestos, and also in the Bible with the description of
that wonderful but fabulous food called Manna. According to the
Old Testament, when the Israelites first saw Manna, they said,
'What is it?' – literally 'Man-hu'. As you will be shown, Manna is a
substance that never existed in reality, despite the mental gymnastics
of the scholars who have sought to rationalise it.

The device PTR survived to become most prominent in the New
Testament as Peter, the disciple. In the old Aramaic and Hebrew
languages, PTR is rendered 'patar', the precise translation of which
has always eluded scholars who know nothing of the art of Hermetic
allegory, although they were forced to conclude that the manuscripts in which it appeared were undeniably connected with the
secrets of some form of initiation. In the New Testament, the word
appears as 'petra' (stone) and thus is the name of the apostle, Peter.
The latter is also derived through the Aramaic word for stone,

'kephas' (Cephus: alternative name for Peter). The only difference between the New Testament and the Papyrus of Ani is that in the former, the inner meaning of the term 'stone' is a reference to the conscious mind which, all unknowingly, holds the key to the subconscious. This is why the Gospel writers tell us that Peter holds the keys to the kingdom of heaven (the subsconscious). But Peter, as a real life character, never existed any more than did the god Ptar. Both were symbols of the Hermetic Science.

And so, the long and significant history of the word PTR, its undoubted connection with 'initiation', and the questioning nature of the phrase in which it is incorporated, all warn us that the text of the Papyrus of Ani, chapter seventeen, holds a hidden meaning, and we must examine it in that light.

The whole tone of the text is an expression of triumph at some achievement which is only explained in terms of the gods connected with it. He (Ani) is said to fly like a hawk (the Hawk-headed god being Horus, Egyptian symbol of the astral body – which explains why he can 'fly'); he cackles like a goose (refer to my remarks about the Great Cackler); he is purified, all defects being driven away (the mind is 'purified', that is, stilled, while the absence of defects means that Ani is now 'perfect', a term which relates to the first matter from which the astral body is composed, considered by the Hermeticists to be 'perfect matter', and which has its parallel emblem in the Virgin, who is 'immaculate'). There is also the mention of a great combat between Horus and Set, the 'battle' to still the mind. Throughout the text, the scribe Ani's name is linked with that of Osiris, the subconscious power. There can be no plainer indication that Ani is rightfully celebrating his successful completion of the long and wearisome meditational process.

Nowhere, of course, does the text openly describe the method by which this may be achieved, but the recognisable hints are manifold. The vignettes illustrating the text include some which are unmistakably Hermetic, one example of which is the first vignette (plate number ten in Wallis Budge's volume) of the chapter. It shows a tree, near which a cat is seen, cutting off the head of a serpent. The subscription tells us

I (Ani) am that cat which is fighting near the Persea tree in Heliopolis, destroying the enemies of Neb-er-tcher (see fig, 6/7).

Neb-er-tcher is an early name for Osiris and was usually employed to represent the complete reconstruction of Osiris's body after it had been hacked to pieces (in one of the legends). The enemies of Neb-er-tcher, in this case personified by the serpent Apepi, are of course, the constantly moving thoughts of the conscious mind which must be 'killed'. The emblem of the cat, to be elaborated upon shortly, was much used to signify the reflective power. In this vignette, the cat (reflection) is seen to be defeating the serpent (the moving thoughts) by cutting off its head (by 'killing' it). The Persea tree is a variation of that in the legend of Osiris and Isis, an emblem of the physical world, later to become prominent in Greek mythology and Alchemy as the Oak. The whole picture is thus an expression of the meditational process.

Another vignette which can be compared to an idea expressed in the Tarot pack, and which should evoke deep thought from those who maintain that the Tarot symbolism does not stem from as far back as the Egyptian cultures, is attached to chapter fifty one. It shows Ani kneeling beside a pool of water (*water* and *reflection*), near a sycamore tree in which the goddess Nut (the *mother* symbol) – another emblem of reflective power) appears, pouring water from a vessel into Ani's hands. This little scene can be closely compared with the Star, the 17th card of the Tarot. Both hold the same concealed meaning, that of initiation in progress, but in the case of the vignette, Ani the scribe has included himself and the sycamore tree.

With these interpretations – and I add that they are but a few of many possibilities – it can perhaps be realised that the Egyptian cult of Death and Resurrection was not evolved as a result of an over-worked imagination, but that there exists a foundation of true knowledge and experience beneath it all, stemming from the transfer of a living, human consciousness into the exalted state of the Universal Mind. Understandably, uninitiated Egyptologists have made errors in their attempts to interpret the strange carvings left on temple walls. For example, when a carving or a vignette shows a supine human form, with its soul (depicted as a bird, or a bee with a human face) hovering nearby, it has been concluded that the picture represents a newly deceased subject, and that his soul is on the point of departure for heaven. From the initiate's point of view, however, the same picture would indicate a fellow adept in the process of developing the 'second body': the 'perfect' part of Man's mind.

The scope for similar interpretation is wide, but recognising that the obscure Egyptian divinity names are of little interest to anyone but a dedicated Eqyptologist, I will close this chapter with a brief annotation of the more familiar emblems.

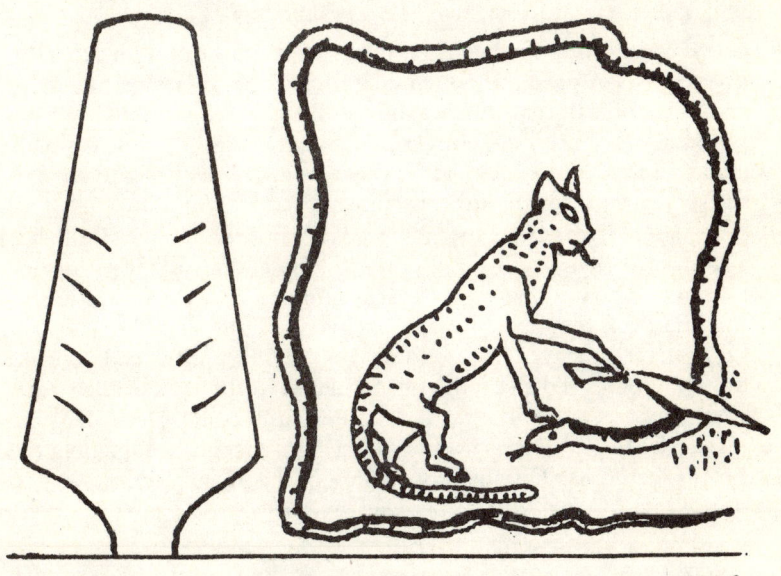

FIGURE 6/7.

The Cat:

Even the casual reader of Egyptian history will be aware that the
domestic cat was venerated during certain periods of the culture,
especially in the city of Bubaste. What went on there has been
partially explained by Herodotus, who wrote

> The Egyptians meet in solemn assembly not once a year only, but
> on a number of occasions, the most important and best attended
> being the festival of Artemis at Bubastis; the second importance is
> the assembly at Busiris, a city in the middle of the Delta,
> containing a vast temple dedicated to Isis, the Egyptian equivalent
> of Demeter, in whose honour the meeting is held.

In this passage, we are alerted by the fact that the names of Isis and
Artemis are invoked, both god names symbolic of the inner reflection, and it follows that the reason for the central symbol, the cat,
must also be Hermetic.

In very early times, the animal was identified with a god of the *Sun*
called Maau, pronounced 'may-ah-oh'. It is at once noticable that the
pronunciation produces a sound similar to that of a cat's 'meow' –
and if you recall that the worship of the sun did not pertain to the
physical orb, but to the Universal Mind, the reason for the animal's
exalted status becomes clear. It was a living phonetic equivalent of
the secret name for the subconscious.

In later Dynasties, the cat-headed goddess, Bast, made her
appearance, being allied this time to the Moon in a very quaint
manner. Every modern motorist is familiar with the little studs in
the middle of the road which reflect his headlights at night. They are
known as 'cat's eyes' for good reason. The Egyptians had no cars,
but they observed the same phenomenon in the eyes of their cats,
which reflected the firelight and torchlight, to emit a greenish glow,
just as the Moon reflects the rays of the Sun. In this phenomenon, the
cat presented itself as a handy symbol of the *Moon* – and by way of
double symbolism, of Hermetic reflection.

The Scarab Beetle

Much has been written about the scarab beetle motif found everywhere in Egyptian drawings, mostly to connect the insect with the
sun. This was done by comparing the rolling of the insect's dung ball
with the daily passage of the sun across the sky, but the motif had a

deeper meaning than the Egyptologists were able to guess, as the following emphasised words will show.

The Hermetic significance given to the lowly beetle is much the same as that of the common egg. In order to *give birth*, to its young, the insect lays its eggs in a ball of dung, which it then rolls about with it wherever it goes. The *internal heat* of the dung gradually hatches out the young beetles, much as the heat of a chicken's body incubates its eggs. Therefore, the beetle was seen to be *self-producing*, the application of a *gentle heat* (comparable to meditation) bringing forth *new life* (the astral body) from a *most unusual place* (few know that the astral body can be produced by the efforts of the conscious mind). In recognition of this hidden significance, the insect was honoured by a beetle-headed god named Khepera.

The Flail: The Crook: The Staff

These three signs appear everywhere in Egyptian pictographs and they represent the earliest known emblems of the three stages of the mental process. All three, in their different aspects, indicate the mastery by the initiate over his own conscious mind. It is worthwhile to note that the Staff and the Crook survived to be widely used in the Bible, along with the 'shepherd', who is really the initiate undergoing the process by 'shepherding' his 'lambs' (controlling his thoughts).

Thoth

I make special mention of this famous deity because his name is found even in England, brought there by North African visitors about four thousand years ago and left to designate burial mounds, some of which are still to be seen scattered across the countryside. They are called 'toots', after Thoth, a name which is properly pronounced 'tote'. In older texts, his name appears more accurately recorded as Tehuti.

In Egyptian inscriptions, Thoth is generally depicted holding what looks like an ink jar, and for this reason has been nominated the God of Writing. However, this is an incorrect translation, for the jar, or vase, is also a hieroglyph for the heart, and the Hermeticists made use of the figure to symbolise the 'heart' of the conscious mind, the inner centre on which the Neophyte must direct his thoughts. Thus, more correctly, Thoth is sometimes known as the god of the *Moon*.

On some monuments, he is depicted with the head of an Ibis and to explain this additional symbol, we must recall that there were two species of Ibis common to the Egyptians, some all *black,* and others a mixture of *black* and *white.* Apart from the obvious emblems of the first two Hermetic colours, there is an additional significance in the fact that the birds were noted for their habit of *killing snakes* and ravaging crocodiles' eggs. In the Egyptian symbolic scheme, the *crocodile* held the same occult meaning as the *serpent* – the conscious mind which must be 'killed'.

The Ladder of Horus

As Horus personifies the astral self, this 'ladder' is a symbol of that which must be ascended in order to reach the exalted, astral state, and is therefore an emblem of the meditational task. It was described as the ladder by which souls of the dead made their way to the Fields of Peace (Sekhet-Hetep), but we can read between the lines and recognise the 'ladder' as being the way to the *silence* (peace) of the mind. The Fields of Peace, incidentally, were always said to lie to the *north* (i.e., the inner mind).

The ladder theme emerges elsewhere; in the Old Testament, it is Jacob's Ladder; the Alchemists of the Middle Ages called it their 'Scala Philosophorum' (philosopher's ladder); and it can still be seen in Masonic tradition as the ladder on the First Degree Tracing Board.

The Game of Draughts

This game was a favourite pastime in early Egypt, but there was a significance attached to it that went far beyond the actual play. The pieces were stylised with the heads of lions, jackals, and gods which related directly to the Hermetic science. In time, it was adopted by the Persians, who embellished the fundamental rules until it evolved into the intricate mental challenge we know today as the game of Chess. From here, it travelled to Europe, brought in by initiates who were fully aware of its concealed meaning.

The significance is the same as that of the elaborate labyrinth constructions scattered here and there throughout the Old World, for both are intended to symbolise the difficult and complicated mental task which faces the would-be adept. In chess, the game is won at the call of 'check-mate' – really 'Shah Mata', Persian for 'the king is dead'. The 'king', of course, is Rex Mundi, the Devil, the

FIGURE 8.

conscious mind. The Labyrinth, on the other hand, calls for the one who enters to find his torturous way to the very *centre* (of the mind).

In the Papyrus of Ani, the initiate himself is shown sitting in the 'hall' playing draughts, an amazingly inconsequential occupation to be included in a so-called funeral rite, unless one reads the picture for what it really intends to show – that Ani is undergoing the mental process, the game being characteristic of the mental effort involved, and the 'hall', the *cave* of the inner mind, where it all takes place (see fig. 8).

The Hermetic meaning of the *black* and *white* intermingled *squares* of the draught and chess board should by now be self-apparent: as representative of the two parts of the human mind which although apparently two opposing paths, are really one in completion. It is the arena where the Hermetic 'combat' takes place – a meaning that is in no way diminished when the samed checkered pattern is seen on the floor of St. Paul's Cathedral, or incorporated in the Masonic Tracing Board of the First Degree.

And before we leave the subject of parlour games, have you ever wondered at the origin of Snakes and Ladders, a game in which the *ladder* helps the contestant upward, while each *snake*, or *serpent* sends him plunging downward again?

The Ankh

A most important and familiar sign, the Egyptian Ankh is composed of a cross surmounted by a loop: an ansated cross. The initiate priests who designed it called it the *Key to the Mysteries* because it was representative of the Hermetic process in action. The loop, or circle, is indicative of the subsconsious power, while the cross is symbolic of the conscious mind in its attempt by meditation to reach the subsconsious, there to intermingle with the higher power. The emblem was secretly perpetuated by the master architects of the Middle Ages who designed the great Gothic cathedrals. Viewed from above, certain of these classic structures will show an outline of the Ankh, the semi-circular apse being the loop, while the main length and the transepts hold the shape of the cross. The Ankh, then, is an emblem of that all-important, Hermetic contemplation which can reach the subconscious powers.

CHAPTER FIVE

The Zodiac

Untold centuries ago, the ancient initiates who possessed the simple but all important formula for ennobling ordinary Man sought for a method by which they could transmit the knowledge to those who might become the Adepts of the future. They saw the need for something even more enduring than hieroglyphics carved in rock, for it was recognised that land masses rise and fall in sporadic, natural upheavals, generally with devastating effects. Finally, in their wisdom, they turned to the one area of Man's environment that could be relied upon to remain virtually changeless for many thousands of years to come: the position of the stars. From the panorma of the night sky, they chose certain star clusters, designating each celestial pattern to represent, in its own way, their mental process. Thus were conceived the signs of the Zodiac.

It has often been observed that the twelve signs, as we know them today, bear little resemblance to the constellations they are supposed to represent and it is apparent that although the stars have moved very little, human interpretation has irresistibly deviated from the original. Despite this, the signs have survived to accomplish the purpose for which they were intended, for such deviation – incredibly restrained when it is considered how many millennia ago the signs were conceived – has resolved in the form of a transposition to a symbol which has the same hidden meaning. This can be no better expressed than by an interpretation of the great earthwork Zodiac at Glastonbury, a feature of past endeavour which shows us the symbols in current use four thousand years ago.

The fascinating story of the giant figures begins in 2,500 B.C., when a contingent of people from the Middle East arrived in England. They stayed to erect many strange monuments, one of which was the great lunar computer, Stonehenge. They set out the network of straight-line trackways about which so much has recently been written, and we may deduce that they carried Hermetic knowledge with them when it is realised that many of the tracks are intersected with still surviving, anciently named points such as *Blackdown, Whitehill* and *Redhill*. Some settled in the area now known as Glastonbury and established a regular camp there. A possible hint as to the land of their origin may be found in the name they gave to the camp. Today, we know it as the village of Somerton, but in the far past, it was called Sumer.

It was in this area that the visitors carefully and brilliantly utilised existing contours of the land to fashion twelve zodiacal figures in the form of giant-sized earthworks. Where the natural terrain failed to supply completely the necessary outline, they constructed banks, mounds and ditches until each figure was unmistakable in form. The finished work lay spread out over the plain below Glastonbury Tor in a great circle, thirty miles in circumference.

The era of these people came and went. Natural upheavals, which took place in 1,500 B.C., brought water sweeping in over the plain to partly cover the figures. But when this inundation eventually subsided, there was a slow but steady reclamation of the land. Those that moved in, however, were ignorant of the pictorial signs laid out beneath their feet, and except to a select few, the knowledge of them was completely lost.

In 1580, the famous astrologer, Dr John Dee, undertook the long journey from London to Glastonbury to examine for himself the unusual arrangement of mounds and ditches. What prompted the expedition is not recorded, but it must be remembered that Dee was a Rosicrucian. He returned to London satisfied that the figures represented the signs of the Zodiac.

Three hundred years or more passed, during which time the giant patterns became steadily less discernible as the land was separated into smaller fields and an ever-increasing network of cart tracks was laid down. Public knowledge of the earthworks seemed to lie dormant.

This suddenly changed in the 1920s, at the publication of a volume entitled THE GLASTONBURY TEMPLE OF THE STARS. The author, Mrs Kathleen Maltwood, described how she too discovered the existence of the great figures, despite that fact that they now blended in so well with the surrounding features as to be almost invisible. Today, thanks to modern aerial photography, we can see them from the best possible position – and appreciate Mrs Maltwood's assertion that the discovery of them amounted to an inner revelation. The patterns are there, but totally indistinct to the casual observer.

The way in which these ancient signs differ from those in current use is of great interest, because it provides corroboration of mythological ideas worked into classic texts which will be found to have a Hermetic basis. The Glastonbury figures are not necessarily copies of star patterns, but rather alternatives with an identical interpretation. Let us now consider and compare each sign and disclose the original meaning.

Aries

Aries, we know, is usually symbolised by the Ram, but the Glastonbury figure is strangely different and far more significant, for it appears as a lamb in a resting position, with its feet tucked underneath its body. Its hornless head is reversed so that it looks along the length of its back. In this sign, we have the first important identification with the classical texts – in this case the Old Testament – and can be compared with the oft-used theme of the sacrificial lamb. This lamb represents the conscious mind, as might have been guessed after reading Jane Leade's account, and its 'sacrifice' as described in the biblical stories was always figurative, never literal. The 'lamb' represents the moving thoughts of the conscious mind which, like lambs, tend to stray from the necessary single-pointed concentration of the practice.

The fact that the Glastonbury lamb is looking rearwards tells us that the first requisite of the practice is to reverse the normal, outward direction of the attention.

Comparable symbols can be found in classical, alchemical writings, especially in the readily available LE MYSTERE DES CATHEDRALES by Fulcanelli, a volume which contains a comprehensive exposition of Hermetic symbols to be found within the great cathedrals of Notre Dame and Chartres. Plate XXVII in the book shows the figure of a *man turning round*, with its accompanying motto

Solve et Coagula

This phrase (dissolve and fix), an integral part of the alchemists's vernacular, indicates the result of turning the mental power inwards, an act that will dissolve the thoughts and fix them into stillness.

The position of Aries in the zodiac as the first of the twelve signs offers yet another clue. The ancient science of Astrology dictated that each sign had dominion over a portion of the physical body, and in this scheme, Aries is related to the head – and so we are advised to begin the process by using the head (mind).

The Ram as a symbol is a less satisfactory alternative and may date from slightly later times, but it does offer a similar clue as to the application of the mental process. Anyone who has observed an angry ram put down his head and charge again and again at the object of his fury will have little trouble in connecting this single-mindedness with the mode of concentration necessary to gain mastery over the conscious mind. Again and again, the Neophyte must direct his attention with the determination and concentration of a battering ram.

Taurus

This sign has remained amazingly constant, although in the Glastonbury circle it appears as the head of the bull only. Students of history and mythology will be well acquainted with the ancient practice of sacrificing a bull, and after what I have just said regarding the lamb, the real significance of the sign should become immediately apparent. Once again we will realise that misinterpretation of the myths by the ignorant has led to unnecessary slaughter of many an animal, for the sign of the *bull* is an emblem of the conscious ego, the personal, outward 'I' which has to be surrendered, or 'sacrificed' before the transmission of consciousness can be made.

Some measure of the antiquity of the symbol can be gained by referring to Plato's CRITIAS, in which he describes the periodic assembly of Atlantean kings in the Temple of Poseidon in order to consider affairs of state. At the height of the ceremony, bulls were brought into the Temple's sacred enclosure and each king was required to hunt one down and kill it, but without the use of metal weapons. As each bull was caught, it had to be dragged to a pillar of Orichalcum (imperfect gold) where its throat was cut, the blood being allowed to run down the pillar and over the laws inscribed thereon. Afterwards, the carcasses were consumed by fire.

This is a typical example of Greek myth, which in its complicated structure, holds many clues to the Hermetic process. The embargo on the use of metal weapons shows at once that it is such an allegory. A similar device is present in the story of King Solomon's Temple, which was built *without the sound of a hammer* – i.e., in the mind. The pillar in Plato's story is said to be of Orichalcum, a mixture of silver and gold, and therefore 'imperfect' gold. The term *gold* (in its perfect state) always represents the subconscious, the Universal Mind, and the astral body, which is composed of the same 'perfect' energy. Thus, the *pillar* is man's mind before he has accomplished the mental task. The same 'pillars' are to be found in the Bible. The 'blood' of the bull is the concentrated power of meditation, symbolised as *dew* in the Bible and certain works of Alchemy.

Gemini:

The Geminian Twins are intended to portray the Dual nature of Man, the conscious and the subconscious, the *evil* and the *good*, the two elements which form the basis of the Old Religion, Dualism. The sign is best explained by turning to the Greek myth of Castor and Pollux. In this legend, Pollux, the immortal part of Man (the subconscious) begs Zeus to save his twin, Castor (the conscious mind). Zeus grants them an alternate immortality, each forced to wait in Hades while the other lived. This is an allegory of Man's daily life, part of which must be spent in sleep. During the day, the conscious mind is active, while the subsconscious lies concealed, but when sleep comes, the positions are reversed.

In the Glastonbury figure, we find only Pollux, the immortal half of Man, depicted with clenched fist raised above his head to show the strength and power of the subconscious. In the course of the mental process, the two natures are pitted against one another, obliged to engage in a conflict which the conscious mind must lose if the transmission of consciousness is to take place. This combat is sometimes incorporated into the Geminian sign, as in Plate XXV of Fulcanelli's book about cathedral symbolism, where the Twins are stylised as two children who are quarrelling and have come to blows.

Cancer

This is one of the major emblems in the zodiacal scheme because it refers directly to the Moon: the prime symbol of inner reflection. In the modern zodiac, the Cancer sign is associated with the Crab, a relationship which may also be seen in the 18th Tarot card, where a crab is shown climbing out of a pool by the light of the moon. This pictorial design is intended to show that *life* can be developed from out of *water*, or from under a *stone*, by the action of the *light* which is reflected from the *Sun*. In the course of the reflective action, we see the *dew* of concentrated thought descending from the moon.

In the Glastonbury sign, however, many investigators have been surprised to find neither the crab nor the moon, but a ship as a representative emblem. In order to unravel this piece of obscure symbolism, we must appreciate that the inward-turned attention invokes a reflective energy which was termed 'light' by the Hermeticist – and by way of an old Sanskrit word 'Argha', meaning 'light', we arrive at the phonetic equivalents 'Argo' and 'Ark'. The Glastonbury ship, therefore, is either the Ark in which Noah rode out the

Flood, or the Argo in which Jason set sail in order to bring back the
Golden Fleece, both stories being allegories that will be interpreted
in their respective places.

There is a significant reference to the Moon-ship to be found in a
manuscript entitled REPUBLICAE CHRISTIANOPOLITANAE
DESCRIPTO, by Johann Valentin Andraea, a German Hermeticist
of the 17th century. The book, published in 1619, describes an
imaginary, Utopian community similar to that in Plato's
REPUBLIC, and Francis Bacon's NEW ATLANTIS. The reference
occurs in the concluding paragraph of the preface, where the reader
is invited to

> . . . embark upon your vessel which has the sign of Cancer for its
> distinctive mark.

The author was, of course, inviting his more discerning readers to
begin the Hermetic process.

Leo

Like Taurus, the Lion is a symbol that has endured unchanged
throughout the centuries. As we have already found, the King of
beasts is the emblem of the Universal Mind, the subconscious. The
mediaeval alchemists used the Lion and its allotted colour, gold, to
indicate the 'celestial' nature of their finished astral body. Not
content with this, however, the Philosophers sought to confuse
seekers by allocating other colours to the lion, depending upon
which part of the process they wished to indicate. At the very
beginning of the process, the lion would be coloured *green* (remember the green glow of reflection from the cats' eyes?) – and at the end,
red. Sometimes, the animal was shown to be entirely black. Incongruously enough, traces of this philosophic representation still linger
to be recognised in the older public house signs: the Black Lion, the
Green Lion (or its alternative, the Green Man), and the Red Lion.

Virgo

Virgo is Mary the Virgin. In the Glastonbury circle, the figure is that
of a woman with a sheaf of corn in one hand, and therefore she is
Demeter, the great Corn Mother of the Eleusinian Mysteries – who
in time still further removed was the Egyptian Isis. At the appropriate place in this volume, you will be shown that the 'corn' symbol
means meditation, while the 'mother' is, of course, the conscious

mind which holds the power to meditate. There is a parallel symbolism to be seen in the Denderah Zodiac, once part of the ceiling in
the Temple of Denderah, Upper Egypt (4,000 B.C.), but now in the
Louvre, brought there by Lelorrain in 1821. Like the Glastonbury
zodiac, the arrangement is *circular*, the significance of which will be
revealed in due course. The Lion is seen *standing on the Hydra* (the
water serpent), and Virgo is represented in a strange manner, for there
are *three* Virgins, the last of which is seen holding an ear of wheat, or
corn.

If the sign of the ear of corn appears to be too obscure, you must
recall that it is produced through the natural action of sunlight and
moonlight, a sequence which lends itself as an example of what can
happen when the *light* of concentrated thought is directed upon the
'earth' of the conscious mind: a *new life* appears. Thus, the Virgin,
that is Isis, is an emblem of the mind's reflective power.

Libra

Where there would be expected the usual pair of scales as Libra's
sign, the position at Glastonbury is occupied by what seems to be the
outline of a bird with outstretched wings, and to resolve this inconsistency we must consult the history of the zodiac. In ISIS
UNVEILED, Madame Blavatsky had good reason to suggest that in
the far past, only ten of the signs were known to the public, the
remaining two being a secret of the initiates alone. One of the secret
figures was that of the Dove, as it appears at Glastonbury, and
therefore suggests that, four thousand years ago, the zodiac was
already undergoing some revision.

The Dove is that which was sent out from the Ark by Noah, and
being *white*, represents the conscious mind just on the point of
making the transmission. The same Dove appears in the Greek myth
of Diana, and as Fulcanelli has pointed out, can be seen over the
central porch of Notre Dame in the figures of the Dog and the
Doves.

The use of the Balance as a substitute must have taken place
subsequent to the building of the earthworks, but nevertheless it
stems from Egyptian mythology where it is prominent in the well
known scene of the Weighing of Souls. In the Papyrus of Ani, a
vignette shows Ani's soul being weighed against Truth and Justice –
or so it has been interpreted – while Horus, Anubis and Thoth
(portrayed both as an Ibis-headed god and a Baboon) look on. In
fact, nothing is being weighed. What is intended to be conveyed here

is a most secret description of the process, for the *balance* is that which the meditator must seek to achieve as he allows his conscious mind to sink into a state of deep reverie, and hold it there in a delicate position between wakefulness and sleep for the period of the meditation. A modern author has compared this feat of mental balance with the art of learning to ride a bicycle, a period during which the Neophyte will fall off many times before he is able to maintain his position. This is the real meaning of the sign of the Balance, and of certain Weighing Scenes in Egyptian drawings (see fig. 9).

Scorpio

Scorpio is quite obviously the Scorpion with its fatal sting and therefore embraces poison and death. It is easy to conclude that this refers to the Hermetic 'death' of the conscious mind.

Sagittarius:

Usurping the familiar Archer, the Glastonbury figure in the Sagittarius position is found to be a horse in the act of throwing its rider. One can appreciate the antiquity of this symbol and render its meaning clear by reference to a passage in the Katha-Upanishad, an Indian manuscript written in Sanskrit thousands of years ago.

> Know thyself to be sitting in a chariot, the body to be the chariot, the intellect the charioteer, and the mind the reins. He who has no understanding and whose mind is never firmly held, his senses are unmanageable, like the vicious horses of a charioteer.

In this ancient analogy, we are shown that the sign of the horse is representative of the uncontrolled thoughts of the conscious mind, dominated as it is by outside impressions. When the Adept begins the process of meditation, he attempts to take control of his conscious thoughts and hold them firmly under control, just as a rider will endeavour to saddle-break a wild stallion. This operation takes a great deal of time and patience, for time and time again, the 'rider' is thrown, until at last – if the Neophyte is successful – the 'horse' capitulates. At this stage, the alchemical 'death' takes place and the mind becomes *silent*. The analogy was a popular one in past times and will be found in various texts, including the Bible.

FIGURE 9.

The Weighing Scene, from the Papyrus of Ani: Ani's soul, represented by the jar ('heart') being weighed against the feather and the
Ankh. Thoth, represented as both Ibis-headed figure and Baboon,
attends on the left, while Horus, as the Hawk-headed figure, is on
the right. Anubis, the dog-headed, 'watches the balance diligently'.

If the reader cares to refer yet again to LE MYSTERE DES CATHEDRALES, he will find that Fulcanelli has drawn attention to the identical emblem, over the central porch of Notre Dame (plate XVIII).

In this concept we also recognise the mythological Centaur, a symbol which should now be self-explanatory: the co-joining of man and horse into one animal. How similar this is to the Sphinx.

The better known emblem of the Archer has exactly the same inner meaning, but stems from a different source. Greek legends tell of Cadmus, son of the king of Phoenicia, who in the course of his many *adventures* was required to pierce the *serpent* Python with an *arrow* and pin it to the *oak tree*. In this theme, the familiar serpent is the same as that in the *Garden of Eden,* a representation of the actively moving conscious mind, while the 'arrow' wielded by Cadmus is no more than the power of reflective meditation.

The Archer appears in folk lore as Herne the Hunter, a mytho-logical entity significantly associated with the *Moon* – and even in Robin Hood's *battle* with the Sheriff of Nottingham, who per-sonifies the forces of *evil*. The story is an Hermetic fable super-imposed over certain historical events, and perhaps this will explain why the legend as told seldom fits the facts.

Capricorn

Of all the zodiacal signs, the Goat is the most obscure, mainly because the most likely comparable references are to be found only in the texts of the alchemical fraternity – not everyone's choice of fireside literature.

The course of the Adept's meditation is long, hard and tedious, and as I have already remarked, was often compared to a task which required strenuous physical exertion, such as Climbing a High Mountain. This analogy is frequently used in the Old Testmanent where the prophets are made to *ascend the mount* before they can *converse with God*. The Goat, a sure-footed climber of mountains, represents the Neophyte who achieves correct depth of meditation without falling off (to sleep). At Glastonbury, however, we see not a Goat, but the mythological Unicorn. This is a far less obscure symbol, for the animal's single horn shows at once how the mind must be focussed in order successfully to complete the process.

Aquarius

The sign of the *water* carrier stems from early Egyptian mythology and can still be seen on wall and tomb carvings as the goddess Nut pouring out the 'waters' of life. Apart from her appearance in the Papyrus of Ani, she is also present in the Tarot cards, Star and Temperance. The water in question is not real water, but the mental power that will produce the required transmission of consciousness. The biblical texts abound with this symbolism, but once again, Glastonbury surprises us with an unexpected substitution, a bird-like figure which most commentators agree is the Phoenix. This legendary bird is supposed to renew itself whole from the ashes of its own funeral pyre – an unmistakable theme of Death and Resurrection by 'fire' (meditation). Therefore, this figure sums up the entire objective of the Hermetic process and so is noticeably centred over Glastonbury's most sacred spot: the Tor.

Pisces

The Fish, the last of the twelve signs, appears in the earth-work circle as a whale, with possibly a pilot fish alongside. It is commonly known that the sign of a fish was used in biblical times to denote Jesus himself, but the whale offers the key to the analogy, for its leads us to an even older fable of the process, Jonah and the Whale.

It is tempting to assess the story of Jonah as a possibility, miraculous though his survival may seem, but in the face of the knowledge that so many of the Testament stories are allegories, rather unwise. Had Jonah really been obliged to spend three days wallowing in the digestive juices of a whale, he would have been in no·condition to set about converting the citizens of Nineveh.

The correct interpretation of the Fish is that it is an emblem of Hermetic knowledge. When the text says that Jonah was 'swallowed up by the great fish', it means that he was swallowed up by the knowledge – that he was initiated. You will notice the clues within the story, which says quite plainly that he was in the 'whale' for *three* days, and that he was presumed *dead*.

Proof that the tale is indeed an allegory is given in the New Testament, when Jesus himself is made to say:

. . . behold a greater than Jonas is here (but look, something more than the superficial story is given here). (Matt. 12; 41)

Glastonbury

I am sure that I have no need to stress the fact that Glastonbury has always been held in great reverence, and that this sanctity has been attributed to the site's connection with King Arthur. But the real significance lies in the legend, not the man. Careful investigation will reveal that the Arthur tradition, the Twelve Knights, the Round Table, the mystic Avalon and the Holy Grail are over-embellishments of yet another allegory of the Hermetic process. In order to show it more clearly, however, it must be recognised that the truth is deeply buried beneath a firmly established mixture of Druidic lore, fiction, and carefully contrived post-Christian myth.

The legendary Arthur did exist, but he was a renowned fighting man of the sixth century, not a king. The glowing accounts of his exploits, propagated both by written and oral traditions, must be recognised as part of the Church's policy of superimposing its own dogma over existing beliefs that were considered to be pagan and therefore undesirable. The Holy Grail, stylised as a cup that never empties, is merely an echo of the earlier Druidic tradition of the magic Cauldron. The early Irish Celts had the same legend, their vessel being known as the Cauldron of Dagda. The subsequent story of Arthur's Quest, if you recall, was centred about the Cauldron of Inspiration. All these magic vessels have identical attributes as the source of miraculous health and wealth – and to receive the Holy Grail, or to drink from Dagda's Cauldron was considered tantamount to receiving the secrets of life itself. As we can appreciate, this is comparable to the results of the initiation process.

All historical records imply that when the first church was built at Glastonbury, the site had already long been steeped in a tradition relating to something 'holy', or connected to a 'secret wisdom'. Without doubt, this was entirely due to the zodiacal circle with its concealed message of knowledge attainable. In accounting for the traditions as they have come down to us, the Round Table is the earthwork circle; the Twelve Knights, the zodiacal signs; and the mystic land of Avalon, the higher state to which the initiate is elevated upon the transmission of consciousness.

Mary

That the famous Abbey's association with the name 'Mary' dates from such an early period has puzzled many scholars. How, they have wondered, did the Mary of the New Testament become linked with Glastonbury so soon after the historical era of Jesus? Almost too soon, it seemed.

We can arrive at the answer to this intriguing question by appreciating that two of the oldest names connected with the Hermetic process are 'Maia' (meaning 'mother', or 'nurse') and 'Mare' (pronounced like 'Mary' and meaning the Great Sea). Both were terms coined long before the advent of the Gospels, the former as an identical symbol to Demeter, or Isis, and the latter to denote the Universal Mind: the great sea of subconscious power on which Noah floated his Ark. When the Christian Church in England set about suppressing the pagan traditions, they found that many of the old god names were so firmly established that to attempt a substitution would be futile. A version of 'Mare' had already been used in the Gospels, and so they fostered their own interpretation of 'Mary' therein, by superimposing it over the existing Glastonbury lore. Thus, the old Maia, or Mare, became the Virgin Mary, an entity eminently suitable in the eyes of the Church because of the part she played in the divinely inspired, virgin birth of Jesus. That those ecclesiastical manipulators were not knowledgeable enough to decipher correctly the original texts of the New Testament is plain to see, for the fable of the virgin birth is itself a direct allegory of the Hermetic process.

Biblical scholars have conducted many a debate over the 'miracle' of the virgin birth, but it is only in comparatively recent times that the weight of opinion has rejected it as a literal event, notwithstanding the conjuring tricks of modern medicine which tend to give the tale credence. The true explanation is simplicity itself. With the correct insight, a study of Hermetic literature will show that the initiates considered the Universal Mind, in its *motionless* state, to be the first matter from which everything material is formed. As such, they termed it 'perfect', 'immaculate', or 'virgin'. Such a state does actually exist, as Einstein has shown by his theory of Relativity, for the energy which moves at the speed of light is known to be not only formless, but timeless. Matter cannot exist at the speed of light, only energy. When an initiate successfully accomplishes the transmission of his own consciousness, he merely extends his thought energy from its restricted position in the waking mind to the freedom of the 'perfect' energy of the Universal Mind. Thus emerges the *new man,* the so-called astral body, and he is said to be *reborn in spirit,* or *born of the virgin*. From this line of symbolism we may see the correct meaning of the Catholic 'immaculate conception', an explanation of which has yet to be given by the Cleric to the congregation.

Armed with this knowledge, we may now account for the

problem of Mary's history, or rather, the irritating lack of it. As Geoffrey Ashe has so rightly pointed out in his volume, THE VIRGIN, it would have been proper to have honoured the woman who gave birth to Jesus in such a miraculous fashion by the erection of a shrine, or the dedication of some relevant spot, yet no place has ever laid claim to her bodily remains. Her sepulchre was assigned to a particular spot, but her bones never were. Geoffrey Ashe goes on to highlight the embarrassment of the Catholic church at this lack of Marian history, to say nothing of some aspects of her life as it is depicted in the Gospel texts.

Proof that Mary's existence is purely allegorical lies in the fact that the Virgin is a sign of the Zodiac, and so was conceived long before the Gospels were written. St. John, in his Revelation, chapter 12, tries to hint at this when he says:

> And there appeared a great wonder in Heaven; a woman clothed with the sun, and the moon under her feet, and upon her head a crown of twelve stars.

Thinking back over the symbolism so far covered, we note that the *woman* is clothed in the *sun,* and therefore must have some connection with both the Universal Mind, and reflection. The latter is confirmed by the statement that she has the *moon* under her feet (she has mastered the power of reflection). But is this woman a Virgo, or a Virgin? The *twelve* stars are an obvious reference to the zodiac, which contains only one feminine sign, Virgo. In the verse which follows on the one quoted above, it is stated that she is about to *give birth,* and so putting these two pieces of information together, we realise that it is not a physical birth, but an Hermetic birth that will take place – the birth of the astral body, which can only be achieved by application of the reflective power symbolised by Isis, Demeter, or the Virgin Mary, whichever initiate name you choose to apply. The woman of Revelation, it is obvious, is Mary of the Gospels.

In yet more support, you may read on to be informed that the great red dragon appears, waiting to devour the new born infant. Naturally, the woman, the *mother,* tries to prevent this and flees into the *wilderness* (descends into deep meditation). There follows a full scale *war in Heaven* (mythical combat indicative of the meditation in progress), at the end of which, St Michael manages to overthrow the dragon. In verse 9, we are told exactly who the 'dragon' really is:

> And the great dragon was cast out, that old *Serpent* called the *Devil*, and *Satan*.

We are therefore left in no doubt that the battle is that which takes place in the mind, and Revelations's new born infant (the astral body) escapes being devoured by the dragon (it is successfully born of the conscious mind) because the dragon was cast out of Heaven (the initiate conquered his thoughts).

The Tarot

Like the zodiacal signs, the twenty two cards which make up the Major Arcana of the Tarot were originally designed as pictorial expositions of the Hermetic process, but so much emphasis has been placed on the divinatory aspect that the true meaning has long ago been submerged.

The origin of the Tarot is uncertain, its documented history stretching back a mere six hundred years, but the weight of opinion places its introduction into Europe at about 1,000 A.D. However, the subject matter, and the designs of the pictures have been drawn from symbolism that existed in far earlier times, some owing their conception to Egypt, others to ancient India. Like the Mystery rites of the former, the Tarot is divided into two sections: the Lesser and the Greater Mysteries.

The Minor Arcana (the Lesser Mystery) was once made up of fifty six cards divided into four suits: Wands; Cups; Swords; and Pentacles (or, in some packs, Coins). It is from this portion of the pack that our present day playing cards have evolved.

The Major Arcana (the Greater Mystery) has twenty two cards, each of which features a symbolic picture – and that these are pertinent to the Hermetic Art is undeniable. I have already made some small correspondences between the Tarot pictures and Egyptian drawings, and I do not propose to prolong this section by interpreting each card individually, for there are more important subjects waiting. Instead, I will briefly bring to your attention a few of the more obvious significances.

The Devil (Number 15)

The Devil in the picture generally stands between the Geminian Twins, as the force that prevents the conscious from reaching the subconscious. Some packs depict the Twins in chains – which they are, of course, until freed by the process.

The Chariot (Number 7):

For an interpretation of this picture, I refer to the previously mentioned Sanskrit text of the Katha–Unpanishad, within the explanation of Sagittarius. The chariot is the physical body of Man, it says, and the vicious horses are the senses which the charioteer must learn to control. Some Tarot cards will show the chariot to be drawn by two sphinxes, one *black,* the other *white*, while the charioteer is seen as a richly cloaked figure wearing a crown and carrying a sword, emblems which are meant to convey triumph in the conquest of the mind.

The Lovers (Number 6):

The two people of opposite sex shown here depict the possible 'marriage' that can take place between the conscious mind and the subconscious (the woman and the man: Mother and Father symbols). The picture is a variation of the Geminian Twins.

Death (Number 13):

The 'death' required of the conscious ego. A.E. Waite's pictorial key makes interpretation all the more easy, for he presents Death as the figure of an armoured skeleton mounted on a horse (the horse of the conscious mind).

The Empress (Number 3):

This Empress is Latona, or to give her more familiar name, Isis: the power of reflection. Look at the picture of this *woman* with the sun, the moon and a halo of twelve stars and turn again to Revelation, chapter 12.

The Fool (Un-numbered Card):

There are conflicting interpretations of this card depending upon whether you see the Fool in the act of stepping off into the Abyss, or if he is pausing at the very brink. If it is the latter, it signifies the lucky man who knows the process and who will soon make the transmission of consciousness. The former, however, is the more conventional explanation and sees the Fool as uninitiated Man, totally unaware of the great potential within his own mind. The noisy, yapping dog at his heels is emblematic of the conscious mind, with its continual agitation, a line of symbolism that can be traced back to ancient Egypt and the *Dog Star*, Sirius.

The tradition of the Fool has survived in other areas – as the Joker in the ordinary pack of playing cards, as the Court Jester of the Middle Ages, as the old fashioned Harlequin, and as the Fool who urges on folk dancers. All have a symbolic basis in the Hermetic process.

The Hanged Man (Number 12):

The Hanged Man is seen suspended upside down in a most unusual manner, hanging by a rope tied to one foot, while his other leg is bent so as to form a cross. His significance must be compared with that of the legendary St Peter, who is said to have been crucified upside down. A further comparison can be made with the Norse god, Odin, who is said to have discovered the secret of the runes (initiation) by suspending himself in a *tree* all *night*. A number of scholars, while not being able to penetrate the secret meaning of this, have commented upon the similarity of the Tarot to the Runes, of Thoth with Odin. They were right. The Hanged Man symbolises the *reversal of the normal procedure* required to begin the Hermetic process.

CHAPTER SIX

The Old Testament

No book in the history of Mankind has had a revolutionary effect on the development of the Western world comparable to that of the 'book of books', the Holy Bible. Translated into more than a thousand different languages and dialects, its texts have exercised a profound influence over human behaviour and affairs for nearly two thousand years. In modern times, collective academic knowledge, patiently amassed amid the dust and rubble of past ages, has served to prove that the book's chronological, historical and geographical statements hold considerable accuracy.

And yet the book remains an enigma.

The reason for this enduring mystique is that the texts, while seeming to relate to locations which unquestionably exist, lapse at times into an almost child-like style of prose which appears to be totally unnecessary. Of course, it has long been deduced that the biblical parables are allegories, but the inner sense of them has remained beyond the reach of most scholars. Many have shrugged off the simplistic ideas as being due to incomplete data concerning the original language in which the texts were first set down, leaving the world at large to be content with the literal word and its doctrine of simple morality. A rare few, more discerning than most, cautiously pointed out that there were inexplicable comparisons to be made with certain other fables – strange texts that were classed as 'Hermetic' – but not being in possession of the key to the Hermetic mystery, they had no way of justifying or enlarging on their suspicions.

As it happens, their intuitive faculties were not deluding them, for the Bible is a collected anthology of Hermetic parables, each one based loosely on a foundation of solid fact. The seemingly incongruous story lines are deliberate inventions, made so as to accommodate the allegory, the cast of characters being fictitious, brought into existence for no other purpose than to express the Hermetic principle. In this respect, Noah, Abraham, David and Solomon have no more substance in fact than Cinderella, Aladdin, Mother Goose and Puss In Boots.

This may be difficult, almost impossible to accept, but once in possession of the key – as you now are – decipherment of the parables will prove the point. And readers will be astounded to find that the Hermetic theme is expressed with such insistence that, in the end, the initial surprise at the discovery is replaced by irritation. Every Adept knows this, and such a revelation will undoubtedly clear the air of mystery from the words of the classic scholar, Maimonides, who wrote:

> Whoever shall find out the true sense of the Book of Genesis ought to take care not to divulge it . . . If a person should discover the true meaning of it by himself, or by the aid of another, then he ought to be silent; or if he speaks of it, he ought to speak of it but obscurely and in an enigmatic manner.

The classic Adepts were bound by the oaths of the secret societies to which they belonged not to reveal the inner doctrine to anyone but those received into their lodges – or so they insisted. However, it was a practice – almost a compulsion – among the initiates to express the form and the existence of their Science in as many obscure ways as they could conceive. Thus, Maimonides, an authority on the Scriptures, tells us outright that there is a great secret to be found within the text of Genesis. With tongue in cheek, he avers that those who discover the inner meaning should remain *silent* – a reference to the conscious mind and not the voice. Let us turn to the Pentateuch to find out what he meant.

Noah's Ark

Perhaps the most debated story in Genesis is that of Noah and his Ark, for archaeologists and geologists alike have striven mightily to place the event satisfactorily in its proper place and time. Not the least astonishing factor is the popularity of the tale, the last count finding upward of 80,000 versions in existence. The legend has been encountered all over the world, and scholars are at a loss to understand why such a story – little more than a nursery tale – should enjoy such widespread recognition.

For a long time, the text was taken literally, causing great speculation as to the scale of the inundation. Was it an event local to the biblical area, or did the description of the rising waters justify the conclusion that it was a global affair? So far, no definite conclusions have been formed, although recent archaeological research has uncovered sound evidence that a flood of some magnitude occurred along the Euphrates in 4,000 B.C. An unprecedented rising of the

great river resulted in a ten feet deep deposit of mud over the ancient
city of Ur. Such a catastrophe, the archaeologists believe, could have
provided the foundation for the story.

It is possible that they have arrived at the correct solution, but
from the wrong direction, for the allegories that appear in the Bible
follow a pattern that was established long before the texts were
written down. The basic rule was to take a literal event, modify the
story line so as to incorporate the hermetic symbols, and add a
fictitious character to play the 'starring' role. The Euphrates flood
was obviously a disaster of some magnitude, one that would live
long in local memory, and important enough to have been adapted
by the initiates.

Taken purely as a literal circumstance, the basic plot of a man, his
family and livestock riding out a severe storm in a boat is quite
credible – until the reader is asked to believe the strange limitation
put on the animals. Only one of each sex to propogate a species after
an all-encompassing catastrophe does not take into account death by
accident or disease. Another strain on the credibility is the way in
which Noah found land.

The real importance of the tale will be understood as we seek out
the hidden clues within the text. You will remember that the mental
task was always stylised as a long and dangerous journey, or voyage
– and so it is with Noah's perilous days on the rising waters. He was
afloat, so it is said, for a period of *forty* days, a length of time which
has nothing remarkable about it until you recall that similar periods
crop up with amazing regularity throughout the whole of the
biblical stories. For example, Joseph embalmed his father for forty
days, Moses was lost on the mount for the same span of time. The
Israelites wandered in the *wilderness* for forty years – and after being
delivered from the whale, Jonah decreed that Nineveh would be
overthrown in forty days. There are other examples, and it becomes
apparent that the number forty holds a significance that has nothing
to do with the days of the month. In truth, it was a symbol, in vogue
at the time of writing, by which the Hermetic writers indicated the
length of their process. Noah was in the Ark for that length of time,
and if I remind you that the word 'Ark' stems from its phonetic
equivalent, Argha, meaning the power of reflected *light*, you will
begin to see that the story refers not to a real incident, but is symbolic
of the Hermetic Art. The animals on board represent the power of
generation within the conscious mind which will produce *new life*.
Even more straightforward clues present themselves, for the Ark has
three decks – and after a *long and dangerous voyage,* Noah sends out a
Raven (a *black* bird). Then a Dove (a *white* bird) is despatched *three*

times to look for land. It does not return on the third time and so
Noah knows that he has found land at last (the process is complete
after the third stage).

Abraham

The rest of the biblical stories follow the same pattern. In chapter 17
of Genesis, we come to a most important text describing the introduction of circumcision by Abraham at the order of Jehovah (verse
10). It is upon the authority of this text that countless generations of
Jewish people have been physically circumcised, the elders claiming
that the hygienic advantages were secondary to the spiritual
command of the Scriptures. But the text was never meant to be read
literally, for the inner meaning of 'circumcision' – the removal of the
'foreskin' – is the same as that described by Alice A. Bailey when
discussing initiation in A TREATISE ON COSMIC FIRE. Speaking of the time in the process when the transmission of the consciousness is made, she refers to a 'burning away of the etheric web'.
By 'web', she means the last barrier of extraneous thought which
prevents access to the subconscious and which is 'burnt' away by the
'fire' of reflected thought. The same barrier is mentioned at the
Crucifixion of Jesus in the phrase

> and the veil of the temple was rent
>
> (Matt 27; 51)

In the Old Testament, this barrier was allegorised as the 'foreskin'.
That the Bible's circumcision is not meant to be read as a literal
practice is a fact that is substantiated by the New Testament itself, for
if we turn to Paul's letter to the Romans (chapter 2; verse 28 – 29), we
find the following unequivocal statement:

> For he is not a Jew, which is one outwardly; neither is that
> circumcision which is outward in the flesh. But he is a Jew, which
> is one inwardly; and circumcision is that of the *heart*, in the spirit
> and not in the letter; whose praise is not of men but God.

I have previously stated that it would be necessary for the reader to
break the habit of blindly accepting the literal meaning of certain
texts, and nowhere does this apply more than to the various adventure stories within the Bible. The one exception that directly
concerns this volume is the writings of Paul, the letters of whom
contain no allegory. In the passages above lie the most amazing
insight into the most prominent themes of Old Testament allegory,

for quite apart from saying that the practice of circumcision as quoted in the older stories has a deeper meaning, Paul outrightly tells us that the use of the name 'Jew' in certain texts refers not to a physical race, but to a spiritual condition. In other words, he is informing the enlightened reader that the term 'Jew' really means 'initiate'. The word 'heart', which I have emphasised, is intended to direct the attention to the centre of the mind, not to the physical organ, an interpretation which is plainly supported by the word 'spirit' which immediately follows it. Thus, the 'Jew' who is 'circumcised' is the initiate who has completed the process.

This device to conceal the truth has given rise to the misconception that the Jewish race were the 'chosen people of God', whereas the term really applies to those who have been fortunate enough to discover and complete the Hermetic process. This application, please note, only relates to the very early use of 'Jew', an appelation which succeeded 'Israelite' after the fall of the ten tribe kingdom. The statement by Paul is based on an event dealt with later, where Jacob receives his revelation of the inner power – allegorised as the famous dream of the ladder. The Scriptures tell us that, not long after that incident, *God* (the Universal Mind) changed Jacob's name to *Israel* (Jacob became an initiate). Subsequently, all 'Israelites' in the Bible were referred to as being descendents of Jacob – i.e., brother initiates, whether they be Jewish or any other race.

Isaac

An allegory more personal to Abraham is given in chapter 22, verse 20 of Genesis, where we read that God said to him

> Take thou thy son, thine only son, *whom thou lovest,* and get thee to the land of Moriah; and offer him there for a burnt offering upon one of the mountains which I will tell thee of.

We are acquainted with the rest of the story, where Abraham does indeed have so much faith in the Lord that he offers Isaac as a sacrifice, but was reprieved from actually carrying out the task. We may now unravel this tale by turning first to the emphasised words; 'whom thou lovest'. As a literal statement, this phrase is by no means out of place, for what father does not love his only son? But we must adjust our thinking to the fact that Abraham did not exist as a real entity, he being a fictitious character placed in the 'starring' role to personify the initiate. So his love for his 'son' in this case, is meant to portray the love, or attraction, of the conscious mind for bodily sensations – the sensations which forever keep the attention riveted on external matters. This 'love' must be 'sacrificed' in order to succeed with the process. Isaac, therefore, personifies the senses of the conscious mind, which is why he had to be offered up.

Next, we examine the order for Abraham to proceed to the 'land of Moriah'. Strangely enough, this rocky eminence turns out to be the site later chosen by King Solomon to build his magnificent temple. Later still, it became Jerusalem, the one place round which almost every major theme centres. Thus, it is apparent that the location holds a very special significance.

Owing to the disclosures of John Allegro in his work THE SACRED MUSHROOM AND THE CROSS, we now understand the name 'Moriah' to be a close phonetic equivalent to the Greek 'Morios', the name of the simple mushroom, a symbol which is prolifically employed in the biblical texts. As we proceed, I shall show how the mushroom symbol relates to the inner mind and not just to the hallucinogenic effects, as John Allegro proposes. From this, we deduce that Moriah, King Solomon's Temple and Jerusalem, although quite possibly places that existed in reality, are in many of the biblical texts meant to indicate *the centre of the mind*.

The rest of the tale needs little effort to decipher. Just as with the Ugly Duckling, the moment Abraham makes up his mind to offer the sacrifice, things change. He was told, instead, to *sacrifice a ram* which had caught its *horns* in a nearby *thicket*. In this short sentence we are given *three* clues to the process: the Ram of Aries; the 'horns', relating either to the crescent *moon* (reflection), or the horns of a *Bull*; and the *thicket*, which in the original Aramaic was a phonetic equivalent of the basic 'mushroom' symbol (the inner mind).

The fact that the whole sequence is made to take place on a mountain has a significance that we have already touched upon. As those familiar with the Bible will know, the theme of climbing a mountain in order to confer with God occurs with great regularity. But now we know that the phrase 'climbing a high mountain' was greatly favoured by the initiates of that period to exemplify the mental task, and so it is with Abraham's Moriah. Elsewhere, the analogy appears as the statement that *Mount Zion* (next to Mount Moriah) was the place where God met *his people,* and at the sanctuary there, all Israelite males (meaning initiates) were made to appear before the face of God (the subconscious) *three* times a year (Ex.23; 17)

Psalm 48, verses 1 and 2, places Mount Zion *in the north,* a direction which, if you refer to previous expositions, is used to indicate the centre of the mind. Other references to the 'mountains of meeting' in the same context, place these eminences in the 'remotest regions of the earth'. Perusal of classic alchemical texts will show that the centre of the mind was allegorised as the 'nethermost regions of the *earth*' ('earth' being the conscious mind).

As before, I point out that there is a real Mount Zion, but the allegory only follows the usual pattern of using real places in order to project the Hermetic theme in a way that will lend credence to the literal word and thereby shield the true meaning.

Jacob's Ladder

Like the story of Noah's Ark, that of Jacob's dream is very popular and known the world over. According to Genesis 28; 11 to 18, he

> . . . lighted upon a certain place and tarried there all night, because the sun was set; and he took the stones of that place and put them for his pillows, and lay down in that place to sleep.

Passing over the literal meaning and scrutinising the text for hidden meanings, we see that it is *night* time, the Hermetic code word for the inner mind. Aware that the symbol 'stone' means the conscious mind, we note the proximity of Jacob's *head* to it and are left in no doubt that the Hermetic theme is being projected. There follows a description of the dream, after which Jacob wakes to say:

> Surely the Lord is in this place; and I knew it not.

Revelation! He has realised that he can reach his subconscious by the use of meditation.

> How dreadful is this place.

Put this down to translation. What is meant here is 'how awesome is this knowledge'. The following sentence supports this interpretation. Then the story continues:

> And Jacob rose up early in the morning and took the stone that he had put for his pillows, and set it up for a pillar, and poured oil on top of it.

These words tell us that he successfully accomplished the mental process. When Jacob 'rose up early in the morning', it quite obviously indicates *sunrise*, which as we have already found, symbolises the appearance of the subconscious power in the mind of the initiate. He then sets up the stone as a pillar, an action which may be interpreted by referring to the priests of On, or Heliopolis, and the fact that their main symbol of the process, a pyramid, evolved from a pillar. As the text of Genesis was written by an initiate who was conversant with Egyptian symbolism, the same interpretation must be applied. The 'pillar' was *annointed* (Jacob was initiated). Thus, in these few verses, the text relates how Jacob, not a real entity but, like Abraham, a personification of the initiate, discovers the process and then carries it to a successful conclusion.

The Ark of Moses

We now turn to the great theme of Exodus, the central pivot around which the entire Jewish religious scheme revolves.

The early life of Moses as depicted in the opening chapters of Exodus begins with a story that strikes the reader as more of a nursery tale than fact, the account of his escape from the Pharaoh's decree ordering the death of every *newborn Hebrew* male. Chapter 2 explains how this was accomplished:

> . . . and when she saw him that he was a goodly child, she hid him three months.
> 3. And when she could no longer hide him, she took for him an ark of bulrushes and daubed it with slime and pitch and put the child therein, and she laid it in the flags by the river.

Subsequently, the infant Moses was discovered by no less a person than the Pharaoh's daughter, who took him into her care and brought him up to enjoy a high position in the royal household. As you will admit, this fable has all the childish charm of such tales as Cinderella and the Ugly Duckling, even to the time-honoured, happy ending. And likewise, it is a vehicle with which to convey the Hermetic theme.

Interpretation begins by noticing that Moses is described as a 'goodly' child, and if you think back to my remarks about the meaning of the word 'good' in the basic elements of Dualism, you will realise that this *child* is no physical person, but a personification of the initiate.

The infant's *mother* (reflection) hid the babe for *three* months (the stages of the process), and then placed him in an *ark* of bulrushes. This 'ark' is just like the one Noah rode in, a symbol of reflection, and we are told that it was daubed with slime and pitch, the latter a substance which everyone knows to be *black*. All in all, the idea of a dirt encrusted basket of bulrushes is a *most unlikely place* to find a *new born* infant.

The ark is placed in the flags, a sentence that can only be deciphered by referring to Egyptian symbolism on one hand and natural lore on the other. The 'flags' mentioned here are better known as the papyrus plant, a tough reed which the Nile crocodile abhorred. As I have had occasion to mention, the *crocodile* was often used as an emblem of the conscious mind which, like the *serpent*, had to be defeated in combat, or like Set, who had to be vanquished. Thus, the verse states that by the *action of the mother*, the *crocodile* was thwarted in its menace to the *newborn* (reflection overcomes the conscious mind, allowing the astral body to be born).

This whole sequence can be compared to a later story, where Jesus escapes from exactly the same decree, this time instituted by Herod. I shall show that neither tyrannical incident is real, but each was a myth concocted to show that if the uncontrolled thoughts of the conscious mind – personified by the Pharaoh and by Herod – were not overcome, then the process would not be successful.

We find a reiteration of the Genesis story attached to the history of Sargon, king of Assyria at about 700 B.C. In the palace of Sennacherib, at Kouyunjik, archaeologists unearthed some fragments of tablets on which were inscribed the legend of Sargon's birth. The relevant stanzas are as follows:

1. Sargon, the powerful king, the king of Akkad am I.
4. My mother the princess, conceived me; in difficulty she brought me forth.
5. She placed me in an ark of rushes, with bitumen the exit she sealed up.
6. She launched me on the river, which did not drown me.
7. The river carried me, to Akki the water carrier it brought me.

Commentators have assumed that Sargon copied the theme from Genesis, wishing to be associated with Moses, and the assumption is likely correct, but not in the way they envisage. In my estimation, Sargon is using the theme to express his own initiateship. Notice how the infant Sargon is not found by a princess, but by a *water carrier*, a direct reference to the zodiacal sign of Aquarius. Yet the two stories have identical meaning at the end of them. If we return to Exodus 2; verse 10, we find that the Pharaoh's daughter gave the infant the name of Moses because he was drawn out of *water*. The antiquity of the basic idea can be realised by comparing the infant sealed in a floating ark to the body of Osiris sealed in a floating coffin, or casket.

The Mythical Exodus

The entire book of Exodus is devoted to the graphic description of
how Moses led the Israelites out of bondage, to wander for forty
years in the desert before eventually arriving at Canaan, the
Promised Land – and as such is the longest and most complicated
allegory of the Hermetic process, for the series of astounding events
portrayed in this famous text never took place in reality.

We have already discovered that Moses was not a real person, but
a character invented to personify the Hermetic initiate, and if you
glance again at the above contraction of that epic journey, you will
perhaps begin to recognise the familiar clues: the *long and arduous
journey* across the *wilderness*, during which many hardships were
experienced and which occupied the space of *forty* years, to finally
terminate in the *Promised Land*, a land flowing with milk and honey,
a virtual paradise which sounds too good to be true.

Serious investigators have never been able accurately to chart this
great trek, nor understand why it should have taken as long as forty
years. Neither have they been able successfully to equate the exodus
of the Israelites with other historical records which, although
describing the movements of various tribes, do not make a point of
corroborating the Pentateuch version.

The simple answer is that it was never a real event.

Space will preclude the interpretation of every single theme within
the whole story, but I will deal with some that are best known,
beginning by asking you to keep in mind our discovery that the term
'Israelite' in the Pentateuch, means 'initiate', and does not refer to a
real body of people.

The Burning Bush

The first major event occurs when Moses confronts the so-called
burning bush to hear the voice of God.

Modern authors have speculated at great length regarding this
strange episode, some even claiming that the prophet saw a flying
saucer. This conclusion was arrived at because the thorn bush is
depicted as flaming with fire, yet not being consumed, and thus
suggests some sort of radiation similar to that featured in UFO
reports. To get to the bottom of this mystery, we are once again
indebted to the expertise of John Allegro, who has deciphered the
ancient Aramaic text to reveal the phonetic puns incorporated in it.
The 'thorn bush' in Aramaic turns out to be identical to Abraham's

'thicket', a word related to the 'mushroom' symbolism – and through it, to the inner mind. So the burning bush is merely another ancient emblem of the human mind and it follows that Moses, the initiate, in communing with this 'bush' is really in the act of meditation, communing with God (Universal Mind) within himself. This accounts for the fact that the voice of God spoke from the bush, and also for the fact that the fire (of concentrated thought) did not consume it.

Moses hears the voice say that it has come to deliver the Israelites from the bondage of Egypt, and asks by what name the voice is to be called. It replies:

I AM THAT I AM

This sentence is intended to convey the existence of the hidden subconscious in every human mind, the subconscious which although in each and every human mind is really but one entity, the Universal Mind. It is the 'I' within us, which is *bound in servitude* to the sensation-seeking conscious mind, just as the *Israelites* were bound in servitude to Egypt.

Moses is then instructed to take his followers into the *wilderness* for *three* days so that they may offer a *sacrifice* to God. After overcoming all resistance from the Pharaoh (the conscious mind), a *battle* which is symbolised by the bringing of the plagues, Moses finally leads the Israelites out of Egypt.

The Red Sea Crossing

Similar speculation has been aroused by the amazing incident reported in Exodus 14, the parting of the Red Sea, with modern commentators again raising the possibility that it was all due to the appearance of a UFO in the shape of a pillar, or a cloud. But logical appraisal of the literal text will force the conclusion that it could never have happened in the way described, any more than Jesus actually walked on water. The fable in which he performs the latter feat, Matthew 14, was conceived to show that great faith is necessary to accomplish *miracles* (i.e. the process). Remember that the incident took place at *night*, after Jesus had *climbed a mount*. When Peter tried to emulate him, he began to sink, but Jesus steadied him, saying:

O thou of little faith, wherefore didst thou doubt? (verse 31)

In the same manner, the magical parting of the Red Sea to allow the Israelites to pass is a parable intended to show the need for a strong faith while undertaking the Hermetic process, but it is harder to understand due to its great antiquity. To comprehend the inner meaning, we accept that the Israelites (the initiates) have set out on their forty year trek (have begun the process). The Neophyte sets for himself a long and repetitive schedule of daily meditation, a wearisome task of mental endeavour, but time passes with no visible sign of advancement towards the desired goal, and quite naturally, he may begin to doubt that such a result is attainable—which is the worst thing he could do, for faith is an emotional energy that aids the process. Doubts and the diminishing of faith only prolong the process, and if strong enough, prevent its accomplishment altogether. The Red Sea story was concocted to stress this fact. Thus the pillar of cloud by day, and the pillar of fire by night which guided the Israelites, is analogous to the certainty and intuition in the mind of the would-be initiate who, having received the revelation that such a process does exist, must believe in it implicitly if success is to be had.

Much emphasis is placed on the fact that the Israelites were pursued by 'all the horses and chariots of the Pharaoh'. In Exodus 14, verse 7, this pursuing force is meticulously numbered:

> And he took six hundred chosen chariots, and all the chariots of Egypt and captains every one of them.

The text of Exodus, having been derived from older Sumerian and Egyptian sources, must be related to the older symbolism, and so in the reference to the 'chariots' we see at once a reiteration of the analogy expressed in the Katha-Upanishad. The 'horses and chariots' of the conscious mind did not belong solely to Indian texts, and as we have found that 'Egypt' is here used to personify the conscious mind, it takes little effort to deduce that the Pharaoh's chariots represent the majority of uninitiated people who cannot believe in the Hermetic Science. You will notice that when these Egyptians tried to follow the Israelites, they had great difficulty with the wheels of their chariots, an interference directly caused by the Lord (Ex 14; 24 – 25). The meaning is clear. Those who cannot believe are not able to follow the path of the initiate.

There are, of course, more clues within this little scenario, not the least of which is the fact that the *Red* Sea was chosen to feature in it, but let them give way to a few more pocket allegories so carefully worked into the whole Exodus theme.

Moses on the Mount

After the interpretations I have already offered, this episode will
need little explanation. The Children of Israel (the initiates) had been
journeying in the wilderness for *three* months before they pitched camp
at the base of the mount (Ex.19; 1). When Moses *ascended the mount*
(yet another exposition of the meditational process), the thunder and
lightning, the trumpeting and the thick cloud, all of which heralded
the *appearance of the Lord* (the transmission of the consciousness) did
not occur until the morning of the *third* day (until the three stages
were completed).

The Tabernacle

The history of the Tabernacle shows that it was the forerunner of
King Solomon's Temple, and indeed, when that magnificent edifice
was completed, the Tabernacle was stored within it. Interpretations
already offered show that the Temple – built as it was on the Mount
of Moriah – really indicates the inner mind; and therefore, so does
the Tabernacle. With its fine fixtures and fittings and its specific
measurements, it represents the 'temple' built in Man's mind by the
labour of the process. The words of the apostle, Paul, tend to reveal
this when he speaks of Jesus as

> a public servant of the holy place and of the true tent, which
> Jehovah put up and not man. (Heb. 8; 2)

The Tabernacle, it will be realised, was the 'true tent' (the mind),
and Jehovah, the Universal Mind.

A further clue is to be found in the instructions given by Jehovah
to Moses regarding the building of the Tabernacle:

> See that thou make all things according to the pattern showed thee
> in the mount. (Heb.8; 5)

On reading this, we recall that before he was able to receive these
intructions, Moses had to *ascend the mount*.

The Tabernacle is described as being in *three* separate parts; the
Entrance; the Holy Compartment; and the Most Holy Compartment – a triple arrangement that is also present in the decks of Noah's
Ark, and can still be seen today in the layout of the great mediaeval
cathedrals. Inside, the Most Holy Compartment was constructed in
a cubical shape – as was the Most Holy Compartment of Solomon's
Temple. The meaning of the symbolic cube is that of the finished

work: the finished 'stone' of the conscious mind, an emblem which has remained prominent in Freemasonry.

The inside of the Tabernacle was veiled from general view, like the knowledge of the Hermetic process, for it was covered over with a layer of *Ram's* skins, dyed *red*, among other things. Because the design of it was so intricate and meticulous, everyone recognised that it was a *work of art,* just like the process of meditation. Finally, the Most Holy Chamber was the place where the *earthly representation of God* was to be found: the Ark of the Covenant (the inlet to the subconscious and the Universal Mind). We must not forget, either, that the Tabernacle could always be easily found, owing to the fact that a cloud by day and a fire by night stood over it.

Manna

In recent years there has arisen a growing dissention regarding the application of the Sunday Trading laws, with merchants on the one hand pointing out that it is no longer the Middle Ages and that a seven day a week option to trade is to the public benefit, whilst on the other, such august bodies who exist to monitor our adherence to this section of ecclesiastic dogma have coldly reminded one and all that to work on the sabbath is to defy the word of God. The crux of the argument can be traced to its source in the sixteenth chapter of Exodus, where the Israelites discover that strange but heaven–sent food called Manna.

Manna is another mystery that has never been solved by the biblical scholars, for it is conceded that no natural substance known to Man will fit the description given. The Scriptures tell us that it appeared on the ground with the evaporation of a layer of dew, as a 'flaky thing, fine like hoar frost'. It is also described as 'white, like coriander seed', or that it is transparent and waxlike, resembling a pearl. In order to prepare it for consumption, it was necessary to grind it in a hand mill, boil it, and then make it into cakes. The sheer improbability of such a substance should alert the reader into the realisation that yet another analogy is being presented.

The story of Manna begins in verse 4, when the Lord promises to 'rain bread from heaven', and it is important to fix in the mind this alternative name for Manna, because it will be essential to the interpretation of later allegories. The name 'manna' is given for the first time in verse 15:

And when the children of Israel saw it, they said to one another, it

is manna; for they wist not what it was. And Moses said unto
them, this is the bread which the Lord hath given you to eat.

We have now established that 'manna' (literally 'man-hu' – 'what
is it?') is some substance never before seen by the Israelites, and
which is symbolised by the word 'bread'.

Manna was gathered at the same rate for five days, but on the
sixth, twice the amount was taken, for

. . . on the seventh day, which is the sabbath . . . there shall be
none.

This is the first point in the biblical texts at which the word
'sabbath' is employed, and it means 'cessation of labour'. It implies,
therefore, that the gathering of Manna was considered to be a labour.
As we are all aware, the foundation of the idea that the seventh day is
a period of rest stems from the opening chapter of Genesis which
deals with God's creation of the Universe. But for the Hermeticists,
the Creation story also holds a very primitive allegory of the meditational process, the *labours* of God being the mental task (because
God did not create with *physical* matter), and the day of rest being the
completion of it. Exactly the same allegory is presented in the story
of Manna, for the *labour* of gathering it is indicative of the daily
period of meditation. When the process is successfully completed,
on the allegorical 'sabbath', the labourer (the initiate) no longer
needs to meditate (gather manna).

This interpretation is also emphasised in verse 35, where we are
told that Manna was gathered for the whole of the *forty* year period
and only stopped when they reached the *borders of Canaan* (the
Promised Land: the end of the process).

You will notice, too, that Manna is a food with strange qualities.
The Israelites were allowed to gather it 'every man according to his
eating', that is, some ate a lot while some ate little, but 'he that
gathered little had no lack'. Manna, therefore, is portrayed as having
the same beneficial effect on everyone regardless of the differing
quantities in which it was taken. Meditation has the same quality.
You can either sit in meditation for half an hour a day, or for two or
three, the result will still be the same provided it is continued to the
end. In a later chapter I will interpret a similar, extremely familiar
story which contains the same truth. For now, all that remains to be
said is that the 'sabbath' has no real relation to a physical rest period
as conceived by the Church.

To conclude my remarks about the mythological basis of the
Exodus story, I would point out that the central character, Moses, a

personification of the initiate, is made to die before he can reach the Promised Land. But this 'death' is an allegorical one, the 'death' of the conscious mind, which *must* take place before one can reach the *Promised Land*. Perhaps this will explain why Moses, as the writer of Exodus, was able accurately to record his own death.

The Real Exodus

It is to be wondered if there is any factual basis for the Exodus allegory, recalling that such themes were worked around actual events, and I may say that I believe there is, but I offer my regrets in advance for any blow to Jewish national pride, for the story has nothing whatever to do with the Jewish race. Instead, it concerns an exodus of the Hermetic fraternity themselves, which is the strongest reason for the invention of the myth. The scene is Egypt of about 1,500 B.C.

Surviving records show very clearly that, at that time, a fierce warrior race swept in from Arabia and completely subdued the whole of Egypt. In the Bible, the invaders were called the Amalekites, but the Egyptian scribes wrote of them as the Hyksos. Barbaric and merciless, they dominated the country for upward of a hundred years before they were finally expelled by Ahmose, Pharaoh of the 18th Dynasty. Their strength and extreme cruelty is graphically recorded, for they smashed everything in their path. The initiate centres, such as those at Heliopolis, would not have escaped attention, and there is little doubt that the Hermetic priests fled into Palestine, where they set up new centres in which to continue their teaching. When the Hyksos were expelled, not all the new generations of initiates felt obliged to return to Egypt, but remained to become the 'Israelites' and 'Jews' of the Old Testament.

Solomon and Sheba

The description of the building of King Solomon's Temple is an allegory of the process which is of some importance to Freemasons, for it was adopted by the first Knights Templars as the doctrine on which to base their initiation rites. In turn, the Templars bequeathed it to the Freemasons. Look closely at the text of the first book of Kings, telling how this great edifice was raised without the sound of mason's tools being heard. Apparently, the *great work* was carried out in complete *silence*. The master builder was named Hiram, and at the inauguration of the Temple

. . . fire itself came down from the heavens and proceeded to consume the *burnt offering* and *sacrifice,* and Jehovah's glory filled the house. (II Chron. 7; 1 – 3)

No sound was heard from the tools because the 'temple' was built in the mind by Hi-*Ram*, the Ram of Aries. As for the mystical entity in the story who was given the name Solomon, a high grade mason once pointed out that this is the name of the *Sun* in *three* ancient languages; SOL OM ON.

The king's legendary wisdom can be accounted for by turning to the text of Ecc. 12; verse 10, where we are told outright that he

. . . did much *meditating* to find the delightful words and the writing of correct words of truth.

We read that the temple is furnished with *gold*, or overlaid with *gold*, and that the treasures within are *three*-fold, *gold, silver* and *precious stones*. The first book of Kings says that

King Solomon exceeded all the kings of the earth for riches.

The inference here is that his 'treasure' was priceless beyond compare. And if this engenders a feeling of dejà vu, we may like to recall the letter written by Louis Fouquet after his talk with Poussin. Of the secret matter they discussed, he said:

. . . nothing on this earth could prove a better fortune, nor be its equal . . .

Finally, we must not forget the fact that the 'temple' was built on the *Mount of Moriah*, close to the *Mount of Zion*, both of which are part of that special area known as *Jerusalem*.

A second royal personage steps briefly into the Solomon story to create a further unsolved mystery: the Queen of Sheba. Unnamed in the Bible, she is thought to have come from the kingdom of Sheba, or Saba, in the south west of Arabia, but a much clearer hint of her original home was given by Jesus, who said she came from the *ends of the earth* (remember the nethermost regions?).

Another clue as to her origin is given by Fulcanelli in LE MYSTERE DES CATHEDRALES, as he endeavours to enlighten readers as to the craft of the allegorisers. Writing of a mediaeval ceremony called the Feast of the Donkey, he states that the lowly Ass, the glorious Christ-bearer, was the focus of a special service which praised it as

This asinine power, which was worth to the Church the gold of Arabia, the incense and myrrh of the land of Saba.

'The priest,' Fulcanelli continues, 'being unable to understand this grotesque parody, had to accept it in silence, his head bent under the ridicule poured out by these *mystifiers of the land of Saba, or Caba*, that is, the cabalists themselves.'

The 'cabalists' to which the author refers are the allegorisers. Thus, the 'land of Saba' – which may well have actually existed as a territory in Arabia – is a name which has been used to represent the art of the cabalists themselves: allegory. Perhaps this may explain why investigators have not been able to pinpoint its physical location with any degree of accuracy.

When the Queen visited Solomon in *Jerusalem*, she brought with her gold, spices and precious stones (*three* gifts, just as the *wise men* brought three gifts to Bethlehem), and after seeing the fabulous Temple, had this to say:

Happy are thy men, *happy* are thy servants. (I Kings. 10; 8)

Referring to the story of the Ugly Duckling, we see that the term 'happy' means initiated. Thus, we arrive at one interpretation of the mythical Sheba's presence in the Solomon legend. The King and his Temple personify the successful initiate, while Sheba is a thinly disguised Queen Isis, the *woman* of the reflective power.

However, there is a greater reason for the inclusion of Sheba, for she relates to the real Queen Hatshepsut, of Egypt.

Hatshepsut, the Initiate Queen

This real life Queen, the daughter of Thothmose I, came to power in 1501 B.C., and what is so unusual about her is that she became an initiate of the process, something which few women achieve. Like the scribe Ani, she celebrated this triumph by leaving a record of her accomplishment – and like Ani, she wrote it in code. She built herself a magnificent temple called the 'Most Splendid of Splendours', at Deir el Bahari, near Thebes, and on the walls within, she ordered a sequence of symbolic pictures to be carved, commemorating her initiation. Following the example of her predecessors, she depicted it as a 'journey', part of which was on *water*, part on *land*, to the place of treasure and rich rewards: Punt.

Expeditions to the mysterious land of Punt were first recorded at about 3,000 B.C., at the time of the Pharaoh Sahu–Re, second king of the fifth Dynasty, but it is interesting to note that no account, either at that early time or subsequently, gives the precise whereabouts of

Punt. In general, the emphasis lies only on the great treasure brought
back from the expeditions.

The visits to this wondrous but undesignated land were frequent
during the ensuing centuries, becoming a regular institution up until
the time of Menu-Hotep IV, in 2,000 B.C. Then the royal records
indicate that the expeditions lapsed, and it wasn't until after the
defeat of the Hyksos that contact was resumed. Some inkling of
what the Land of Punt really is can be gained when it is observed that
the Egyptian records alternatively call it the 'Land of the Gods', or
the 'Divine Land'. Punt, inscriptions tell us, is in the *east*. Note the
words of Amon, in the time of Amenhotep III, at the latter end of the
18th Dynasty

> When I turn my face to the sunrise . . . I cause to come to thee the
> countries of Punt.

Knowledge of the Hermetic symbolism, such as we have so far
examined, will allow us to interpret the *sunrise* as the inner mind,
thus putting the mysterious Punt in its proper perspective as a
mythical name like those of Avalon, Shangri-La and Atlantis.

Certain clues which substantiate this are present in Queen
Hatshepsut's inscriptions, such as a relief which shows a flotilla of
five sailing ships about to depart for Punt. On close examination,
however, it will be seen that only *three* of them are actually under sail
(indicating the three stages). It is also significant that the hieroglyph
for Punt was written without the usual sign indicating a foreign
country, and leads the observer to conclude that Punt was a land far
away, yet somehow connected with Egypt.

The inscriptions say that Queen Hatshepsut undertook the *voyage*
at the bidding of an *inner voice*;

> A command was heard from the great throne, an oracle of the god
> himself that the ways to Punt should be searched out, that the
> highways of the myrrh-terraces should be penetrated. ('Records',
> Vol. II, Breasted)

The 'myrrh-terraces' are elsewhere described as the 'glorious
region of God's Land': obviously not a real location, but relating to
the goal of the Hermetic process.

Space precludes a complete review of all the clues, but the most
decisive piece of evidence is in the form of a wall carving, showing
Hatshepsut standing between the hawk-headed god Horus and the
Ibis-headed Thoth. Both gods are in the act of pouring the contents
of their vases over her head. But it is not liquid which issues from the
vases. Instead, two streams of *ansated crosses* fall down each side of the

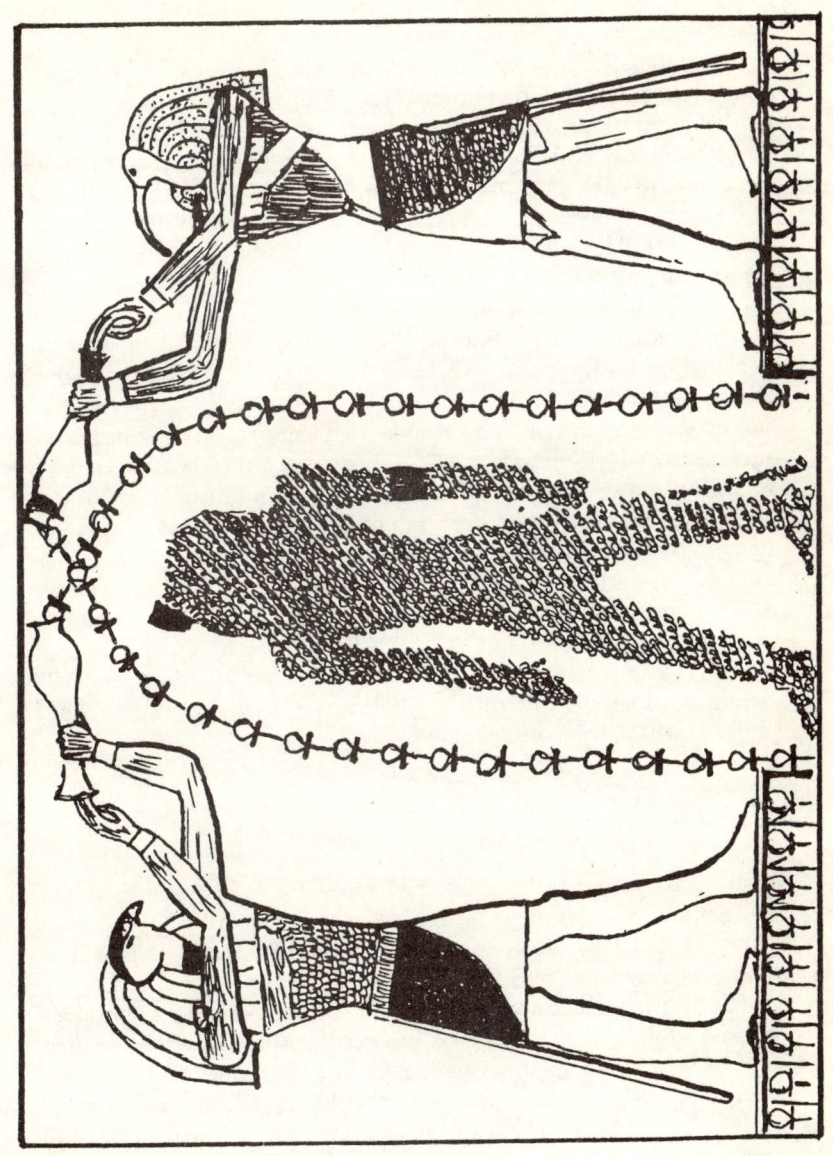

FIGURE 10.

figure, intersecting above her head in a large cross – no plainer indication of the Queen's initiateship (see fig. 10). The figure of the Queen was originally dressed as a man, and was defaced after her death at the order of her husband, Thothmese III.

Immanuel Velikovsky, in his AGES IN CHAOS, has gone to considerable lengths to connect Hatshepsut with the biblical Sheba in the hope of proving that *Punt* was actually another name for *Jerusalem*. How close he was, had he thought of the names as figurative instead of factual! In his thorough investigation into the origin of the name, Punt, he found reason to suggest that it is in some way linked with 'pontifex', a term of obscure origin meaning 'high priest'. He quotes an ancient authority as regarding the word to be derived from the Latin 'pontis' (a bridge), and 'facio' (I make). Thus, the conjecture is that a Pontifex is a man who builds bridges, an explanation which Velikovsky finds very strained. However, in the language of the initiate, a man who *builds bridges* (between the conscious mind and the subconscious) is a handy term to describe the successful Adept, so it is not so surprising to find it connected to Punt. Although Velikovsky is perfectly correct in believing that the biblical Sheba is a personification of Hatshepsut, the fact is that the Egyptian Queen did not go to Jerusalem under the name Sheba. She did not physically go anywhere. But she accomplished the Hermetic process and immortalised it as the mythical 'journey' to the Land of Punt: the inner mind.

I can only add that, until scholars accept this explanation, they will continue to search in vain for the last traces of Punt, or for that matter, Saba, Ophir and Atlantis.

David and Goliath

Even this familiar little fable, the famous battle between the giant Philistine and the youngest son of Jesse has a Hermetic basis, and to interpret it, all we need do is to think of Goliath as the dull giant of the conscious mind, and David as the subconscious, or initiate.

The text describes how the Philistine armies, ranging themselves against Saul, had taken a position *on top of a mountain*, while the men of *Israel* stood on an adjoining peak. The Philistines sent out their champion, Goliath, to issue a challenge. His appearance was *frightful* (same as *ugly* in the Duckling story), for he was a giant (the 'dull giant' figure is often used in Hermetic allegories to portray the uninitiated mind), and he wore a *brass* helmet (as you will see in later expositions, the term 'brass' is another well-worn symbol of the conscious mind), along with a coat of mail that was extremely *heavy* (allied to the colour *black*).

Goliath demands that the Israelites send out their own champion against him (to begin the 'combat' between the two minds);

9. 'If he be able to fight with me, and to *kill* me, then will we be your servants.' (I Sam. 17)

The giant didn't just say this on a single occasion, but kept repeating it for some considerable time

16. 'And the Philistine drew near morning and evening and presented himself *forty* days.'

The Israelites began to despair, until young David, a *keeper of sheep* (initiated) offered to meet the challenge. Saul armed him with a brass helmet and a heavy coat of mail like his adversary, but David put them aside saying that he didn't require them. He asked

Who is this *uncircumcised* Philistine?

He then went out to meet Goliath with only his sling and his *staff* in his hand, at which the giant disdained him

. . . for he was but a *youth* and *ruddy* (red) and fair of countenance.

43. 'And the Philistine said unto David; am I a *dog* (another emblem of the conscious mind) that thou comest to me with staves . . .'

Then David *killed the giant* with a *stone* from his slingshot.

Absolom

I conclude this all too brief look at the Old Testament allegories with the quaint story of the death of Absolom, as recorded in chapter 18 of II Samuel. Once again, the fairy-tale, almost laughable quality of the narrative leaves it open to comparison with the Ugly Duckling.

After a long and distinguished career, Absolom, the *third* son of David (an initiate) apparently suffered a rather bizarre death. While riding on a *mule*, he passed beneath a great *oak tree* and inadvertantly caught his *head* in the lower branches. The mule continued on its way, leaving the unfortunate Absolom *suspended*. There was only one witness to the incident, who straightaway ran to inform Joab, the captain of David's armies. Far from being helpful, Joab forthwith took *three* darts and thrust them through Absolom's *heart*, while he was still alive and hanging in the tree. Absolom was then finished off by *ten* men.

At this stage of the expositions I have no need to dwell on the obvious clues of the process, the three darts (stages) thrust through the heart (the centre of the mind), or the fact that like the Norse god, Odin, he was suspended in a tree (meditation in progress). However, the fact that Absolom was finished off by ten men places the story at the time when the signs of the zodiac were ten in number as far as the public were concerned.

Just as obscure is the fact that he is depicted riding on a mule, a symbol comparable to that of the *Ass*. The significance of the ass lies in the fact that it is generally representative of *fool*ishness, or unawareness – which is strange when it is remembered that they are really very intelligent creatues, recognised by those who handle them as more knowing than a horse. The answer to this inconsistency rests in the animal's distinctive bray, a sound which closely resembles the pronunciation of certain ancient names for God and the Moon, depending on the era and the language employed.

Iao, or Yao, are names for the Sun (Universal Mind) and are spoken as 'eeyow'. Io, Ievo and Evoe are all names for the Moon (reflection) and are pronounced in much the same way. The name for the ass in Coptic is 'ao', and in Egyptian, 'eo', again both phonetically similar to the 'hee-haw' sound. Therefore, just as in the case of the cat, the initiates made use of the ass, this time as the emblem of the uninitiated conscious mind. The symbol is most prominent in the New Testament, where Jesus is made to ride into *Jerusalem* on an *ass*. Sometimes, as in the story of Absolom, the creature's little half-caste brother is used: the mule.

Having seen that the fundamental concepts of Dualism are adequately, if furtively represented, we move on now to the era of the Greeks, some four or five centuries before, and leading up to, the Christian Era.

CHAPTER SEVEN

The Classic Greek Initiates

Almost all the classic Greek scholars, text book names of the Philosophy class, were initiates of the Hermetic Science: Plato; Pythagorus; Plutarch, and even the poet Homer; and although the greater part of their writings mention the Art only in the established allegorical manner, there are to be found certain passages which are frank statements intended to help the aspiring Neophyte. In the text of DE ISIDE ET OSIRIDE, for example, Plutarch attempts to explain the existence of the astral body:

> While we are here below, encumbered by bodily afflictions, we can have no intercourse with God save as in a philosophic thought we may faintly touch him as in a dream. But when our souls are released and have passed into the region of the pure, invisible and changeless, this God will be their guide and king, who depend upon him and gaze with insatiable longing on the beauty which may not be spoken of by the lips of man.

Quite naturally, commentators without knowledge of the process have taken this passage to relate to a state attained only after death – but if this is so, how did Plutarch know of it?

In speaking of the Egyptian Mysteries (the Mysteries of Isis, the Hermetic schools), he outlines the goal of the process, the transmission of the waking consciousness:

> By these means they may be better prepared for the attainment of knowledge of the First and Supreme Mind, whom the goddess (Isis) exhorts them to search after.

Plato too, propounded the doctrines of the astral man hidden within the physical body, and which could be invoked by the intiates' process:

> In consequence of this divine initiation, we became spectators of single and blessed visions, resident in pure light; and were ourselves made *immaculate* and liberated from this surrounding garment that we call a body and to which we are bound like an oyster to its shell.

I have emphasised the word 'immaculate' in order to prompt the memory in respect of my previous comments about the 'immaculate Virgin'.

The poet Homer referred to the astral body in an oblique manner, but the meaning is nevertheless clear to those with Hermetic insight:

Haste, let us *fly* and all our sails expand
To gain our dear, our long-lost native land.

This analogy, which compares the execution of the process to a voyage, is a theme which the ancient writers often used. The myth of Jason and the Argonauts is just such a vehicle, the tale being a complete allegory of the mental process. Jason sets out on his *voyage* across the *Black* Sea in his ship, the *Argo* (Argha – Ark, symbol of reflection) in order to bring back the *Golden Fleece*, the magical *Ram's* skin (the goal of the process). In order to accomplish this, he was obliged to undertake a *long and adventurous journey*, half of which was on *water*, and half on *land*, and then enter into *combat* with the *Dragon*. The Golden Fleece was hung on an *Oak Tree* (the same tree in which Osiris was imprisoned).

Hercules

The same foundation is in the story of Hercules and his *Twelve Labours*, except that he brought back the *golden apples* in place of the Fleece. The descriptions of the various labours are interwoven with symbolism, some of which is obscure and would require a great deal of space to explain, so I therefore intend to restrict myself to a single example, the Twelfth Labour, because it employs emblems that will be recognised elsewhere.

The Twelfth Labour required Hercules to capture the dog Cerberus (the *dog*, as we have discovered, is the conscious mind), and to bring him up from Tartarus (Hell, or the state of non-initiation). As a preliminary, he went to Eleusis to become initiated into the Mysteries, and thus prepared, he descended into Tartarus – some versions saying that he departed from the Archerusian penin-sular, near the *Black* Sea, to be guided by Athene (the *Moon*) and Hermes (Mercury, or thought power). Terrified by his *ugly* scowl, Charon ferried him across the Styx (a *voyage across water*).

At the gates of Tartarus, Hercules *rolled away a stone* under which Demeter (reflection, same as Isis) had imprisoned Ascalaphus; wrenched away the chains that bound Theseus; *killed* one of Hades' cattle and *wrestled* with the herdsman, Menoetes – all feats of strength symbolic of the mental task. He was then told that he could have Cerberus if he could *master the dog without using his club or arrows*. Hercules found the dog at last, chained to the gates of Acheron, and seized him by the throat, upon which Cerberus immediately sprouted *three* heads, each covered by a mane of live *serpents*. The dog's barbed tail flew up to strike, but Hercules was protected by his *lion's pelt* coat, and *did not relax his grip until the dog had succumbed* (continued the meditation until a successful conclusion was reached). On his way back, Hercules wove himself a wreath, the outer leaves of which remained *black* because it is the *colour of the Underworld*. Those next to his brow, however, were bleached *white* by his *sweat* (same symbolic significance as *dew* – concentration of thought).

As you can now plainly see, the Greek philosophers turned the art of allegory into a virtual sport, each one contending with the other to make the concealment of the process more devious.

Psyche and Amor

Take for example, the tale of Psyche and Amor. Psyche enjoys the love of the divine god each *night* (the conscious mind is animated by the subconscious each waking day), and although she is aware of his presence, she is not allowed to see him (uninitiated minds are unaware of the potential within). At a time when the god is sleeping, her curiosity gets the better of her and she lights a lamp in order to see him (Man searches for God outwardly, in the material world). But the moment she looks, the god disappears (the more Man looks outward, the less likely is he to know the truth). Terribly disappointed, and now ready to die (just like the Ugly Duckling), she is saved by the power of Love (attraction: the inward–looking reflective power that will attract the subconscious to the conscious).

Medusa and the Minotaur

There are easier allegories to decipher, especially at this stage of the book. The Medusa, for example, was one of *three* Gorgons, creatures whose *heads* were covered with *crawling serpents* (the moving thoughts) instead of hair. Perseus was able to *kill* the Medusa by cutting off her *head* (like the cat in Ani's vignette), whilst looking at her *reflection* in a mirror. Had he looked directly at her, he would have been turned to *stone* (remained uninitiated).

The Minotaur, a monster that had to be slain by Theseus was an *ugly* creature, having the body of a *Bull* and the head of a *man*. It was kept in a *Labyrinth*. We have already encountered the emblem of the Bull and the Labyrinth, and all that remains is to compare the *dual nature* the creature with the Sphinx.

Prometheus Bound

The legend of Prometheus as dramatised by the classic playright, Aeschylus, is worthy of investigation, if only because of a minor mystery attached to the author himself. Aeschylus, the story line informs us, was born of a *noble* family at Eleusis, near Athens, in 525 B.C. He wrote more than seventy plays, but only seven of them have survived as part of our heritage from the classic era. Like the other scholars, he was an initiate, and some interest is aroused by the persisting story that he was once prosecuted for divulging the secrets of the Eleusinian Mysteries – which were, of course, the same as the Egyptian Mystery rites, the Hermetic process. It is not known how, but he was able to prove himself innocent of the charge and thus escape the ultimate penalty of death.

The play opens with *four* characters on stage: Strength and Violence are seen, dragging Prometheus, their prisoner, and followed by Hephaestus, the god of fire. The first words of the dialogue alert the knowledgeable that Hermetic allegory is present. 'Here,' Strength is made to say, 'we have reached the *remotest region of the earth.*'

Having discovered the use to which previous initiate writers have put this phrase, we are now aware that Strength is speaking of the inner mind, a place reached by few. As the dialogue continues, we learn that Prometheus has committed the unforgivable sin of stealing fire from Hephaestus and giving it to mortal man, and for this crime he has been brought hither to be chained for all eternity to a large rock. Aware that the scene is the inner mind, we easily interpret 'fire' as the reflective power, and the 'rock' as the *stone* of the conscious mind. The whole scenario, therefore, is intended to portray the hidden potential of the reflective power.

In this particular version of the myth, the chained god is endowed with prophetic powers, and into this situation steps Io, the *woman with horns* (again the reflective power). In the latter pages of the playlet, Prometheus prophesies that she will go on a *long and adventurous journey*, after which she will *marry Zeus*, and from this union will descend a *child* who will *free Prometheus from the rock*. The child, incidentally, will be famed as an *Archer*.

In this we have the outlines of the process, for the child (the astral body) is an Archer, like Sagittarius, or like the fabled Cadmus who used his arrows to pin the *snake* to the *oak*. In the fact that he is an offspring of Io and Zeus, we have the emblem of reflection in the woman, and the subconscious or Universal Mind in Zeus, for this entity was the Supreme God of the Greeks.

So, in 'Prometheus Bound', the process has most certainly been allegorised, but it is doubtful if Aeschylus would have been indicted on the strength of the play's dialogue, for without the knowledge of the key to these allegories, they will remain as they always have been, merely a myth. Indeed, it is more than likely that the story of his persecution is just another device by which to draw attention to the allegory – like the biographic statement that he was from a noble family. The term 'noble' is often used to indicate an Adept.

Hermes

The mention of Zeus brings us to another familiar name, that of Hermes, son of the Supreme God. Known as the god of *good fortune* and ambassador for his father, he was also patron of all *travellers*, and was depicted wearing *winged sandals* (symbolic of the astral self which can 'fly'). He generally carried the Caduceus, or Staff, an emblem that can be related to the staff of Moses with which the latter struck the *rock* to bring forth *water*. Traditionally, Hermes, used the Caduceus to conduct the souls of the dead to Hades, a legend which corroborates the idea that it is an emblem of the power used to produce the astral body. This interpretation is supported by the visual aspect of the Caduceus: two intertwining *serpents* surmounted by *wings*. Hermes is familiar to all principally because it is his name which has been lent to the secret science, the Hermetic Science.

The Druids

The inference by Diodorus that Stonehenge had once been a temple of the Druids seems to be at variance with the tradition that they worshipped the oak tree in their sacred groves, and it is a point of Druidic lore that has never been satisfactorily resolved. In order to get at the truth, it must be understood that the real Celtic magi were not at all like those described in the works of the Greek scholars. Today's conception of the Druids as a mysterious caste is drawn mainly from the speculations of a few seventeenth century anti-quarians – speculations that were not always hand in hand with the truth.

Post-war archaeological research has yielded up a broad outline of what tribes were like in the era of the Druids, their customs and their level of primitive technology, but this evidence relates to the Celtic inhabitants as a whole. What we really seek is knowledge of the select band of priests who were important enough to be mentioned in the Greek texts – and it is at this stage that we encounter a difficulty.

It is a strange fact that the name 'Druid' is not evident in any Celtic inscriptions, but seems to have sprung from the Greek writings alone. Pliny, for instance, relates it to the Greek word 'Drus', meaning 'oak tree'. We may also consider the Gallo–Britonic word 'nemeton', which has the meaning of a 'shrine', or 'sacred place'. Strabo writes that the meeting place of the Galatian Druids of Asia Minor, was Drunemeton, a name which thus implies 'shrine of the sacred oak'. And after what we have learned regarding those philo-sophic writers and their love of deep allegory, it does not take long to realise that we are once more at the centre of an involved, Hermetic joke.

Having discovered the inner meaning of the 'oak' symbol, there can be little doubt that the 'druid' who worships at it is merely another name for the initiate. The oak tree itself, an emblem descended from the Persea tree of Ani, was chosen to represent the physical/conscious because these sturdy old growths were often found to be *hollow*, like a *cave*, and therefore a good place in which to hide *treasure*.

A detailed account of a druidic ceremony is given by Pliny, and it is to this that we must turn to lay bare the hidden message. The rite, we are told, takes place at *night* (in the inner mind), and required a *white*-robed Druid to *climb the sacred oak* (instead of the mount), where he used a *golden sickle* to cut off a branch of mistletoe, which was caught as it fell, in a *white* cloak. After this, *bulls were sacrificed*. Connected with this ceremony, there were a number of strange actions to be religiously followed: gathering the samolus with the *left* hand; plucking selago *without using an iron knife*, while standing barefoot with the *right* hand through the *left* sleeve of a *white* tunic, and similar oddities. Each one of these incongruous conditions conceals certain clues to the process, some of which will be recog-nised now, others at a later stage – and the remnants of such traditions may even be experienced today by the candidate for Freemasonry, the ritual of which requires him to present himself with the *left* breast and leg bared, while blindfolded.

Another version of the Druids' ceremony can be culled from the story of Ram, the Indian mystic. As a young man, *Ram* was in the habit of *meditating* beneath an *oak tree*. One particular evening, after pondering long on the *evils* of Mankind, he drifted off to sleep and dreamed that he was called by name. Looking up, he saw a *white*-robed Druid standing before him, who took him by the hand and showed him a branch of mistletoe at the foot of the oak. Taking a *golden* knife, the Druid cut a sprig and gave it to him, saying:

This is the remedy you seek.

He whispered the secret way in which the plant should be prepared, and then vanished.

There are variations of this theme, but the basic allegory remains as described. Close examination of the bardic preoccupation with mistletoe will lead to the conclusion that a literal interpretation is unlikely. It is true that the plant is anciently regarded as a 'heal-all', but how much of this is due to tradition rather than its medicinal qualities is open to question. What draws the attention is the unlikely routine the Druids went through to obtain it: climbing a tree at midnight on the night of the full moon to cut it with a sickle made of gold. Professor Stuart Piggot, in his book, THE DRUIDS, says that he finds this idea inexplicable. And well he might!

The *sickle*, by its shape, represents the *Moon*, in crescent form but still a symbol of reflection. The *Mistletoe* as a secret symbol has slightly more depth and to reveal the true meaning it is necessary to consider the natural cycle of the real plant. The berries are *white* in colour and, like the robes of the Druids, relate to the second stage of the mental process. Nature dictates that these berries are eaten by birds and, by way of their natural functions, the seeds are ejected with birdlime to become attached to the branches of other trees. On germination, the seeds pierce the bark, penetrating the wood, and then flourish into maturity. So the mistletoe, the berries of which are representative of the astral body, is born due to the agency of birds – and if you recall the symbol of the Dove, you will realise that the classic writers are once again using the emblem of the bird to signify 'spirit'. To sum up the allegory, this wonderful plant, with its miraculous 'berries' is generated by the industry of birds (the astral body is generated by the agency of spirit).

The above interpretations should now account for the Greek-based traditions that the Druids worshipped in *oak groves* (the 'oak groves' of their own minds). As for the connection with Stone-henge, the Celtic magi were the people who held the knowledge of the monument's function as a lunar observatory. Such computive activity, and the high knowledge of the initiates' process, although linked symbolically by the Moon, must be considered as entirely separate sciences.

The Oracle at Delphi

Just as the classic writers amused themselves by inventing their own version of the Druids, so the famed Oracle at Delphi was another one of their little jokes. In case any reader in unfamiliar with the story, let us quickly review the essentials.

According to the historian, Diodorus Siculus, the site of the great temple at Delphi was once open countryside where sheep and goats were put to graze. The temple, erected later, was constructed to commemorate a wonderful discovery at that very spot. A herdsman noticed that every time one of his flock approached a certain place, it would suddenly begin to skip about, bleating in a manner that was quite removed from normal, and upon investigation discovered a chasm in the ground. When the puzzled herdsman himself drew near and peered down the hole, he was similarly affected and began to prophesy the future. Soon, all the peasants were visiting the hole to put the phenomenon to the test, and sure enough, whenever one of them came too close, he or she fell into a trance and began to prophesy. Thus the place soon came to be regarded as miraculous.

The practice was dangerous, however, for many were so entranced that they fell into the chasm and their bodies were never recovered. To avoid this, the local people constructed a special chair, supported by three legs, in which one person alone could be hoisted over the chasm to become entranced in safety. They chose a woman for the job, calling her the Pythia. The chair itself was known as the Tripod. 'And indeed,' Diodorus blandly adds, 'The bronze tripods that we have today are almost exact replicas of it.'

In time, the site of the chasm was so venerated that the great temple of Delphi was built up around it, and many were the tales of the oracle's prophetic powers.

Archaeological researchers of the present day have looked in vain for the mysterious chasm, and not finding it, have concluded that it must have been since closed by volcanic action. But, acquainted now with the way in which Hermetic myth is laid over real locations, we might guess at the true reason for the lack of evidence. The story is of the same order as that of the oracle at *Argos*, where the priestess was supposed to go into a frenzy of prophecy after drinking the *blood of a lamb sacrificed at night*: an Hermetic fable.

The chair in which the Pythia sat had *three* legs, and Diodorus was at pains to point out that the same kind of 'tripod' still existed. Of course it did, because it was indicative of the three stages of the process, and those emblems certainly do exist, even in our day. The word 'bronze' introduced by the Greek writer is merely a slight deviation from the older tradition of calling the conscious mind 'brass', as in the story of Goliath, or to go even further back into the past, where Tubal Cain is said to be a *founder of brass* (someone who 'works' on his conscious mind – i.e., an initiate). In a chapter to come, you will see the symbolism recur in its 16th century form.

After the passing of Thoth as a male deity, the reflective power of the conscious mind was ever afterwards represented by a woman, notably Isis, and it is for this reason that the story tells us a *woman* was selected as the prophetess. She was called *Pythia*, a name derived from Apollo's other name, Pythian, after the *Python* he was supposed to have *killed*. Thus, in the Pythia, we have symbolic reference to both the conscious mind and the reflective power within it.

Certainly there was a great temple at Delphi, but it was constructed not because of an 'Oracle' that never existed, but because the place was selected as a school of Hermetic knowledge, like a latter day Heliopolis.

Atlantis:

Of all the Greek initiate writers, perhaps the greatest influence has been exterted by Plato, and this mainly due to his famous discourse on the lost continent of Atlantis.

It has been estimated that well over two thousand books have been written on the subject of the mysterious continent, every one of them founded solely on the material supplied in TIMAEUS and CRITIAS, a dialogue set down by Plato some three hundred years before the Christian Era. Equally often, the single most pertinent question has been posed: was Plato recounting fact, or fantasy?

No one knows, and it is doubtful if anyone will ever succeed in determining, if there was a land mass in the middle of the Atlantic prior to the end of the last Ice Age. As for its disappearance in 'a single day and night', the best explanation proposed so far is that the continent fell victim to a stray but sizeable meteor, there even being a certain amount of evidence to support the theory in the form of great meteor scars still visible across Carolina.

Geological research has shown that about ten thousand years ago, the eastern seaboard of the United States projected much farther out into the Atlantic than it does at present. And barely one hundred miles east of Miami, off the coast of Andross island on the Bahama Bank, many square miles of Inca-like buildings, walls and even pyramidal shapes, have been found in the shallow waters, showing that in the far past, a thriving civilisation existed there. But is it the Atlantis of Plato? I'm afraid that I must shatter many a visionary's dream of a once great society as depicted by the classic scholar, by showing that the detailed description of Atlantis and its capital city, Poseidon, is yet another allegory of the initiates' process. If the reader cares to refer to the easily accessible paperback edition of TIMAEUS and CRITIAS, I will point out the clues concealed within the text.

In the opening pages of TIMAEUS, the subject of Atlantis is introduced and we are told that it was eventually destroyed in a single dreadful day and night. But then Critias is made to add a rather odd statement:

> That is why the sea in that area is to this day impassable to navigation, which is hindered by mud just below the surface.

Commentators of classic literature have never been able to rationalise this implication that the Atlantic is shallow, for every ancient mariner knew that it wasn't, especially in the Sargasso Sea area to which Plato seems to be referring. It is hardly surprising, for the statement is a deliberate error, the first clue to the hidden allegory, and it warns the reader that there is something hidden 'just below the surface' of the text.

Atlantis is then presented as an *ideal society*, similar to that which is described in the author's REPUBLIC – and equally similar, I may add, to those other lands of fantasy where all is *perfect*, Shangri-La, Avalon, Shamballa, and the Garden of Eden. Atlantis is lost, we are told, but there are signs of it just below the surface. Other obscure hints follow, but let us move forward to CRITIAS, where interpretation can proceed on lines which are by now becoming familiar.

In the exposition of the zodiacal sign of Taurus, I mentioned Atlantis, referring to Poseidon's *Temple*, or *Palace*, which is located in the *centre* of the city, and where the assembly of kings met to *sacrifice bulls*. We now read that this inner temple is surrounded by *three* circular causeways, which are constructed of *black, white* and *red* stone. The houses in the city were built of the same coloured stones, sometimes with the colours mixed, so as to *divert the eye*. The three circular causeways, with *three* channels of *water* to separate them, become apparent now as the three stages of the process, complete with the Hermetic colours. Plato seems to have drawn this allegory from the ancient inscriptions of Ramses III (about 1200 B.C.) on the wall of the temple now known as Medinet Habu.

The three causeways, it is made plain, must be crossed before access can be gained to the *central shrine*. This is achieved by way of bridges built over the channels and tunnels cut through the causeways – each bridge having a guardhouse, each tunnel a garrison. This makes for a *difficult but not impossible* passage to the centre. Once having arrived there, it will be seen that the Temple of Poseidon is surrounded by a *golden wall*.

The circular design of the causeways has a significance all of its own, it being the most basic symbol of the reversal of thoughts necessary to begin the process: sending them back (inwards) from whence they came, thus forming a 'circle'. As I will later show, the use of the circle for this purpose was far more prolific than is realised.

The text says that when the Atlanteans constructed their city, their *first work* (Hermetic phrase meaning meditation) was to bridge the rings of water round their *mother's original home*. Ostensibly, this phrase refers to Cleito, the wife of Poseidon, but remember that we are dealing with myth. The passage has the deeper meaning of the original Mother, Isis (the *mother* of reflection). We are also informed that they proceeded to build the central palace at once, 'in a place where their ancestors lived'. When this statement is compared with the favourite description by the Chinese alchemists of the centre of the mind – the 'cave of one's ancestors' – it will be conceded that Plato was not writing of a material dwelling.

Outside the three main city walls, there were houses and a large harbour, crowded with constant use

> . . . and from which rose a constant din of shouting and noise, day and night.

This rather unnecessary remark inserted into the description of the city's layout has been put there to indicate the material world of the conscious mind with its constant 'noise' of moving thoughts, and which will be required to become like the central shrine, completely and utterly silent, with all thoughts stilled.

The philosopher's description of the rest of the island contains a number of obvious clues, such as the statement that the *mountains* in the *north* were more numerous, higher and more beautiful than any that existed today, an assertion that seems to hold unwarranted emphasis. Poseidon city was surrounded by a flat plain, rectangular in shape and situated high up above the level of the sea, from which it rose precipitously. For irrigation purposes, the Atlanteans had cut channels across the length and width of the plain, 'uniformly and regularly spaced out'. Thus, the text hints, if viewed from above, the plain would resemble a giant *chessboard* – and so you will now be aware that the mythical plain is a further vehicle with which to express the mental task of the Hermeticist.

Philosophy

With the passing of Plato's era and the advance into the Middle Ages and beyond, the average person's conception of what a Philosopher really was became far removed from the original meaning. To the mediaeval mind – and indeed, to most today – a philosopher was an experimental chemist, or metallurgist, spending hours in the laboratory conducting experiments in order to discover the true nature of matter – and the possible transmutations that may be accomplished once the knowledge is gained. The work of this brand of 'philosopher' is wholly material. But the original Philosophers, like Plato and his contemporaries, were those who, through long hours of carefully directed meditation, had arrived at the knowledge of the eternal truth of Nature.

The Black Virgins

Before concluding this section, I would like to throw some light on an enigma that has become prominent in recent times – the question so often asked about the origin of the Black Virgins, the many black-coloured statues of the Virgin Mary that hold places of dubious honour within Catholic cathedrals. I say 'dubious' because these mysterious icons have a tradition that is steeped in paganism, despite their attachment to the Church. They are surrounded by an aura of legendary power which supercedes by far any attributed to the conventional representations of Mary. And the enigma is heightened by the fact that the statues are more often than not to be found in the crypt – not consigned there by the Catholic authorities, but by the intent of those who conceived them.

There are nearly forty such black idols scattered about Europe alone, although they have been found as far afield as Mexico. The

Roman Catholic Church, in whose cathedrals and churches many of the Madonnas repose, accords no special status or significance to them, but the local people and the many who make the pilgrimage to see and touch them, hold them in so high an esteem as to be an embarrassment to the Catholic hierarchy. Miraculous powers of healing and fertility are accorded them, a belief which borders on outright Paganism, and which has prompted some Church authorities to go as far as covering their Madonnas with a coat of 'purifying' white paint.

All the Madonnas are seen holding a *child*, usually on the *left* knee – and all are decked out in rich apparel which, on festive occasions, may be supplemented with precious stones.

The mystery may be solved by examining some of the legends attached to the various statues and by tracing their sources. At Tindari, in Sicily, for example, the Madonna there is said to have been *washed ashore in a casket,* a phrase which immediately links with the Egyptian legend of Osiris and Isis, and thus accounts for the fact that many of the statues are Egyptian in appearance.

The Black Madonna at Montserrat is said to have been discovered by *shepherds* in a *cave*, after they had been led to it by *lights seen in the night* and had heard an angelic choir. At Avioth, the Madonna is reputed to have materialised in a *thorn bush*.

Some statues are identified as the *Queen of Heaven,* a name more often given to the *Moon* – while at Chartres, in France, the Madonna is called the *Queen of the Underworld*. And then there is the fact that all the statues are *black,* the colour of the first stage. This can be coupled with the legend of Osiris, whom the Egyptian priests maintained to be a *black* god. The Old Testament tells us that Solomon was a passionate devotee of the *Queen of Heaven,* and as we have already discovered that the name Solomon personifies the initiate, we understand that the appelation 'Queen of Heaven' and its connection to the Moon must be taken to its ultimate hidden meaning, the reflective power present in the conscious mind of Man. Thus we see that the Black Madonnas are representations of Isis, the Egyptian Queen who is emblematic of the meditative power, and it is because of this that the statues are credited with 'miraculous powers'. She is seen holding the child Horus, because it is through her action that the infant (the astral body) will be born.

The inscription beneath the Chartres Madonna verifies this:

To the Virgin about to give birth.

Saint Bernard, the Abbot of Clairvaix, propagated a tradition which said he experienced a most illuminating revelation from a black Madonna at Chatillon. While he was reciting the Ave Maria, so his story goes, she suddenly pressed her breasts, whereupon *three* drops of milk spurted out and fell into the monk's mouth. From this miniature allegory, we may appreciate that Saint Bernard was an initiate, but owing to his membership in a faith which decried the Hermetic Art, he felt it more prudent to express his initiation in a way that only brother initiates could understand.

The fact that some Madonnas are to be found in the crypt can be accounted for when it is remembered that the Gothic cathedrals were in most cases built to the architectural design of Hermetic initiates, who carefully planned the construction to represent the human mind, just as the Tabernacle was supposed to. The crypt is the most secret and *silent* part of the church, *hidden from public view*. It is therefore symbolic of the centre of the mind, the subconscious, where utter *stillness* prevails.

With the gradual growth of Christianity, the Roman Catholic Church adopted the sign of the Virgin Mary, little realising that it was a symbol of reflection, and not a living entity from the past. This marvellous power of reflective thought has been given a long list of different names, as we are beginning to find out, but perhaps no better idea of the nomenclature's scope can be gained than by referring to the classic Greek tale of the GOLDEN ASS, as told by the 2nd century writer, Apuleius.

In this story, the author – an initiate – personifies himself as Lucius, a bawdy young man who has the misfortune to be turned into an *ass*. After *many strange adventures* Lucius, still in his asinine shape, reaches a sandy shore and lies down to sleep at the onset of *night*. Later, he awakes to find a dazzling full moon rising from the sea and was inspired to pray to the *visible image of the goddess*. Then he returns to sleep and dreams that the goddess herself appears to address him. In both the prayer and the address, a wide but by no means complete range of names are quoted, all of which pertain symbolically to the power of reflected thought. They are: Queen of Heaven; Ceres; Venus; Paphos; Artemis; Prosperpine; Nature; Mother; Pessinuntica; Aphrodite; Dictynna; Corn Mother; Juno; Bellona; Hecate; Rhamnubia.

'But both races of the Ethiopians,' says the Moon Goddess, 'whose lands the morning sun first shines upon, and the Egyptians who excel in ancient learning and worship me with ceremonies proper to my godhead, call me by my true name – Queen Isis'.

The story of Lucius culminates in a remarkable *transformation*, like that of the Ugly Duckling, and as you have no doubt guessed, is an Hermetic allegory. Pertinent to this section of our investigation is the way in which Apuleius describes the appearance of the goddess Isis:

> Her many coloured robe was of the finest linen; part was glistening *white*, part crocus *yellow*, part glowing *red* . . . But what caught and *held my eye* more than anything else was the deep *black* lustre of her mantle.

These are, it is plain, the Hermetic colours of ancient Egyptian times, the most emphasis being placed on the black mantle of Isis – the Black Madonna.

CHAPTER EIGHT

The New Testament

As the story of the Exodus dominates the Old Testament, so the Crucifixion is the centrepiece of the New, and the suggestion that the death of Jesus, like that forty year trek in the wilderness, is an event which took place only in the imagination of an initiate, will be totally unacceptable to most Christian thinkers. But for some time, a nucleus of scholars have had their reservations, for they have been unable to ignore the inexplicable lack of support for the Gospel story in non-biblical, historic documents. Quite rightly, they have expressed the view that an episode of emotionally charged importance such as the Crucifixion, the deliberate and cruel execution of a much loved miracle worker, should warrant an honourable mention from sources other than the New Testament itself.

However, this is a point that we will explore and answer in the appropriate place. For now, let us continue to unearth the hidden message of the initiate. As with the Old Testament, space will limit our enquiry to the most prominent texts and in respect of this, it will be helpful to divide the New Testament into two separate sections: those which are of an allegorical nature, and those that are not. The letters of the apostle, Paul, for example, contain many hints as to the author's own initiateship, but the texts are in the nature of sermons rather than allegorical myth. Of the hints, that which has caused the most brow-furrowing speculation among biblical enthusiasts occurs in Galatians 2, when Paul says:

> 20 I am crucified with Christ; nevertheless I live; yet not I but Christ liveth in me . . .

Throughout the apostle's letters, such enigmatic statements are thrown in among the argument for the attainment of knowledge, and it is not hard to deduce that those to whom the texts were directed were guilty of reading the Gospel story literally, and that Paul was warning against it. Although it is highly unlikely that his real name was 'Paul', there is little doubt that he existed as a real entity at the time designated, and that he was an initiate of the Hermetic practice.

On the other hand, the Gospels, Acts and Revelation are entirely allegorical, with a cast of characters who although perhaps loosely based in living entities, never existed as the texts portray them.

To give a brief instance of the difference between the texts, we can consider the life story of Paul as given in his own letters. He was famed as a missionary and for the travels he undertook for the purposes of spreading the inner knowledge, but careful assessment will reveal that the apostle himself, while describing certain of his movements, was hardly a stickler for detail. Far more 'information' can be gleaned from the Book of Acts, a text which was written by Luke and is in allegorical style. Acts will tell us that Paul made *three* missionary *journeys,* during which certain *miraculous happenings* took place. The third journey sees Paul revisiting the city of Ephesus, this time to *labour* there for *three* years. Ephesus was a city built on the slopes of the *mounts* near the mouth of the Cayster River, and as such, was a place of both *land* and *water.* The main feature of the metropolis was a magnificent temple dedicated to Artemis (one of the *Moon* goddesses), an edifice of striking aspect because it was roofed with *white* marble similar to that used in the construction of the *Temple of Solomon.* It was also alleged that *gold,* not cement, was used to join the marble blocks together.

Of course, there is a real city of Ephesus, and it did have a temple – but not quite as opulent as the text of Acts would have us believe. As usual, real names and places have been cunningly utilised to project the fact that Paul was one of the Hermetic brotherhood.

In both the Old and the New Testaments, there are two methods by which the initiate message was enciphered. The first, and the easiest to detect is that which we have so far studied, the carefully prepared allegorical theme, with its constantly recurring clues, examples of which can be culled from any standard, English version of the Bible.

There is, however, a second fundamental encipherment which is only recognisable in the original Aramaic and Hebrew of the Testament texts. With the translation into English, these were lost, for the coded words depend upon phonetic equivalents in the original language – the same form of word play so loved by the Egyptians, and which I have briefly outlined in chapter 4. Exactly the same puns and equivalents can be found in the original Sumerian script from which the biblical Aramaic descended, and thanks to the work of John Allegro and his brilliant study of these ancient languages, some of the missing code words have recently come to light.

The Sacred Mushroom

When THE SACRED MUSHROOM AND THE CROSS was published in 1970, it provoked a veritable storm of adverse criticism from the established stream of academic thought. Such censure was extremely hostile but hardly surprising under the circumstances, for however erudite the author was known to be and however comprehensively he presented his arguments, the theme was one that could not help but arouse controversy. In brief, John Allegro told his readers that, by way of a prolonged study of the ancient Sumerian script upon which the original Bible texts were founded, he had discovered that the allegories within the Testaments referred to a secret cult centred around the imbibing of the hallucinatory drug extracted from the common mushroom, Amanita Muscaria. With a multitude of examples, he showed how the word play of the biblical scribes conceals references to the Sacred Mushroom in even the most innocuous of texts. He achieved this in such a scholarly way that no one without the same degree of education in the subject could hope to offer any coherent argument. The sum effect of the book was to infer that the whole of the Christian edifice is based on a drug-taker's cult. Hence the academic fury.

As this masterly volume is still available, there is little need for me to repeat anything but the basic principle as outlined by the author. Instead, let us come at once to the crux of the question raised: it is possible that he is right?

The answer is that his interpretations, even the educated guesses, are indubitably right – but there remains one final, all-important conclusion that John Allegro has yet to reach.

The fundamentals of his research resolve in the common denominator of a dual symbolism which is presented in its basic aspects. With the mushroom, the two parts are the stem and the cap, while in the very ancient Sumerian, he makes a comparison with the oft used 'penis and vulva' emblem. Relating also to the biblical stories are the ball and socket joints of the leg and thigh bones. As we are wholly aware that we are dealing with a long established practice which employs double, and even compound, symbolism, it is but a short step to relate the above to the most basic Dual system of all, the conscious mind against the subconscious – evil against good – the metaphysical foundation which can only be expressed symbolically by material objects. John Allegro has failed to take this final step, and in searching for an answer, has selected the mushroom as the root of the symbolism due to its known hallucinogenic effects, which could be construed as a temporary removal from the earthly plane to the 'realm of the gods.' It was an understandable error, for there is no denying the appearance of the 'mushroom' symbol as described, and we have already seen how it applies in the text of the Old Testament where I have identified its true meaning. And yet, the correct solution was available to him in the form of an alternative to the 'mushroom', an emblem which he calls the 'bolt plant' symbol.

Through the interpretation of various names which, by word play and punning, hide the 'mushroom' code word, he brings the reader to a common denominator of the 'bolt plant', so called because of the shape of the fungus. The large, circular top surmounting the slender stem was alike in outline to a primitive door key, an implement that consisted of a rod with a small right-angle bend in it, while the other end terminated in a knob which could be grasped by the hand. This key was simply pushed through a hole in the door and manipulated so as to lift the latch on the inside. Thus we are presented with a 'knobbed bolt' imagery which might have been used to hide the real meaning, the mushroom and its drug.

Seeing no religious significance in the idea of a key with a knob at one end, the author returns to the mushroom and its phonetic equivalents, by quoting that well-known paragraph in Matthew 16:

And I tell you, you are Peter, and on this rock I will build my church, and the gates of Hades shall not prevail against it. I will give you the keys to the kingdom of heaven.

John Allegro sums up his interpretation by saying:

The sacred fungus was the 'bolt', or 'key' that gave access to heaven and to hell, a double reference to its shape as a knobbed bolt for opening doors, and to its ability to open the way to a new and exciting mystical experience.

So near to the truth, this statement is based on the word play between 'Peter' and 'rock', compared to the mushroom ('petra' compared to 'pitra'), followed by the outright mention of the keys to the kingdom of heaven. But the real answer lies in a simple reversal of this conclusion – more in the shape of the knobbed bolt and its use as a *key* than in the hallucinatory substance extracted from the mushroom. The key, with its single stem surmounted by a knob, was visually similar to that most ancient key of keys, the Egyptian Ankh – the Key to the Mysteries (the potential within the human mind).

The aspect of Dualism present in the symbols of the mushroom, penis and vulva, and in the primitive door key, are resolved in the sign of the Ankh, the Cross surmounted by the Circle. These two are

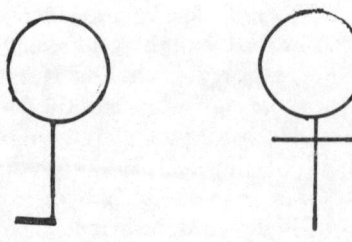

The door key   The Key to the Mysteries

age old emblems of the conscious mind (the cross) and the sub-conscious (the circle). When, by means of the Hermetic process, the two are made to intermix, the result is signified by one of the oldest symbols of the Rosicrucians, the Rose Cross:

And so, in order to arrive at the correct foundation of the inter-pretations given by John Allegro, every reference to the sacred 'mushroom' must of necessity not stop there, but be carried to its true root, the Ankh (the mind). We have already encountered one phonetic equivalent (in the original Aramaic) in the name 'Moriah', and to remind you how complex the symbolism can become, re-member that Mount Moriah is the site on which Jerusalem was built. By inference, therefore, the name *Jerusalem* can hold the same hidden meaning, simply because it is *in the same place*. Another example of the 'mushroom' emblem was found in the Burning Bush story, and as we proceed, you must keep in mind that the inner meaning is similarly extended to any 'bramble', 'thicket', or 'thorn bush' – a prime example being the *crown of thorns* placed upon the *head* of Jesus.

It must have been with great irony that the old Hermetic masters utilised the common mushroom as a representative of their science, for the temporary and wholly uncontrolled release of the astral self was little compensation for the nauseating and often dangerous effects of the drug – a frustrating way in which to become appraised of the potential within the mind. The visual symbolism is not hard to explain, the most obvious being that the fungus displayed the three alchemical colours in its *black* underbelly, *white* stem, and *red* cap.

The latter was comparable to the Phrygian Cap of both the Eleusinian and Mithraic Mysteries. This red-coloured headgear, with its shape identical to the mushroom top, was placed on the Neophyte's *head* at the beginning of the Eleusinian initiation rites. The same hat, in the Mithraic rituals, was called 'Liberia' and was a mark of the finished process. The significance of the cap lies also in the fact that, in early times, it was worn by *freed slaves,* and so is emblematic of the astral body being freed from the physical.

Some mushrooms have a spotted cap, and this too, was drawn into the symbolic scheme as a sign that *fermentation* was taking place in the mind of the Neophyte. The spots looked very much like bubbles in a boiling pot, you see. This facet of symbolism can be traced back to Egypt where it is present in representations of Horus. Alternatively called Heru-p-khart, Horus (the child) is a person-ification of the new born astral body or *Infant* – and this may solve the mystery of why the god is consistently portrayed with his finger to his mouth, the action of an infant. The same deity is often seen dressed in a *spotted* leopard skin.

Continuing with our comparisons, it can be recalled that the mushroom is a plant that *grows at night,* and if further evidence is required, we can look up the Greek name for mushroom: Morios. I have already pointed out that 'Moriah' is a phonetic equivalent of this, and now, with a simple transposition of the 'i', permissible in the rules of word play, the name becomes Morois, the mythical *forest* of Tristan and Isolde. This in turn, is comparable to the French 'Mort Roi', the 'dead king' of the Hermeticist and the Shah Mata of the winner at *chess.*

Finally, may I point out that the consonants present in the Aramaic word for 'mushroom' are PTR, which takes us back to Egypt and the god, Ptar.

Turning to comparable emblems in Latin and Greek, John Allegro cites the Navelwort plant (Latin, 'cotyledon'; Greek, 'kotuledon') as part of the 'mushroom' symbolism, showing that the name means any socket shaped cavity, such as that of a hip joint, the inside of a cup, or the hollow of the hand. The source of these various emblems is traced back to a Sumerian phrase meaning 'ball and socket', or as applied to the fertility cults, 'penis and vulva', both of which should be taken to their true root in the religion of Dualism. It is remarked that the specific reference in Greek of 'kotuledon' to 'hip joint' gave rise to certain myths in which the central figure has his hip put out of joint, or was pierced either in the hip or the side of the body – the last named being the treatment meted out to Jesus while on the cross. In this myth, the Dual aspect was reiterated in the Gospel of John, where both *blood* (red) and *water* (white) were seen to run from the wound.

The alchemist, Fulcanelli speaks of the mystical fountain of youth, the Fountain which the Arabians call Holmat, and then draws attention to a version of the theme to be seen in a little church at Brixen, in the Tyrol. A painting within shows Jesus making the blood flow from his pierced side, to fall into a large bowl. Nearby, the Virgin squeezes her breasts to make the milk (*white*) fall into the same receptacle and *intermix* with the blood (*red*). Below is the inscription:

While the blood flows from the blessed wound of Christ and the Holy Virgin presses her virginal breasts, the milk and blood spurt out and are mixed, and become the Fountain of Life and the Spring of Well-Being.

I doubt very much whether the effects of the mushroom drug would ever have been designated the Spring of Well-Being.

What this particular aspect of the symbolism does show is that the long sought after Fountain of Youth is no more than a myth, the result of the Hermeticists' process, the intermixing of the conscious mind with the subconscious.

The Gospel Story

The first of the Gospel texts was that written by Mark, the general opinion of scholars being that it was set down about 70 A.D. Some ten years later, came the texts of Matthew and Luke – the latter penning the Acts at the same time – while the fourth Gospel, that of John, was thought to have been written somewhere between 90 and 110 A.D. The twenty years between Mark's work and that of John may perhaps account for certain subtle refinements of the original story that will come to our attention as we proceed.

The term 'gospel' refers, as everyone recognises, to the *good* news about the kingdom of God, and if you recall the basic aspects of Dualism, one evil (the conscious mind), the other good (the sub-conscious), you will be left in no doubt that the texts relate to that *kingdom* to be found in the inner mind. Perhaps this may explain why the gospeller's side of the church altar is always on the *north*.

We now turn to the prominent points of the Jesus story and uncover the truth that so many people deny.

The Birth of Jesus

At the outset of this exposition, the reader is required to grasp the fact that Jesus and his twelve apostles were never real entities, but are characters brought into existence purely for the purpose of expressing this particular version of the Hermetic theme. Peter, for example, was carefully characterised to portray the conscious mind which is undergoing the process, but has not quite realised its accomplishment. This is ably expressed in a fable previously mentioned, when he tries to emulate Jesus by walking on water, but fails. Throughout the whole of the Gospel texts, Peter is portrayed with the traits of the average conscious mind. He was generally the one who spoke first in any situation, impulsively, sometimes impetuously. Equally often, he is reproved or rebuked by Jesus, as in the oft-quoted verse of Matthew 16:

> 23 But he turned and said to Peter, get thee behind me, Satan; thou art an offence unto me; for thou savourest not the things that be of God, but those that be of men.

You may now understand why Peter was called 'Satan' (the conscious mind). The rest of the disciples each personified the conscious mind in the same way, the whole *twelve* being the significant number of the zodiacal signs.

In the same way, the name of Jesus Christ has the meaning of 'initiate', for Jesus represents the conscious mind, and Christ, the subconscious. When the two are linked together as one name, it tells us that the two minds are linked and so the whole name represents the completed task. The use of 'Jesus' in this sense was not an innovation peculiar to the New Testament, but appeared in the earlier texts as 'Joshua'. 'Christ', on the other hand, comes from the Greek 'Khristos', the equivalent of the Hebrew 'Mashiah' (Messiah) and means 'anointed'. We have only to refer to the story of Jacob to find that 'anointed' really means 'initiated'. Counterparts of the Christ name exist in other countries: in India, it was Krishna, with the Asiatics, Buddha, and in Egypt, it was Horus.

I have already fully explained the true meaning of the virgin birth and so we pass on to pick out the various other clues enciphered into the account of Jesus's birth. We are told that he was born in a lowly manger, a place where *sheep* are normally kept, and therefore a *most unlikely place* for a future Messiah to be found. Present at the time of birth were *three kings, bearing gifts,* a trio who represent the three phases of the process and the end reward. In order to be there at the appointed time, these kings *followed a star,* and it is pointed out that they came from the *east*. Sometimes, the kings are alternatively known as *wise men,* an appelation which means 'initiate'.

The *child* in the manger is the astral body, said by the initiate to have been 'reborn in spirit'. Alternatively, the child Jesus is said to be a 'babe in swaddling clothes' (an infant concealed), or an 'innocent'. In respect of this last synonym, the story of King Herod's slaughter of the first born, or 'innocents', takes on an entirely new meaning, and will be fully explained at the proper juncture.

The Star of Bethlehem

This mysterious star, which the *wise men* were said to have followed, has been the subject of much conjecture and erroneous conclusion. Many have sought to equate the legend with a real, stellar event taking place at the stipulated point in time, such as the passage of a comet, the fall of a meteor, the flare of a distant supernova, or even a triple conjunction of the planets Saturn and Jupiter, a natural enough phenomenon known to have occurred at about 7 B.C. – and in truth, the writers of the Gospels may well have made convenient use of any one of the named events in order to lend more authority to this single item of symbolism. The fact is, however, that the *star* as an Hermetic emblem, predates the supposed birth of Jesus by many centuries. The very knowledgeable Greek philosopher, Plutarch, whilst re-lating the allegory of Isis and Osiris, informs his readers that the ancient Egyptians considered the star to be *exempt from old age,* thus confirming that it was used as a symbol of *immortality*. Something of the very same tradition can be recognised in the Old Testament dream of Joseph (Gen 37; 9), in which his parents were represented by the Sun and the Moon, and his eleven brothers each by a separate star. Joseph, having acquired a *coat of many colours* (having passed through the stages of Black, White and Red and therefore attained initiateship), himself represents the twelfth star – the whole dozen hinting at the full zodiacal circle, a symbol of the completed process. And Balaam, the man whose *ass* miraculously spoke to him after he had beaten it *three* times, had already referred to the initiate tradition depicted in Genesis with the words 'a Star out of Jacob' (Numbers 24; 17).

In the New Testament, we recall that the *resurrected* Jesus pro-claimed himself the 'bright morning star' (seen at *sunrise*). This very same star is mentioned in Revelation 2; 28 and 22; 16, as the 'offspring of David', an Old Testament character who personifies initiateship, as does Jesus Christ.

Of the four Gospel scribes, Matthew alone chronicles the episode in which the *three* wise men emerged from the east (Matt 2; 1 – 18), following the star, a heavenly body which was also seen *in the east*, and which continued to be observed there until it 'came and stood over where the young *child* was' (verse 9). So illogical is this reported phenomenon that reason dictates the event to be a symbolic representation of something not explained, rather than a real one. According to Bible commentators, the wise men who came to see the infant Jesus were members of a priest caste called the Magi (Greek 'Magoi'), an elite band of astrologers or soothsayers, although Matthew does not confirm this and it remains but a conjecture. However, these mysterious Magi, if really astrologers, would warrant the alternative title of 'star-gazers', an occupation which certainly lends itself to the conditions set down by Matthew.

Of course, the same symbolic star is found elsewhere, as in nursery rhymes, where it manifests at the tip of the wand wielded by the fairy Godmother, and with which she performs her miracles. Often the emblem is shown as a five pointed star, but the true *Star of the Magi* has six points and is therefore exactly the same as Solomon's Seal, the *Star of David*, the Hermetic emblem appropriated in later times by orthodox Hebrew priests. A further clue is offered in the simple tradition of placing a star at the top of a Christmas *tree*. Like the Egyptian persea, or the Druids' oak, the Christmas tree is a symbol of physical man, and so the star's position at its top obviously signifies the head, and thus the mind of Man.

In enigmatic alchemical tracts, you will find recommendations to use *star mucus* as the first matter for the work of illumination, a fitting directive if we take into consideration the fact that a star is but a distant *Sun* and is therefore representative of the Universal Mind. Elsewhere, the star can be seen in the Tarot, and – most apt – at the top of the ladder – the scala philosophorum – in the First Degree Tracing Board of Freemasonry.

The most revealing morsel of information regarding the true identity of this 'star' comes from the work of John Allegro, who points out that the Greek name for the 'Christ' mushroom symbol (Korkoron) is phonetically similar to the Hebrew word for 'star' (Kohkhav) – and that our own word for 'star' is derived from the Greek 'aster', which itself is descended from a Sumerian root word for 'knobbed bolt' – i.e. 'mushroom'.

The Star of Bethlehem, then, denotes the Hermetic process, the immortal illumination to be found within Man's mind, the pure consciousness, an inkling of the great subconscious powers which lie dormant in the uninitiated. Thus the Magi of Matthew, the *star-*

gazers who have *fixed their attention* on this heavenly light (of understanding), are initiates who are undergoing the process. The *star* is the intuitive course they must follow, and thus there is no real mystery in the fact that Matthew's star came to a halt over the place where the *child was born* (the process was completed).

Christmas

The supposed birth of Jesus is celebrated all over the Western world by the annual festival of Christ's Mass on December 25th, but this date has no basis in the Scriptures, and in fact our Christmas Day was originally the date on which pagan Mithraic rites commemorated the birth of the sun, a festival which existed a long time before the Gospels were written.

Biblical commentators who question the December date have remarked that it is unlikely because the New Testament texts say that at the very hour of the birth, shepherds were in the fields tending their flocks by night. They point out that in the colder months, it was common practice to keep sheep inside during the night. This minor mystery can be solved if we apply the Hermetic key and extract the inner meaning from the familiar lines of Luke 2:

8. And there were in the same country shepherds abiding in the field keeping watch over their flocks by night.
9. And, lo, the angel of the Lord came upon them . . .

Compare these lines with the traditional cure for insomnia which advocates the counting of sheep. The 'sheep' here mentioned are the wayward thoughts of the meditator – the *shepherd* – who is *keeping watch* (meditating) by *night* (in the mind). He succeeds in the process when he has all of his 'flock' under perfect control, and it is only then that the *angel of the Lord* comes upon him (the transmission of consciousness). The initial phrase in verse eight – 'and there were in the same country' – has the connotation, 'in relation to what has secretly been explained before'. This refers to the information given in verse seven, where Mary (reflection) wraps the *infant* in *swaddling clothes*.

The Christmas celebrations as we know them today were not related to Jesus until about four hundred years after his 'death', and then at the order of the Catholic Church, who failed fully to appreciate the significance of the pagan date. The concept of Father Christmas came even later, although it may be recognised that his function of *bringing gifts* and spreading *good*will is related to Hermetic mythology.

Certain hymns are vehicles for the initiates' message, for when the choristers sing that well loved carol about the *watching shepherds,* they are unwittingly expounding the allegory of initiation. Another carol that holds the secret message is *Silent Night.*

I have no doubt whatsoever that the foregoing will not sway the opinion of the sceptics who adhere rigidly to the literal word of the Scriptures, and therefore direct them to the sacred texts themselves, to the words of Paul, who openly declares the real message to be hidden.

> If, now, the *good news* we declare is in fact veiled, it is veiled among those who are perishing, among whom the god of this system of things has blinded the minds of the unbelievers, that the illumination of the glorious good news about the Christ, who is the image of God, might not shine through. (2 Cor. 4; 3 – 4)

King Herod

No sooner had the infant Jesus been born than he was threatened by Herod, who decreed death to all children under the age of two years. Matthew, in whose text the tale appears, makes Joseph and Mary flee to Egypt, taking their child with them.

We have come upon the myth before, some thousand years in the past, and there is little doubt that Matthew took the bare bones of the legend and revamped it at the inspiration of the real Herod's unenviable history. This king was known to have executed his own sons for fear that they would usurp him. But the inclusion of his name in the Gospel text has caused some consternation among biblical scholars who have read it at face value, for other historical records show that Herod died in 4 B.C., and thus could not have been alive at the time of Jesus's birth.

Perhaps we should allow the 16th century father of German mysticism, Jacob Boehme, to answer the question. In the second volume of his theosophical work, the Book of True Resignation, he says:

> 46. A man must wrestle till the dark centre that is shut up close, break open and the spark lying therein, kindle; and from thence immediately the nobly lily-branch sprouteth as from the diving grain of mustard seed, as Christ saith . . .
> 47. And then when Christ is born, Herod is ready to kill the child,

which he seeketh to do outwardly by persecutions, and inwardly by temptations, to try whether this lily-branch will be strong enough to destroy the kingdom of the devil which is manifested in the flesh.

As this extract plainly shows, the name of Herod has been adopted to personify the ever moving thoughts of the conscious mind, and also the doubting effects of scepticism which is constantly hurled at the would-be initiate. The meditator must wrestle with the dark centre of his own mind until he reaches a special point at which he is able to put the process into motion. This is the 'lily-branch' of which Boehme speaks, and if it is strong enough to subdue all outside interference, it will eventually produce the required transmission of consciousness.

A further indication that the decree of Herod was never issued in reality lies in the fact that the Jewish historian, Josephus, who lived between 37 and 100 A.D., makes no mention of it at all. As Josephus, in his own words, was a native of Jerusalem, it seems inconceivable that such an act should have escaped his notice, especially as he left us a full account of the king's reign, including the murder of his sons.

A number of other significant clues connected with the days subsequent to the birth of Jesus are there to be considered: his *circumcision* on the *eighth day* (a little used term meaning the accomplishment of the process); and the fact that Luke tells us he was *brought to the temple at Jerusalem forty days after birth* (merely another way of expressing the time of the process).

The Ministry of Jesus

After the events surrounding his birth, little is heard of Jesus, except for an episode described in Luke 2, where he became *separated from his parents* (he was not as they were) on a visit to Jerusalem. But he was found after *three* days, sitting in discussion with learned men who were said to be astounded at his *understanding*, especially as he was only *twelve* years old (again, the signs of the zodiac indicate initiate-ship).

The next most important event in his life was the baptism by John, marking the beginning of his ministry. It must be noted that he was baptised in *water*, and that straightaway, the *heavens opened* (the process was revealed to him and he understood the power of the subconscious). According to the text of Mark, a spirit within Jesus drove him at once into the *wilderness*, where he remained for *forty* days, *tempted of Satan* (complete allegory of the process).

Scholars have amused themselves for centuries by endeavouring to pinpoint accurately the chronology of the years leading up to the Crucifixion, forced to rely only upon the vague outline given in the various texts, but such meticulousness is profitless. It would have been more rewarding to consider the fact that the ministry lasted for approximately *three* years, or that Jesus was baptised when he was thirty years old, a number significant because of the *three* within it.

The outstanding features of the ministry period were the various miracles, but a brief look at these will serve to show that they too, are myth, and that the same hidden truth is encoded in them.

The Feeding of the Five Thousand

The text of Matthew 14 relates that this miracle occurred in a *desert place* (same as *wilderness*), and that immediately afterwards, Jesus *ascended a mount*.

Logical appraisal of the story, the distribution of the five loaves and the two fishes among 'five thousand men, beside women and children', will render the conclusion that it could not have taken place as described, and so we must seek for clues to the real meaning. That it is Hermetic is beyond doubt, for the fragments of food were said to have filled *twelve* baskets. But what kind of food can it be to appear so small and yet satisfy so many? The answer is found in the fact that the loaves were bread – the same 'bread' that fed the Israelites on their way to the Promised Land – meditation. The two fishes were included because the sign of Pisces was the dominant zodiacal emblem of the period, as Aquarius is ours, and was thus used to designate an initiate.

The Raising of Lazarus

The account of the miraculous recovery of Lazarus is one of John's own refinements of the Gospel story, for it will not be found in the earlier three, although Luke does express his own variation of the theme in the raising of the widow of Nain's son (Luke 7; 11 – 15).

The Lazarus story is plainly one of Death and Resurrection, and the only minor deviation from the normal run of symbolism occurs when Lazarus is said to have been dead for four days, instead of the expected three. The fact of it means nothing to the average reader, but such a pointed departure from the time-honoured would bring a smile to the lips of an initiate. The rest of the tale, though, remains with the familiar. The body of Lazarus is in a *cave* (the inner mind) which is blocked by a great *stone* (the conscious mind blocks the entrance to the subconscious). When the stone was rolled aside (by the process), Jesus *lifted up his eyes to his Father* (reversed his thoughts) and prayed (meditated). It is at this point that John injects into the story a clue of great significance, but one which must be left until a later chapter if the full value is to be realised from it. When Lazarus emerges from the cave, he is

> . . . bound hand and foot with gravecloths; and his *face was bound about with a napkin* . . . (John 11; 44)

Is it coincidental that all this occurred in the little town of Bethany, which sounds very similar to the name of Sauniere's guest house, Bethania? And Bethany, the Gospel tells us, is but a little way from *Jerusalem* – only fifteen furlongs, in fact (John 11;18).

Prior to the resurrection of Lazarus, we are told about his two sisters, *Martha* and *Mary*, two entities who hold a concealed clue relating to the Hermetic theme. In Luke 10; 40, Martha receives a rebuke from Jesus which seems strangely unjustified:

> 40 But Martha was cumbered about much serving and came to him and said; Lord, dost thou not care that my sister hath left me to serve alone? bid her therefore that she help me.
> 41 And Jesus answered and said unto her, Martha, Martha, thou art careful and troubled about many things.
> 42 But one thing is needful; and Mary hath chosen that *good* part which shall not be taken away from her.

In these passages we once again discover the fundamental aspects of that other religion, Dualism – the conscious mind, personified by Martha, and the subconscious, by Mary. Martha is the noisy one, full of worry and bustle, as 'noisy' as the conscious mind's restless thoughts. But Mary does nothing – that is, she remains *quiet* (contemplative).

This interpretation is corroborated by John, who says:

> Then Martha, as soon as she heard that Jesus was coming, went and met him; but Mary sat *still* in the house (John 11; 20).

Cleansing the Lepers

Some of the miracles performed by Jesus are based on instances of faith healing that can still be witnessed today, such as causing the blind to see and the lame to walk, incidents so described that they have only an indirect allusion to the power of the subconscious mind. But there is also the cleansing of the lepers which, while not featuring any of the usual clues to the Hermetic process, refers instead to an already long established analogy from the Old Testament.

It seems highly improbable that the loathsome disease of leprosy should have been utilised as a vehicle to carry such a message, but perhaps your doubts will fade as I uncover the connections.

We can begin with the statement by Manetho, who claimed that Moses was a leper. At the same time, however, we must recall that the Egyptian historian was himself an initiate, and so his words must be read carefully. Leprosy and Moses are two factors that come together in Exodus 4; 6 – 7, where the Israelite leader is instructed to place his hand in his *bosom* (where the *heart* is). When he does so and pulls it out again, it is as *leprous as snow*. On repeating the gesture, the hand returns to normal – and as this is obviously an impossibility, we are warned to look for a deeper meaning to the incident. It is almost self-evident, for the author is indicating the fact that Moses was an initiate, but that this knowledge was generally kept hidden from public view.

There are two forms of leprosy, *black* and *white*. In some cases, the hair turns *white*, or there is a *white* skin erruption with patches of *raw* (red) flesh, and thus the victim's skin is seen to be *spotted*. Finally, the hair and nails fall away, and so the sufferer literally *loses his flesh* as it is slowly eaten away.

The most comprehensive statement about the disease occurs in Levictus 12, where all the symptoms are listed and such cures as a priest might attempt are recommended. It may be thought only a coincidence that all four of the ancient, alchemical colours are mentioned, therefore I will draw your attention to verse 13:

> Then the priest shall consider: and behold if the leprosy have covered all his flesh, he shall pronounce him clean that hath the plague: *it is all turned white: he is clean.*

This message is repeated for good measure in verse 17, ostensibly to infer that, at its advanced stage, the disease is no longer contagious. But the lines contain also the Hermetic inference that when the *white* stage is reached (the moving thoughts are ultimately stilled), the *leper* (the initiate) is *clean* ('purified') – an intepretation that will make the incident of Moses's leprous hand become more clear.

A similar sequence can be found in 2 Kings, 5, where Naaman the Syrian leper was instructed to plunge himself into the Jordan (*water*) *seven* times (another expression of the length of the process). When he did so, his flesh came back '*like the flesh of a little boy*' (he was reborn). Miriam likewise had to be quarantined for *seven* days, just as Joshua (early form of the name Jesus) had to march round the walls of *Jericho* for *seven* days before the *walls fell down* (before the transmission of the consciousness was made).

To sum up, leprosy was seen as a disease in which the victim lost his flesh, a phrase seized upon to analogise the accomplishment of the mental process, when the astral body ceases to be bound to the physical. Thus, to all those who can read it so, the cleansing of the lepers by Jesus offers the same interpretation.

The Last Supper

Each little event that preceded the death of Jesus contains its own clues to the Hermetic theme and as the most important of these will be dealt with at the appropriate place, I will begin at the point where he enters *Jerusalem* on an *ass*. The emphasis on these words, relating to that which has previously been explained, will appraise you of the fact that the mental process is being projected, and that the ride through Israel's most famous city on the back of a donkey was an event that never took place in reality.

The next most notable event is that of the last supper, where Jesus met with his *twelve* disciples in a *large, upper room* (the human mind), and in order to understand fully the inner meaning of the scene, it is necessary for you to envisage Jesus and the twelve as merely symbols which collectively represent the conscious mind of a Neophyte just on the point of making the transmission, for this, remember, is the feast of the *Passover*. Another glaring clue lies in the fact that Jesus distributed *bread* among his disciples – the 'bread' of meditation. The *wine*, which was also given out, is merely a reiteration of the same theme. This is the *last supper*, the last hour of meditation before the transmission is made.

Judas, who betrayed Jesus, is required to do so in order that the Crucifixion may take place (so that the process can be completed). As everyone well knows, the price of his betrayal was *thirty pieces of silver*, the inner meaning of which can be determined by referring to the symbolism of the old Babylonian astrologers. They assigned to the sun, the moon and five of the planets, seven different metals, of which Silver was coupled with the *Moon*. Recalling that the lunar orb is the prime symbol of reflection, it is but a step to associate silver with the same power. In the figure thirty, there is once again the prominent number *three* – and thus the 'thirty pieces of silver' stand revealed as the three stages of the reflective process. Supposedly filled with remorse at what he'd done, Judas later hanged himself (Matt. 27; 5), the real meaning of which can be deduced by comparing the episode to the Hanged Man of the Tarot. It is in fact, just one more reiteration of the mental process theme.

Peter, the main emblem of the conscious mind, is made to deny Christ *three* times before the *cock crew*. As with the betrayal of Judas, the inner meaning of this scene is simplicity itself if you accept that Peter, as the conscious mind not quite fully initiated, cannot know Christ (the subconscious) until the cock had crowed three times (until the three stages were complete). As to why the cock was used as an emblem in this manner, you may recall that it is a *bird* (indicating inner spirit) and that it generally crows to herald the *sunrise* (the dawning of the Universal Mind within the ordinary consciousness).

The Crucifixion

This theme was written during an era of intense persecution of the native Jews by the Romans, but you may notice in the biblical account that Pilate, representing the Romans, has no wish to condemn Jesus to such a fate. He was forced to do so by the Jews themselves, who demanded a crucifixion. The hidden meaning behind this little charade lies in the interpretation of the name 'Jew'. As I have shown, both 'Jew' and 'Israelite' could hold the meaning 'initiate' on occasion – and so it is in this instance. The story makes the Jews (the Hermetic Brotherhood) demand a crucifixion (the mental process) which, from the point of view of the initiates, was highly desirable.

It is quite apparent that the fable of the Crucifixion was conceived by those who were familiar with the locale in which the story has been set, but it must be recognised that the usual liberties have been taken in order to accommodate the required clues.

Golgotha, the place of the *skull*, is a site which has never been satisfactorily pinpointed by historians or archaeologists, and while the traditional spot within the city walls is marked today by the Church of the Holy Sepulchre, all investigators concede that the location remains highly questionable. A second choice of location, known as Gordon's Calvary, has the necessary requirements mentioned in the Scriptures – a garden tomb and a road nearby (Matt 27) – but cannot be unreservedly designated as the correct spot.

The truth is that the 'tomb', or 'cave'; the 'garden' and Golgotha were ficticious necessities in order to portray the Hermetic process, and looking for them as real places will be as rewarding as searching for the lost continent of Atlantis.

Gesthemene is the name of the *garden*, a term which had been used centuries earlier by the initiates to indicate the inner mind, the subconscious. Right in the beginning of Genesis, we read how Adam and Eve (early personifications of the subconscious and the conscious minds) were in the *Garden of Eden* – another locality that archaeologists will never discover in the material world. And the Koran speaks often of that divine place, the *Gardens of Delight*, a wondrous spot comparable to the *myrrh-terraces* of Hatshepsut.

Thus, Jesus's *agony in the garden*, was never a moral torment, but symbolises the effort of concentration required for successful meditation – and it follows that Gesthemene is the *garden* in which the mythical Jesus (Neophyte) will be finally *crucified* (undertake and finish the process).

The Cross

In the Crucifixion account, we stumble over another enigma in that the word 'cross' is not found in the Bible texts. The Greek term 'stau-ros', which was rendered by the translators as 'cross' actually denotes an upright stake, or pole, and there exists no outright statement that the authors of the Gospel intended it as anything else. The earliest known representation of Jesus as we see him today, nailed to a cross, did not appear until five centuries after the supposed event.

The conception of death by being nailed to a stake is partly due to the actions of Alexander of Jannaeus, of about 100 B.C. In the course of his persecution of those who followed Dualism, he seized upon one of the initiates' own myths – a Hermetic 'death' by being nailed to a tree – and put it into practice literally, killing many by use of the single stake method. This was carried out by simply impaling the victims on the stake, but in certain cases, nails were used to fasten the prisoner's wrists to the stake in a position above his head. The ensuing pain, especially if the victim's legs were broken so that he could no longer take his weight on his feet, was generally enough to make death slow but inevitable. But this was accomplished without the use of a cross bar.

That the writers of the Gospels failed to mention the cross outright, does not mean that they did not have one in mind, however, for their 'cross' was purely figurative – the lower section of the Egyptian Ankh. This cross signified the conscious mind undergoing the Hermetic process, and was subtly indicated by the fact that *three* nails are said to have been used on Jesus instead of the normal two. The nails themselves are emblems of the process, their true meaning having been derived from a long established symbolism which connects the metal Iron with the sign of the Ram. *Iron*, therefore, becomes a symbol of the concentration necessary for correct meditation – and this is why Doubting Thomas did not believe that Jesus had been resurrected until he saw the *marks of the nails in Jesus's flesh* (one cannot produce the transmission of consciousness until the 'iron nails' of meditation have been applied). The 'nails' thus signify the stages of meditation. That is why there are *three*.

At his Crucifixion, Jesus is led towards Golgotha, a walk that requires him to travel *uphill* (the mount), but the text of Luke 23; Mark 15; and Matthew 27; tell us that a man named Simon, a Cyrenian, is made to carry the cross.

This is an example of obscure symbolism that can only be interpreted by relating to the situation that existed at the time of writing. Cyrene was at that period, a Greek colony in North Africa, but which had fallen under the domination of the Romans. Bringing to mind the fact that the Romans were active persecutors of the initiates, the mention of this colony in an initiate text should be read in the same light as the Pharaoh's chariots of the Red Sea Crossing – representative of the unbelievers. But, as the name is coupled with that of Simon, meaning 'hearing' – or in this particular instance more aptly translated as 'now ready to listen' – the entire cameo represents a former unbelieving conscious mind now ready to undergo the process of Hermetic initiation. Thus, it no longer remains a mystery as to why Simon (Peter's other name) was made to *shoulder the cross*. And speaking of Peter, we can now appreciate the supreme irony of II Peter, verse 16, when the disciple avers that he was an eye witness to the transfiguration of Jesus, and says:

> For we have not followed cunningly devised fables when we made known to you the power and the coming of our Lord, Jesus Christ, but were eyewitnesses of his majesty.

The power of the Lord (the subconscious/Universal Mind) is certainly a reality, but as the writer well knew, the Bible is composed almost wholly of cunningly devised fables.

The Crucifixion

In chapter three, I briefly outlined the predominance of the number three attached to the Crucifixion, a repetitive clue intended to symbolise the stages of the process. Elsewhere, I have touched on the inner meaning of the spear wound in the side of Jesus, with its Aramaic basis in the 'mushroom' emblem. Now let us examine the last words of Jesus, uttered just before he expired:

My God, My God, why hast thou forsaken me?

This phrase translated from the original as *'Eloi, Eloi, lama sabachthani'* – leaves the Gospel reader with the feeling that the trust which Jesus has placed in God has been sadly misdirected, a most unsatisfactory turn of events for a crusader who has spent thirty years extolling the virtues of the Lord.

To rationalise this situation, we must accept that the Gospel stories have been indisputably constructed round the lines of certain Psalms, notably number 22, where the themes of verses 1, 8, 15, 16, and 18 have been reiterated in one form or another. Present too, are ideas expressed in Psalms 31, 34 and 69. Many early Bible commentators have laboured under the misapprehension that the Psalms were prophetic, but the truth is that the Crucifixion myth was carefully fabricated to accommodate these earlier ideas.

With the help of John Allegro's THE SACRED MUSHROOM AND THE CROSS, we discover that *'lama sabachthani'* is equivalent to the Sumerian phrase for the 'mushroom' symbol. Further, it is pointed out that the cry, *'Eloi, Eloi'* is a corruption of a cultic invocation used by the Bacchantes, *'Eleleu, Eleleu'* – better known to us all in the Bible as 'Halleluia'. This cry was chanted at their secret ceremonies.

As the figurative Jesus would hardly have been made to cry

My God, my God, the sacred mushroom.

we find it far more logical to accept that he said instead

My God, my God, in my mind.

The cry *'Eloi, Eloi'*, is echoed in the alternative Bacchanal shout of joy, *'Evoe, Evoe'*, which if traced to the root of its symbolism, will be found to refer to the *Moon* (reflection). It is beyond doubt, therefore, that the cry of Jesus – copied directly from Psalm 22; 1 – is a reference to the Hermetic process.

Much of the symbolism used in the Crucifixion can be traced not only to the Psalms, but beyond, to ancient Sumeria and Egypt, for the Psalms themselves are no more than incantations from these sources, slightly modified by time.

Let us consider the strange fact regarding the legs of Jesus. The two criminals who were crucified with him had their legs broken, but Jesus did not, and we must wonder why, irrespective of the reason given in the text.

This aspect of symbolism stems directly from Egypt, where the Leg and the Thigh were names given to certain constellations in the same manner as the zodiacal signs. In the Egyptian funeral rites, in which the clues to the process are concealed, Osiris was made whole again by the collection of his scattered members, or *bones*:

> . . . I have made the offering of Osiris, who hath triumphed with victory, gathering his bones and bringing together his limbs. (Chapter CXLVII: Papyrus of Ani)
>
> . . . I have *knit together my bones,* I have made myself whole and sound. I have become *young once more.* I am Osiris, the Lord of Eternity.
> (Chapter XLII – Ani's advice to others about how they should complete the process).

In order to convey this ancient message, but in an inverted manner, the Gospels indicate that the legs of the two criminals were broken because they were *not yet dead* (had not accomplished the process), but those of Jesus were not touched, because he was already dead (the process had been completed – the 'bones' of Osiris were therefore whole and could not be shown as broken).

The Resurrection

We know that the body of Jesus, like that of Lazarus, was placed in a *cave* and the door blocked by a large *stone*. However, at this point, the collective renderings begin to disagree. All are concerted in the statement that *three* days elapsed before the stone was rolled away, but Luke 24 names those who witnessed the event as the women who came with Joseph of Arimathaea and 'certain others' – while John 20 reports that only Mary Magdalene was present. Matthew 28 admits to Mary Magdalene, but includes the 'other Mary'. Mark 16, on the other hand, lists those present as Mary Magdalene, and Mary, mother of James, and Salome. Biblical scholars have been disconcerted by this lack of unanimity, but the situation can be resolved by the appreciation of two related facts. The first of these is that all accounts agree that only *women* were present at the opening of the tomb, and to decipher this we need only remember that since the time of the Egyptian 'mother', Queen Isis, the conscious mind and its power of reflection has always been represented as a *woman*. The emblem occurs time and time again in the Bible, especially in the Old Testament, but is seldom seen for what it really is.

The second fact is, that of all the women present, Mary Magdalene is the most prominent, being mentioned in three out of four accounts, and thus we must penetrate the inner meaning of the name.

Mary Magdalene is so called because she is said to be a native of the area near the Sea of Galilee called Magdala, a Hebrew word culled from 'migh-dal', which means 'tower', or 'fort'. And as the towers, or forts, of the biblical period were invariably made of *stone*, we call on the Hermetic symbolism to find a comparison in the Tower card of the Tarot. This Tower is representative of the uninitiated conscious mind which, when struck by lightning as it is in the Tarot picture, throws its occupants from the top (enlightenment over-throws all previous misconceptions). Thus it becomes easy to see that our Mary Magdalene personifies the enlightened conscious mind, undergoing the meditation (Mary = reflection), and so it is hardly surprising to find her present at the 'resurrection' of Christ (the appearance of the astral body).

Matt. 28 relates that while Mary Magdalene and the 'other Mary' (reflection in progress) were *watching the sepulchre* (meditating), there occurred an *earthquake* (an upheaval in the conscious mind) and the 'angel of the Lord descended from heaven' (the astral body appeared – the transmission of consciousness took place). Mark 16 describes the event in a different way, for he says that when the *stone was rolled away from the cave entrance* (the transmission of consciousness was made), Mary Magdalene and the other women entered to find a *young* man (a reborn initiate) sitting on the *right* side clothed in a long *white* garment.

Within this sentence, we happen across an area of symbolism not yet fully touched upon, but which is continually employed. So innocuous is it that it can be easily missed. I refer to my emphasis on the word 'right'.

We are all familiar with the sinister phrases to be found in certain occult literature which announce that a person has taken the 'left hand path', meaning that the one concerned is indulging in evil, or the black aspect of magic, and while these texts have little or no real substance in truth, they do point us towards the correct inter-pretation of the emblem, for the superstition attached to the left hand stems directly from the symbolic aspect of Dualism. In this scheme, the left hand represents evil, or the conscious mind, while the right hand is indicative of good – the subconscious. It is with this quaint piece of symbolism in mind that Mark carefully portrayed the *young man,* the new born initiate, sitting on the *right* side. You will find no other explanation for it.

As alternative examples of the symbolism, I will quote the Tarot once again and ask you to look closely at the various pictures. The MAGICIAN holds a wand (power) in his right hand, *pointing to heaven,* while his left hand is directed down at the *earth* (the conscious mind). The DEVIL holds a flaming torch, which is sometimes in the right hand pointing up and at others in the left, pointing down. Sauniere's statue of Rex Mundi follows the former, for it once held a torch, a flaming fire which represented the *ever burning lamp* of the subconscious. The STAR card shows the goddess with her left knee on *land* and her right foot in *water,* a pictorial design which can be compared to Fulcanelli's description of St Christopher, who is seen with his right foot in a stream, while his left remains on the bank.

Still with Fulcanelli, we may ponder on his description of plate XXII, which shows;

> An old man, stiff with cold . . . Weak and feeble, he is leaning on a block of stone, his left hand hidden in a sort of muff. ('Le Mystere des Cathedrales')

This quaint picture depicts the conscious mind undergoing the process, for the left hand (conscious mind) is being subjected to the *gentle heat* (meditation) of the muff.

Quite obviously, it would be possible to continue with examples of the same symbolism within the Crucifixion theme, for the texts are so carefully contrived that almost every line holds a word or phrase of Hermetic import. However, as this volume is intended to cover the widest possible range of the symbolism's application, we now move on to the post-crucifixion period, leaving the questions raised to be answered at a later stage of the book.

CHAPTER NINE

Hermetic Brotherhoods

The Hermetic religion of Dualism, with which Berenger Sauniere became so unaccountably involved, has now been shown to have existed at every historical age prior to the advent of the Christian Era, and indeed, if it is interpreted on the basis that I have outlined – that it represents the two facets of the human mind – then it can be clearly admitted to be the true root of all religions.

Similarly, history shows that those who follow the true concept of Dualism, have at every period been subjected to consistent and active persecution by those who do not – *as if such disbelief is a natural emotion implanted in the mind at birth*. In this concept we arrive at one reason why the uninitiated conscious mind has been always symbolised as *evil*, for it is the lack of belief that presents the biggest obstacle to Man's own advancement. The initiates, by discarding the faculty we call reason, and turning instead to that far superior power, intuition, have managed to surmount their built-in prejudice and thereby glimpse the truth. But the initiates are few, the persecutors many. Is it any wonder that such a vast panorama of secret encipherment exists?

When the Roman Catholic Church was instituted subsequent to the appearance of the Gospels, it carried on the tradition of persecution with a new fervour – and in this respect, it will be as well to examine the basis on which the papal regime lays claim to be the leading, true church formed by Jesus Christ.

Traditionally, the Roman Catholic Church is said to date from 43 A.D., when St Peter went to Rome to become the city's first bishop, but this claim is nowhere substantiated by fact – not something to be wondered at, now that we know the apostle to be completely fictitious. The story appears to be one of the many attempts by the Church to establish its foundations in close association with the Gospel characters. But the Dualists weren't idle, either. Contemporary to this, there exists a legend that St Peter was martyred at Rome, an event that if true, would seem to negate the purpose of the first story – which was undoubtedly the intention of the initiate who concocted the tale. Having already revealed the true meaning of St Peter's head-downward crucifixion, and shown that the disciple is a literary symbol only, we can deduce that his 'martyrdom' is a veiled way of saying that the newly established Catholic Church was ignorant of the real message in the Bible, and that it was continuing to persecute initiates.

The legend was most likely founded on the real events that overtook Paul in Rome, for this initiate was imprisoned there and it is probable that he died while enduring this incarceration. It would be logical for the Hermeticists to superimpose the mythical Peter over the real life story of Paul in order to get their message across.

The factual story of the Catholic establishment is less romantic, motivated more by the normal human desires for power and wealth rather than spiritual enlightenment. Its foundations may be said to have been laid in the 4th century, when the Roman emperor, Constantine, having decreed toleration of Christianity, moved his headquarters to a new city called Constantinople. This left the Roman bishop in a position of importance that otherwise would never have been his. Before he went, Constantine convened a body known as the Church Council of Nicea, to settle once and for all the great controversy raised by the Gnostic priest, Arius, who insisted that Christ was not of the same substance as God. This assertion shows that Arius, if not actually an initiate, was certainly in possession of the secret knowledge of Dualism. In any event, although he was right, the Council decreed otherwise and condemned him – yet another example of the blind persecution of the 'heretics'.

The Church hierarchy, emboldened by the position in which they found themselves after Constantine's departure, made the presumptive declaration that the bishop of Rome had authority over all other bishops – and the Catholic regime was on its way. The bishop changed his title to that of Pope, land and money was donated or bequeathed, and thereafter Roman Catholicism became increasingly powerful. At a later stage, it boldly assumed the right to crown kings, one pope making good this prerogative by crowning Charlemagne in 800 A.D. It was an occasion which firmly cemented the alliance between the Church and the State, but the final move to complete domination came only in the 11th century, when the popes – especially Gregory VII – asserted that the State was subject to the Church. All such claims were made, don't forget, in the name of Jesus Christ.

Thus the Catholic Church embarked upon a long career, its foundations firmly entrenched in the literal word of the Scriptures and, in its early years, committed to a policy of torture and death towards those responsive to the hidden wisdom within the texts. In the face of such unassailable power, the initiates were to remain well in the background for many years. But they were by no means inactive.

The Templars

The story of the Templars begins in 1090, when Christendom remobilised to capture the city of Jerusalem. When it fell, Godfrey Bouillon of Boulougne, the knight who had led the victorious armies, was offered the crown of the city by a mysterious group of religious figures known as the Order of Our Lady of Mount Zion. Look closely at the title. 'Our Lady' is none other than the Virgin – in former times, Isis – while Mount Zion has the inner meaning of the subconscious. The Order was obviously one that followed the Hermetic path. And it was from the ranks of this mysterious sect that the Templars evolved.

The origin of the Knights Templars is mentioned in an historical document, the chronicle of William of Tyre (1160), and it is in this screed that the discerning reader will encounter traces of a hidden message. According to the text, the first Templars were *nine* in number. Led by Hugh de Payens, they went to Jerusalem, their appointed task being to *keep the roads to the Holy Land safe* – with especial regard for the protection of *pilgrims*. The king of Jerusalem looked favourably on their ideal and allowed them to stay in one whole wing of his palace, which happened to have been built on the very spot occupied by the original *Temple of Solomon*. Hence the name Templars.

To extract the real message from this slightly fictitious item of history, we have only to centre our attention on the introduction of the Temple of Solomon, and knowing that famous edifice to be a symbol of the inner mind, we extend the symbolism to the palace of the king of Jerusalem. Aware now of what to look for, we read the text again to find that the Templars were *nine* in number (a reference to the 'scala philosophorum', the Hermetic Ladder which has nine rungs). The Templars' task was to keep the roads to the Holy Land safe, and as the 'holy land' is another reference to this inner mind, we gather that the Order's intention is to maintain the secret tradition of the Hermeticists. Especial regard, it is pointed out, is afforded pilgrims. In the Hermetic parlance, a 'pilgrim' is a Neophyte – one who wishes to undertake the mental process.

The number nine is repeated later in William's document, in a statement declaring that the Templars pursued their activities for nine years, during which time they excavated the ruins under the palace and came upon the ruined stables of King Solomon. To decipher this, I ask you only to recall the Katha-Upanishad with its 'horses' of the conscious mind and you will see that this is just one more way of saying that the Templars were in the Hermetic business. The document also notes that five of the original 'nine' Templars were brothers of the founder organisation, the Order of Our Lady of Mount Zion.

As you can now appreciate, the document of William of Tyre was written by an initiate, and in the formation of The Knights Templars we are presented with a situation where a secret organisation (Our Lady of the Mount Zion) remains in the background, but initiates and controls another, more open society to which non-initiates might be attracted. In this scheme you will find the beginning of a recurring, historical pattern.

For its inner doctrines, no doubt selected by the parent organisation, the Templars adopted the biblical allegory of Solomon's Temple, the real meaning of which was revealed only to selected members. The Hermetic colours were not absent in the scheme, for the Templar crusader's uniform was *white*, over which was worn a coat of *iron* (black) mail. A *red cross* was emblazoned on the smock, and they carried a *white* and *black* banner. Accompanying the cross, there was a motto which read;

"In this sign shalt thou conquer."

Outwardly, this conveys a sterling sentiment, well suited to a Crusader, but its real significance lay in its connection to the special initials which always accompanied the cross; I.N.R.I., translated exoterically as;

Iesus Nazarenus Rex Iudeorum (Jesus of Nazareth, King of the Jews).

However, the initiates had another interpretation of the initials;

Igne Natura Renovatur Integra (By Fire, Nature is Renewed Whole).

Knowing that the 'fire' herein mentioned means the mental power of inner reflection, we realise that this short phrase is a concise description of the Hermetic practice.

The Templars, like the Cathars, were considered to be heretics because they 'denied Christ' and 'trampled on the cross'. Let me explain the meaning of the latter term, for it was totally misunderstood by the accusing Catholics. In biblical times, the Hebrew name for a Laundryman came from a word which means 'to trample' – that is, to trample with the feet in order to loosen the dirt, as was the practice. The early Launderer also processed new clothes by bleaching them *white*, and so from these two facts arose the phrase used by the Templars. To 'trample on the cross' means to wash or bleach (purify to white) the cross (the conscious mind).

Outwardly, the Templars aims were couched in a language which the Church hierarchy could only read as above reproach, and it must have given the parent organisation much satisfaction when, in 1128, the Templars were officially recognised as a religious, military Order, answerable only to the Pope himself. From this period, the Templars grew unrestrainedly, recruiting the sons of noblemen and receiving vast sums as donations, until by the end of the 13th century, the Order numbered some 15,000 and owned 9,000 strongholds.

The Church had watched this unprecedented expansion with growing trepidation and finally resolved to curtail or remove for good what they saw as a threat to their own supremacy. Applying pressure to King Phillip of France, they engineered the suppression that took place in 1307. Long before this happened, however, the parent group, the mysterious Order of Our Lady of Mount Zion, had felt that the Templars had outgrown themselves, and that the Hermetic knowledge was in danger of corruption and loss. In 1187, they quietly extricated themselves, moved into deeper secrecy, and left the Templars to go their own way. After this withdrawal, the secret group modified its title, becoming thereafter known as the Priory of Sion. And in this action of withdrawal after founding a popular Order, we have the second part of the recurring pattern.

The Jesuits

Moving forward in time to 1534, we have a repetition of the Templar sequence in the history of the Society of Jesus. This Order, more familiar by its abbreviated title, The Jesuits, was formed by a Spanish Knight named Ignatius Loyola, and like the Templars, it soon gained in popularity and wealth, finally to be awarded recognition by the Pope. Spreading to Europe, it continued to expand until it was powerful enough to exert a significant political influence. In short, it replaced the vanished Templars as the leading 'secret' society.

What is seldom realised is that the founder, Loyola, and a select few of the central lodge, were initiates, and that the Jesuit Order was founded on the Hermetic principle, but just as with the Templars,

the rapid expansion of the main body brought the inevitable lessen-
ing in understanding of the initiates' aims. So the Adepts withdrew,
leaving the non-initiates to their own devices. History records that
they followed the same luckless path as their predecessors, for they
were suppressed in 1773. Once again, the pattern had been worked.

The Rosicrucians

Superficial history informs the scholar that Rosicrucianism began
in Bohemia in 1612, with the appearance of the Manifestos, two
strange documents which set the great Furore in motion, and so that
we may unravel the true intent of them, we will give them some
attention. Should the reader wish to see the entire texts of the
Manifestos, far too long to reproduce here, they are easily to hand in
the appendix of THE ROSICRUCIAN ENLIGHTENMENT, by
Francis Yates (1972).

The 'Fama Fraternitas' (1614) The First Manifesto

The reader is alerted to the Hermetic value of the Fama, in the
opening lines, by the statement that the world at large is likely to
scoff at the idea of a Librium Naturae (Book of Nature), or a perfect
method of all arts. We know from experience that even in this
modern age, paranormal powers and the talk of astral travel are
greeted with the greatest scepticism.

There follows a fable, a vehicle designed to carry the familiar clues
of the process, just as they are carried in the Gospels and the Greek
myths. The name of the Rosicrucian founder, Christian Rosencreutz, is obviously an adaptation of the age old symbol of the Rose
and the Cross, a sign which was the property of the original Order,
Our Lady of the Mount Zion. The great significance of the symbol
as expressed in the Manifestos was that, for the first time, it was
being made public.

The second Hermetic clue is offered in the idea that Christian
Rosencreutz was a man much *travelled*, especially in the *east*, where
he gained knowledge not previously available to him. The first
Brothers of the Rose Cross, the original founders, are said to be only
four in number, and that their first task was to write out their total
knowledge into a book;

> which yet we daily use to God's praise and glory, and do find
> great wisdom therein.

This book sounds uncommonly familiar, and we realise that the Bible is being referred to. The 'four' clearly relate to the books of the Gospels, in which the Death and Resurrection theme is so cleverly allegorised. After increasing their numbers to eight, the members of the Rose Cross disperse to teach others – and here the text emphasises the fact that none of the initiates suffers disease or pain (the astral body doesn't, you see). Although they do not live beyond their appointed span, they were able to heal themselves and others, as initiates are capable of doing.

There follows an imaginative fable, the section which describes the discovery of the perfectly preserved body of Rosencreutz, and which is interpreted thus:

One of the Brothers, the story begins, was making some *alterations to his building*, meaning that the mystical brother was readjusting his normal outward thinking, turning his mind inwards so that he could begin the process. Soon, he finds a brass plate on which was inscribed the names of 'the Rosicrucian brothers and other things besides' ('brass' is indicative of the conscious mind). The Brother decided to remove the plate to a more fitting place, but an *iron nail*, so deeply embedded that it required great force to dislodge it, causes a further *stone* behind the plate to become uncovered. This 'iron nail' is a duplicate emblem of the 'nails' in Jesus's Crucifixion, and constitutes the effort of concentration required to still the conscious mind, here symbolised both by the brass plate and the stone. The displacement of the stone reveals a *concealed vault* (the hitherto unappreciated subconscious powers). And this vault is said to be in *three* parts.

Of the upper part,' says the text. 'You shall understand no more of at this time.'

Allegorised here are the three stages of the process, the last of which is the most secret of all and can only be fully understood by one who has successfully accomplished the first two. The three parts of this vault are identical to the three compartments in the Tabernacle, or the three sections of the Gothic cathedrals.

In the centre of the vault, the tale continues, there is an altar (the centre of the mind) under which was found the body of Rosencreutz (the inner knowledge). His perfectly preserved body (the knowledge never dies) holds a Book in one dead hand, a word picture which reiterates the idea that total knowledge is to be found in the centre of the mind.

The Confessio (1615)

The second of the manifestos repeats the ideals expressed in the first, openly stating that all those who joined the Brotherhood would be shown more wonderful secrets than they had ever experienced before. It hoped that such an offer would arouse the curiosity of men to take advantage of it. The knowledge that Christian Rosencreutz wished to share, it said, was so comprehensive that if all the books in the world were suddenly lost, everything would still be found in the Rosicrucian teaching. As we can at this stage appreciate, this is tantamount to saying that the Rosicrucian teaching is an inlet to the Universal Mind.

The gaining of this great knowledge would not be so hard to do;

> as if one should begin to pull down and destroy the old ruinous building, and then enlarge the forecourt, afterwards bring lights in the lodgings, and then change the doors, stairs, and other things according to our intention.

Here again, the reconstruction of a 'building' is presented as analogous to the change of thinking necessary for the would-be initiate.

The Confessio then annotates some of the benefits to be obtained by joining them (by which is meant undertaking the process). These are put in the form of a series of questions.

> Were it not good that we needed not to care, nor to fear hunger, poverty, sickness and age? Were it not a precious thing that you could always live so, as if you had lived from the beginning of the world, and moreover as you should still live to the end thereof? Were it not excellent you dwell in one place, that neither the people which dwell beyond the River Ganges in the Indies could hide anything, nor those which live in Peru might be able to keep secret their council from thee? Were it not a precious thing that you could so read in only one book, and withal by reading, understand and remember all that which is in all other books (which heretofore have been, and are now, and hereafter shall come out)? How pleasant were it that you could so sing; that instead of stony rocks you could draw the pearls and precious stones; instead of wild beasts, spirits; and instead of hellish Pluto, move the mighty princes of the world?

How reminiscent is the querulous phrase 'were it not' to the much older 'what, then, is it?' of the Papyrus of Ani!

The Confessio says that it is aware that such secrets are normally kept from the common masses, reserved more for the noble and princely, but to those who are concerned, it states that the Rosicrucian secrets will never become commonly or generally known. The implication here is that those who wish to learn such secrets must break away from the common stream of thought. And with regard to the phrase 'noble and princely', which may appear to invoke a certain class distinction, I refer you to the fact that *noble* has always carried the inner meaning of 'initiated'.

The text of the Confessio also makes it plain that many would lack the perspicacity and faith necessary to find and accomplish the process:

> Although the FAMA be set forth in five languages and is manifested to all, yet we do partly very well know that the unlearned and gross wits will not receive or regard same.

And further on:

> Although the Great Book of Nature stands open to all men, yet there are but few that can read and understand same.

Like the 'Fama', the Confessio advocates a study of the Bible as an insight to the truth of Nature:

> Wherefore we do admonish everyone for to read diligently and continually the Holy Bible, for he that taketh his pleasure therein shall know that he prepared for himself an excellent way to come to our Fraternity.

But in case it should be thought that the literal word of the Scriptures was to be followed dogmatically, it is added:

> And not only to have it continually in the mouth, but to know how to apply and direct the *true understanding* of it to all times and ages of the world.

From the initiates' point of view, the inclusion of this passage reaped a twofold benefit. It unquestionably directed the discerning reader to find the secret hidden within the texts – and it forestalled any action by the Church authorities to mount accusations of ungodliness in the words of the Manifestos.

The Confessio ends with a stern warning about the spurious literature of those who imitate the Hermetic texts without being in possession of the inner knowledge.

> We must earnestly admonish you that you put away, if not all, yet the most books written by false alchemists who do think it but a

jest, or a pastime when they either misuse the Holy Trinity, when they do apply it to vain things, or deceive people with strange figures and dark sentences and speeches, and cozen the simple of their money, as there are nowadays too many such books set forth.

The two Manifestos were followed one year later by a third manuscript entitled THE CHEMICAL WEDDING OF CHRISTIAN ROSENCREUTZ, and had there been any doubt as to the Hermetic foundation of the previous texts, it was completely removed by the style and content of the new contribution. 'Chemical Wedding' was presented in the form of a romance about a husband and wife who lived in a fairy-tale castle full of marvels and images of *lions*. The narrative divided the depicted events into periods of seven days, reminiscent of the Creation theme in Genesis, but set out in a nursery tale, folk fantasy style.

Historical evidence strongly suggests that the author was Johann Valentin Andraea, the Hermeticist who had previously written THE REPUBLICAE CHRISTIANOPOLITANAE, a fable which portrayed a *perfect society* on lines similar to that of Plato's REPUBLIC. It is not thought, however, that Andraea was responsible for either the Fama or the Confessio, and thus it suggests that all three manuscripts emanated from a select group of initiates whose identity was never revealed. The one clue we have to this secret group is that the name Andraea is on the list of Grand Masters of the Priory of Sion.

Thus was the Rosicrucian movement publicly born, although some time was to elapse before non-initiate lodges began to be formed. Like the Templars and the Jesuits, however, once the idea was put into practice, membership quickly grew, an abundance of lodges springing up throughout Europe and Britain. It may be said that the movement in this form came to maturity in the 1750s with the establishment of the Order of the Gold and Rosicrucian, a hierarchial lodge which remodelled the existing rituals, surrounding them with an aura of fantasy and mystique that inevitably attracted an even larger membership, none of whom understood the inner meaning of the rites they so readily swore to.

The few small lodges of Freemasonry that existed at the time, remnants of the old Templars, were similarly influenced and rose collectively to supercede Rosicrucianism as it declined towards the end of the nineteenth century, thus resulting in the dominant Masonic Order of the present day. But long beforehand, the pattern had been worked once more. The initiates had taken care to withdraw from their fast developing offspring, their true Rosicrucian powers imperceptible to the 'profane'.

The initiates of the past can only be detected through their writings, where their accomplishment is stated by way of the established repertoire of literary devices. Most of these manuscripts are the alchemical enigmas over which scholars have pored in vain, for they are totally undecipherable to those without the knowledge; but certain prominent men found less confusing ways of indicating their affiliation to the Brotherhood.

Francis Bacon

Sir Francis Bacon (1561 – 1626) is most regarded in history as the originator of modern experimental research, but it is the manner in which he stated his aims that tends to catch the eye. In his NOVUM ORGANUM, published in 1620, he advocates a 'true and patient *understanding of Nature* through phenomena and facts'. What he proposed was a 'total reconstruction of sciences, arts, and all human knowledge . . . to extend the power and dominion of the human race . . . over the universe'. Once this goal was achieved, it would result in Man commanding the *serene tranquillity of abstract wisdom*, something which could only be obtained by 'building in the human understanding a model of the world *such as it is in fact, not as man's own reason would have it be*'.

In words of the same ilk, Bacon made it clear that he wished Mankind to achieve Ultimate Knowledge – just as the Rosicrucian Manifestos had described. And in comparing the date of his publication with the advent of the Manifestos, it is instinctive to conclude that Bacon had read them, become fired with enthusiasm for their ideas, and then produced a Manifesto of his own. Thus the question arises; did he copy the idea, as any educated person could, or was he a true Rosicrucian?

Few of his letters give any hint that he possessed the inner knowledge of the initiate, but his books contained many ideas that could only emanate from a Rosicrucian source. Like Newton, he expressed the concept of the Universal Mind, but he called it the 'Incomparable Verulam', a term which has Hermetic significance if one stops to work it out. Near to St Albans, where Bacon lived, there were the remains of a Roman city called Verulamium – and thus in the adaptation of this name, he obliquely paralleled the 'ancient city' with the 'holy city' of the inner mind, a tenuous link as far as the non-initiate reader is concerned, but by no means unknown and quite sufficient for an initiate.

Add to this the fact that Bacon possessed an inventive flair that was incredible by normal standards, proposing a myriad of technical innovations. In 1941, F. Sherwood Taylor, the director of the Science Museum in London, drew up a list of discoveries which had been previsioned by Bacon. At the time it was a phenomenal collection, and in the intervening forty years, many more have been added. You might like to compare this ability with that of Leonardo da Vinci, known to be a Rosicrucian and a Grand Master of the Priory of Sion. It is well known that da Vinci's interests extended beyond art to the theory of flight, as his drawings demonstrate. The sketches may not satisfy a modern aeronautical engineer, but we must ask by what means the artist arrived at the idea of a helicopter. Are such ideas previsions of what is to come? To answer that, you will need to become a Rosicrucian.

Bacon's most outright expression of Rosicrucian links are found in a book that was not published until after his death. Entitled NEW ATLANTIS, the narrative is in the form of a fable comparable to the Greek myth of Jason and his epic voyage, except that Bacon's sailors discover not the Golden Fleece, but a *perfect society*. These adventurers, while making their way through *uncharted waters*, become lost in a veritable *wilderness* of ocean, but eventually chance upon an island 'full of boscage' (*forest* – like the forest of Morois) which made it show up more *dark*. They came close to the shore, hoping to land, but the inhabitants warned them off 'without any cries' (in other words, they were *silent*).

Later, however, they were allowed to land, but were *confined to a large house for three days* (expression of meditation), at which they were visited by a man. They noticed that he was wearing a *white turban* (round the *head*) on which was the sign of a small *red cross*. Some time after this, they fell into the company of a man named Joabin. He was a *Jew and circumcised* (an initiate), and he told them that the *Father of Solomon's House* (the Universal Mind) would be coming to see them.

The narrative continues in the same style, with Hermetic clues scattered here and there throughout the text. NEW ATLANTIS, as even its title infers, is the work of an initiate, without doubt.

The Freemasons

There exists a long held tradition that, shortly before his execution, Jacques de Molay, Grand Master of the Knights Templars, passed on the secrets of the Order and the hiding place of their wealth to Templars who subsequently transmitted them from age to age, to be preserved in the form of Freemasonry. The legend, while exerting a great psychological appeal and the vague promise of monetary gain upon affiliation to the Masonic Order, has been dismissed by sceptical historians as no more than the usual kind of folk fable that becomes attached to a figure of persecution. But as we have discovered, such legends often serve to conceal a foundation laid in truth – and there does exist an indisputable link between the Templars of long ago and present day Masonry. As William of Tyre's document shows, the use of the fable of King Solomon's Temple is common to both, and thus it is to this link, the Masonic initiation ceremony, that we must turn in order to unearth the long lost secrets of the Templar 'treasure'.

Masonic candidates are told that the basic objective of the Order is to overcome death and ascend to immortality, an ideal that is undoubtedly akin to the Hermetic principle. The 'death' and 'resurrection' theme is exemplified in the *raising* of the candidate from the dead level to the perpendicular, while the three stages of the process are to be plainly glimpsed in the three degrees of initiation.

The First Degree Tracing Board has already been equated with the Ladder of Jacob, the Star (of Bethlehem, if you like), and the checkered pattern of the chessboard. There are also to be seen the *three* immovable jewels, and the *rough* and *perfect* Ashlars (*stones* – symbolic of the unfinished and finished mental process) (See Fig. 11).

The Second Degree Tracing Board shows a *three* storied *building*, part of King Solomon's Temple, which was built *without the sound of a hammer*. There is a winding staircase leading to the second floor, or chamber, symbolising the second stage of the process. Above, at the top of the third chamber, the *Star of David* is seen shining (see Fig. 12).

The Tracing Board of the Third Degree, however, is most explicit in its simplicity, for it shows the *coffin of Hiram Abiff*, thus depicting the *death* of the *brass founder*, the conscious mind.

Masonic ritual also features the symbolic use of the left and right, mainly expressed by the *pillars* of Boaz (left) and Jachin (right). These pillars are to be found in the description of King Solomon's Temple (I Kings, 7; 15–22), where they are said to be *hollow* and made of *copper* (both emblems which point to the inner mind).

A Masonic candidate is presented for initiation with his *left* leg and breast bared, ready to be symbolically *killed*, while in other sections of the ritual, he is required to take a step forward with his *left* foot and place his *right* heel in the *hollow* of his left, thus not only forming a 'T' shape – the Tau, or cross – but symbolically bringing together the

FIGURE 11.
The Freemasons' First Degree Tracing Board.

Three pillars represent the stages of the process, while the Ladder
(compare with the Mutus Liber Plate 1) symbolises the whole mental
task. Above is seen the Dual aspect of the human mind – the Sun (the
subconscious) and the Moon (reflective power of the conscious).
The chessboard floor is another emblem of the mental task. In the
centre, at the top of the Ladder, is the Star – the goal which the
Neophyte must follow.

FIGURE 12.
The Second Degree Tracing Board of the Freemasons.
Note the flight of steps leading to the second floor, denoting the
second stage of the mental process, while above, on the *third* floor,
the Star of David is visible (the end of the process in sight at the third
stage).
Both the entrance to the Temple and the door to the second floor are
made under an *arch* (see chapter 13).

conscious mind (left) and the subconscious (right) in the inner mind (the hollow).

In the Third Degree, the candidate must cross his *right* foot over his *left* to signify that Hiram Abiff (the conscious mind) was slain just before the Temple was finished (the conscious mind must 'die' to allow the subconscious to harmonise, that is why the *right* foot is dominant).

It is in the interpretation of this ritual that the Templar secret is contained, the transmission of the coded knowledge of the early initiates. All the Masonic candidate has to do is to learn to read it correctly.

It will be a worthwhile exercise at this juncture to compare the Masonic rituals with those of the late Rosicrucians, as far as historic records permit, for like the Freemasons, the latter day Rosicrucian lodges either knowingly or unknowingly preserved the Hermetic message in their own ceremonies. The interest arises because some schools of Masonic thought consider the Rosicrucian rites to be blasphemous.

Walton Hannah, in his book, DARKNESS VISIBLE, discloses that the reason for Masonic distaste lies in the fact that the Rose Croix based their ceremonies directly on the Crucifixion, expressing the event as a dire calamity. Christian Masons have interpreted the mourning depicted in the rites to be for Satan, not for the death of Jesus. They were, of course, arguing in the dark, both factions being ignorant of the mythical nature of the Crucifixion, or the real meaning of the name Satan. It is with the advantage of such enlightenment that we can re-examine the Rosicrucian ceremony. I will emphasise the key words in the usual manner.

Three rooms are required for the 18th Degree of the Rose Croix of Heredom. The first is a *black* room in which there is an altar overhung with black, and on which are represented *three crosses*. The centre cross is embellished by a *black rose* (this symbol has an early foundation in Arabia and can be found employed in a classic text of Arabian Nights' Entertainments, all tales with an Hermetic foundation). The rose is surrounded by a *crown of thorns* (remember the 'mushroom' symbolism). The other two have the *skull and crossbones* depicted at their feet (another well known facet of 'buried treasure' myth that we shall shortly examine). There are *three pillars* in the room, representing – so the candidates are told – Faith, Hope and Charity. Thus the first stage of the Hermetic process is symbolised.

Strangely enough, the Heredom rites do not express the second stage with a predominance of white, but the emphasis is placed instead of the *death* of the conscious mind, for the second room is called the Chamber of Death. It is liberally decorated with the appropriate signia, skull and cross-bones, and possibly even a figure in a winding sheet.

The third room is called the *Red Room* and is *brilliantly illuminated* in that colour. It contains a super-altar, profusely decorated with *red roses*, while on the *fourth* step leading to the altar, there rests a *cubic stone* (the finished process). There is also a *ladder*, this time with only seven rungs (an alternative to nine but with the same fundamental meaning) on which are placed the movable letters F.H. and C., followed by I.N.R.I.

The opening ceremony contains the following passage:

Most Wise Sovereign:	Excellent and *perfect* Generals; what is the hour?
First General:	The *ninth* hour of the day.
Most Wise Sovereign:	Then it is the hour when the *veil of the temple was rent* in twain and *darkness overspread the earth*, when the true light departed from us, the *altar was thrown down*, the *blazing star was eclipsed*, the *cubic stone* poured forth *blood and water*, the *Word* was lost, and despair and tribulation sat heavily upon us. (a solemn pause) Since Masonry has experienced such dire calamities it is our duty, Excellent and Perfect Prince, to endeavour, by renewed *labours* to retrieve our loss . . .

The Hermetic iniate who conceived this passage has implanted the message that the true light has departed – meaning that the true knowledge of the mental process has remained hidden. Hence the mourning. An identical theme is present in Masonic ritual when the brothers mourn the death of Hiram Abiff and the *lost secrets of the master*.

The ritual of the Rosicrucian lodge is somewhat richer than that of the Freemasons, even culminating in the use of strontium chemicals to produce a vivid, red flame. Walton Hannah sees deadly heresy in the ceremony which requires the candidate to give his age as *thirty-three*, as he *journeys* for *thirty-three* days through the Black Room, the Chamber of Death, and the Red Room, there to be *resurrected*. It is a heresy that is viewed as blatant because that candidate achieves (symbolically) both *light* and *perfection*, not through Christ but *by his own efforts*.

Although the Masons' Lost Word seems to have remained lost to them in modern times, there were undoubtedly initiates in the earlier

lodges, and I take this opportunity to bring a most unusual example
to your attention.

Jonathan Swift

In the preface to the second edition of LE MYSTERE DES
CATHEDRALES, Eugène Canseliet closes with some remarks on
the application of the caballistic art, and the key to it which can be
found, so he says, in Fulcanelli's text. Canseliet writes:

'. . . *the Language of the Gods, the Language of the Birds*. It is a
language with which Jonathan Swift, that strange Dean of St.
Patrick's was thoroughly familiar and which he used with so much
knowledge and virtuosity.'

The suggestion that Jonathan Swift was an Hermeticist may be
just a little too much for some to credit, but I remind you that in
GULLIVER'S TRAVELS, he wrote about a *flying island*, worked by
a *giant magnet*, and which was *cut off from the rest of the world*. I have
gone to some lengths to show that Rosicrucianism – the true
brotherhood – was always invisible and that its members were
where you would least expect to find them.

Being the brilliant satirist that he was, Swift's manner of con-
veying the Hermetic meaning is unique, making cunning use of the
established devices and enhancing them with his own ingenuity. The
usual clues, therefore, are not easy to unearth unless the reader has a
firm grounding in the Language of the Gods – allegory.

I begin with an autobiographical manuscript deposited by Dean
Swift (a younger relative of Jonathan) in the Trinity College Library,
Dublin. Entitled FRAGMENTS OF AUTOBIOGRAPHIES, it is
an unfinished piece, and the first thing that strikes the eye is that the
text is written on the *right hand* half of the manuscript only. Swift
purports to describe brief, historic episodes in the lives of the early
Swifts, notably Thomas, his grandfather. Thomas, he says, was a
clergyman of 'small estate' who suffered the misfortune of being
plundered by the Roundheads on no less than thirty six occasions,
but he remained stoutly loyal to King Charles 1st's cause. As part of
Thomas's story, Jonathan blandly writes

. . . being informed that three hundred horses of the Rebel Party
intended in a week to pass over a certain river upon an attempt
against the Cavaliers, Mr Swift having a head mechanically
turned, he contrived certain pieces of iron with three spikes,
whereof one must always be with the point upwards; he placed

them overnight in the ford where he received notice that the Rebels would pass early next morning, which they accordingly did, and lost two hundred of their men, who were drowned, or trod to death falling off their horses, or torn by the spikes.

No doubt this quaint tale was penned with tongue firmly in cheek, and would normally be accepted by the reader in a like manner. But examine the text in light of the Hermetic clues so far covered and you will find a number of them to be present. The figure *three; water* (the river – which the Roundheads were going to *pass over); death* (of the Rebel horsemen); *iron* (the spikes – of which there were *three); night* (the time at which the operation took place); and *sunrise* (the time at which the Rebels died). Finally, the ford is a place where one *crosses from one side to the other.*

If this is to be labelled a coincidence, we may examine a later stage in the manuscript where Swift – writing as his own biographer – speaks of himself.

He was born in Dublin on St Andrews Day, and when he was a year old, an event happened to him that seemed very unusual; for his Nurse, who a was woman of Whitehaven, being under an absolute necessity of seeing one of her relations who was then extremely sick, and from whom she expected a legacy; and being at the same time extremely fond of the infant, stole him on shipboard unknown to his Mother and Uncle, and carried him with her to Whitehaven, where he continued for almost three years. For when the matter was discovered, his Mother sent orders by all means not to hazard a second voyage till he could be better able to bear it. The nurse was so careful of him that before he returned he had learned to spell, and by the time he was three years old, he could read any chapter in the Bible.

Here again, the reader will frown at the improbability of the tale – and so again we examine it for a hidden meaning. It seems that the *infant* Swift was undertaking a *voyage* with his *Nurse* (ancient term for Isis – reflection), who took him to *White*haven. The obvious clue is the second Hermetic colour which constitutes part of the town's name, but there exists an even more significant association from Swift's point of view. Whitehaven, if you consult the map, lies but a few miles from a point of land known as *St Bees Head.* The Bee is a symbol of the astral body, much used by the Egyptians, and with which Swift was well acquainted, as I shall demonstrate. The symbol of *death* (impending) is present in the nurse's sick relative, from whom she expects a *legacy* (a *good* fortune, or *treasure*), and the figure three is featured twice. The final assertion that a *three* year old would be able to read any passage in the Bible can hardly be taken literally. Rather, it is a statement intended to convey the fact that Swift had gained *unusual knowledge*.

Swift was known to possess an extensive library of books, including many classic, Hermetic texts, and therefore it is not to be wondered that he used even the most obscure and ancient symbolism. The bee presented a ready made emblem for the early initiates, as certain references in the Bible corroborate. In Exodus, the ultimate goal of the Israelite initiates was a land flowing with milk and *honey*. Bees are also said to build their nests in *cavities* in walls, or in *clefts in the rock* (Deut. 32; 13 and Psalms 81; 16). Sometimes they built them in *trees* that were *hollow*. The *honey* eaten by Jonathan, son of Saul, was found *in the woods*, a term with the same concealed meaning as *forest, grove* or *garden*, i.e., in the mind. Perhaps you recall the story of Jonathan as recorded in I Sam 14; 25 – 27, where Saul has ordered his people not to eat, but his son, not hearing the order

> 27 . . . put forth the end of the rod that was in his hand and dipped it in an honeycomb, and put his hand to his mouth; and his *eyes were enlightened*.

I suppose it could be legitimately said that one's eyes would be 'enlightened' upon tasting ordinary honey, but I'm sure even the most sceptical reader would agree that something deeper is inferred in this passage.

A more familiar reference to the bee, and one which has provoked intense puzzlement in scholars who have considered the story, is that found in Judges 14; 5–9, and relates how Sampson *slew the lion*. When he later returned, he found 'a swarm of bees in the lion's corpse and honey'. Academic scepticism arose because it is well known that bees have a strong aversion to dead bodies and carrion. The figurative meaning, however, is not hard to interpret when the Hermetic key is applied.

Bees are seen to be incorporated in Egyptian wall carvings, notably on a bas relief in the Temple of the Sun, and it is on the strength of this that scholars assume domestic beekeeping to date from very early times, although the first written evidence of apiculture dates only from about 200 A.D., at the time of the Jewish Mishna. As with wild bees, the domestic variety provide a handy line of symbolism for the initiate.

The early hives of Palestine were constructed of a wicker cylinder thickly plastered over with mud or cow dung – and it was therefore a *most unusual place* to find *nectar*. The true mode of the bee's existence lends itself to symbolism, for the insect falls into two categories, social and solitary. The solitary bees, like the initiates who are set apart from the rest of humanity, are *builders*, being called *carpenters*, *masons* and *miners*. As for the social bee, there are *three* classes, the Queen, the drone and the worker who bends all her efforts towards the production of a *new life* – the Queen's eggs. It is the worker who *gathers the nectar*.

All this and more was common knowledge to Jonathan Swift, and perhaps the best evidence I can provide in support of that statement is to reproduce in the appendix the contents of one of his satirical letters. Therein, he shows quite clearly that few Masons of his day understood the significance of their Order's traditions as he did.

Let us now pay some attention to Swift's major work, GULLIVER'S TRAVELS, and in particular to that section entitled 'Voyage to Laputa'. Commentators have pointed out that the basic idea for GULLIVER'S TRAVELS stemmed from discussions between Swift and some of his cronies, who had formed themselves into a select group known as the Scriblerus Club. Robert Boyle, the famous chemist, was an earlier member of this group, and it has been claimed that his essay, UPON THE EATING OF OYSTERS, led eventually to the conception of Swift's volume. This may be so, and parallel to this theory, I would like to bring to notice the fact that Boyle was known to have been deeply immersed in Hermetic studies, in pursuit of which, he was also in communication with Isaac Newton. Thus, the undeclared activities of the Scriblerus Club will be left to the reader's imagination.

To the lay public, Swift's volume was received as he had intended, as one of the most savage pieces of satire ever written about Man and his ideas of Government and Society. In modern times, the art of interpreting allegory has been almost lost, as we must now admit when considering how the Bible and the Greek myths have consistently been misinterpreted. Swift's book is no exception, and today it is relegated to the children's library to be appreciated only in its most superficial sense. Yet many an adult would gain valuable insight to himself and his fellows were he to trouble to read it with penetration.

'Voyage to Laputa'

The epics of adventure endured by Gulliver were portrayed as *voyages*, or *journeys*, in the course of which, *strange events* took place.

'Voyage to Laputa', you will notice, is the *third* of Gulliver's journeys and occupies the first *three* chapters of part *three*. The tale begins with Gulliver engaging in a voyage during which a great storm blows up, driving the ship to the *east*. Later, they are boarded by pirates, one of whom was a *Dutchman*. The inner significance of this birthright may be appreciated by consulting a well known alchemical tract of 1673 called 'The Testimony of Helvetius'. Therein, the author describes how he transmuted *lead into gold* with the help of a stranger who called unexpectedly at his house one day. The stranger was *beardless* (indicating youth and therefore, by association, a *child* – an initiate), and was said to have been born in *North Holland*. He was also, he maintained, a *founder of brass*. This last sentence alone will indicate the stranger's initiateship, and it follows that his birthplace must have a significance. This is revealed to us when we remember that Holland is also called the *Netherlands* (the nether regions of Prometheus). Gulliver's 'Dutchman', it is quite clear, personifies the initiate.

Gulliver is set adrift in a canoe and it took him *three* hours to reach a nearby island, which was all *rocky*. After *roasting some eggs* (meditating) he slept under the shelter of a *rock*. In the days that followed, he visited several adjacent islands until he arrived at the last of the chain, but he found it *difficult to land* until he entered a small creek just *three* times the width of his canoe.

He became very despondent (just like Jane Leade and the Ulgy Duckling), and as he walked the desolate island, the *sun became so hot* (meditation began to have its effect) that he was forced to *turn his face from it* (reverse his outward thoughts). It was at this point that Laputa, the flying island appeared, seeming to *eclipse the sun* (well-used term to indicate that the first stage had been completed), but Gulliver remarks

I did not observe the air to be much colder, or the sky more *darkened* than if I had stood under the shade of a *mountain*.

When the island neared, he was able to see people on it engaged in *fishing* (biblical expression meaning meditation), while others looked on (*watched* – again meaning meditation). He waved his *cap* (Phrygian) and called to them, but although they saw him, all remained strangely *silent* (just like the people in Bacon's lost island).

Once aboard Laputa, he saw that the inhabitants were *not as ordinary people are*, and that their outer garments were adorned with the figures of the *sun, moon and stars* (the zodiac = initiateship).

'I observed here and there many in the habit of servants, with a blown bladder fastened like a *flail* to the end of a short stick, which they carried in their hands.

In each bladder there was a quantity of dried peas, or pebbles, so that a rattle was produced, the servants employing this device to *attract the attention* of their masters, who were always so wrapped up in cogitation (meditation) that they were in danger of *falling down every precipice*. The bladder described is, of course, the Sistrum used in Egyptian and Greek Mystery rites, and as a rattle carried in the festival processions, it symbolises the constantly moving thoughts of the conscious mind. The Sistrum was only *stilled* at the very culmination of the ceremonies. The servants described by Gulliver are identical to the mediaeval *Fools*, who urge on the dancers of the *Nine* Men's Morris, an intricate dance pattern which resembles the torturous path of a *maze*, or *labyrinth*. As for the *masters* falling down every precipice, that is exactly what the Fool of the Tarot seems about to do.

Gulliver ponders on the derivation of the name Laputa, and as his conclusions are deliberately misleading, it is as well to find out from what source Swift might really have coined it. The answer is given to us in the strange little verse at the opening of his letter from the 'Female Masons' (see appendix), and which begins;

Ixion, the Impious, Lewd, Profane . . .

Ixion is a character in Greek mythology who, having murdered his father in law, is taken to heaven by *Zeus* for *purification*. For subsequently attempting the virtue of Hera, wife of Zeus, he was condemned to be bound to a *continuously rolling wheel* in the *nether world*. In this theme we cannot help but notice the parallel to the fate of Prometheus, who was bound to a *rock* in the *nether regions*, and it is plain that Ixion, like Prometheus, personifies the potential within the conscious mind (the continuously rolling wheel). In the myth, Ixion is said to be king of Lapithae, in Thessaly. Laputa, a near phonetic equivalent, obviously has the same significance – the mind.

The island itself is described in chapter *three*, it being exactly *circular* (like the walls round Poseidon) and *three* hundred yards thick. The underside appears to all those who view it *from below* as a plate of adamant (an old name for 'lodestone'), while at the top, the island has a declivity from the circumference inwards, so that all rains and *dews* will be conveyed towards the *centre*. At this centre, there is a large chasm into which Gulliver is taken. One hundred yards *below the surface* they enter the Astronomer's *Cave*, where there were *lamps continually burning*, the lights of which *reflected* strongly from the adamant walls.

Without labouring the point further, it is plain that the profligacy of clues within this text is something more than just a coincidence, and so I have no hesitation in proclaiming Swift to be in full possession of the Hermetic knowledge – the traditional 'treasure' of the Templars and of the Freemasons.

CHAPTER TEN

The Alchemists

The name 'Alchemy' inevitably brings to mind mediaeval cults depicting the gloomy laboratory of the ancient Adept. He is surrounded by retorts and crucibles, while a pumping bellows keeps the furnace glowing at red heat. The Alchemist himself, in his long flowing cape, looks expectantly at the ladle of molten metal with which he is working. Invariably, there are astrological representations of the sun, moon and stars within the picture. Ostensibly, our Adept is engaged in the highly secret task of transmuting base metals like common Lead into the purest Gold – and this is exactly what the initiates of the Middle Ages wished everyone to think.

Roger Bacon, the thirteenth century Adept, defined the three stages of the Hermetic process and the end result thus: distillation; sublimation; calcination; followed by separation. This summing up may throw some light on the reason why so many mediaeval manuscripts have been thought to conceal a lost process for making gold out of other metals. In the terminology of the Metallurgist and the Chemist, the Hermeticist found a ready made symbolism with which to project the mental process, but in such a manner that the Church would be unable to prove a charge of heresy. In the same way that the 'lamb' of the Bible personified the conscious mind which had to be 'sacrificed', so common metal (the conscious mind) had to be subjected to the furnace (the 'fire' of meditation) in order to be melted down and rendered raw (dead) before it could be brought back to maturity and transmuted into fine gold (the transmission of the consciousness). The range of symbols employed by the Rosicrucian writers is so comprehensive that I will be able to cover only a bare minimum here, but acquainted as you are with the real key to the Hermetic puzzle, a little careful cogitation on your own account will decipher all but the most obscure manuscripts. For success, however, all aspects of the symbolism must be considered. Word play, for example, was even more popular in the 16th century than it was in ancient times, the passage of time extending it to include comparisons in a number of languages. To demonstrate in a small way, we may say that the laboratory retort, the chemical flask known as a Matrass, was often used as an emblem for the reflective power. The name of this round retort, which is used in the process of *distillation*, is phonetically similar to the French 'Maitresse', meaning 'mistress', in the sense of 'governess' or *Mother*, an obvious connection with Isis and the Virgin.

Much the same interpretation can be put on the Three Armed Still of Mary the Jewess, described by Zozimus, an Alchemist of 300 A.D. The chemical still was a favourite article by which the initiates could symbolise their mental process because, like a Matrass, it was an instrument of distillation. The still, therefore, was the Adept's mind. The specification by *Mary* the *Jewess* – who is, according to Zozimus, the transmitter of the Art – requiring three outlets, or arms, is merely a way of expressing the three stages of the mental task. Yet the description of this Tribikos and the unorthdox use to which it was supposedly put, has baffled chemists for centuries, leading them to the false conclusion that the Hermetic masters were incompetent in the basic skills of chemistry.

Another symbol employed with great frequency was that of Vitriol. In the New Testament, this acid which putrifies and *kills*, appears as the *vinegar* given to Jesus on the cross. The Alchemists, ever ready with their word play, even constructed a Latin acrostic with the initial letters;

> Visita Interiora Terra, Rectificand Invenies Occultum Lapidum (Visit the interior of the *earth*; by *purifying* you will find the hidden *stone*).

The term 'earth' in this instance refers to the conscious mind, while 'stone' should be more fully described as the Philosopher's Stone, the end result of the process. This application of the 'stone' symbol heralds a change from the way it is used in the Bible, so an investigator must be wary of that when deciphering Alchemical texts.

A further conception of the cunning way in which the ancient initiate writers concealed their process can be gathered from the text of an early Adept named Synesius. He comments on instruction given in a (now irretrievably lost) book by the philosopher Democritus (470 B.C.), showing how to complete the process.

> What he (Democritus) says, O Dioscorus, is as follows; 'And put it into a flask on a hot-ash bed, not having the fire direct, but on a gentle hot-ash bed, which is a Kerotakis. During the action of the heat, there is adapted to the flask above, a glass apparatus having a Masterion fitted to it. And put it on top of it and receive the water which comes up through the breasts and keep it and putrefy it. This is called divine water'.

We begin to interpret this obscure text by noting that Democritus insists on a *gentle heat* (meditation) being applied, like that used in a Kerotakis. This unfamiliar piece of equipment turns out to be a paint palette used by early artists. It was fitted with a small lamp, or burner, the heat of which kept the colours of those times fluid, as they were a mixture of pigment and wax. The Kerotakis, therefore, employed a *gentle heat* in connection with *colours* and was used by *artists* (initiates). The Masterion was a breast-shaped cup of glass used by the early chemists, and in this we have an oblique reference to the breasts of the Virgin from which the *white* milk would flow. Note also that the *divine water* had to be *putrified* (killed).

By now, I will have no need to tell you that Democritus was an initiate, the first man to expound atomic theory. Any manuscript by him must be read with care for the hidden message. I recall one modern author claiming that human eyesight is better today than it was in times past because Democritus had written that he could only see four colours – *black, white, yellow* and *red.*

To open the pages of almost any Alchemical work is to plunge headlong into an ever-deepening morass of parable and allegory, obscure emblems and literary cul-de-sacs. Nearly all of the mediaeval texts, each one of which boldly proclaims that within its pages alone is the Great Secret revealed, can be meticulously and studiously perused only to find that the beautifully worded contents are totally incomprehensible. A brief example of these literary convolutions will suffice, for there is no point in unnecessary labour. The reader who is interested enough to experience the mental quagmire of such manuscripts at first hand will have little trouble obtaining reprints of the better known works.

Witness this quote from the TURBA PHILOSOPHORUM, a compendium of alchemical papers.

> Divide the elements by fire, unite them through the mediation of Mercury, which is the greatest arcanum, and so the magistery is complete, the whole difficulty consisting in the solution and conjunction. The solution, or separation takes place through the mediation of Mercury, which first dissolves the bodies and these are united again by ferment and Mercury.

Some sages, just to confound the issue even further, inject the chemical vernacular with an alternative terminology. Ascansius, for instance, blandly tells us

> . . . stir up war between copper and Mercury till they destroy and devour each other. The copper then coagulates the quicksilver, the quicksilver congeals the copper, and both bodies

become a powder by means of diligent imbibition and digestion. Join together the red man and the white woman till they become Ethelia, that is quicksilver. Whoever changes them into spirit by means of quicksilver, and makes them red, can tinge every body.

Even the results of the final stage of the process are contained in this quote, but no uninitiated person will be able to penetrate the inner meaning. In both the above quotes, Mercury, or quicksilver, is the power of reflection, the reversed *attention*, while copper is made, like brass, to represent the outward thoughts of the conscious mind. An oft-quoted piece of advice to be found in Hermetic texts is

Burn your books and whiten your latten.

This is meant to convey the fact that the answer will not be found in any text book, but in the seeker's own mind. Latten is a brass alloy and was seized upon by the pun-loving scribes because it is phonetically similar to the name Latona, the woman of Revelation, the alternative Isis. The phrase therefore advises that the conscious mind must be brought to the *white* stage of the process.

Thankfully, there do exist straightforward texts which point the Neophyte in the right direction. Of these, the most illuminating is a paragraph in a book by Johannes Tritheim, the Benedictine scholar known as the Abbot of Spandheim and renowned for his researches into Alchemy. First printed in 1506, the significant lines run

If you wish to succeed in such a work, you must know how to separate the spirit and life in Nature and, moreover, to separate the astral soul in yourself and make it tangible . . .

In speaking of the art of Divine Magic, by which he meant the mental process, Johannes stated positively that such processes take place according to an established law:

You will learn the law by which these things are accomplished if you learn to know yourself.

On the same subject, Paracelsus, the 16th century Physician-Alchemist, and a pupil of Johannes Tritheim, says

This emanation, or separation, takes place by a kind of digestion, and by means of an interior heat.

In these few sentences alone, the key and the objective of the process is given – that it is a mental process which will result in the production of the astral body.

The Artist and the Labourer

The initiate, because of his use of the mental process which employed the Hermetic colours (the three, or four, stages), was often called an 'artist'. Alternatively, using a term culled from the Bible, he was known as a 'labourer'. To show the application of the first term, I quote from a little known text by the French writer, Jacques Breyer.

> The mine of precious stones is well guarded. Each door is defended by a Dragon. In order to find it, one must have Humility, Disinterestedness, Purity. These are three infallible clues WHEN THEY ARE FULLY UNDERSTOOD. The F.F. (King) to be captured by the artist is therefore to be found; 'in the air'; the real mine is above! Poor puffer and blower! Why are you going astray? . . . Come . . . Think more closely, the great art is light.

As one can appreciate, even in possession of the key, this text is hard to decipher. Without it – impossible. The 'mine of precious stones' relates to the 'treasure' of the subconscious power, the mythical treasure of King Solomon. The King (Lion) represents the Universal Mind (subconscious) which must be captured (reached). The term 'puffers and blowers' is a derogatory reference to those who consistently misread the manuscripts and search for a way to transmute lead into gold by means of a physical, metallurgical process, the puffing and blowing being the sound of their furnace bellows.

In LE MYSTERE DES CATHEDRALES, Fulcanelli gives an apt example of the second name when he describes a relief showing the symbolic combat between the *eagle* and the *lion*, and which was mounted above the main door of a Paris mansion. Underneath was the inscription

> By a *labourer* I was built. Disinterested and zealous, he called me 'the beautiful stone'. In the year 1762.

The curious use of the word 'disinterest' in both inscriptions refers to the mental state adopted by the Neophyte as he proceeds with the task, his thoughts becoming less and less bound to outward, worldly impressions, and more and more centred in the inner mind, until he reaches the desired state of perfectly controlled consciousness. This is not implying that he wanders about his daily life in a daze, but rather he adjusts his mind so that the centre of his attention is no longer claimed by external influences alone.

Another interesting aspect of the latter quote is the use of the word 'zealous', for it is culled from the works of the Jewish historian, Josephus, who coined the name 'Zealots'. Outwardly, this name signifies a race of brigands as described by Josephus, but the inner word play will show that its root is in Hermeticism. However, this will be dealt with at a later stage.

The Mutus Liber

One item of Hermetic literature that deserves special mention is the Mutus Liber, the *Silent Book* of the alchemists. Within this enigmatic tome the process is not described, but illustrated instead by a series of symbolic pictures on the same lines as those of the Tarot. But they are more difficult to decipher without a considerable knowledge of the Hermetic key and therefore I will content myself with a single, pertinent example. Plate One shows a picture which has a familar theme (see Fig. 13).

The scene shows a *bound man*, *sleeping* against a large *rock*. On a *ladder* extending down from the *night* sky, in which are seen the *Moon* and *Stars*, two angels are blowing their Horns of Revelation. The whole cameo is surrounded by a *circlet* of *thorn branches*, with two *roses* at the bottom. Readers will have no difficulty in identifying this picture with the text of Genesis 28, in which Jacob dreams of just such a ladder. The same pictorial idea is present in the First Degree Tracing Board of Freemasonry.

Chinese Alchemy

In considering the impenetrability of some manuscripts which have survived from the European Middle Ages and before, it will be realised that the publication of such works developed into a contest to see who could become the most obscure. To review and interpret these at length would be possible, but would place an unnecessary strain on those of you who are waiting to see what part Rennes le Chateau plays, and so I intend to remain with the more quaint works which can be clarified in a few sentences. There is a charming little legend connected with the Taoists, the Chinese initiates, and concerns one Wei Po-Yang, who is said to have lived in the present province of Kiangsu at about 120 A.D.

Wei Po-Yang *went into the mountains* to make a *special medicine*, taking with him *three* disciples and a *white dog*. Having made the medicine, Wei Po-Yang turned to his disciples and said;

FIGURE 13. The Mutus Liber – Plate One
Compare this Alchemical picture with the text of Genesis 28, depicting Jacob's dream, and also with the First Degree Tracing Board of the Freemasons.

'It must be tried out on the dog, and if no harm comes to the animal, then we may take it ourselves.'

Po-Yang fed the medicine to the dog, which *died* instantly. He then asked the disciples:

'What is to be done? Shall we take the medicine, or not?'

'Would you take it yourself, sir?' they asked.

'I have committed myself,' Po-Yang replied. 'I have forsaken my home to come here and I would be ashamed to return if I could not become immortal. I must take it.' Thereupon, he took the medicine and died instantly. On seeing this, one of the disciples said;

'Our teacher is no ordinary person. He took the medicine and died of it. He must have a special reason.' So saying, he too, swallowed the medicine and died.

The two remaining disciples *reasoned* that it would be better not to take the medicine, which instead of making the others immortal, killed them. So they returned home.

After they had gone, Wei Po-Yang, the disciple and the dog, all *revived*, and as the Chinese text describes it, 'went the way of the immortals'.

In this little fable, we not only have the usual clues to the process, but also the main theme of death and resurrection. Present too, is the example of the intense faith required, once the Neophyte has committed himself to the mental task. The reference to 'immortality' does not apply to the physical body – it never did – but to the astral body, which once 'born' by means of the process, does not disperse at the event of physical death. It is for this reason that the Chinese initiates referred to the transmission of consciousness as the Elixir of Life, a theme which spread to Europe and led many unsuccessfully to search for a material well, or spa, the waters of which would confer eternal youth on the drinker. The two disciples who were unfortunate enough to lose this chance of immortality did so because they 'reasoned', i.e., they thought outwardly.

English Alchemy

Alchemy flourished secretly in England as it did elsewhere, the most noteworthy Adepts being Roger Bacon, George Ripley, Thomas Charnock and Edward Kelly. The latter was famous for his name being connected to Dr. John Dee, and the 'astrological experiments' they were supposed to have performed together. A.E. Waite's preface to THE ALCHEMICAL WRITINGS OF EDWARD KELLY discloses that while still a young man, Kelly travelled to Glastonbury where he was shown a strange manuscript said to have been taken from the violated sepulchre of a bishop. Kelly apparently recognised it for what it was, a treatise of Alchemy, and after a study of its contents, discovered the Great Secret. You may put two and two together here and come to the realisation that, despite the correspondence which may indicate the contrary, Kelly and Dee were one and the same person, and that the rather despicable 'Kelly' is a literary invention of Dee, the Rosicrucian, so that if anyone came too close in attempting to probe the secret, Kelly would have been the entity on which the blame was to be laid. The reasons for this charade, and the elements of proof which support it, are unfortunately beyond the scope of this book. What does concern us are the writings left by 'Kelly' for posterity. They are un- doubtedly the work of an initiate, outlining the Hermetic principle in verse, likening it to the making of bread (a subtle reference to the 'bread' of meditation). When meal and water are joined together, he explains, they are no longer meal and water, but become dough. All this is expounded in 'Sir Edward Kelle's Work'. The 'prima materia', the power of the Universal Mind, is obtained by Grace, he says, by which he means divine influence. Further on he lists some of the now familiar names applicable to the various stages of the work:

This very place is cal'd by many names –
As imbibition, feeding, sublimation,
And rightly it is termed exaltation,
When all is nothing else but circulation.

   And a few stanzas later:

This black, this white doe we call separation,
Which is not manuall but elementall;
It is no crude mercuriall sublimation,
But Nature's true work consubstantiall;
The white is called conjunction naturall,
Secret and perfect conjunction, not grosse,
Which bringeth profit, all other losse.
When thrice yee have turned this wheel about,
Feeding and working as I have said,
Then it will flow like wax without doubt . . .

Thereafter, he discourses on the white becoming red, until the *perfect medicine* is obtained.

Thomas Charnock left two manuscripts describing the Art – his BREVIARY OF PHILOSOPHY, written in 1557, and ENIGMA OF ALCHEMY, in 1572. The 'Breviary' claims to describe all the instruments required for the Art, adding that the services of a potter, a joiner and a glass-maker would be necessary. All are symbols to conceal the real meaning, as is the information left in a memorandum saying that he attained the gold producing powder when his hairs were *white*. The fact that a joiner is mentioned as a symbol of the mental science may cause readers to remember that Jesus was said to be the son of a carpenter, or that he was a carpenter himself. To analyse this, it is only necessary to recall that a carpenter, or joiner, is one who *joins* (the conscious with the subconscious).

Roger Bacon was an accomplished initiate. Born in Somerset in 1214, he rapidly became versed in languages, mathematics, medicine and philosophy. His grasp of scientific possibilities was prodigious, and like Leonardo da Vinci and Francis Bacon, he proposed many inventions that came only centuries later. In one letter, still available to present day researchers, he assures his readers that it is possible to construct machines for navigation without the aid of rowers, and which have extraordinary velocity. Equally possible, he maintains, are cars which move with great rapidity, independent of horses or other animals. Flying machines may be made, with a man seated in the centre, and by means of certain contrivances beating the air with artificial wings.

Of Alchemy, he recounts how a man may become a great prophet and predict the future by means of a 'mirror' which he called Almuchefi;

> composed in accordance with the laws of perspective under the influence of a benign constellation, and *after the body of the individual has been modified by alchemy*.

Once again we may read between the lines and conclude that the inventions Bacon listed were in fact drawn from his prophetic facility, made available to him by the accomplishment of the Hermetic process.

After Bacon, came George Ripley, a native of Bridlington who, in 1471, wrote TWELVE GATES OF ALCHEMY. In it, he declared that the principle, or 'prima materia', may be found everywhere. It flies with the fowls, swims with the fishes, it may be discovered by the reason of angels, and it governs man and woman. He was talking of the all-encompassing energy of the Universal Mind. An astronomical year, he maintained, was necessary in order to manufacture the 'stone' – a statement that must not be read literally, but with the signs of the zodiac in mind.

The Prophetic Power of Nostradamus

I am sure that every reader is acquainted with the name of Michael Nostradamus, 16th century Europe's most celebrated prophet. His 'quatrains', four line verses of concealed prophecy, have been the subject of concerted academic scrutiny in an effort to decipher those events which yet remain unfulfilled. Many have already been seen to be uncannily accurate in their forecast of historically notable occasions. Like the Alchemists, though, Nostradamus buried the true meanings under an obscuring mantle of word play so that he would not be accused of sorcery.

The name of Nostradamus has never been openly connected with the Hermetic Fraternity and the fact that he was an initiate may come as a surprise – but how else did he 'see' like Roger Bacon? The clues to his initiateship are left to us by Nostradamus himself, right from the opening verse of his book.

The first and second quatrains are supposedly intended to describe the method by which his divination was achieved, but we must never forget that he was more than liberal in his application of word play. Here is Erika Cheetham's translation of quatrain number one, but with the key words emphasised:

(Century One; quatrain one)
Sitting alone at *night* in secret study;
it is placed on a *brass tripod*.
A *slight flame* comes out of the *emptiness*
and makes successful that which should not
be believed in vain.

Disregarding modern academic argument over the accuracy of the translation, for others render it with slight variations, I make the point that many have read this at its face value and assumed that the seer employed a brass tripod on which something was heated. A similar process is described by the 4th century Syrian writer, Iamblichus, in his DE MYSTERIIS EGYPTORUM. Unfortunately, it has not been realised that Iamblichus himself was an initiate, and that both men were utilising an earlier, well established aspect of the symbolism. You will at once know what this is when I ask you to recall what I have said regarding the Oracle at Delphi, with its special *tripod* chair. The same tripod, used by Nostradamus, indicates the three stages of the process, while the fact that it is made of *brass* reminds us of the conscious mind. The *emptiness* suggests the thought-free condition necessary before the subconscious power of prediction can be drawn upon, and even the phrase 'that which

should not be believed in vain' has the connotation of the absolute
faith required.

For further proof of the Hermetic connection, attention may be
drawn to the name 'Nostradamus', the seer's adopted name. It is a
slightly modified version of what is said to be his true name, Nostra
Domina, but neither is likely to be his original family title, for both
are Latinised, and both are uncommonly close to Notre Dame (Our
Lady, i.e., the Virgin). Other clues are scattered throughout his life
story, which must be read with great care.

By his own admission, he was born of simple people from the
region of Avignon. The first clue comes when he relates that his
Grandfather was named Peyrot, or Pierre; that he was an established
grain dealer; and that he married a Gentile girl named Blanche. This
information, sandwiched as it is between similar less than startling
revelations about his ancestry may arouse little comment, but look
carefully. The term *Grandfather* projects the idea of the Old Man,
Saturn (the conscious mind undergoing the process), and the fact
that his name was Pierre (French for *stone*), will now throw more
than usual significance on the statement that he was a *grain dealer*.
Outwardly a trivial piece of information, we must compare this with
the many instances where Isis, the Virgin, has been depicted holding
an ear of wheat, or corn – the symbol of meditation.

The girl that he married was described as a Gentile, inferring that
the grandfather was a *Jew*, the biblical interpretation of which we
have already encountered. Furthermore, the girl's name was
Blanche, which in French, means *white*, or 'to *purify*.'

Nostradamus tells us that he was a healer – not particularly
significant a piece of information in itself, until he claims to have
once prescribed an Elixir of Life for a local bishop, a tongue in cheek
statement aimed at the ignorance of the Clergy. He reports that he
became a doctor of medicine, but his remedies were so unorthodox
that his successes made him a number of enemies among the faculty
in which he enrolled. The renowned Paracelsus suffered the same
fate – a strange coincidence, don't you think, that both men were
required to suffer this kind of *persecution*?

Eventually, Nostradamus set off on his *wanderings*, a journey
somewhat reminiscent of that undertaken by the Israelites, for it was
to last most of his life. He describes himself as dressed in a *dark*
scholar's *cap* and gown, a morsel of information in which we may see
a reference to the Phrygian Cap of the initiate underlying the surface
innocuity.

In 1538, so we are told, he was accused of heresy due to a chance
remark made some years beforehand. To a workman casting a
bronze statue of the Virgin, Nostradamus commented that 'devils were

being made'. The Church demanded that he present himself in Toulouse and explain the remark, but the prophet immediately set out on his wanderings again, avoiding any contact with the Catholic hierarchy for the next six years.

Perhaps at this stage of our enlightenment about the Hermetic symbolism, the inner meaning of the tale will be easy to appreciate. The conscious mind, the emblem of which is copper or brass, is to be seen in the 'statue of the Virgin', and therefore it is no wonder that Nostradamus called it a 'devil'. There is no way in which this incident can be confirmed as a real event, but in view of its inner meaning, it is likely to be just another Hermetic fable.

By the 1550s, Nostradamus writes that he had ceased practising medicine and had settled in Salon to concentrate on his prophetic writings. He *converted the top room of his house* into a study where he worked *late at night* with his occult books. He mentions that he burned a lot of books, once he had finished with them, a statement which later scholars have great difficulty in bringing themselves to believe. They were intuitively right, for no such desecration took place. Nostradamus was in fact making an oblique reference to that much repeated piece of alchemical advice;

burn your books and whiten your latten.

No; there is no doubt that Nostradamus was a Rosicrucian initiate. It is simply a matter of reading the hidden meaning of his own words. You must not forget that he was the master of the occult word, as his predictive verses ably testify.

Jacob Boehme

Up until the end of the 16th century, knowledge of the Hermetic Art was considered to be a divine secret in the keeping of God alone, and only to be revealed to the Neophyte in a vision, or a revelation. But it was known that the masters of the Art did, on certain occasions, pass on the secret by word of mouth to those whom they considered strong enough in character to attempt the task. This attitude began to change after the publication of the works of Jacob Boehme the self-made initiate from the little German town of Gorlitz. Unlike other Hermeticists, Boehme did not conceal the process wholly in allegory, but set down certain dialogues that were an open door to the truth. In his Theosophical Works, which are written for the *true Israelites*, so he says, he expresses the method of the process by way of a dialogue between initiate master and pupil:

Pupil: 'How can I succeed in arriving at the supersensual life in
           which I may see and hear the Supreme?'
Initiate: 'If you can only for a moment enter in thought into the
           formless where no creature resides, you will hear the
           voice of the Supreme.'
Pupil: 'Is this far, or near?'
Initiate: 'It is in yourself, and if you can command only for one
           hour the silence of your desires, you will hear the inex-
           pressible words of the Supreme. If your own will and
           self are silent in you, the perception of the Eternal will
           manifest through you. Your own hearing, desiring and
           seeing prevents you from seeing and hearing the
           Supreme.'

The 'supreme', is of course, the Universal Mind. The desires
which must be suppressed are those of the conscious mind, the
continuous thoughts – and it may be of interest at this juncture to
compare the above answer with Matthew 26; 36. Jesus leads his
disciples to a place called Gethsemene, where he stops to pray.
Gethsemene as we know, is a garden (the inner mind) and finding
Jesus praying in it, we become aware that he is in the act of
meditation. But as he prays, his disciples fall asleep, and Jesus asks
Peter (the conscious mind);

. . . What, could ye not *watch with me one hour?*

(Matt. 26; 40)

Having seen their secret so openly expressed, the Hermetic
Fraternity despaired of keeping it to themselves any longer. And yet,
as history shows, so few took advantage of this valuable key.

Jacob Boehme did inject a certain amount of allegory into his text,
especially in respect of his background and origins, which no doubt
he preferred to keep to himself. Of his early introduction to the
Hermetic Art, he is said to have passed into a hypnotic trance one
day, by accidentally *fixing his eye* on a *burnished pewter dish* that was
reflecting the sun. Another revealing tale, and one that will have
familiar overtones, tells how a youthful Boehme went into a *cave* in a
rock called Land's *Crown*, where he discovered a *large wooden vessel*
full of money. He *drew back* from it, *as if it were evil.* Subsequently, he
told his companions about the experience, but although they visited
the spot many a time afterwards, in search of the *concealed treasure*,
they could not even find the cavern at the place in question.

CHAPTER ELEVEN

Magic

If the Church stands guilty of blind obeisance to the literal word of the Scriptures, no less misguided are those who promote a similar misinterpretation of the Grimoires, the so-called Books of Magic Spells. As a scientifically orientated culture, we have developed astounding medical techniques to prolong life, and equally astounding weapons with which to annihilate it; placed a man on the Moon, and sent space laboratories to the very edge of the solar system. Yet our booksellers still enjoy a brisk trade in volumes purporting to explain the reality of the wand-waving magician, with all the accompanying nonsense concerning the use of signs and pentacles, talismans and incantations. It is regrettable that this welter of misinformation has been allowed to prey on the imagination of the gullible to the point where some have actually attempted to put it into practice. At the least, they have made fools of themselves, at the worst, they run the risk of psychological contamination of themselves and others.

Because of the strength of such superstition, not a few have been ready to believe that they can be possessed by 'demons', while an egotistical elite have acted out the incantations on the assumption that they will be endowed with supernormal, occult powers, for good or for evil, as they see fit. Ironically, the powers they seek are fully described within the texts they work from – but in a code which, for all their exhortations, they are unable to read. To show how the reality is hidden behind the rigmarole, I consult one of the foremost 'magical' books, the Key of Solomon the King.

The 'Clavicula Salomonis' is available in a number of languages and is widely accepted to be of considerable antiquity, although its true origin remains unknown. The British Museum holds seven versions of it in manuscript form, the oldest being dated about the end of the 16th century. But it is without doubt a copy of a copy, and the Grimoire in its original form is likely to have come into existence in the early centuries A.D. Traditionally, the Key is attributed to the legendary King Solomon on account of his great wisdom, but it is an attribution that has no basis in fact. We have already discovered that the biblical King Solomon was a mythical character conceived to personify the Hermetic initiate, and this alone should prepare us to accept the Grimoires in the same light. Should the reader be curious enough to wish for a sight of the text himself, there is no need to make the journey to the British Museum, for a composite volume of all seven manuscripts is still in print. Compiled by MacGregor Mathers, at one time head of the Order of the Golden Dawn, one of Britain's most influential magical groups, its contents lay out in entirety the process of summoning up invisible spirits. It details the exhaustive complexity of the mediaeval rituals, the correct time and place, the prayers, the fastings, the drawing of circles and pentacles, and the use of the various magical weapons such as the lance, the wand, the sword and the staff. Within the pages can be found complete the long and impassioned incantations with which the magician concentrates his inner resources in the hope of calling down the invisible but all-creative power.

The plain and simple truth is that should a person devote enough obsessional fervour to the performance of the ritualistic task, there is undoubtedly a likelihood of him succeeding in inducing the appearance of spirits or demons by means of self-delusion and hallucination, according to the strength of his imagination. He would, however, have no power to influence anyone other than himself – and that most probably to his detriment.

For true insight on this matter, let me quote the words of the Rosicrucian initiate, Paracelsus;

> The exercise of true magic does not require any ceremonies or conjurations, or the making of circles and signs; it requires neither benedictions nor maledictions in words, neither verbal blessings nor curses.

We should also mark the words of Alice A. Bailey, in her A TREATISE ON COSMIC FIRE:

> . . . no man is a magician, or worker in white magic until the third eye is opened, or in the process of opening . . .

The 'third eye' is the Hindu term for the transmission of consciousness to the Universal Mind. It is only when this transmission has been successfully accomplished that man's mind attains certain powers.

In the Key of Solomon, therefore, we need to seek out the clues to the real art of magic, the Hermetic process. And as with all other texts that we have scrutinised, it requires us to ignore the literal meaning. In the introduction, which is set out as if the great King Solomon is addressing his son, Roboam, we are told that on a certain *night*, Solomon lay down and prayed (meditated) for wisdom and when he began to *close his eyes* (shut off his outward thoughts), an *angel appeared* (revelation). When Solomon understood the words of the angel, he knew that the *knowledge of all things was in himself*. He therefore composed the Key and preserved the secret in it.

Solomon commanded that his son should fashion an ivory (white) casket in which the Key should be hidden (compare this with the casket of Osiris, the ark of Moses in the bulrushes, etc). This was duly carried out. In a later period a certain sect of Babylonian philosophers came to the sepulchre wherein the casket rested and opened it but none of them could understand the Key on account of its obscure text (surely the most outright clue to the fact that the Key should not be read literally?). One man, however, plainly distressed at the lack of ability to decipher the hidden message, waited until the others had retired (he set himself apart from the rest – thought on different lines) and then *prayed fervently* (meditated for a long time) to be allowed access to the secret. At the height of his prayer, an angel appeared and charged him to keep the secret to himself. The man promised and the angel disappeared – and when the man looked again at the text of the Key, he suddenly saw and recognised the true wisdom concealed therein.

In chapter 1, Book 1, a short statement tells us that if we wish to acquire magical knowledge, it is necessary to have prepared the order of hours and days, and of the position of the *Moon, without the operation of which, nothing can be effected*. If this is done with *diligence*, an effect will be attained. Concealed in this statement is the fact that *reflection* will produce the required result.

Chapter 2 contains a long and meaningless catalogue of the times of the day which are good for specific purposes. The one piece of real information appears in the last paragraph, which tells the reader that nothing can be done without a *circle* being prepared. The classical misinterpretation of this advice needs no further elaboration from me. In reality, the making of the circle means that the outward attention must be reversed, sent back to the centre of the mind from where it came. This is the inward concentrative reflection that will produce the astral body. The circle symbol has been utilised in countless texts, many of which will be familiar – the circular walls round Plato's Poseidon, or the walls round the biblical Jericho, for example; the spinning wheel of the Alchemists, the folk tales and of the Hindus; even the great circular windows of the Gothic cathedrals.

Hardly anyone spoke openly about the act of thought reversal, and even Paracelsus, who was a great deal more forthcoming than his brother Rosicrucians, never described it in a totally straight-forward manner. In his ARCHIDOXES OF MAGIC, for example, he refers to it thus:

> Whosoever desires to have the tincture of metals (to accomplish the process) ought to take the Philosopher's Mercury (the outward attention) and let him cast the same into its own ends, into quick Mercury, from whence it proceedeth.

Returning to the text of the Key, we may find many similar references to the circle. In chapter 14, for instance, we are told how to render ourselves master of a treasure possessed by the spirits. Of the manner by which this may be accomplished, we are instructed to *describe a circle with the sword of the magical art*, at a time when the *Moon* is in the sign of the *Lion*. Disregarding the literal intent of this direction, we can see that in these few words lie hidden the bare bones of the Hermetic process, the *sword* being the power of con-centration necessary. It is made to describe a *circle*, an act which is associated with the *Moon* (reflection) and the *Lion* (Universal Mind). The rest of this particular text, in which we are asked to procure a lamp, the oil of which should be mingled with the fat of a man who has died in July, and secret characters written in blood on the skin of a newly slain goat, is just so much fanciful rubbish intended to throw the undiscerning off the track.

The balance of the book must be examined in the same light – in search of the same hidden references. They are to be found, but I think it unnecessary to detail them here, having adequately proved the point.

Folk Lore

Similar misconstruction has added to the superstition attached to folk lore tales and the many weird legends connected to places and animals. The significance associated with the cat by the ancient Egyptians was carried over to the Middle Ages, where the animal was usually coupled with warlocks and witches as their 'familiar'. In folk lore, the cat is invariably said to be *black*, and we are now aware of the reason for the colour, but superstition has endowed the hapless feline with all kinds of Satanic powers – not the least because of its supremely independent mien and nocturnal habits.

The toad is another unnecessarily maligned animal, being de-picted as closely linked with the Devil and therefore evil incarnate. This very legend should alert us to the possibility of the Hermetic theme being involved, for we are now appraised of the fact that the

Devil is the conscious mind of Man. We therefore apply the Hermetic key in order to unlock the folk fantasy of the unfortunate toad.

There is a legend that the toad, when used as an ingredient in the evil concoctions brewed by mediaeval witches, would confer the power of flight. The explanation of this story is simplicity itself and is derived from the fact that the toad excretes a poison through its skin glands to repel attackers. These poisons are hallucinogenic, and are thus able to free the astral self, just as the mushroom drug can, in a temporary but uncontrolled 'flight' according to the imagination of those who imbibe. Another legend that has a more positively Hermetic basis is the 12th century belief that toads carried a precious gemstone within their heads, like a pearl in an oyster shell. The toad, being *black and ugly*, is a symbol of the first stage of the process for the Hermetic story teller. So is the fact that it ejects poison, for this means *death* to the assailant. And if the toad is emblematic of the Hermetic task, it follows that the *gemstone* must be merely a symbol of the end result, and not real fact. Said to exist within the toad's *skull*, or *head* (mind), this 'gemstone' is the same as the 'pearl of great price' in the Bible, or the Philosopher's Stone, about which so much has been written and for which so many have unsuccessfully searched.

Clovis, the king of the Franks at the end of the 5th century, is said to have held pagan beliefs, carrying a banner on which were emblazoned *three toads*. There exists a legend that while he was on his way to fight the Visigoths at Toulouse, he saw a vision in the sky, a representation of his own banner. *As he watched*, the three toads changed to *three lilies* – and thus was born the oriflame of France, the fleur-de-lis. These lilies represent the Blessed Virgin – and thus can the Hermetic principle be traced back to the lowly toad.

An interesting example of the way in which the Hermetic message seems to survive to be presented in the most unexpected places, can be found in the folk lore of the Isle of Man. In particular, I will recount one such legend attached to Rushen Castle, the fort at the southern end of the island.

Between the years 1720 and 1730, George Waldron, an English Government agent sent to thwart the activities of the smugglers, was resident on the island. He didn't succeed in his official mission, but he did find time to develop a consuming interest in Manx folk lore, collecting a wide variety of anecdotes and eventually publishing them in his DESCRIPTION OF THE ISLE OF MAN. The legend of Rushen Castle tells how the fortress was first inhabited by fairies and then by giants, who held it until they were cast out by the magic

spells of the great wizard, Merlin. It was strongly rumoured that
certain underground chambers existed, of exceeding magnificence,
but entirely secret. In the past, several brave souls had ventured
down to explore the subterranean passages, but none had ever
returned to tell of their experience.

Because of the fairy-tale quality of the tale, commentators have
laughingly dismissed it, pointing to the gullibility of Waldron for
printing it. It is an attitude that is understandable in the circumstances. Rushen Castle, unlike many other early fortresses, is
positioned on low ground, close to the sea shore. There are a couple
of underground rooms, not secret, but open to public inspection,
and it is common knowledge that unusually high tides will fill them
with two or three feet of water. The likelihood of there being deeper,
more elaborate chambers, therefore, is improbable, and it must be
concluded that the tale is no more than a fable – but to what end?

Waldron goes on to tell of one man who, determined to find for
himself what mysteries lay beneath the castle, gained permission to
make the descent. Providing himself with a 'clue of packthread' to
help him find his way back, he entered the secret apartment. Travel-
ling through rough, winding passages and dark caverns, he eventually came to a lighted house where a servant led him through and
sent him on his way:

> He then walked a considerable way, and at last beheld another
> house, more magnificent than the first; and the windows being all
> open, discovered innumerable lamps burning within every room.
> Here, also, he designed to knock, but he had the curiosity to step
> on a little bank which commanded a low parlour; on looking in,
> he beheld a vast table in the middle of the room, of black marble,
> and on it, extended at full length, a man, or rather, monster; for
> by his account, he could not have been less than fourteen feet long
> and ten or eleven round the body. This prodigious fabrick lay as if
> sleeping with his head on a book and a sword by him, of a size
> answerable to the hand which 'tis supposed made use of it.

The traveller prudently gave up all attempt at an entry and made
his way back. During the return journey, he met the servant once
more, who told him that if he had knocked on the second door, he
would 'have seen company enough', but that he would never have
returned to daylight.

Most readers will uncompromisingly categorise this as a fairy tale,
but those who are familiar with the Hermetic symbolism will
recognise yet another projection of the theme. The details are
comparable to better known allegories; the *journey* into the *under-*

world; the innumerable burning lamps (reminiscent of the Festival of Lamps, a segment of the Egyptian Mystery rites); the 'clue of pack-thread', a duplication of the theme found in Greek mythology where Ariadne uses her Thread to find her way through the *Labyrinth* (the inner mind). There is a great table made of *black stone*, on which lies a *sleeping giant* (a potential initiate). His *head* lies on a *book not yet opened* (Rosicrucian Book of Knowledge – i.e., knowledge of the process) and there is a *sword* by his side (the 'sword' of reflective power).

As we marvel at the way in which this tale has survived, we must wonder if Waldron was aware of its special significance. There is an interesting rider to the story. Further on in his quaint volume, now held in the library at Douglas, the author writes;

> I have been shown a hole in the side of the rock near Kirk Maroan (now spelt 'Marown') Mountain which, they say, was formerly the habitation of one who has chosen to *mortify the body for the sake of the soul*. . . . There is still to be seen a *hollow* cut in the side of the *rock* with a round *stone* at one end, in the shape of a pillow.

The obvious comparison to Jacob's dream in Genesis 28 can hardly be regarded as coincidental.

Nursery Tales

Just as the Hermetic process is cunningly allegorised within the Papyrus of Ani and the Bible, so it is contained within the plots of familiar nursery tales. We have already encountered an example in the story of the Ugly Duckling, and the hint of Mother Goose's ancestry.

Aladdin's lamp, with its powerful but hidden genie, represents the conscious mind with its unexplored potential. The lamp, remember, led the way to a *cave* filled with a *vast treasure*. The story is contained in a volume of legendary tales called the Arabian Nights' Entertainments, the plots of which are centred around Arabia and which undoubtedly project the Hermetic principle in the usual, concealed fashion. But strangely enough, a cursory examination of the book's history will reveal that Aladdin's tale, although found in the French and English versions, is not present in the Arabian texts, and it leads to the conclusion that the story was created in Europe, possibly France, at sometime during the 17th century. Significantly, France at this time was the centre of Hermetic thought.

Aladdin is widely known today as the plot for a Pantomime production, and it is to this art form that we next turn to uncover more Hermetic links. The history of Pantomime can be traced all the way back to ancient Egypt, where the basic idea was present in the dramas, or mystery plays, enacted in honour of the 'gods'. The very name means that it is a work of dumb show, and was later presented as such by Roman mimers.

In the 17th century, French pantomimes traditionally ended in a transformation scene called a Harlequinade. The principal character, the Harlequin, was flamboyantly dressed as a Fool, carrying a visor and a magic wand, an entity which can be immediately linked to the Fool and the Magician of the Tarot. His scene of dramatic transformation was originally intended to portray the transformation which can take place in Man's mind. Time, however, has gradually eroded this piece of symbolism and Harlequin is no longer part of the modern Pantomime, except possibly in a revamped form, such as Buttons, in Cinderella. That the character was intended to represent man's conscious mind is irrefutable and is corroborated by the fact that, in Old French, his name was Hellequin, and he was regarded as the Devil.

Not all pantomime stories originated in Europe, and some of them have remarkably long histories, considering that they are regarded today only as entertainment for children. Of them all, Cinderella seems to have been the most popular and can be traced back to 855 A.D., the earliest version appearing in a Chinese book of that period. But even then, the tale was described as being from a distant time. The basic plot is to be found in a book called COMPLAYNT OF SCOTLAND (1540), while in Germany, the Brothers Grimm knew the story as 'Aschenputtel' (Cinder-fool), a heroine who had a little *white bird* to magically supply her needs, instead of a fairy godmother. This white bird can be compared to the Dove sent out from the Ark.

The earliest European version of Cinderella was published in Italy, in Basile's PENTAMERONE (1643). Here, the girl is called Zezolla, her domain the kitchen (where there is *heat*, or *fire*) and she is known as La Gatta Cenerentola (the Hearth Cat). The present form of the tale stems from HISTOIRES DU CONTES DU TEMPS PASSE, a volume by Charles Perrault published in France in 1697, and translated into English some thirty odd years later.

The basic message concealed within the various versions is unreservedly Hermetic. The heroine, a beautiful young girl, is kept in a repressed state, although she is really of *noble* birth, and as such she represents the hidden power of the subconscious. She is kept in the kitchen (heat), a lowly position, where one would *least expect to find such beauty*, by the *ugly* sisters, who symbolise the conscious mind not yet initiated (as the Ugly Duckling does). The Prince is made aware of her because Cinderella has been aided by supernatural powers (the fairy godmother) to attend the ball (the aspiring initiate has experienced the revelation which shows him how to carry out the process). He embarks on a *quest* to find out whose foot will fit the slipper (he embarks on the process – compare this analogy with Osiris in the casket), during which he is almost thwarted by the actions of Dandini, whom he thought to be his friend (the forces of the conscious mind rebel against the discipline of the process, but are finally overcome). After the Prince's quest is over, he and the heroine live *happily* (initiated) ever after (the process is complete).

Other well known nursery tales will, upon comparison with the above, be found to contain the same message. Jack and the Beanstalk compares favourably with the older legends like Jacob's Ladder, or the Asiatic Bo-Tree of Buddha which, on being planted, sprang up to the sky – and even the Prose Edda's mighty Ash Tree, Yggsdrasill, which stretched up to heaven. The printed publication of the tale is comparatively recent, however, first appearing in THE HISTORY OF JACK AND THE BEANSTALK, by Benjamin Tabart, in 1807.

A tale in which the Hermetic theme is more cleverly stated is Puss in Boots, due mainly to the special adjustments made to the plot by those who contrived the modern version. Once again we have to thank Charles Perrault for this, although the basic story was not an invention of his time, for it is found in Basile's PENTAMERONE and in Straparola's PIACEVOLE NOTTI (1553). But prior to 1697, the time of the Perrault version, the cat in the plot was always depicted without the boots, and it is the strange, apparently motiveless addition of the footwear that has so intrigued scholars. There appears to be no reason at all for them, and none is given. Nor is the theme developed in any way, except in Perrault's text, where there is a single, rather facetious reference to the fact that the cat trod the tiles with some danger, for its *boots were an impediment while in its natural, rooftop habitat.*

To get to the bottom of this mystery we must first recall the traditional Hermetic signficance of the cat as a symbol of either the conscious mind (Isis) or the Universal Mind (Maau). Next we apply the phonetic cabala, the word play so beloved of the initiate writers, to the problem of the 'boots'. Puss in Boots, in French, is 'Le Chat Botte' (pronounced 'sha-bo'), a phrase which has its equivalent sound in Sabot ('sa-bo'). The Sabot, in modern French, means merely a clog, or hoof, but in the 18th century, it was also the name of the child's *Humming Top* – as the text of Fulcanelli's LE

MYSTERE DES CATHEDRALES will confirm. With its motion, the spinning top ideally portrays the constant and noisy motion of the conscious mind. As the Humming Top is whipped into motion, so the conscious mind must be *flailed* into *silence* – and thus, by the devious route of the phonetic cabala, the 'boots' are an emblem of the conscious mind. In this nursery tale, the cat is representative of the subconscious, the Universal Mind, until he wears the boots, and then he becomes uninitiated Man. This is why it is made clear in that one facetious sentence that the cat was in danger while wearing them. The conscious mind, with its constant activity, is an 'impediment' to the would-be initiate in his efforts to become one with the Universal Mind.

In case it may be thought that this explanation is too involved to be credible, I must point out that the symbolism of the 'boots' occurs elsewhere, but generally remains unrecognised. As an example, we might look at the early life of certain initiates, as it is related for us to believe unquestioningly. Jacob Boehme was reputed to be a poor *cobbler*, or *shoemaker*, a statement that was not meant to be taken literally, but which held a special significance for a brother initiate – in the same way that Jesus was said to be a *carpenter*.

An alternative title for Puss in Boots was 'The Master Cat' – 'Le Maistre Chat' in Old French. Phonetically, this is rendered 'Me-troh-sha', and we might note the similarity to 'Me-tree-zay', which means to subdue, control, or to *master* (the mind).

The theme of the plot conveys the message that certain persons, generally those in a lowly or underprivileged state, will come into *good fortune* through the works of a cat. The cat generally carries out *three* operations in order to achieve the well-being of his master.

The same idea prevails in the story of Dick Whittington, who was *three* times Lord Mayor of London, due only to the good works of his cat. Factual history, while confirming that Whittington did take office as Lord Mayor at least once, nowhere mentions his famous cat. As for the statue that exists to honour the mythical animal, it was erected long after the tale had gained its widespread popularity. Add to this the fact that the cat is always said to be *black*, and we can safely assume that the whole pleasant little scenario was concocted by an initiate who made use of the real Whittington's basic history.

The Tales of Mother Goose, a book which originated in France, has a title which will yield a hidden meaning if the phonetic cabala is applied. In French, 'Mother Goose' is 'Mere l'Oye'. By dropping the last 'e' and replacing the 'y' with an 'r' (quite permissible in the rules of word play because the two sounds are almost identical), it becomes 'Mere l'Or', which means 'Mother of Gold' – a reference to the *gold* of the astral body and the *mother* of inner reflection. This interpretation is supported in the story because the Goose is made to lay the *Golden Eggs* (compare with the Golden Apples of Hercules). The magic *Goose*, the central character of the tale, is a symbol which all initiates will immediately recognise, owing to its illustrious, Egyptian ancestry.

Tradition and Myth

To attempt a comprehensive analysis of mythology peculiar to Britain would be futile, as most of it would be found to have its roots in the Hermetic principle already described, but I will conclude this chapter by remarking on a few of the most popular.

The holiday at Easter is intended to celebrate the Ascension of Jesus Christ and relates to a date that has been carefully worked out by scholars of the past – well after the supposed event. If you can bring yourself to agree that the Ascension story is not factual, then this Spring holiday can be seen in its true light, a pagan festival to honour the sign of Aries on the 21st March, the beginning of the yearly, zodiacal cycle. The significance accorded the first sign of the zodiac has nothing to do with either the position of the stars, or the changing of the seasons, but rests solely with the Hermetic meaning of the Ram as I have previously explained. Aries signifies the head (the mind), as well as the commencement of the yearly cycle, and therefore the basic import of the Easter festival is, 'the process has been started' – surely something to celebrate!

In spite of the manipulation of 'facts' by the early adherents to the Catholic ideal, tradition has seen to it that the truth has remained in plain view for all those who wish to read it. The Easter Egg, for example, is a piece of Hermetic symbolism that can be traced back as far as the early Chinese Dynasties, and has much the same explanation behind it as that of the Egyptian scarab beetle. We have already seen that its *father*, the cock, always signals the approaching *sunrise*. The hen (the *mother* – Mary), by application of a gentle but sustained heat (meditation) will hatch out the egg (give birth to new life – the astral body).

The Hot Cross Bun too, is not without its special meaning. A traditional delicacy in the form of a little cake was the custom among the Egyptians, Greeks and Romans as part of their Mystery celebrations, one such becoming known as the Epiphany Cake. Invariably, it was in the form of a little pastry, sometimes enclosing a bean, a custom that endured into the France of the Middle Ages. The cake represented the conscious mind, while the bean was the emblem of the hidden subconscious, an interpretation which can be corroborated by use of the French cabala. In this language, the word 'galette' (cake) is very similar to 'galet' (pebble, or *stone*).

In Britain, the cake evolved into the Hot Cross Bun, but the inner meaning remains. The word 'bun' is derived from the older 'boun', meaning Oxen, and was used in relation to the delicacy because they were at first marked with the outline of horns. This Ox (or Bull of Taurus) had to be *roasted*, or *cooked* before the delicacy was ready for consumption. The Bun was also *circular* in shape, and the *cross*, which was introduced later, is an emblem that has already been fully explained.

Dragon myths are almost commonplace and a great deal of romanticism has lately been employed in order to explain them. More especially I refer to those tales about sacred sites which are reputed to possess a mysterious and hidden energy called the Dragon Force. Intense speculation and sporadic research forays have so far failed to uncover any visible, or measurable sign of anything but natural phenomena of a magnitude far below that which would register on a physical body and I would therefore humbly remind all such enthusiasts that the sources from which their Dragon myths have been culled may well have been subject to the influence of the Hermetic initiate. The earth does conceal a mysterious force which will harmonise with heaven – the *earth* of the conscious mind.

In post Christian times, the myths of Dragon slaying, stemming directly from the Book of Revelation, were allegories inspired by the Hermetic theme. The combat in which the *dragon* of the conscious mind is killed, is the same age old battle in which Hercules and Jason engaged, the symbol of the fire-breathing monster superceding that of the Egyptian *crocodile* and the Old Testament *Serpent*.

To interpret but one of many Dragon myths, we may refer to the church of St. Michael, at Trull, in Devon. A long held tradition relates that a *dragon* was *killed* on nearby Castlemen's Hill (a *mount*). To commemorate the event, a window on the south side of the church shows *three saints*, each *slaying a dragon* (the three stages of the process).

Just as the great earthwork figures at Glastonbury hold the secret of the Hermetic process, so do other monuments of ancient date. The great conglomeration of standing stones at Avebury, in Wiltshire, once assumed the shape of a gigantic *serpent* weaving its body through the main *circle,* as early descriptions testify. While most of the stones belonging to the great circle remain, those of the serpent's body have been largely scattered and broken up, but this does not preclude us from interpreting the true meaning of this impressive, Neolithic 'church'. At the head of the serpent, at the southern end of the Kennet avenue of stones, there used to be a circular enclosure, the purpose of which cannot at this length of time be properly defined, although it has been suggested that a dolmen was placed there. We may possibly find the true answer by comparing a similar figure on the other side of the Atlantic, the Serpent Mound of Ohio. There, one of the great earthworks has been constructed in the form of a great *serpent* just about to devour an *egg*. In respect of the egg's significance, just discussed, it can easily be realised that the Serpent, the pre-Christian dragon, personifies the evil force that will prevent the egg of the astral body from hatching out because he is about to devour it. The same lore may be applied to the Avebury serpent, a monument erected in honour of the Hermetic principle by the same people who were responsible for the Glastonbury earthworks. This is the 'secret wisdom' of tradition, attached to all such monuments.

Slightly later in date, but still of the pre-Christian period, is the well-known hill figure, the Cerne Abbas Giant. Paying no regard to the imaginative superstitions attached to the figure, historical research will show that he is Hercules of early Roman times. Recent archaeological activity has revealed that the mysterious erasures under, and attached to, the left arm, were the outlines of a *lion's skin*, as portrayed on early Roman coins. This discovery, coupled with the figure's strength and display of generative potential, shows that he is not, as many have suggested, a sign of physical fertility, but an emblem of the greatest power of all, the subconscious, the Universal Mind. The *Giant*, then, who has *slain the lion*, is the initiate who has accomplished the process.

CHAPTER TWELVE

'Buried Treasure'

In the very popular FAIRY MYTHOLOGY, by Keightley (1850), the author mentions a story of some interest to us, relating to the great array of Neolithic standing stones at Carnac, in Brittany. He culled his information from a volume called MONUMENS CELTIQUE, by Monsieur de Cambry, a writer of the early 1800s.

In discussing the folk tales inevitably associated with the monument, de Cambry states that an old sailor told him that one of the standing stones covered an immense treasure, and that the rest had been set up the better to conceal it. He added that a calculation, the key to which would be found in the Tower of London, would alone indicate the spot where the treasure lay.

It is apparent that if M. de Cambry was not an initiate himself, he must have received the story from one who possessed the necessary knowledge to concoct the myth in such a fashion. We interpret it thus.

The story was told to him by an old *sailor*. This statement is the first clue indicating a Hermetic basis to the yarn, for while it is possible that a seafaring man would have knowledge about the monument, it is most unlikely that a thousand odd standing stones would have been set up just to conceal a single one. Wiser now to the methods employed by the initiate, we relate the 'old sailor' to Jason, that sailor of old, who embarked on the quest for the Golden Fleece. The 'immense treasure' is the Golden Fleece itself, the transmission of consciousness. This 'treasure' lies buried beneath the *stone*, or *pillar* of the conscious mind, while the reference to the Tower of London as the holder of the key is a clever deviation from the usual run of themes and can be linked with the *Tower* of the Tarot – that is, the conscious mind. The 'calculation' is representative of the mental effort required to complete the process.

There exists a number of such myths relating to a treasure concealed beneath Neolithic standing stones, with the result that not a few have been uprooted in a futile search for a non-existent cache. But these stories are insignificant compared to certain other, nationally known sagas which have exerted a profound influence.

The Relatorio

In 1841, Brazilian historian and archivist, Senhor Lagos, was poking about in the musty corners of the old National Library in Rio de Janeiro when he chanced upon a document addressed to one Dom Luis Peregrino de Carvalho Menezes de Athayde, a personage who had been the Viceroy of Rio some sixty years previously. As the addressee had long since been deceased, Senhor Lagos decided to open the document and examine the contents. With great care, he loosened the binding and unrolled the ten sheets of faded parchment, noticing as he did so that it had been damaged in places by the Copim, a small South American insect with a voracious appetite for paper.

Then he began to read:

'Historical relation of a hidden and great city of ancient date, without inhabitants, that was discovered in the year 1753. In America. . . (here the document has lines missing due to the Copim). . . in the interior. . . adjoining the. . . Master of Cam . . . and his followers, having for ten years journeyed in the desert country in the hope of discovering the famous silver mines of the great explorer Moribeca, which through the evil intentions of a certain governor, were lost – and to deprive him of this glory, he was imprisoned in Bahia till death, and so they remained undiscovered.

This letter reached Rio de Janeiro in the beginning of the year 1754.

After long and troublesome wanderings, incited by the insatiable greed for gold and almost lost for many years in the vast interior, we discovered a cordillera of mountains so high that they seemed to touch the ethereal regions, and serve as a throne for the Wind and Stars. Their glittering aspect from afar, excited our wonder and admiration, especially when the sun was shining, turning to fires the crystals of which the rocks were composed. The view was so beautiful that none could take their eyes from the reflections. It began to rain before we came near enough to fully appreciate these crystalline marvels, and we saw water cascading over the rock faces, precipitating itself from the heights, looking like snow on which the sun reflected its rays of fire.

Delighted by this pleasing vista . . . shine . . . of the waters and the tranquility . . . of the day or weather, we resolved to investigate this admirable prodigy of Nature. Arriving at the foot of the cordillera, without hindrance of forest or rivers which might have barred our passage, we were disappointed to find no apparent way in which we could ascend into these Alps, or Brazilian Pyrenees. We made camp, intending to retrace our steps on the following day, but one of the negroes who had been sent to gather firewood, chanced on a white deer which he chased. The deer ran into a small canyon between two hills, in which the negro discovered a road, a man made trail, not one made by nature. We were overjoyed at this news and began the ascent. As we climbed we noted that the road had once been paved, but was now littered with broken stones, probably due to some extremely ancient earthquake.

The ascent took us a good three hours, during which we mar-velled at the crystals as they blazed forth in many colours. At the summit we halted. Spread out before our eyes, we saw an open plain – and scenes of even greater interest. About four miles away, we could see a great city of such size that we concluded it to be one of Brazil's capital cities. Intrigued, we descended to the plain, and with the caution demanded of such a situation, sent scouts ahead to investigate, with instructions to look carefully for the smoke of cooking fires, a sure sign of habitation.

We waited two days with growing restlessness, until the scouts returned, but they had been unable to see anyone. We were greatly puzzled at this, and uncertain. Then an Indian in our company volunteered to try to enter the city. He soon returned, frightened, but affirming that he could see no one, nor could he discover any human tracks. At this, the whole body of scouts retraced the Indian's steps and saw that the city was indeed deserted.

At dawn the next day, and well armed, we all moved towards the city, seeing no one to hinder us, nor any other road than that which led directly to the city. We entered under three arches of great height; the middle arch being the greater, while the two at the sides being of lesser height. On the central and largest arch we could make out some letters cut in, but which we could not copy owing to their great height from the ground. Beyond was a street as wide as the three arches, with upper storied houses on either side, whose facades of carved stone were blackened with age . . . inscriptions all open to the day . . . of lesser . . . observing that, by the regularity and symmetry of their construction, it appeared to be one long house; but in reality it was a great many. Some had terraces and all without tiles, the floors being of burnt brick and others of freestone slabs.

With great care and not a little fear, we went into some of the houses, and in none did we find any vestiges of personal goods or furniture which might, by their appearance, give some clue as to the nature of the inhabitants. The houses were all dark inside; there was scarcely any gleam of light and the echoes of our own voices struck fear into us.

Moving on down the broad street, we came upon a well-laid-out plaza, or square, and in the centre, a column of black stone of extraordinary height and size, and upon which was the statue of an ordinary man. This figure had his left hand on his hip, while the right arm was extended, pointing with the forefinger to the north pole. In each corner of the square was an obelisk, or needle, like those of the Romans, but which were now in a damaged state, as if struck by a thunderbolt.

On the right side of the plaza was a superb building, like the principal house of some great lord of the land. At the entrance, there was a great vestibule, but still in awe, only a few of us dared to enter . . . being so numerous and the . . . to form some . . . we found a . . . mass of extraordinary . . . had some difficulty in raising it . . . The bats were extremely numerous, making an astonishing noise as they fluttered in swarms about the faces of our people.

Upon the principal portico of this street we saw a half relief figure carved in the solid stone, representing a beardless youth, naked from the waist up and crowned with laurel. He wore also a girdle and a lower garment. Beneath a shield with this figure, were some characters badly defaced by time, but we made out the following:

$$KU\varphi I\lambda$$

On the left side of the square stood another totally ruined building, but the vestiges remaining showed us that it had been a temple. Most of the facade was still intact and there were some stone naves and some aisles. It occupied much space and on its ruined walls we could see carvings of superior workmanship, with pictures and figures inlaid in stone; also crosses of various sizes, curves and other figures too numerous to describe.

Beyond this building, the greater part of the city lies in complete ruin, some parts buried under masses of earth, or fallen into great crevasses. And in this desolate spot, no vegetation is to be seen, only heaps of stone, some raw, some worked and carved. We concluded . . . because still among . . . of corpses which . . . is part of this unhappy . . . and forsaken, perhaps on account of some earthquake.

In front of the square, there ran a river deep and swift, quite wide and with spacious banks that were pleasing to the eye. Almost straight at this point, the width we judged to be eleven or twelve fathoms, and not cluttered with fallen trees which the floods usually bring. We sounded its depth and found the deepest parts to be from thirteen to sixteen fathoms.

Beyond the opposite bank, the country consisted wholly of a green and flourishing plain, so thick with a variety of flowers, it was as if Nature herself had gone out of her way to create a perfect garden of Flora. There were also lakes covered with wild rice, from which we benefited, and numerous flocks of duck which breed in these fertile plains, they being easy to catch that we had no need of shot.

We journeyed down the river for three days until we came to a cataract of such roaring noise and foaming waters that it could only be compared to the mighty Nile. Below this fall, the river spread out so that it appeared to be a great ocean. It was full of peninsulars covered with green grass, with trees here and there, which makes . . . Here we found . . . for want of it . . . much variety of game . . . many created beings without hunters to hunt and chase them.

On the eastern side of the cataract, we found deep shafts and cuttings, the depths of which we attempted to plumb, but no matter how long our ropes were, we could not touch the bottom. We found certain broken stones, and lying on the ground as if carelessly abandoned, some silver nails, or ingots. We saw one cavern that was covered by an enormous slab of stone upon which were carved the following figures, and which suggest a great mystery;

Over the portico of the temple, we saw besides, the following;

Distant a cannon shot from the abandoned city is a building like a country house, with a frontage of 250 feet. It is approached by a great portico, from which a stairway built with stones of various colours is seen to lead into a large chamber, and from there, fifteen separate chambers, or rooms can be reached, each room with its own connecting door and with its own water spout . . . which water meets . . . in the exterior courtyard . . . colonnades in a . . . squared by art and overhung with the following characters;

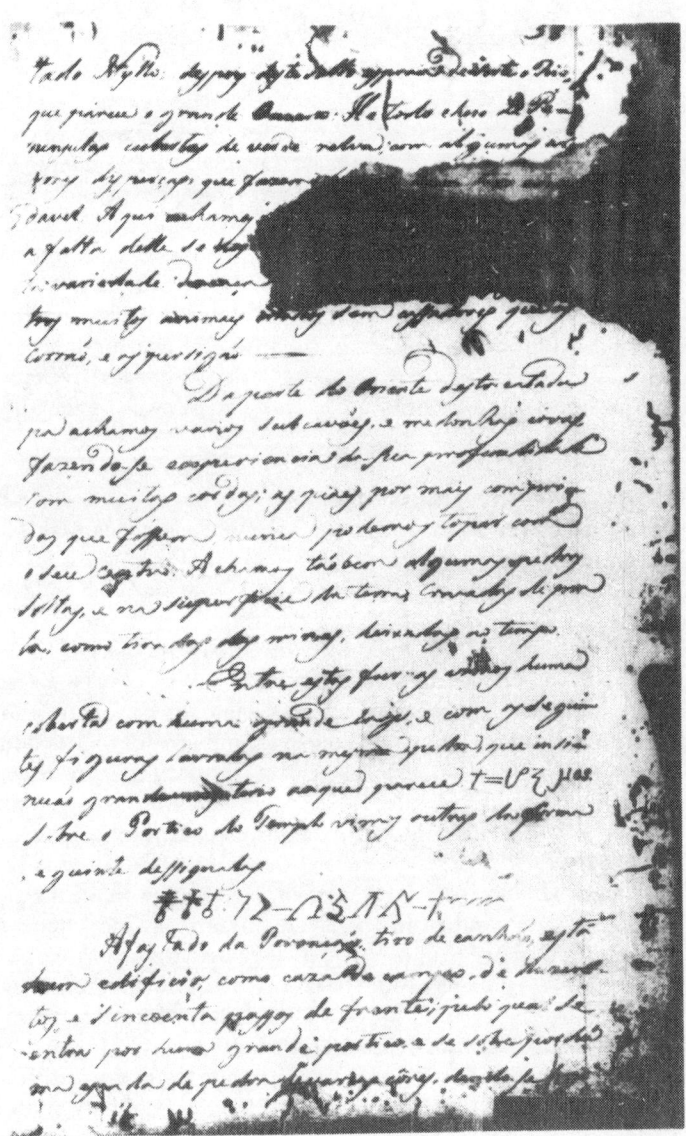

FIGURE 14.   A page of the RELATORIO

Leaving this marvel, we went down to the banks of the river to see if we could find any traces of gold, and we soon saw rich paydirt, promising a great wealth of gold as well as silver. We wondered why the inhabitants had left such a place, for in spite of our zealous searchings we had not met a single person who might tell us of this deplorable marvel of an abandoned city, whose ruins, statues and grandeur attested to its former populousness, wealth and its flourishing in centuries past. Today, it is inhabited only by swallows, bats, rats, and foxes that, fed on the innumerable swarms of hens and geese, have become bigger than a pointer dog. The rats have tails so short that they leap like fleas and do not run or walk as they do in other places.

From this spot, a companion, in the company of others, left us and after nine days hard march, sighted at the mouth of a large bay formed by a river, a canoe carrying two white persons with loose black hair and dressed like Europeans . . . a shot as a signal, in order to . . . for they escaped . . . They had . . . shaggy and wild . . . and their hair is plaited and . . .

One of our company, Joao Antonio, found in the ruins of a house, a piece of gold money, round and larger than our pieces of 6,400 reis. On one side was the image of a youth kneeling; on the other, a bow, a crown and an arrow; of which coins we doubted not to have found many in the abandoned city because if it had been destroyed by an earthquake, the people would not have had time to put their treasure in a safe place. But it would require a powerful arm to turn over the ruins, as we saw.

This news I send to your Excellency from the interior of the province of Bahia and from the rivers Paraguassu and Unna, and assuring you that we will not impart it to any person as we think whole towns and villages would be empty (as the inhabitants went in search). But I have brought your Excellency the news of these mines, mindful of the much that I owe you.

Supposing that from our band, one has gone forth with a different idea. He, with great harm to your Excellency, could abandon his poverty and come to use these things for his own benefit and bribe that Indian. So as to spoil his purpose and lead your Excellency to these great treasures . . . would find in the entrances . . . flagstones . . .

(The manuscript concluded with the following characters;)

ONE
TWO
THREE
FOUR
FIVE
SIX
SEVEN
EIGHT
NINE

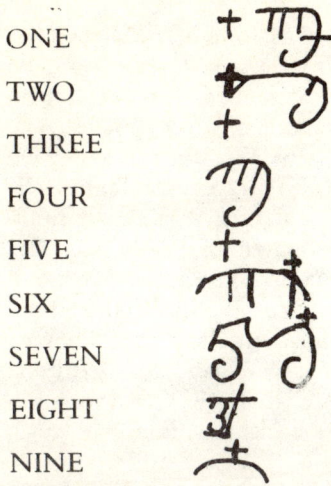

Not unnaturally, the discovery of this document generated intense speculation as to its veracity, and to the whereabouts of the lost city. The tale seemed genuine, for a perusal of surviving records verified that there had existed a man named Moribeca, or Murebecca; there are various spellings.

The history attached to the Relatorio, as the document is now called, began in 1516, when a Portuguese mariner was shipwrecked on the wild coast of Bahia at the site of the present day city of Salvador. Marooned, he eventually married an Indian girl named Paraguassu and established the first settlement there. Other Portuguese and Spanish explorers found him and moved in, one of whom married the sister of Paraguassu. From this marriage was born Melchoir Dias Moreya, the man later known to the Indians as the Moribeca. They were able to show him ancient mine workings located in the interior, pits which still contained great quantities of ore, and with the help of Indian labour, Moribeca worked until he had acquired a fortune in gold, silver and precious stones, thus becoming the envy of incoming colonists.

Yet Moribeca was not a happy man, for he was conscious of his half-caste origin, and that he lacked the pedigree of the Spanish and Portuguese nobles who frequently graced his table. He sought to rectify this sense of inferiority by offering the location of his rich mines in exchange for a title of nobility to be conferred on him by the Court of Portugal. The authorities in Lisbon noted this offer and, in

1591, sent out a new Governor to the fast growing state of Bahia, one Dom Francisco de Souza.

De Souza had been promised the title of Marquis of the Mines if he could persuade Moribeca to reveal their location. Moribeca himself would be allowed to assume the position of Administrator, a title which had no nobility attached to it. When this proposition was put to him, Moribeca angrily refused. De Souza's answer was to throw him in prison until such time as he came to his senses and imparted the location of the mines. But Moribeca was made of sterner stuff than the Portuguese had imagined. Although an elderly man, he remained silent, eventually to die without gaining his freedom. Thus, in 1622, the secret died with him. The only others who knew where the mines lay were the Indians, and it was already well known that no Indian could be made to speak if he didn't want to, regardless of the cruel torture that the conquerors of the New World were so quick to use. From that time on, the ancient workings became known as the Lost Mines of the Moribeca.

There are variations to this account and at this distance in time, it is clearly impossible to say how much of it rested in fact. All I ask is that you recall all the symbolism that you have had explained so far – and then read the account again, this time looking for the same kind of clues. You will find a number of them.

The Relatorio itself is more important. When the news of the document's discovery was circulated, a steady stream of adventurers presented themselves in Rio to read it before setting out to find the lost city and the mines attached to it. One of the first was a canon of the Theological college in Bahia, Senhor Conego Benigno Jose de Carvalho e Cunha. From the clues given in the text, the names of the rivers and the description of the quartz mountains, he concluded that the city lay one hundred miles or so inland from Bahia city, in a range of hills known as the Serra do Cincora, and thereupon set out to track it down. Throughout 1842, the luckless priest wandered about in the inhospitable interior, questioning farmers and cattlemen for some hint of the deserted ruins. Eventually, he fell victim to a severe fever, which laid him low in a remote estancia for six months. On recovering – weak, and without funds – he was forced to abandon the search, although certain travellers had obligingly hinted at the existence of a city somewhere nearby, they weren't quite sure where. Benigno's letters, with his pathetic plea for more Government assistance, were put with the Relatorio and contained in a collection of similar documents, the whole being known as the Revista Trimensal.

It was to see this collection that the noted English explorer, Sir

Richard Burton, came to Rio in 1865. He studied the Relatorio and
had this to say in his EXPLORATION OF THE HIGHLANDS OF
BRAZIL (1868).

> The reader will find in the appendix a translation of this curious
> document. Its allusions to the Great Rapids of Paulo Affonso are
> evident, but the tale of the deserted city is popularly supposed to
> be a romance.

Sir Richard also disclosed that, at the area of Paulo Affonso falls,
some 200 miles up river from the mouth of the Sao Francisco, a range
of mountains there used to be named after the central figure in the
Relatorio – the Serra da Moribeca.

In 1920, the legendary Lieut. Col Fawcett, a British army sur-
veyor turned explorer, arrived in Rio to examine the documents for
himself. He had already formulated a theory that the highland
plateau of Brazil had at some time in the remote past been inhabited
by a white culture of far more advanced knowledge than the Indians,
and that the remnants of their cities could well be hidden away in the
vast tracts of unexplored interior, at locations known only to the
wild Indian tribes. The sight of the Relatorio served only to add to
his conviction, and he devoted all his energies towards a planned
exploration of the most probable areas. In 1925, at the age of fifty-
seven, he set off into the wild regions of the Xingu, accompanied
only by his son Jack and one of Jack's friends, Raleigh Rimell. The
party's disappearance and the fact that their fate remains unverified,
is a matter of historical record. Many others risked their life in the
same way and, although returning to tell the tale, none ever found
the elusive city.

As for the Relatorio, it is now listed as Manuscript No. 152 in the
Bibliotec Nacionale in Rio and is still available for the curious to
examine. It has been subjected to tests by experts who agree that it is
at least as old as its date indicates. The truth of the story, however, is
now increasingly in doubt, for although many have searched,
especially in the latter years of improved transport and comprehensive aerial survey, no trace of the city or the mine shafts have ever
been seen. The Relatorio thus remains an unsolved enigma.

Let us look once again at the contents of this beautifully worded
romance. Careful scrutiny will disclose a number of recognisable
correspondences between the Relatorio text and the older Hermetic
manuscripts.

We are presented with the first clue when we are told that the
searchers have endured *long and troublesome wanderings* (just like the
wandering 'Israelites'), having been ten years in search of the

Moribeca Mine (in search of 'treasure'). After having been so long in this vast *desert*, they finally reach a range of *high mountains*. Much is made of the fact that the *sun* is seen to *reflect* from the quartz crystals of which the mountain is composed. The view was so beautiful, it is asserted, that none could take his *eyes* from it. When it rained, the *water* was seen to cascade down the *rock* face, looking like *snow* (*white*) in the *reflected rays of the sun*.

At first, they *could not find a way up* and were extremely disappointed (just as Jane Leade was when she couldn't find her way into the 'holy city'), but by chance, one of the negroes in the party, (a *black* man) chased a *white* deer, and in doing so, discovered an *ancient road* (how to accomplish the process). They began to *ascend the mountain*, which was difficult and took them *three* hours. Once at the top, they were amazed to see a *great city* some distance away. Cautiously, they waited *three* days before entering, which they did by way of the main gate. It had *three* arches.

The city, they soon saw, was *dead*. The facades of the houses all *blackened* with age and were all *dark* inside. On a column of *black stone* (a pillar) there was a statue of an *ordinary man* (not a god).

Shall I go on?

A river (*water*) runs through the city, its banks pleasing to the eye, and opposite, a flourishing plain like a *perfect garden*. The explorers journeyed *three* days down river where they found shafts of *unplumbed depths* on the *east* bank. It was the *abandoned mines* (the secret of the subconscious).

Like the allegorical city of Poseidon, the ruins with their carvings, statues and grandeur of architecture, all attested to the lost city's populousness, wealth and flourishing state in the centuries gone by.

The author of the Relatorio seems to have borrowed a number of ideas from Plato's description of Poseidon: the beautiful mountains, the stairway in the country house built of coloured stones, and the great plain. Even the philosopher's description of the 'noisy harbour' can be compared to the 'roaring of the falls'. The central theme of Death and Resurrection is also present – the 'death' of the city due to an *earth*quake (upheaval in the conscious mind), and its possible 'resurrection' when the 'treasure' is found.

These are the main points only, but there are many other references to the Hermetic process concealed within this cleverly devised text. Of the special ciphers, or hieroglyphs, which are meaningless in themselves and belonging to no known language, the last has its significance in that there are *nine* of them.

The question of the Relatorio's authorship will remain an enigma, for the precise origin of the document can never be traced, but we must conclude that the disciples of the Hermetic Art were not confined to the Old World alone. Many of the society of Jesus came as missionaries to the Americas. Certainly, the manuscript was conceived by someone who was acquainted with the territory at first hand. The Serra do Cincora is a mountain range which features a considerable amount of white quartz – and we have noted Sir Richard Burton's comment about the similarity to the great falls of Paulo Affonso. The desert land areas of western Bahia State contain many examples of natural erosion into rock formations that look uncannily like the ruins of ancient buildings. Clearly, the exotic description in the manuscript is based on these existing features, and is therefore another example of allegory being superimposed over natural conditions, just as the Crucifixion myth was overlaid on features which exist in Jerusalem.

In case any reader wishes to contest this assertion, I must point out that the Relatorio is not unique, but merely the most outstanding of half a dozen similar fables. In 1601, Barco Centenara, a Spanish scribe with the Conquistadores, wrote about a city called El Gran Moxo, supposedly situated somewhere near the source of the Paraguay River, in the Mato Grosso. I will quote the relevant passage and emphasise the key words as usual.

In the middle of the *lake* was an *island* on which were *buildings of great beauty and splendour, beyond human understanding.* The *mansion of the Lord*, El Gran Moxo, was built of *white stone* right up to the very roof. It had *two very high towers* at its entrance and a stairway in the middle. At a *pillar* in the *middle*, on the *right*, were two live *lions*. They crouched at its sides, *in chains*, whose links were of *gold*. On the summit of the pillar, 25 feet high, was a great *Moon*. It illuminated all the lake, *dispelling darkness* and *shadows* by night and day, so that all appeared very bright.

No sign of this mysterious city has ever been discovered, even though its purported location lies in an area that becomes more populated each year. Many searched for it, preferring to ignore the fairy-tale quality of the text, especially the ever-burning lamp on the pillar, a facet of allegory that can be compared to that of the Tabernacle.

The continent of South America is noted for its treasure legends, especially that of the 'golden man' of El Dorado. Not quite so familiar to the public eye, but equally fabulous, is the story of the Great Tunnel of Peru, a bizarre tradition related in detail by Madame Blavatsky in her ISIS UNVEILED, Vol I, chapter 15. It concerns an *underground tomb*, the Tomb of the Incas, which is built into a vast subterranean passage running south from Lima. The only way to enter into this finely carved mausoleum is from a hidden cleft in the *northernmost* of *three* peaks, 'which form a curious *triangle*', and which are situated near a river known as the Pay'quina. In a footnote, Madame Blavatsky points out that the river is so called because its waves used to drift particles of *gold* downstream from Brazil.

We are warned of the fabulous nature of the tale when Madame Blavatsky says that, *without the secret* of the landmarks to the *hidden entrance*, a 'regiment of titans might rend the rocks in vain'. The symbol of death is also present as we are told that any attempt to blast out the huge door of the tomb would result in the superincumbent rocks falling in to bury 'a thousand warriors in one common ruin'. Other clues consist of hieroglyphics carved in *rock*, which are only visible when the *rays of the setting sun* fall across them.

A document known as the Derrotero Valverde and lodged in the archives of Ecuador, was investigated for several years by the British botanist, Richard Spruce, who found indisputable proof that it had originated in Spain. It describes a route to the Llanganati Hills, which have *three* peaks, and on the *right* flank of which lies an artifical *lake*. In the *water*, will be found the *golden treasure of the ancient Indians* (the Incas).

The most remarkable facet of this story is the fact that almost all of the landmarks so cunningly utilised are real, most of them being in evidence to this day. But, as detailed as the manuscript is, the trail peters out just towards the end and so no one has ever been fortunate enough to find the missing hoard. For those readers who are interested, a full transcript of the Derrotero was given in INCA GOLD, by Jane Dolinger. Like the Relatorio of Brazil, it abounds with Hermetic clues.

As to why the Hermetic writers indulged in this form of literary endeavour, the answer is the same as for those who wrote the Gospels – to project the Hermetic theme. Do not forget that the threat of persecution by the Church was as strong in 17th century America as it was in Europe, with unpleasant penalties imposed on the 'heretic'. By reason of the mineralogical finds in certain areas of the New World continent, the 'lost city of gold' theme was immediately grasped by the initiate writers as a suitable vehicle with which to carry their hidden message. It was then presented in the hope that some would be astute enough to comprehend the inner meaning. The tendency of those with an insatiable lust for gold to take the texts at face value was an unfortunate side effect, eliciting little sympathy from the Hermeticists, who considered all unbelievers to be all too aptly portrayed by the un-numbered Tarot card.

Mahe

On Mahe, a pleasant island in the Indian Ocean, search for a buried hoard was commenced in 1948, after the discovery of strange signs on the sea shore at Bel Ombre. The signs, cut into pieces of rock, were found to correspond with certain documents of a secret and mysterious nature, hinting at the concealment of a treasure cache by an 18th century pirate captain. A retired Grenadier Guardsman, who became involved, raised the necessary financial backing and began to dig. But the treasure proved elusive. By the '70s, seven hundred tons of rock had been carefully removed at the cost of £30,000 – a considerable sum in those days – but no pirate chest had been brought to light.

Our suspicions about this cache deepen when we consider the clues given regarding its precise location and the method by which it must be recovered. After decipherment of the documents concerned, the theory was formed that the secret of the location had to be worked out according to a plan based on the story of *Hercules and his Twelve Labours*. The treasure was supposed to be located in a *cavern*, and it was contained in *three* chests. Significantly, the approach to the cache would have to be made from the *north*, there being many traps set which could result in *death*. Finally, it was made quite clear in the documents that the pirate captain who placed the cache was a member of a *French Masonic lodge*.

The Kidd Maps

Author Rupert Furneaux, an avid investigator into the legend of Captain Kidd, has remarked that the popular association of pirates with buried treasure is fictional, for the Buccaneers were notorious spendthrifts. Were the famous Kidd maps, he wonders, just an elaborate hoax? Like many other researchers, he is reluctant to concede that anyone would go to such lengths with no apparent motive other than to mislead. Yet the fact remains that the enigma of the maps is one that has not been resolved by the discovery of a buried chest full to the brim with doubloons.

For modern readers the story begins in 1929, when Hubert Palmer, a retired lawyer living in Eastbourne, purchased a heavy, 17th century oak bureau from a London antique dealer. Palmer, himself a dealer, was an avid collector of pirate relics and he had been attracted to the piece by a brass plate affixed to it, and which bore the inscription:

Captain William Kidd. Adventure Galley 1669.

Palmer knew that the Adventure Galley was the name of the ship captained by the famous William Kidd in 1695. Familiar with the deviousness of such buccaneers, the lawyer examined the chest carefully in search of secret compartments – and found three. They were disappointingly empty, but during his search, he accidentally applied pressure to one of the brass runners on the chest, causing it to break off. To his surprise, he saw revealed the outline of the words;

Captain Kidd – His chest.

Inside the runner, he found an ageing piece of parchment which turned out to be a crude chart of an island. There were no clues to its location, but the drawing bore the words 'China Sea' and the date, 1669.

Keen to acquire further relics, Palmer let it be known to his friends in the antique trade that he was a prospective buyer and in 1931 was offered a chest reputed to have been the property of Captain Thomas Hardy of the Victory, Nelson's flagship at Trafalgar. Palmer was told that Hardy had bought it from the grandson of Ned Ward, Kidd's bosun, to whom the condemned pirate had bequeathed it on the night before his execution. The chest seemed authentic enough, for carved on the lid was the sign of the skull and cross-bones, the date 1669, and the words;

Captain Kidd – His Chest.

Eagerly, Palmer examined it for secret compartments and came upon a false bottom, under which he found an old book dated 1662 – and a further map of the same unidentified island.

By this time, Palmer had acquired a reputation among dealers as a man who would be prepared to buy genuine relics attached to the Kidd legend. In 1932, he was approached by a retired ship's captain named Daniel Morgan, who offered him a third chest. Palmer was told that it had been taken from Newgate Gaol by Morgan's ancestors, one of whom had been a gaoler there. The chest bore a brass plate inscribed with a skull and cross-bones – and behind a mirror at the back of the chest, Palmer found a third parchment map of the same mysterious island. This time, however, the chart showed considerably more detail, with the addition of woods, hills, a lagoon and some compass bearings.

In 1934, Palmer encountered a fourth chest, this time while in the Channel Islands. It bore the legend;

William and Sarah Kidd – Their Box.

It too, had a secret compartment containing a chart of the island, but larger and far more detailed than any of the previous parchments. It also provided a totally different set of directions for locating the elusive isle.

All four charts were sold privately in 1950, after Palmer's death, but not before they were photographed by the British Museum. The Museum expert on Cartography gave the opinion that all were genuine 17th century products, conforming in type, ink, parchment and handwriting of the period. There seemed to be no doubt as to their authenticity.

Various islands have been linked with the Kidd saga, notably Oak Island, off the coast of Nova Scotia. Other tenuous links have been made with the Philippines, and with an island off the southern tip of Japan. In 1957, Rupert Furneaux, who has undertaken extensive research into the subject, visited Providenciales Island, one of the southernmost of the Bahamas Group. He found no treasure, but located three caves that could well be those depicted in the fourth, most comprehensive chart, a copy of which is included here (see fig, 15). The size and shape of the island agreed comfortably with the outline of the chart's 'treasure island', and a pile of rocks, placed by human hands, seemed to link up with an inscription round the edge of the map. As a final, convincing piece of evidence, a flat rock bearing a scratched letter 'K' was brought to light. But there was no treasure.

It is a matter of official record that, while in the condemned cell in London, Kidd wrote to the Speaker of the House of Commons, offering to lead an expedition to recover a treasure cache worth £100,000. It was a last desperate bid for freedom which the Government rejected, but it fired the imagination of treasure seekers the world over.

Did it also fire the imagination of those with an entirely different interest?

Let us now examine the fourth map closely – from the point of view of the Hermetic initiate. It will be seen immediately that there are a number of correspondences with symbolism already interpreted in this volume. On the *left*hand side of the island, the southwest according to the chart's compass position, you will see a short series of marks intended to indicate a range of hills. Close scrutiny of these will show that among them, seemingly as an accidental formation, are *three* letters, O, A, and K. To the casual observer, this may be shrugged off as an unpremeditated slip of the cartographer's pen, but we must not overlook the fact that 'oak' is a known Hermetic emblem, as well as a possible reference to Oak

Island. The central indicator of the compass is aimed directly at *three circles*, thought by many to be the 'three stumps' mentioned in the inscription round the chart's edge. Is it a coincidence that the three are indicated by the compass point *north*?

The island is drawn roughly in the shape of a *crescent moon*, possibly an oblique reference to reflection, a symbol which is duplicated in the word 'lagoon', meaning shallow *lake* – while the enigmatic '20 Turtles' (the nautical term 'to turn turtle' meaning capsizing or turning *upside down*) may indicate the reversal of thoughts necessary for the process. The instructions for locating the treasure, written round the edge, contain the words; North; Centre; Rocks; and Skeleton. All these are familiar as part of the Hermetic symbolism, as far back as the New Testament.

As we have already discovered the true origin of the pirate's well known sign, the skull and cross-bones, and are aware that it emanates not from the whim of the buccaneers who were supposed to have sailed under it, but from the inner symbolism of the Rosi-crucians, we may now see the maps as a form of Hermetic cipher for the education of those who can read them.

Far fetched?

I ask you to recall the whole panorama of emblems upon which we have touched during the course of this exposition, and then look again at the contents of the third Kidd chest as it came into Hubert Palmers hands. I quote my own text;

> The chest bore a *brass* plate inscribed with the *skull and cross-bones* – and *behind a mirror* at the back of the chest, Palmer found a third parchment . . .

An amazing parallel to this can be found in the ancient festival of the Mystery called Thesmophoria, where the priests carried the 'sacred objects' in a cistus (a casket, perhaps reminiscent of Osiris, and about the size of Kidd's chest). The objects were a ball; a mirror; and a pine cone. In the Hermetic Mysteries of Eleusis, similar objects were treated with the same veneration: an egg; a spiral serpent; and a pine cone. Each object had its significance in relation to the sym-bolism currently in favour with the Hermetic Fraternity – the mirror being the most obvious to us as an emblem of reflection.

Yet another parallel can be drawn between the Kidd chests and an ancient symbol of knowledge featured in numerous pictorial and literary allegories, including the famed Rosicrucian Manifestos. I refer to the second chest in which Palmer found, as well as the chart, an *old book*.

The fourth chart carries the words 'China Sea', and in an effort to

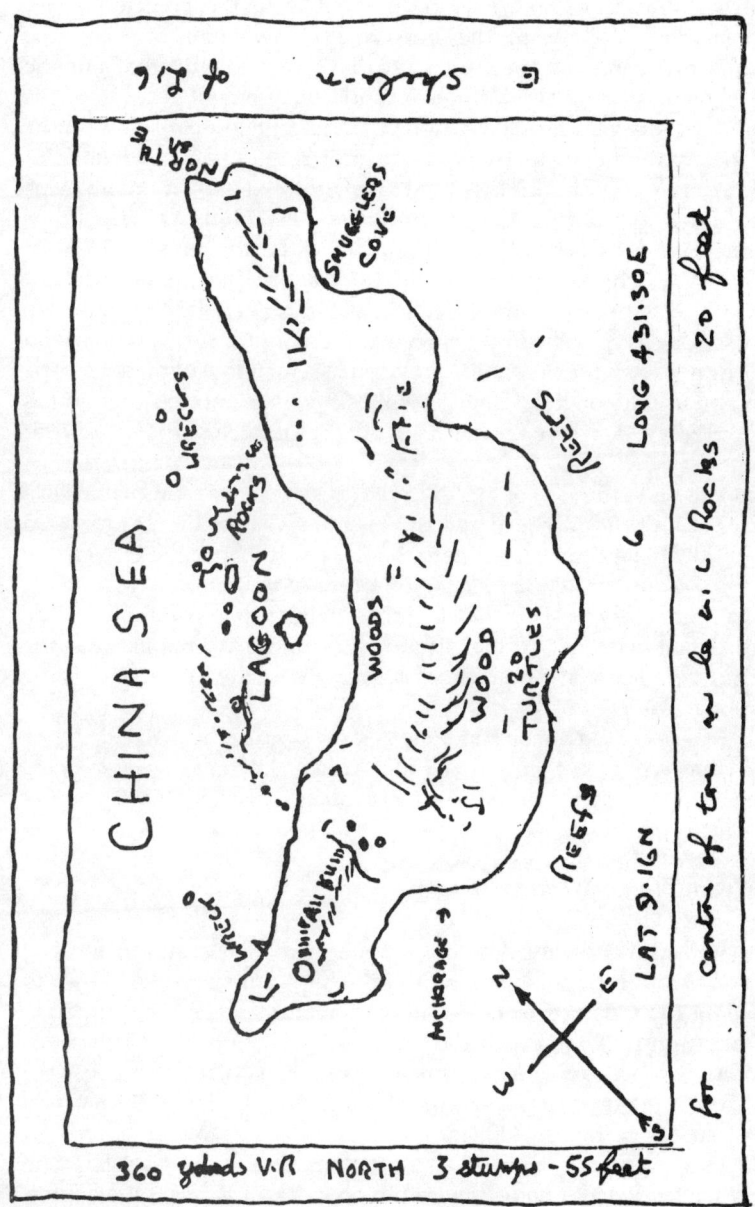

FIGURE 15.

link it with Oak Island, Rupert Furneaux rightly brings to the attention that 'China' may be derived from the French 'chêne', meaning 'oak'. From the treasure hunter's point of view, the solution would certainly seem to have been discovered, but the Hermeticist would look at it in an entirely different light.

Rupert Furneaux makes another significant comparison when he remarks on the last line of the inscription round the edge of the map. He draws attention to the word 'Skele(ton)' and mentions an identical theme in Edgar Allen Poe's story, THE GOLD BUG. In this tale, Poe describes how a treasure, which he attributed to Kidd, is found by dropping a line through the *eye hole of a skull suspended in a tree*. Poe wrote this story in 1828, while living in South Carolina. He is said to have picked up the legend there, but it is this writer who penned the significant line 'the eyes are the window of the soul'. The inner import of this sentence will escape you until chapter 14 has been reached, where the mechanics of the Hermetic process are dealt with.

The *skull*, the sign of 'death' and the fact that it was suspended in a tree (recall Odin/Thoth and the Hanged Man of the Tarot), is so obviously Hermetic in content that it raises the intriguing question: did Poe appreciate the inner significance of what he was writing, or was he merely repeating a legend? Certainly, this writer displayed a remarkable talent, having a first volume of poetry published at the age of eighteen, and thereafter becoming virtually the founder of the modern detective story.

As a last word on the Kidd maps, I will say that they were drawn at a time when the 'buried treasure' and 'lost island' themes were popular among the initiate writers as allegorical vehicles.

Rennes le Chateau

And so at last, armed with some enlightenment gained in our long trek through the wilderness of Hermetic symbolism, we return to Rennes le Chateau to take a more perceptive look at the enigma. Having now appreciated the incredible lengths to which the Hermetic scribes went, it will not now be so hard to accept that the carefully contrived labyrinth of clues will lead not to physical treasure, but to knowledge.

The most basic legend of the affair is that of the *shepherd*, who while *watching his flock*, chanced upon a *concealed cave*. Upon entering, he found *skeletons* and *gold* (compare this with the story told about the young Jacob Boehme). When he returned to the village to relate his amazing discovery, he was *not believed*, and the villagers, accusing him of theft, *stoned him to death*. Thus, apart from the basic emblems that have now become familiar to us, the tale also projects the idea of the shepherd's persecution. Add to this the fact that his name was said to be Paris, the same as that of the Greek mythological *hero* (Greek emblem for initiate), and the evidence for the fable's Hermetic content is overwhelming. And so we must look at the rest of the items in the same light.

The Parchments

Of the *four* parchments found within the *three* cylinders, only two are available for public examination and we may begin by noting that the first enciphered message was contained within the Gospel story of the visit by Jesus to the house of Lazarus, in Bethany. I have already dealt with the Hermetic content of this, not only in the parts played by Martha and Mary, but also in the 'raising' of Lazarus from the dead, and it is quite apparent that this is the real secret to be found in this text. But just as the originators planned, the attention of the investigators has until now been focussed solely on the decoded message – which in itself, does not provide much of an answer.

The second parchment consists of the parable of the disciples plucking the ears of corn on the sabbath, put together from *three* separate versions. But as before, little or no significance has been attached to the original text, once the inner cipher was decoded. We have seen that this is a mistake, so let us remind ourselves of the tale as it is presented in Matthew 12; 1 to 8; Mark 2; 23 to 28; and Luke 6; 1 to 5.

The Pharisees, seeing Jesus and his disciples plucking ears of corn to eat, protested that such an act was unlawful, for it was the sabbath – at which Jesus referred them to an incident recorded in the Old Testament describing how a hungry David went to the temple, where the priest could only give him 'shewbread' (hallowed bread) because it was the sabbath and no common bread was available.

The term 'bread' is the clue that will provide the inner meaning to both parables, for it links us immediately with the 'bread' of the Israelites – manna. The *plucking of the corn* and the *eating of shewbread* are alternative phrases for *gathering manna* – that is, meditating. The fact that in the latter case the meditation seems to be taking place on the sabbath – a charge which Jesus must answer – is explained by realisation of the meaning attached to the word 'sabbath'. In this case, it pertains to the ordinary day (of our week) the seventh, a day in which the Neophyte does not cease his meditation period, for success in the process depends upon there being no interruption from start to finish.

This explanation may appear to be contrived, but it so happens that an item of historical evidence exists which will give further support to it. There exists a parchment called the Codex Bezae, presented to the University of Cambridge by Bezae the Reformer in 1581, and obtained so it is said, by Bezae himself from a monastery in the Templar dominated region of south eastern France. The manuscript is bi-lingual, containing beside the Greek text of the Acts and the Gospels, a parallel Latin version of great antiquity. But the most remarkable thing about it is a number of peculiar textual variations, one of which has no parallel to be found anywhere else. It concerns the parable we are discussing. First, there comes the standard text of Luke 6.

1. And it came to pass on the second sabbath after the first, that he went through the cornfields; and his disciples plucked the ears of corn and did eat, rubbing them in their hands.
2. And certain of the Pharisees said unto them, Why do ye do that which is not lawful to do on the sabbath days?
3. And Jesus answering them said, Have ye not read so much as this, what David did when himself was hungered and they which were with him;
4. How he went into the house of God, and did take and eat the shewbread, and gave also to them that were with him which it is not lawful to eat, but for the priests alone?
5. And he said unto them, That the son of man is Lord also of the sabbath.

It is at this point that a unique insertion into the text has been made, which reads;

And on the same day, seeing someone working on the sabbath, he said unto him. 'Man, if thou knowest what thou doest, blessed art thou; but if thou knowest not, thou art accursed and a transgressor of the law'.

This passage has baffled bibilical scholars, but if the original text of Luke is, as I have shown, speaking figuratively of meditation, then it can be seen at once that the insertion – obviously the work of an initiate – implies that *work* (labour – meditation) on the sabbath to be justified, *providing you know what the sabbath and work really mean.*

The Pentacle

The pentacle is a symbol which has been given great emphasis in the Rennes story, and that which has been laid out over the Languedoc countryside is supposed to lead the investigator to the long lost treasure. But we have examined adequate examples of such deliberately placed red herrings. Without doubt, there is a cave at the designated spot and there is certainly the possibility that it was once used as a hiding place. Henry Lincoln, aware of the pentacle's astrological links, has drawn attention to the Rennes figure and the synodic period of the planet Venus. However, this avenue of search is misleading, for the ancient art of Astrology, of which the pentacle is a part, was purely symbolic and has no real connection with the physical stars. The five pointed star represents Man, or rather, his conscious mind with its reflective power, symbolised by Venus (Love = attraction = meditation).

Further elucidation on this point comes when it is realised that certain Hermetic writers have made use of the name Geometry to represent the *perfectness* of form required to complete the mental process, as in the six pointed Star of David. This *geometry* is the formula by which *sacred temples*, or *holy cities* might be built – edifices such as *Solomon's Temple*, *Jerusalem*, or *New Jerusalem*. Thus, when a text claims that *geometry* was discovered before the Flood, you can be sure it is not the ability to draw correct angles that is being discussed.

The point brings to mind the controversy which arose between two notable Rosicrucians, the astronomer Johannes Kepler and Robert Fludd, the alchemist. In his HARMONICA MUNDI (1619), Kepler took great care to state that his work on astronomy was purely from the mathematical point of view, with no Hermetic overtones. He accused Fludd of confusing true mathematics with the symbolism of the Hermeticist, feeling that the two should be kept separate for the sake of material astronomy. Thus, the pentacle of Rennes may point to a material location, but for the Hermeticist, it indicates the manner by which he may find the 'treasure' of the mental process.

Et In Arcadia Ego

In the course of the foregoing expositions we have found the inner mind to have been symbolised by many flowery names, most of which indicate an idyllic place of natural beauty, like a *garden* or *grove*, a *grotto* or *forest*. Alternatively, the mental centre is characterised as a faraway land where everything is *perfect*, and which is cut off from the rest of the world, and if we look at the phrase 'Et in Arcadia Ego', we find just such a spot. Arcady, or Arcadia, is portrayed in historical texts as a country of ancient Greece which, due to its *mountainous* terrain is very hard to reach, and is therefore *isolated from the rest of the world*. This lack of outside contact resulted in the people remaining unspoiled, or *innocent*, spending much of their time in simple pursuit of *happiness*, like singing and dancing.

In English, the phrase is rendered 'I too, live in Arcady', and if we now apply the correct interpretation to the mythical name, we arrive at 'I too, live in the subconscious'. There is no denying that the phrase is a statement from an initiate, proclaiming his successful accomplishment of the mental task. And as Poussin made great use of the phrase, we must suspect that he was a Rosicrucian, and investigate his connection with Rennes.

The Shepherdess

The history of the 'Shepherds of Arcadia' theme is tracable to the 1st century B.C., when the Roman poet, Virgil, wrote of a 'tomb' in Arcady. From the same period, there is a mural which is strongly reminiscent of the theme. Set in the inner sanctum of the Temple of Isis, at Pompeii, it shows *Argus*, guardian of Io (both emblems of reflection) leaning on a large *rock*. Io is sitting on a smaller rock, looking up at Hermes, who is offering her a set of pan pipes. It is plain that Io is the *shepherdess*, for she is seen with her *staff*.

In 1502, the Neopolitan poet, Sannazaro, wrote a pastoral entitled 'Arcadia', in which he described the *tomb of a shepherd*, to which other shepherds made *sacrifices*. Nearby, was the river Alphaeus *(water)*.

The first known painting of the theme was by Guercino, in 1620, and shows two young *shepherds* leaning on their *staffs*. They are *gazing thoughtfully* (contemplatively – meditation) at a small *square tomb of stone* blocks, on which rests a human *skull*. For the first time, the phrase 'Et in Arcadia Ego' appears, carved on the side of the tomb.

Poussin's early version, painted about 1629, combines most of these ideas, for it shows a *shepherdess*, with two shepherds gazing with interest at the tomb. At the monument's base, sits a personi-fication of the River God, Alphaeus, holding a pitcher from which water is being spilt (Aquarius). The tomb is pictured larger and more ornamental than that of Guercino, and is set in the *shadow* of a towering *rock* face, but the *skull* still reposes on top of the tomb. The phrase also is present, with one of the shepherds pointing to it with his *right* hand. The attitude of the shepherds is notably different, their former contemplative stance replaced by an air of excitement as they lean forward to examine the tomb.

The second version, thought to have been completed at some time in the mid-1650s, is in greater contrast, for there are now *three* shepherds, while the shepherdess looks on from the *right*. In the latter figure we have confirmation of the interpretation placed on the pentacle as an Hermetic symbol, for this *shepherdess*, who occupies the *centre* of the pentagonal foundation of the painting, has already been seen to be Io, the *Moon*, the feminine emblem of inner reflection.

The *skull* has gone, and the tomb is now a *squared* monument, the likeness of which actually exists some kilometres off from Rennes le Chateau. This, and the similarity between the painted background and the real landscape in which the monument is situated, is fair evidence that Poussin visited the Rennes area personally. The painter lived most of his working life in Rome, but it is known that he spent the period between Oct. 1640 and Nov. 1642 in Paris, and so it is not improbable that he took the opportunity to make the journey to Rennes and sketch the necessary preliminaries. What is certain is that Poussin was in possession of the 'secret', the matter mentioned in Louis Fouquet's letter, by the year 1656, the date of the letter.

Apart from its portrayal of the Rennes area, the second version does offer certain clues to indicate Poussin's own accomplishment of the process, for it features *three* shepherds, whereas the earlier canvas depicts only two, and thus may be a hint by the artist that he had reached that vital third stage by the time the second version was painted. This is supported by the fact that, in the later picture, the tomb is *squared* (sign of the finished process) and that the skull is not there (no longer necessary as the process is complete). (See fig. 16).

Applying the Hermetic key to the work of Teniers, there will be little difficulty in deciphering the pictorial truth in the *Temptation* of St. Anthony. The saint (personifying the initiate-to-be), is shown in a *stone cave*, or *grotto*, kneeling before a *rough stone* altar (sign of the process not yet complete), on which rests a human *skull*. He is trying to read a book (focus his mind on the centre at which the knowledge lies –meditate), but his attention is constantly distracted by *devils* and goblins. The picture represents the Hermetic task at its first stage, the 'temptation' to which Anthony is subjected being the uncontrolled thoughts of the conscious mind which, if not subdued, will hinder the process.

FIGURE 16.   The Shepherds of Arcadia. Second version by Poussin

It is now child's play to extract the meaning from the painting of St Anthony and St Jeromy, the only canvas by Teniers in which St Anthony is not being tempted. As Henry Lincoln has pointed out, there is a *shepherdess* in the *background*, indicating that St Anthony has achieved the necessary stilling of the thoughts and is on the point of making the transmission of consciousness.

The Spider

Another emblem of the Rennes mystery, and one that I have not yet had the opportunity of discussing, is that of the *spider*. The motif of the spider is prominent on one of Marie de Blanchefort's grave-stones, and also at the church of Rennes le Bains, where the painting of Jesus shows the *crown of thorns* stylised as a gigantic spider. As we recall, the 'thorn' emblem relates to the Aramaic 'mushroom', really the inner mind, and thus the spider obviously holds the same concealed meaning. To the initiate, the insect represents the trans-mission of consciousness, the so-called astral body, for as the spider flies out into the wind on the end of his silken cord, so the astral body of the initiate flies out on its 'travels' in the Universal Mind, but tethered to the physical body by means of the silver cord mentioned in Ecclesiastes 12; 6. This cord is regarded by the initiates as comparable to an umbilical cord, accounting still further for the astral body being thought of as an *infant*.

The spider, when it weaves its web, moves in a *circular* motion, and the web is constructed with an unmistakable *centre*. In Le MYSTERE DES CATHEDRALES, Fulcanelli devotes some space to the phonetic equivalents of the spider names, and asks;

Is not our soul the spider which weaves our own body?

The Church of Sainte-Madelaine

Another art work of Hermetic import is that which was painted by Sauniere himself, the picture set into one panel of his church altar. The scene depicts *Mary Magdalene* kneeling in a *grotto* with her *gaze fixed* (meditation) on a rough *cross* made from the branches of an *acacia bush* (same emblem as 'bramble, or 'mushroom' – the inner mind). Beside her, on the ground, is an *open book* (denoting knowl-edge of the process) and a bare *skull*. (See Fig. 17). All these are now easy to interpret, but the scene presents a further, unique expression of the process. Mary is shown with her hands in her lap, but with the fingers interlaced in a prominent and far from natural manner. If you bring to mind the significance attached to the *left* and *right* hands, you will appreciate that this is a most ingenious way of representing the *interlacing* of the two minds, the conscious and the subconscious, at the point of transmission. If Sauniere conceived the idea of this scene for himself, there remains no doubt that he had gained full knowledge of the Hermetic secret, irrespective of whether he was able to make us it or not.

His acquisition of this knowledge is further confirmed in the relief of Christ on the Mount, with its unexpected addition of the little, golden sack tied with rope and lying at the foot of the mount.

First, let me say that that the whole sermon, as rendered in the biblical texts, holds concealed references to the mental process, and to quote just one, supportive instance, verse 8, in Matt. 5, states:

Blessed are the pure in heart, for they shall see God.

Outwardly read, the implications are just as we have always thought them to be. If we are good, we shall go to heaven instead of the other place. But this interpretation is for the uninitiated. Our deeper insight into the meaning of the word *good* enables us to translate 'heart' not as the physical organ, but as the *heart*, or centre of the mind, which if made *pure* (thoughts stilled) will most certainly result in the sight of *God* (transmission to the Universal Mind). The subject of Sauniere's relief, therefore, is a statement of the Hermetic practice, but the golden sack is the priest's own addition. It is obviously a sack meant to contain treasure, but what kind of 'treasure'?

Beneath the relief, there is a text which runs;

Come to me, all ye that are heavy laden, and I will give you rest.

The words 'ye that are heavy laden' in French read

vous qui etes accablés.

Some writers, versed in the cunning use of word play, have extracted from this sentence the following;

'ete' (summer); 'sac a cable' (sack with rope); and 'ble' (corn – but also slang for treasure).

It is the last of these three extractions that paves the way to the truth, for we have already witnessed how 'corn' and 'treasure' are long established emblems in the Hermetic scheme. The *corn* is really

FIGURE 17.   Mary Magdalene.
Painting by Sauniere, placed in one panel of the altar of Sainte-
Madelaine church. Note the unusual interlocking of the fingers.

meditation, the *treasure* being the end result, the transmission of consciousness and the acquisition of mental power. The sack, therefore, contains corn – the key to the process.

Applying our wealth of symbolic knowledge still further, we need no longer wonder why Sauniere relaid the floor of his church with a black and white, tiled pattern which resembles a *chessboard*. The same special floor design is present in certain other churches – St Paul's Cathedral, for one.

The words of Jacob, at Bethel – 'terribilis est locus iste' – (how awful is this place) are carved significantly on the *keystone* of the *arch* at the entrance to the church, and refer to the great wonder in the mind of the initiate as he makes the transmission to a superior state of consciousness.

The grotesque representation of Asmodeus, or Rex Mundi, the devil who once held a flaming torch in his *right* hand, is an emblem of the conscious mind with its hidden potential, and as if to support such a conclusion, there is written above the figure, a motto which reads;

> Par ce signe tu le vaincras (In this sign shalt thou conquer – or, *I.N.R.I.*)

The great slab which once laid at the foot of the altar was found, when raised, to have its underside carved in an archaic style which dated from the 6th century. There are two scenes, both of which are placed underneath an *arch* (a sign which has great significance, as the next chapter will show). The *left* hand picture shows a *knight* on a *horse* (a Neophyte). He is sounding a horn (revelation), while his horse (the conscious mind) lowers its head to drink from a trough (*water*), a design intended to show that the Neophyte has discovered the method of the process and is putting it into practice.

The *right* hand scene shows the same knight, but this time with a *staff* in one hand (sign of a conquered mind) and a *child* in the other – a clear expression of the completed process.

Grave inscriptions

At least one of the gravestones of Paul de Fleury presents an entirely new meaning as we apply the symbolism. Recall the rather mystifying inscription:

> He passed away doing *good*
> The *transferred* remains of
> Paul Urbain comte de Fleury
> Died 7 August 1856 aged 60 years

Following the time honoured ritual, the initates have diverted the attention from the important clues, which I have here emphasised, by giving both stones conflicting dates. If these are ignored, and we read the emphasised word in light of the Hermetic knowledge, it becomes clear that Paul de Fleury was a Rosicrucian initiate.

The other gravestone inscriptions will now yield their respective messages. 'Mort Epee', means 'sword of death' and is recognisable as the inner reflection which 'kills' the conscious mind, while we have satisfactorily translated 'Et in Arcadia Ego'. The remaining quotation which may give pause for thought is that of 'Reddis, Regis, Cellis, Arcis', which in English is rendered; 'Rennes, of the King, in a concealed shrine, in safe keeping'.

Most investigators have construed this to be a positive indication of a material treasure secreted at Rennes le Chateau, but there is an alternative interpretation. We must not forget that the sign of the *spider* appears prominently displayed on the same gravestone, and it obviously has a part to play.

The French word for 'spider' is 'araignée', which in the local dialect is pronounced 'arenn'. Those attempting to decipher the inscriptions have quite rightly drawn attention to the phonetic similarity between 'arenn' and 'Rennes', claiming that it supported the theory that Rennes was the spot where the treasure was located. The sign of the spider, they maintained, meant Rennes le Chateau. But a simple reversal of this conclusion will provide the true answer – that by its very name, it is Rennes that points to the *spider*, the soul within us all, the subconscious which contains the real treasure.

The Message

Thus we re-examine the cryptic message extracted from the second of the parchment texts:

SHEPHERDESS. NO TEMPTATION. POUSSIN AND TENIERS HOLD THE KEY. PEACE DCLXXXI BY THE CROSS AND THIS HORSE OF GOD, I REACH THIS DAEMON GUARDIAN AT MIDDAY. BLUE APPLES.

Even a casual appraisal of this farrago will now show it to hold some of the Hermetic clues we have discussed. The *Shepherdess*, we know to be reflection, the creative power used in the meditational task, which if continued for a long time without interruption, will 'kill' the conscious mind, and so there will be *no temptation*. The paintings of both artists mentioned unquestionably hold the key to the Hermetic process, as does the sentence 'by the cross and this

horse of God, I reach the daemon guardian at midday'. In effect, this
means 'by taking the conscious mind (the horse) and nailing it to the
cross (subjecting it to the mental process) the *evil* of the moving
thoughts (the daemon) will be overcome at *midday* (when the *Sun* of
the Universal Mind has fully risen).

The phrases which remain, 'peace 681' and 'blue apples', are
meaningless, inserted with the express purpose of confusing seekers
even more.

The whole outward expression of the Rennes symbolism, hinting
at a material treasure, is like that of the Kidd maps, or the Brazilian
Relatorio, deliberately misleading. The real treasure will only be
yielded up at the correct interpretation of the clues – a statement that
applies just as much to the Gospels as to the story of Rennes le
Chateau.

Indisputably, Sauniere came by considerable wealth – and at first
sight it does appear that he stumbled upon the key to a carefully
guarded, centuries-old hoard. But the greater part of this book has
been devoted to showing that things are not always as they appear to
be on the surface. Intuitively, this seems to have occurred to some
perceptive investigators, who now hold the opinion that Sauniere
did not actually find gold, but was financed by a wealthy organisation which managed to keep its name from being openly connected
to the transaction. In other words, Sauniere found something, and
was paid to keep silent – and paid more than handsomely.

If this is the case, we must ask the reason why. Was it because a
cache of gold had been unearthed; because a secret Rosicrucian lodge
had been discovered; or because an ancient religion had been found
to have survived, and once found, offered shattering revelations
about the whole structure and conception of Christianity? If you are
capable of finding the true answer to the question you will know
where Sauniere's wealth came from.

The Priory of Sion

There is an interesting post script to the Rennes le Chateau saga.
After many years of research, Henry Lincoln discovered the existence of the Priory of Sion and, like the persistent investigator he is,
persevered until he was at last able to confront two persons who
confessed to membership in the Order. One of these was no less a
person than the present figurehead of the Priory itself, Pierre
Plantard de Saint Clair.

From discussions with Monsieur Plantard, and after even more painstaking research into the history of the Frankish kings, Henry Lincoln developed a hypothesis to explain the core of the mystery, setting it out at length in his recent co-authored work, THE HOLY BLOOD AND THE HOLY GRAIL. Fundamentally, he theorizes that Mary Magdalene was, in reality, the wife of Jesus, and that their marriage produced at least one child. After the Crucifixion, the Magdalene was smuggled into France, where she took refuge with Jewish communities already established there. Her child survived to carry the Jesus line, which became the royal Frankish lineage, the Merovingians.

Had the events portrayed in the Gospels been real, not mythical, it is a hypothesis unquestionably worthy of the most meticulous research.

However, it is fair to say that Henry Lincoln was at least half-right. There *was* a transmission from Palestine to France all those years ago – but it was the knowledge of the Hermetic process passed on by the initiates, not a real life Mary Magdalene and her child.

We have already dealt with the inner significance of the Magdalene in chapter eight (the New Testament), finding that she personifies the conscious mind of the enlightened Neophyte undergoing the mental process. In the same way, an Hermetic significance is to be detected in the concept of 'Merovee', the original Merovingian king. As Lincoln himself has already discovered, Merovee was the subject of a Frankish myth in which he is declared to be of *miraculous origin*, (just like Jesus, or John the Disciple) because he was born of two fathers, one of which was a 'creature from beyond the sea' (i.e. a divine being). Thus Merovee had two kinds of blood flowing in his veins, one human, the other supernatural. In this, we can immediately detect the fundamentals of Dualism (the conscious mind = human; the subconscious = supernatural), and no effort of deduction is required to conclude that the myth is yet another expression of the Hermetic theme.

Further, the name 'Merovee' has more than a passing phonetic similarity to the French word for 'Mother', as well as both the Latin and French for 'sea' (*water*). I need hardly remind you that both symbols are oft-used by the Hermetic writers.

Outwardly, the aim of the Priory of Sion appears to be the restoration of the Merovingian line of descent – of which Monsieur Plantard is a member – as rightful kings of France, an aspiration which today seems pathetically outdated and pointless if accepted in its literal sense. But if interpreted symbolically, as we are required to do, the true goal at once becomes perfectly clear. The old name 'Merovingian' personifies the Rosicrucian initiate, just as 'Jew' does in the Bible, and the aim of the Priory is to perpetuate the hidden, mental science of the Hermetic initiate.

As for the 'Jewish' community in France to which Mary Magdalene hypothetically fled, this has been linked by the author's research to the biblical Tribe of Benjamin – and once again he is half right, for another Hermetic root presents itself. The name 'Benjamin' means 'son of the right hand'. Thus, if we recall the symbolism pertaining to the left and right hands, the name translates easily as 'son of the subconscious', an initiate of the process.

There is one final interpretation to be made. First, we may look carefully at the gravestone of Marie d'Hautpoul to see her described as 'noble Marie de Negri d'Arles dame d'Hautpoul de Blanchefort'. Applying our accumulated knowledge, we recall that the word 'noble' has the hidden meaning of 'initiate'. 'Marie' is *Mary, the Virgin*, and 'negre', or 'negri' can also yield *black*. 'D'Arles' should correctly be spelt 'd'Ables', a word which is a close phonetic equivalent of 'diable', the *devil*. Finally, 'Blanchefort', besides being a common family name, has the connotation '*extra white*' (or perhaps bleached – purified). Thus, in this one name, there are five unmistakable references to the Hermetic theme.

In the same manner we now look at the name of the Paris head of the Priory of Sion, Pierre Plantard de Saint-Clair. 'Pierre' means *stone*, while 'Saint' was extensively used at the time of the Gospels to denote an *initiate* for a saint, you see, was a *good* man. The Hermetic significance tended to be lost in later times when the Church applied it unknowingly to non-initiated clergymen. The word 'Clair' in French, means *light*, being associated in this sense with the *Moon*, and thence by double symbolism to *reflection*. You may care to recall that Claude Debussy, one of the Priory's Grand Masters, wrote a popular piece of music entitled 'Clair de Lune' (*light of the Moon*). The name 'Plantard' is a phonetic equivalent of 'planteur', which means 'farmer', or 'grower' – and if you recall that the mental task has often been designated 'celestial agriculture', you will see the significance at once.

I do not doubt that Pierre Plantard de Saint-Clair is the man's family name, established generations ago, but neither can I ignore the four blatant symbols of the Hermetic Art contained within it.

CHAPTER THIRTEEN

The Real History of Christ

The greatest single question raised by the foregoing exposition – and one that relegates the Rennes le Chateau enigma to a mere triviality – is that seeking a true account of the events which resulted in the writing of the Gospels and the gross misinterpretation to which they were later subjected.

A long succession of scholars has pondered on the vague and conflicting testimony bequeathed to us from the past, almost all of them falling into the same sticky trap – that of assuming the Bible texts to be factual accounts. It was easily done, for the general detail, the topography and geography of the biblical lands as reported, is accurate. Many of the tribes and the cities they occupied actually existed, their historical backgrounds authentic. But it is upon this solid foundation of fact that the allegories have been cunningly laid, the central characters being wholly fictitious, invoked solely for the purpose of personifying the Hermetic initiate and his mental process. This proposition is doubly hard to accept in view of the fact that certain of the entities have been given names borrowed from real life persons, as in the case of King Herod, whose biblical exploits bear no relation at all to the real events. So as to avoid making the same error, we are required to rebuild a picture of the times from sources entirely divorced from, or which are not in any way influenced by, the allegories within the Bible.

Further, we must be wary that these alternative sources are not the works of other initiates, for if they are, there will almost certainly be passages open to the same classic misinterpretation. Two instances of this are Manetho and Josephus, whose writings have been used as a foundation on which the historian has built our present day picture of the past. Manetho was an Egyptian priest of the 3rd century B.C., keeper of the sacred records of Heliopolis, a writer, historian – and an initiate. None of his works has survived except as quotations by later historians such as Josephus, Eusebius and Sextus Julius Africanus. However, there is no reason to suppose that what little is available is not accurately transmitted, even to the Hermetic references of the original. For example, when Josephus quotes Manetho as saying that a *leper* named Osarsiph changed his name to Moses, you can appreciate the hidden significance of the word 'leper' and know that Manetho is indicating the Hermetic content of the Moses story.

Similarly, Josephus inserted one or two allegories into his works, especially his Jewish Histories, and therefore his text must be read with the same perception and penetration.

The scene we wish to reconstruct is that of the biblical lands in the century prior to the supposed birth of Jesus – the general area known to the writers of the time as Syria, a term which includes the Palestine we know. And we are required to view it not through the eyes of the average man, but from the point of view of the Hermetic initiate.

Just as the Rosicrucians of the 18th and 19th centuries were a shadowy Order, invisible to the rest of the populace, so were the biblical initiates. To define themselves, they employed the names 'Hebrews', 'Israelites', and later, 'Jews', and we can show the truth of this by looking carefully at the origin of the names.

The term 'Hebrew' came first, mentioned in Genesis in relation to Abram, or Abraham, thus distinguishing him from his Amorite neighbours, the dominant tribe of the era in which the story is placed. Historians have concluded that the name implied a real tribe, but it is written 'Ivri', a word of undetermined origin, although the most favoured theory is that it was derived from 'a-var' (to pass over), because it would then relate nicely to Abraham as the one whom 'God took from the other side of the flood' (water) (Josh.24;3). Translators of the Septuagint version of the Old Testament understood the name in this way and referred to Abraham as the 'passer', rather than the 'Hebrew'. In the expositions so painstakingly covered, we have discovered that the phrase 'crossing the river (water)' is often used by the initiate to exemplify the transmission of consciousness. Thus 'Hebrew' is a code word for the initiate, and not the name of an uninitiated tribe of the biblical past.

Perhaps the most perceptive insight to the Hermetic meaning of 'Israelite' can be gained by reading Genesis 32, where Jacob discards his *old name* (uninitiated) for a *new* (reborn, as an initiate).

. . . Thy name shall be called no more Jacob, but *Israel*: for as a *prince* hast thou *power with God*. . .

A 'prince' is a *noble* person, you see, and Jacob, having become ennobled by accomplishment of the mental task, has power with God (is in harmony with his subconscious power). Thereafter, the descendents of Jacob were called *Israelites* (fellow initiates).

The name 'Jew' is first encountered in II Kings, and it has the meaning 'lauded'. It is not hard to equate this interpretation with that of 'annointed' (initiated), but if that is too tenuous to accept, then I remind you that Paul, who did not write in allegory, openly drew attention to the fact that the name had a concealed significance.

The earliest references to the Jews by other sources tend to corroborate Paul, as in the works of the Greek philosophers, Theophrastus, Clearchus of Soli, and Megasthenes, classic writers of the 3rd and 4th centuries B.C. Theophrastus wrote;

> They are a race of philosophers; they do not cease to *occupy themselves with the divinity*.

Mindful that the classic scribes of ancient Greece were invariably brother initiates, we read between the lines of that statement to understand that these 'philosophers' (initiates) do not cease to think about the divinity (they meditate).

Clearchus of Soli drew a parallel between the initiates of the Bible lands and those in India;

> The Jews are descended from a race of philosophers of India; the philosophers in India are called Calanians and in Syria, Jews . . . The name of their capital is very difficult to pronounce: it is called Jerusalem.

Megasthenes echoed the India connection;

> All the opinions expressed by the ancients about nature are found with the philosophers foreign to Greece, with the Brahmins of India, and in Syria, with those who call themselves Jews.

It is also recorded that Pythagorus and Plato were in close contact with the Jews and were anxious to learn from them.

I must reiterate that the 'Jews' to which the Greek writers were referring are not the mass of people from whom the Israeli race of today is descended, but a select group of initiates who maintained centres of Hermetic teaching in the biblical lands and who were responsible for perpetuation of its traditions. It is from this group that the writers of the various Old Testament books emanated. The origin of the Jewish race proper is something that may never be satisfactorily determined, although conjecture has it that they are descended from the Hyksos/Amalekites who, when expelled from Egypt, settled in southern Palestine. But this is unproven.

So far, we have covered the exodus of the initiates from Egypt and their consolidation in Judaea up until the time of Ezra, roughly about 470 B.C.

The next period of some significance is that of the Greeks in Judaea, which lasted from 330 to 167 B.C. During their occupation

they became aware of Jewish Hermetic tradition and wrote the
whole of the Old Testament out in their own language to preserve it,
a work of translation undertaken in Alexandria in 250 B.C. Seventy
scholars were employed to carry out this task, and for this reason
the finished work became known as the Septuagint.

The Greek period is important because it is from their language
that the word 'Christ' is derived. It sprang from 'Chrestos', a term in
use in the 5th century B.C., and employed by a number of classical
scholars such as Herodotus and Aeschylus. As John Allegro plainly
shows, the word can be traced by way of its Aramaic/Hebrew
original, back to a Sumerian root as one of the 'mushroom' symbols,
the same Aramaic word being used in the Old Testament to indicate
someone who is *annointed*. Thus 'Christ' means 'initiated'.

Another point of importance stemming from the Greek period is
their references to India and its religious legends, in which they
compare favourably the philosophers of both countries, for an
examination of Indian legends will reveal the foundation from which
the Christian Crucifixion theme evolved.

Buddha, the Asiatic Christ, is a miracle worker born from an
immaculate virgin. Persecuted, he is driven out of his country to die,
so it is said, under a *cruciform tree*. The Indian Kristna is also born of
a virgin and becomes a worker of healing miracles until he is
persecuted by the orthodox clergy. Some traditions state that he died
nailed to a tree by an arrow, an aspect of Hermetic myth that is
repeated in the Greek story of Cadmus, who must pin the *serpent* to
an oak tree with his arrow. A comprehensive comparison of these
legends and the Christian myth has been given by Madame
Blavatsky in Vol. II of her ISIS UNVEILED, and so needs nothing
more from me here.

Thus, we see that at the time of the 1st century B.C., the initiates
in Palestine were using the old themes of Exodus and Solomon's
Temple less and less, although the traditional stories were preserved
as sacred lore from which the uninitiated could still learn. Instead,
they were turning to a mixture of Egypto-Indian myth in which the
act of the mental process was symbolised by the initiate being nailed
to a tree. With the appearance of the Septuagint and the Greek word
'Christ', the myth gradually built until it was Christ, the personification of the initiate, who was nailed to the tree.

The cruelty of Alexander of Jannaeus, who persecuted the initiate
Essenes and put barbaric action to the word of their sacred myth by
actually nailing many of them to the stake, gave impetus to the
tradition until by the opening years of what we like to call Anno
Domini (the years of our Lord), it was well established among the
circle of Judaean initiates.

The situation prevailing in Judaea at that time was one of almost constant civil turmoil. From 167 B.C., there came the period of the Maccabeans and their revolt against the Assyrians, followed by the Roman occupation and its subsequent unrest, a time of persecution and revolt which eventually culminated in the destruction of the city of Jerusalem in 70 A.D.

It is during this critical period that Jesus Christ is said to have been born of a miracle birth, held his ministry and then died a martyr's death on the cross. But Philo Judaeus, an historian who left a long account of the Essenes of that period, and who having been born earlier than Jesus, died in 50 A.D., never mentioned the episode at all. Although he lived all his life in Palestine, he had apparently never heard of the Messiah.

The same can be said of the apostle Paul, whose early letters were written somewhere between 50 and 60 A.D. Bible historians have never ceased to be amazed that this writer said little or nothing about Jesus as he is depicted in the Gospels. Nowhere is there any mention of the miracles worked by Jesus, or even a mention of the all important Lord's Prayer. Paul speaks of *Jesus the Christ*, but it evidently is not the same person featured in the four Gospels – and when he does describe the death of Jesus, there is no reference to Pilate; instead he says that he was crucified at the instigation of wicked angels, 'the rulers of this age' (I Cor.2; 8).

Paul may perhaps be forgiven for this astonishing lapse, for at the time of his writing, the full details of the first Gospel myth were still in the mind of Mark, who was just about to set them down. As an initiate, however, Paul was quite conversant with the prevailing innovation in Hermetic lore, the crucifixion to a tree myth, and it is to this tradition that he is referring when he says;

I am crucified with Christ; nevertheless I live; yet not I but Christ liveth in me.

This statement only becomes crystal clear if you apply the Hermetic principle to it.

In searching for a reason which might have impelled Mark to set down his cleverly devised version of the myth at the time he did, the most obvious appears to be the devastation of the initiates' teaching centre at Jerusalem. It was a traumatic enough event. As the onslaught of the Hyksos of long ago had forced the initiates to flee from Egypt, so the crushing victory of the Roman army precipitated a second Exodus – and there was no hesitation. When the centurions finally broke through the temple defences to lay their hands on the great treasure, the initiates had already departed, the gold and silver temple trappings disregarded, the real 'treasure' taken with them.

Jerusalem was conquered in 70 A.D., the same year that Mark is
thought to have written his Gospel – and it is at this critical date that
we consult the work of the Jewish historian, Flavius Josephus.

Masada and the Sicarii

Josephus was born in Jerusalem in 37 A.D.; later he became one of
the leading figures in the Jewish rebellion. At the fall of Jerusalem, he
was captured by the Romans, but there seems to have been little
enmity between himself and his captors, for he subsequently went to
Rome where he was eventually granted citizenship. There, in his
later years, he wrote several historical works, one of which was THE
JEWISH WARS, a long and very detailed account of the events
which preceded the attack on Jerusalem.

As with Philo and Paul, Josephus would seem to have been ideally
placed to transmit vital information about Jesus, but in his entire
works, there are only two references to 'Jesus the Christ' – and
modern theologians are suspicious about the veracity of those, for it
is well known that the early Church was in the habit of inserting
spurious passages into such works in order to support their own
beliefs. But this is old ground. What remains is the fact that once
again, it is as if Jesus the Messiah who was crucified only four years
before the birth of Josephus, had never existed.

THE JEWISH WARS offers a comprehensive account of the turmoil in Judaea, from the 1st century B.C., up until the final assault
on Jerusalem, and as such, is considered to be a relatively accurate
historical document, an assessment which makes the omission of
information about Jesus all the more aggravating. But Josephus
places before us information of another kind, for if the text is
interpreted from the point of view of the initiate, it will be realised
that the historian was not at all unfamiliar with the language of the
Hermeticist. He opens his account – written, so he tells us, for 'the
barbarians up country' – with an apparently innocuous statement of
personal data. The text, he informs us, is written by;

> Josephus, son of Matthias, a Hebrew by race and a native of
> Jerusalem, and a priest . . .

As we have now discovered, the name *Hebrew*, and the phrase
'native of Jerusalem' can hold an inner meaning, but is it enough to
justify acceptance of the writer's initiateship? Josephus obviously
thought it wasn't, so he included the phrase 'son of Matthias',
thereby invoking a name with a Hermetic basis. 'Matthias' has

significant phonetic equivalents in the Greek language, which the reader can verify for himself by consulting LE MYSTERE DES CATHEDRALES. Fulcanelli demonstrates that 'Matthaeus' (St. Matthew) Μαrθαιος and 'Matthias' Μαrθiou stem from the word Μάθημαros which means 'science', or 'knowledge'. Thus, right at the beginning of his work, Josephus informs his readers that he is a *Son of Science*, i.e., an intitiate – and that his text must be read in that light.

THE JEWISH WARS, therefore, while indisputably an authentic historical transmission of Judaean history, does contain certain passages that have been deliberately embellished in order to carry the Hermetic myth. I will interpret one, and perhaps that which is the best known is the historic last stand of the Sicarii/Zealots at Masada.

Yet again we are indebted to John Allegro for his deep study of the older texts, for he shows that the roots of both 'Zealot' and 'Sicarii' lie in the 'mushroom' symbolism, and so we are warned that whatever the real Zealots, or Sicarii may have been, their name has been utilised to personify the Hermetic initiate. Support for this will be found in the fact that the name Sicarii comes from the 'sica', a curved dagger carried by them, and you will notice that there is a comparison to be drawn between the Sica and the Sickle, the curved knife of the Greek Druids. The inference is plain.

The account tells how the Sicarii and their leader, Eleazar, at the fall of Jerusalem, refused to surrender, but retreated southwards to take refuge in the fortress of Masada, a rocky eminence near the shores of the Dead Sea. Its inhospitable terrain has been used by Josephus in order to convey the difficulty of the Hermetic task, as my emphasis on certain words will show. Masada, he writes;

A rock of no slight circumference and lofty from end to end, is abruptly terminated on every side by deep ravines, the precipices rising sheer from an invisible base and being *inaccessible to the foot of any living creature*, save in two places where the rock permits of *no easy ascent*. Of these tracks, one leads from the *Lake* Asphaltitis (the *Dead* Sea) on the *east*, and the other by which the approach is easier, from the west. The former they call the *snake*, seeing a resemblence to that reptile in its *narrowness and continual windings* (a tongue in cheek description of the conscious mind); for its course is broken in skirting jutting crags and returning frequently upon itself and gradually lengthening out again, it makes *painful headway* (like meditation). One traversing this route must firmly plant each foot alternately (the meditation periods must be consecutive with no break). Destruction faces him, for on either side yawn chasms so terrific as to daunt the hardiest. After following this track for *thirty* furlongs one reaches the summit which, instead of tapering to a sharp peak, expands into a plain.

The western approach, Josephus points out, is easier but it was barred by a great *tower* erected by *Herod*, who once occupied the plateau. The king had a palace built there and enclosed the entire summit with a wall of *white stone*.

The Sicarii took possession of Masada in 70 A.D., and found Herod's vast stores *in perfect condition*. Thus, they were able to hold out against the Romans for *three* years. However, when the attackers finally breached the walls with *fire*, Eleazar and his Sicarii decided on *self-massacre* rather than surrender. And so they *died nobly* for their beliefs.

It might be argued that if the Crucifixion was indeed an Hermetic myth, why did not Josephus – an initiate – make the effort to perpetuate it in his work on Jerusalem? The explanation to this is that the Gosepls did not assume the euphoric importance placed on their literal word until more than two or three centuries afterwards, and so Josephus was doing what other initiates did, concocting his own allegory by making use of an historical incident. We can be sure that some sort of battle took place at Masada, but the real event was not quite as Josephus has portrayed it.

If further evidence of such manipulation of facts is required, may I refer you to an amazing parallel to the Masada story. I have already described how the Cathars were persecuted in 13th century France, and how the last remnants of them retreated to the rock fortress of Mont Segur, an eminence of astonishing similarity to Masada, if the historical account is to be believed. The story goes that, surrounded and beseiged, the Cathars were given a few days in which to decide their own fate. Either they must give up their 'heretical' faith and go free, or be burned at the stake. It is said that, during this truce, *three* men climbed down the sheer rock face under cover of *darkness* and managed to slip through the enemy lines to escape, taking the Cathars' 'treasure' with them. The rest elected to be *put to the fire* ('fire' = meditation). Thus, they *sacrificed* themselves – a *self-inflicted death* which took place on a *mount*.

The Gospels

Following Mark's initial transcription of the Crucifixion myth, there came the Gospels of Matthew and Luke, judged by modern scholars to have been written in 80 A.D. At the same period, Luke also penned the Acts of the Apostles, a subsidiary text which serves to embroider the main tradition and has the effect of adding credibility to it as a 'real' event. A decade later, the initiate John added his Gospel, a version which contains a number of notable embellishments to the original idea. Lastly, there is John's Revelation, a book of the deepest allegory and the hardest to interpret successfully.

The special names given to the four writers – they are obviously pseudonyms – offers some enlightenment as to the basis on which they were selected. Matthew (Matthaeus), as we have just discovered, is coupled with the Greek word for 'science'. The Hebrew name, Mattithyah, from which it is also derived, means 'gift of God', a phrase much used by later alchemists to denote the successful completion of their practice. In the Gospel of Mark (2; 14), Matthew begins life as Levi and is said to be the son of Alphaeus, the river god. It may be coincidence, but just like Moses, Matthew was 'drawn out of water'. When Levi achieves his initiateship, he becomes Matthew (a son of science – the Hermetic Science).

Luke is a contraction of Lucius, meaning 'light' – which in the case of the Hermeticist, refers to *understanding*.

John means 'God has been gracious', a phrase which suggests successful initiateship, a Hermetic view which is further supported by the fact that, like Jesus, John was the product of a *miraculous birth*.

Mark, or Marcus, is Greek for 'mighty hammer', a little used term within Hermetic lore, but nevertheless denoting strength through initiateship – the might of the subconsious power, once invoked.

Beginning with a special synod convened near Jaffa at about 100 A.D., the 2nd and 3rd centuries were a critical period in which the secret religion of Dualism fought a losing battle with the birth of Catholic Christianity. As we now understand, the latter concept was founded purely on the literal words and ideas of the Gospel texts. It was a struggle in which the classic arguments of Athanasius and Arius, the two bishops of Alexandria, finally came to a head to be settled by the Council of Nicea in 325 A.D. That Arius was condemned and the Catholic Church began its rise to power is a matter of historical record, and in retrospect, it seems a monumental act of misfortune for the Gospels to have been set down at all. And there is still the question of exactly why they were written. To be sure, the fall of Jerusalem saw the disintegration of Jewish culture in that centre, but after all, there still remained the Old Testament, a book of sacred law that had sufficed for fifteen hundred years, in spite of the fact that it too, was myth. Why try to improve on it?

As it happens, there exists a very good reason to explain the advent of the Gospels. The clues are thin on the ground, owing to the secrecy which prevailed at the time – but they are there.

The Shroud of Turin

Recent international publicity given to this sacred relic has made us all aware that the Shroud bears an image purported to be that of Jesus after his crucifixion, an image somehow transferred to the cloth as it was wrapped around his body in the cave. In 1978, increasing academic interest in the origin of the Shroud culminated in a detailed photographic analysis by scientists using the most up to date techniques available. The result showed that, whatever was used to impress the figure on the linen, it was a process entirely unknown to modern science and cannot be duplicated in any of our laboratories. Technicians have ascertained that the image is comparable to a scorch mark, yet such heat that was used appears to have been applied so fleetingly that it did not penetrate the linen threads, but only marked the surface. The conclusion of the scientists in Los Alamos Scientific Laboratory is that the image was made by a 'burst of radiant energy'. Both front and back images are a perfect negative, as might have resulted had the Shroud been wrapped over a body – and then the body had somehow been made to emit a brief flash of heat energy.

Such is the enigma presented to Science.

Let me remind readers at once that the Shroud can only be documented back as far as the year 1353, when it suddenly turned up in the ownership of Geoffrey de Charny, a French nobleman who resided at Lirey, some twelve miles from Troyes. By a strange and possibly revealing coincidence, Geoffrey de Charny's family name appears in earlier historical documents, for it was a Geoffrey de Charny who was burnt at the stake in 1314, a companion knight to Jacques de Molay, Grand Master of the Templars at the time of their suppression. Although no documented evidence has come to public scrutiny which would link the two Geoffreys, it is not in the least unreasonable to assume that the de Charny in whose keeping the Shroud was found in 1353, was of the same family line – and therefore a hereditary guardian of a sacred Templar relic.

The idea of the Shroud being a secret inheritance from earlier Templar lodges is supported by the fact that the sacred cloth only came to light by sheer accident. De Charny was killed suddenly on the battlefield, before he had time to arrange his affairs, and his surviving relatives allowed the Shroud to be seen, perhaps not realising its import. The attention of the Church was aroused, and thereafter the Shroud was annexed by them.

For the general public, the Shroud's earlier history remains obscure. There are scattered references to it in Church manuscripts which date back to the 1st century – and a recent pollen analysis shows that the cloth had at one time been exposed to the air in the Jerusalem area. There exists some comparison in historical references to the Mandylion, the Image of Edessa, the 'image not made with human hands', a relic that was on view in Constantinople until 1204, but which disappeared completely when Templar Crusaders sacked the city. Again, a Templar connection.

The difference between the Mandylion and the Shroud is that the former, according to the historic reports, showed only the face of Jesus, whereas the Shroud contains the full length figure. Modern investigators, however, have proposed that the Edessa cloth showed only the face because it was folded in four and placed in a special frame so that it appeared as a head and shoulders portrait. Ian Wilson, in his book THE TURIN SHROUD, makes a very good case for the present and the Mandylion being one and the same – and perhaps I can support his conclusions with no less an authority than the Bible texts themselves. However, these references are most obscure and secret.

The Mandylion

To reconstruct the sequence of events which led to the writing of the Gospels, we begin with some historical documents attached to Abgar V, king of the city of Edessa from 13 to 50 A.D. Edessa lies to the north of Judaea, inside the borders of Turkey, and is nowadays called Urfa. The relevant documents are no longer extant, but verbatim copies of them were recorded by Eusebius, bishop of Ceasarea at the end of the 2nd century, in his 'Ecclesiastical Histories'. They take the form of two letters, the first sent by courier from king Abgar to Jesus in Jerusalem:

Abgarus, prince of Edessa, sends greetings to Jesus the excellent Saviour, who has appeared in the borders of Jerusalem. I have heard the reports respecting thee and thy cures, as performed by thee without medicines or the use of herbs. For it is said that thou causest the blind to see again and the lame to walk, and thou cleansest the lepers, casteth out impure spirits and demons, heal those that are tormented by long disease, and raise the dead. Hearing all these things, I have concluded that you are either God, having descended from Heaven to do these things, or that by doing them, you are the Son of God. Therefore I have written and besought thee to visit me, and to heal the disease with which I am

afflicted. I have heard also, that the Jews murmur against thee and
are plotting to injure thee; I have, however, a very small but noble
state which is sufficient for both of us.

The reply from Jesus, received by Abgar, said:

Blessed art thou, O Abgarus, who, without seeing, hast believed
in me. For it is written concerning me, that they who have seen
me will not believe, that they who have not seen, may believe and
live. But in regard to what thou hast written, that I should come
to thee, it is necessary that I should fulfil all things here, for which
I have been sent. And after this fulfilment, thus to be received
again by Him that sent me. And after I have been received up, I
will send to thee a certain one of my disciples, that he may heal thy
affliction, and give life to thee and those who are with thee.

For many years, historians have assumed the letter from Abgar to
be proof that he forsook his eastern religion to become a Christian, in
the hope that he would be granted a miracle cure. But think back on
the panorama of symbolism that I have revealed to you. Bring to
mind the casual but concealed manner by which a Freemason may
indicate his membership during the course of conversation, using
such phrases as 'on the square'. Is it to be thought that the initiates of
the far past never employed such a technique? No, because I have
adequately proved that they did. Look at the letters once more and
you will begin to see that they constitute an exchange between
Hermetic brothers. Abgar's references to the *cleansing of lepers*, the
raising of the dead, and the *Son of God* are glaring examples of initiate
'catch-phrases', and as such, are merely an identifying prelude to the
important part of the message. This lies in the very last line, where
Abgar extends sanctuary to the initiates of Jerusalem, who are on the
verge of their second, enforced exodus.

The reply, couched in the same esoteric language, acknowledges
Abgar's initiateship in the sentence 'they who have seen me will not
believe, that they who have not seen, may believe and live'. This is
an inverted way of saying that those who believe the Gospel story to
be a literal truth are uninitiated, while those who know it to be a
myth, *believe and live* (in the third state of consciousness). Ostensibly, the letter indicates to prying eyes that Jesus cannot make the
journey, but that one of his disciples will do so at a later date.
However, as every initiate knew that 'Jesus' did not exist as a person,
Abgar would ignore that part. Reading that a disciple would come,
he would take it for granted that his offer of sanctuary had been
accepted.

The initiates of strife-torn Jerusalem, therefore, came to Edessa, bringing a 'treasure' with them. This is made quite clear in a further screed attached, so Eusebius informs us, to the two letters. But as before, the text holds one meaning on the surface and another underneath. After the ascension of Jesus, it is said, a disciple named Thaddaeus came to Edessa and began to *perform miracles*, healing the diseased and infirm, so that all were amazed. Abgar soon heard of this;

> and began to suspect that this was the very person concerning whom Jesus had written saying 'after I have been received up again, I will send to thee one of my disciples, who shall heal thy affliction'.

Arrangements were soon made for Thaddaeus to be brought to the palace, and immediately upon entering into the presence of the king;

> Something extraordinary appeared to Abgar *in the countenance* of the apostle Thaddaeus; which Abgar observing, paid him reverence. But all around were amazed, for they did not perceive the vision which appeared to Abgar alone.

Reading between the lines, as we are required to do, it is apparent that the initiates from Jerusalem showed something to Abgar, telling him a truth concerning it which no non-initiate should know. The 'treasure' they displayed was the Mandylion, the 'face not made by human hands', and the three documents are proof that the Mandylion came to Edessa from Jerusalem some time in Abgar's reign – a time critical to the initiates.

Support for this assertion can be found in a tenth century text recovered from a monastery in Lower Egypt during the 1840s. It is another version of the Abgar story, but with a slight variation concerning the king's vision. The original letter quoted by Eusebius warily refers to the sacred relic as something which Abgar saw 'in the countenance' (meaning the 'face'). According to the 10th century text, when summoned to the palace, Thaddaeus took the Mandylion with him and placed it 'on his forehead, like a sign'.

> Abgar saw him coming from a distance, and thought he saw a light shining from his face which no eye could stand, which the portrait Thaddaeus was wearing produced.

So dumbfounded was Abgar that he forgot all about his affliction – a paralysis of the legs – and ran to meet the disciple. As he did so;

> He felt the same feeling, though in different way, as those who saw that face flashing with lightning on Mount Tabor. And so,

receiving the likeness from the apostle, immediately felt his leprosy cleansed . . . '

   After recovering from the shock, Abgar

asked about the likeness portrayed on the linen cloth. For when he had carefully inspected it he saw that it *did not consist of earthly colours*, and he was astounded at its power . . . At this, Thaddaeus explained about the *time of the agony* and that the likeness was *due to sweat, not pigment*.

I have emphasised certain phrases in this text because they are of tremendous importance in relation to discovering the true nature of the Mandylion/Shroud. The first proposes the portrait to be in some way of paranormal origin, while the latter, apparently casual connection to the appropriate biblical passage leads us to the carefully devised clues which show exactly how the portrait was made.

Before interpreting them, however, let us complete the history of the Mandylion and link it up with that of the Shroud.

Abgar died in 57 A.D., but prior to his death and during the short reign of his first son, the portrait remained on display in Edessa. But when Abgar's second son ascended to the throne, he reverted to pagan worship and the guardians of the Image hurriedly concealed it so that it would not fall into non-initiate hands. No surviving document of the period describes the location selected for the hiding place, but some hint may be gleaned by the knowledge that, from 58 A.D. onwards, the west gate of the city was then and ever afterwards held in special reverence. It was known as the Kappe Gate – the gate of arches, or vaults.

The Mandylion remained concealed thus, all but lost to knowledge for nearly five hundred years, until a severe flood caused extensive damage to the city's buildings in 525 A.D. During the period of reconstruction that followed, the Kappe Gate was examined, and a hidden vault situated above the main arch was discovered. Later documents describe how the Mandylion was found resting inside, together with a red tile – on which there was also a picture of Christ's face – and a lamp, said to be still burning at the time the vault was opened. It can be accepted, of course, that the tile and the lamp are figurative addition, but the Mandylion was real enough.

The portrait remained in Edessa for many years, but in 944, when it seemed likely that the Persian armies then laying seige to the city, were about to force an entry, the relic was secretly transported to Constantinople. It was held there for the next two and a half centuries and documented evidence suggests that it was in this period that the Mandylion was taken out of its frame, allowing the full length figure to be viewed by all.

In 1204, Constantinople itself was threatened and ultimately sacked by the Crusaders, of whom many were Templars. It is at this point that the Mandylion/Shroud disappeared, only to return to public view at the untimely death of Geoffrey de Charny.

This history is, of necessity, nothing more than a brief annotation, but should the reader wish to ascertain the ground on which it is given, I suggest Ian Wilson's book, THE TURIN SHROUD, where all the relative details are comprehensively laid out. On my own account, I can add a few details which do not appear in Ian Wilson's analysis, but stem instead from initiate sources and which refer indirectly to the Mandylion and its hiding place.

The first of these has already been dealt with in the exposition of the Rennes le Chateau symbolism where, if you recall, we discussed the carved pictures on the great slab raised from the foot of Sauniere's altar. Both right and left hand scenes take place in an *arched vault*. Another obscure clue occurs in the fact that the name 'archangel' appears only in the New Testament. The prefix 'arch' has always been interpreted to mean 'chief', but it is significant that the texts in which it is found (I Thess. 4 and Jude 9) were written either at the time the Mandylion was hidden, or a few years later.

Other areas of Hermetic symbolism will be found to contain references to an 'arched vault', but by far the most comprehensive is that found in the initiation ritual of Freemasonry.

The Royal Arch

As we have seen, the ordinary lodge rites of initiation take the form of three degrees, the basis of which is the myth of King Solomon's Temple. But there is a fourth, even higher degree, open only to Master Masons. It is called the Royal *Arch*, and is considered to be the supreme degree.

In the initiation ceremony, the candidate is required to mount seven steps to a sacred shrine, which is situated at the *crown of a vaulted chamber*. There, he wrenches out two of the arch stones so that he can be lowered into the vault, to 'attend to a portion of the writings of our Grand Master, King Solomon.' He is also ordered to *search for something*, and finds a scroll of vellum which he is unable to read because there is not enough *light*. To overcome this, he wrenches out a *third stone* and sees that the scroll contains the first *three* verses of Genesis, chapter 1.

A part of the ceremony required the Principal Sojourner, one of the accompanying master masons, to relate how they found a vault beneath a dome at the site of the former Temple, which had been burned down. Gaining entry, they discovered an altar of *white marble*, on which were mystic symbols covered by a white *veil*. The ritual continues until Zerubbabel, the master directing the initiation, congratulates the candidate on his exaltation into Royal Arch Masonry, which is the 'foundation and keystone of the whole Masonic structure'. The new initiate is warned that though he may think he has taken a fourth degree in Masonry, it is not the case, for it is merely a higher part of the Third Degree (because there are only three stages to the Hermetic process).

At this point, a significant statement is made;

. . . when you were raised to the Third Degree, you were informed that by the untimely death of our Master, Hiram Abiff, the secrets of a Master Mason were lost, and that certain substitute secrets were adopted to distinguish all Master Masons until time or circumstance should restore the genuine. *These secrets were lost for a period of nearly five hundred years*, and were regained in the manner which has just been described to you, somewhat in a dramatic form, the more forcibly to impress on your mind the providential means by which those ancient secrets were regained.

There is little doubt that this speech relates to the rediscovery of the Mandylion after its five hundred year disappearance.

The historical texts which relate the story of King Abgar name the disciple sent by Jesus as Thaddaeus, a name which in the original Syriac in which the documents were written, is Addai – and there exists a fourth century version of the tale, entitled 'The Doctrine of Addai'. Other versions tell how Thaddaeus preached Christianity in Edessa, aided by a person named Aggai. Both these historic names are reflected in the Royal Arch ceremony by the presence of a character named Haggai, whose duty it is to deliver a symbolic lecture to the successful candidate;

The form of the Royal Arch Chapter, when properly arranged approaches – as nearly as circumstances will permit – that of a Caternarian Arch; thus we preserve a memorial of the vaulted shrine in which the Sacred Word was deposited, whilst from the impenetrable nature of this strongest of all architectural forms, we learn the necessity of guarding our mysteries from profanation by the most inviolable secrecy. It also strongly typifies that invariable adherence to social order and spirit of fraternal union,

which has given energy and permanancy to the whole consti-
tution of Freemasonry, thus enabling it to *survive the wreck of
mighty empires and resist the destroying hands of time.*

The significance of the Caternarian Arch is that it is not like an
ordinary arch, but is *inverted*, its form as that of a chain hanging
between two pillars. Whilst the arch is not shown thus outside
Masonic rituals, this special inversion symbolises for the Royal Arch
candidate, the *reversal* of thoughts necessary to complete the process.
I think you will have to agree that there are sufficient indications in
the above ceremonies to show that the 'Sacred Word' is really the
Mandylion/Shroud, which was the property of the Hermetic
initiates.

As a footnote to this, I add that in the opening degrees of ordinary
Masonry, there is a character known as the Tyler, whose function is
that of a guard, or door-keeper. Nowhere in the myth of Solomon's
Temple is there a guard mentioned, nor a 'tyler', or 'Tiler'. But there
is in the historical discovery of the Mandylion.

The Origin of the Shroud

Having shown that Templarism, Rosicrucianism and Free-
masonry have a common ancestry of which the Shroud was indisputably a major part, it should now be conceded that the Mandylion
and the Shroud are one and the same thing, despite the absence of
written proof (for what it would be worth) that will tie the two
together. And in considering the Shroud, which exhibits every
aspect of the symbolism annotated in the Gospels and elsewhere, we
are inevitably confronted with a two-handed question: If Jesus really
was a mythical character invented to act out a part in a grand
Hermetic allegory, it follows that the Shroud was never wrapped
about his body. So how was the Shroud made, and why?

The latter part of the question is relatively easy to resolve, especially when we recall the troubled times in which the artifact came
into existence. Judaea was slowly being torn apart, not only by the
Romans, but by quarrelsome civil factions, with the result that the
long established traditions of the initiates were on the point of being
totally submerged. Something drastic was required – an innovation
that would restore the waning influence of the Old Law of Dualism.
The Crucifixion myth, already in current favour with initiates, was
seized upon as the new vehicle to promote the Hermetic secret, the
underground religion of Dualism – and action was put to the word.
The Shroud was manufactured and then the first Gospel was written

out to support the verbal tradition.

It is the answer to the first part of the question that will be a stumbling block to those sceptical of Rosicrucian powers. I have indicated that one advantage to be enjoyed by the full initiate, at the transmission of the ordinary mind to an exalted state, is a form of mental communication. I now add that such powers – considered to be 'paranormal' by the average person – extend to other spheres, and that the impressed figure seen on the Shroud was put there by a high initiate focussing his exalted consciousness in the necessary manner.

To those who will immediately object that such a proposition is absurd, I ask for a consideration of the phenomenon known as Stigmata, an aspect of the paranormal which has been comprehensively documented, so much so that there is no denying its reality. It is known that certain deeply religious persons quite unexpectedly evince all the physical wounds said to have been suffered by Christ on the cross – the nail marks in the hands and feet, an issue of blood from the spear thrust in the side, and even the scratch marks on the forehead from the crown of thorns. The phenomenon lasts for a short time 'and then disappears, leaving the victim unmarked. Medical and scientific supervision of a number of Stigmatics has shown that the victim descends into a religiously inspired trance in order to allow the phenomenon to manifest – and here we have a classic example of the subconscious power at work *while the conscious mind is subdued*. In the conscious mind of the misinformed devout, the myth of the Crucifixion is a reality, and so as the conscious mind becomes deadened by the state of trance, the *idea* is externalised by the subconscious power. When the victim comes out of the trance state, the conscious mind assumes its dominance once more and the Stigmata disappear.

If this can happen to an uninitiated person, do you not think it possible for an exalted consciousness of the initiate to exert the same power, *but in a controlled fashion*? And further: is it so surprising that, with all the technology at their disposal, the scientists can only conclude that the Shroud image was made by a 'burst of radiant energy'?

I leave the sceptics to their protestations and move on to the clues hidden in the New Testament text which relate directly to the Shroud and the way it was made.

The Linen and the Napkin

There has been a great deal of academic agonising over the Shroud and its possible connection with the few sparse lines in the Gospels describing the finding of Jesus's burial linen;

7.   And the napkin that was about his head, not lying with the linen clothes, but wrapped together in a place by itself. (John 20)

The word 'napkin' was originally written 'soudarion' – literally 'sweat-cloth', and it holds a concealed significance for the Herme-ticist. We may recall that the tenth century text of Abgar's story attempted to hint at how the Mandylion was made.

'. . . Thaddaeus explained about the time of the agony and that the likeness was due to sweat, not pigments.

Following this unmistakable line of enquiry, we turn to the rele-vant passage of Luke 22 which tells of the agony of Jesus in the *garden*;

44   . . . being in agony he prayed more earnestly; and his sweat was as it were great drops of blood falling to the ground.

By now, we are familiar with the Hermetic sense of the word *garden* in that it relates to the inner mind, and its application in this instance immediately enlightens us as to the real meaning of verse 44. The *agony* which Jesus suffered as he *prayed* was the effort of concen-tration exerted during his deep meditation. Do not forget that this episode took place not long before he was 'crucified' and therefore is intended to portray the initiate in the last stages before the final transmission of consciousness. As for the *sweat*, I ask you to look at the 18th Tarot card, the *Moon*. In this pictorial design you will see the *sweat*, or *dew* of the Moon (reflection), which is sometimes referred to as the *blood of the moon*, and which is really the energy generated by deep meditation. You will now know why the Rosicrucians are sometimes called the Brothers of the Boiled Dew.

Applying this key to the mysterious sweat–cloth described by John, we realise that the napkin was the *sweat-cloth* (the Mandylion) that absorbed the *sweat* (mental energy) of Jesus's head (from the mind of the initiate who made the Mandylion).

John even leaves us a clue to the way in which the Mandylion was presented while it was in Edessa, for he tells us that the napkin was not lying with the linen clothes, but that it was wrapped together in a place by itself. Recalling that the Mandylion was not at that time displayed as a full length figure, but was folded and placed in a frame so that only the face was exposed, we can now discern the inner sense of John's statement;

And the napkin that was about his head (the face of the

Mandylion), not lying with the linen clothes (the rest of the figure
was hidden), but wrapped together (folded up) in a place by itself
(Edessa).

The 10th century manuscript relating to Abgar provides a second
line of investigation in the passage describing the king's vision;

He felt the same feeling, though in a different way, as those who
saw that face flashing with lightning on Mount Tabor.

This relates to a tradition that Mount Tabor was the height upon
which Jesus stood when he went through the *transfiguration*, and so
we are guided to that section of the Gospels – the text of Matthew
17.

1. 'And after six days Jesus taketh Peter, James and John his
   brother and bringeth them up into an high *mountain* apart.
2. And was *transfigured* before them: and his *face* did shine as the
   sun, and his raiment was *white* as *light*.
3. And behold, there appeared unto them Moses and *Elias* (Elijah)
   talking with him.'

The Hermetic key allows us to see that this *ascent into the mountain*,
with Peter and the others (all personifications of the conscious mind)
after six days (the time taken by the process) is just one more
expression of the mental task which will end in the *transfiguration* (the
transmission of consciousness). This is plain to see, but we must
search for some significance in the inclusion of Moses and Elias.
Moses directs us to the Old Testament, and Elias – a name for the
Universal Mind by way of the *Sun* – refers to the prophet Elijah. And
it is with Elijah that we find an oblique connection to the Mandylion,
in I Kings, 19, where the prophet arrives at Horeb, the *mount of God*,
after a *journey* of *forty days and forty nights*. This is obviously a
reference to the Hermetic process, so we read on to find the link with
the face in the Mandylion. While the prophet is in the *cave*, hearing
the *still*, small voice of the Lord, he does a strange thing.

13.   'And it was so, when Elijah heard it, that he *wrapped his face in
      his mantle*, and went and stood in the entering of the cave.'

'Every Rosicrucian knows that the phrase 'wrapped his face in his
mantle' is not to be read literally, for it is a device to show that the
conscious mind must be deadened (wrapped, or covered up) in order
to allow the 'still, small voice' of the subconscious to come through.
The analogy is found elsewhere, as in the *adventures* of Apollonius of
Tyana who, when he desired to hear the voice, wrapped himself in a

mantle of fine wool. Thus, the *face* of Elijah is actually another term with which to represent the conscious mind.

In his own text, Matthew has used the same analogy, except that as Jesus has been *transfigured* (the process is complete), his *face* is said to *shine as the sun* (it is full of the light of the Universal Mind). In this double reference to the *face* of the conscious mind – the invocation of the name Elijah – we are given the key with which to understand the real import of the 10th century text when it says that Abgar 'felt the same thing' (initiateship). But there is an added comment, 'though not in the same way', which warns us of some alternative. And the only other 'face' that held any special significance for the initiates of that period was that on the Mandylion.

Finally, I would like to offer an item of evidence which is of some importance, for it relates to an edition of the Gospels which has remained uninterpreted.

In his book, THE SECRET GOSPEL, Professor Morton Smith of Columbia University, USA, describes an expedition undertaken by him to the biblical lands in 1958, during which he visited the monastery of Mar Saba, some twelve miles south east of Jerusalem. Browsing through the library of old documents held in the monastery's archives, he chanced across a letter written by Clement of Alexandria (circa 125 A.D.), and which was directed to a person named as Theodore. Theodore, it appeared, had been desperately worried by the manner in which certain factions were interpreting a copy of Mark's Gospel, held at that time in the church of Alexandria. In his letter of reply, Clement had tried to allay these fears, and in doing so, included a verbatim copy of a passage inserted into the Gospel in question, and which is not found in the generally known text. This special insertion is made in chapter 10, in the middle of verse 32;

(Normal Text)

32.   And they were in the way going up to Jerusalem . . . (insert begins here)

(Special Insertion)

'. . . and they came into Bethany, and a certain woman, whose brother had died, was there. And coming, she prostrated herself before Jesus and said to him, 'Son of David, have mercy on me.' But the disciples rebuked her. And Jesus, being angered, went off with her into the garden where the tomb was and straightaway a

great cry was heard from the tomb. And going near, Jesus rolled
away the stone from the door of the tomb. And straightaway
going in where the youth was, he stretched forth his hand and
raised him, seizing his hand. But the youth, looking upon him,
loved him and began to beseech him that he might be with him.
And going out of the tomb they came into the house of the youth,
for he was rich. And after six days, Jesus told him what to do and
in the evening, the youth came to him wearing a linen cloth over
his naked body. And he remained with him that night, for Jesus
taught him the mystery of the kingdom of God. And thence,
arising, he returned to the other side of the Jordan . . .'

(Continuation of original text of Mark, at verse 35)

35.   . . . And James and John, the son of Zebedee, came unto him
         . . . etc.

The gist of Clement's reply was to allay the fears of Theodore,
who had drawn attention to the interpretation of the passage by a
sect known as the Carpocratians. This group, Theodore darkly
pointed out, had stated that such activities could only be concluded
to be those of a homosexual, and it was for this reason that this copy
of the Gospel had been kept secret. Thus, Clement – a man who well
knew the inner meaning of the text – was required to explain away
the apparent literal meaning to an uninitiated Theodore.

Although Professor Morton Smith was not in possession of the
Hermetic key, he quite rightly deduced that the passage deals not
with homosexuality, but with some sort of initiation. Readers will
quickly recognise that the insert is a variation of the Lazarus story
found in John 11. And it is in the text of John that we find a reference
to that famous *napkin:*

'And he that was dead came forth, bound hand and foot with
graveclothes: and his face was bound about with a napkin . . . '
(John 11; 44)

However, in the special insertion, Lazarus is designated as a *rich
youth*. In the ordinary text of Mark, there appears a *rich youth*, first in
chapter 10; 17, as the 'one who came running', and who was advised
to *give up all his worldly possessions* (transfer his attention from outward things to the inner mind). The act of running is, of course, a
feat of endurance, and therefore exemplifies the Hermetic process.
Notice too, that this whole episode takes place in a *garden* at *night*.

In Mark 14, the youth makes his second appearance:

51.   And there followed a certain young man, having a linen cloth
      cast about his naked body; and the young men laid hold of him.
52.   And he left the linen cloth and fled from them naked.

The secret text connects this young man with Lazarus, who was
raised from the dead (resurrected – initiated), and as the insertion into
the secret Gospel is indisputably the work of an initiate – a fact
supported by Clement's reply – we are left in no doubt that the same
young man (a reborn infant) of Mark 14 is an initiate. The youth is *rich*
because he has accomplished the process. This fact throws further
light on the strange affair of the linen cloth, for we can now appreciate that the young man (an initiate), who is caught by several other
young men (also initiates), leaves the linen cloth behind him (manu-
factures the Shroud image). As the 'face' represents only the facial
image on the Shroud, so the full length figure is denoted in the Bible
by the term 'linen cloth'.

The Shroud's Symbolism

I conclude this chapter with a few words regarding the image on
the Shroud, for it tells its own Hermetic story. The figure bears all
the characteristics annotated in the New Testament texts; the marks
made by the crown of thorns; the scourge marks; the imprint of the
nails and the wound in the side. All these are emblems which have
been duly interpreted in relation to their Hermetic import. Now it
must be brought to the reader's attention that throughout the whole
of the New Testament, there exists not one solitary word that will
indicate the physical appearance of Jesus, either in stature, looks, or
colouring. And nowhere does it specify if he was normally bearded
or clean shaven – but the figure on the Shroud sports a *full beard*.
    Irrelevant, you might think, as most thirty year old Judaeans of
the period would not have bothered to shave. But the beard is yet
another symbol employed by the Hermetic writers.
    The astral body, remember, is depicted as a *child* because it has
been reborn, and so if an initiate wished to portray himself, either
pictorially or literally, he would show himself as a full grown man,
but *clean shaven* as a sign of his new found *youth*. Alternatively, if the
Hermeticists wished to portray a person undergoing the mental
process, but not quite having reached the point of transmission, they
would give the figure a beard. This has been done in the case of the
Shroud, and the figure thereon – like the Emperor of the Tarot – is
intended to show the conscious mind undergoing the 'suffering' of

the process and drawing near to a successful conclusion. This is why the *face* of the Mandylion/Shroud was emblematic of the conscious mind.

Interested researchers will be able to uncover various other examples of this quaint symbol to compare with that of the Shroud. As an instance, we may look at the text of Herodotus, who says that the Egyptians shaved off the hair of both face and head, an assertion that is not always substantiated by other sources. The clue to the real meaning is given when the historian maintains that to the Egyptians, a beard represented an *undesirable condition* (incomplete initiation is undesirable). The words of Herodotus must be read with care.

LE MYSTERE DES CATHEDRALES offers a first class example when Fulcanelli discusses a figure known as the Alchemist, to be found in the *north tower* of Notre Dame.

> Wearing a Phrygian cap, the attribute of the Adept, negligently placed on his thick, curling hair, the scholar, dressed in his working cape, is leaning with one hand on the balustrade and stroking his full silky beard with the other . . .

The photograph accompanying this text offers the clue we are searching for. It shows the Adept's *left* hand to be the one stroking the beard, a double symbol of the conscious mind.

Another application of the emblem can be found in the Old Testament, by referring to Joab, the man who 'killed' Absolom. In II Sam. 20; 8 to 11, we read that Joab kills again, the victim this time being Amasa. But it is the unusual method by which this slaying is carried out that captures the attention. Approaching Amasa as if to greet him, Joab allows his sword to fall from its scabbard, seemingly by accident. Casually, he stoops to pick it up in his *left* hand and stepping closer, grasps Amasa's *beard* with his *right* hand as if to kiss him (a customary mode of greeting in those days). Caught off-guard, Amasa takes no heed of the sword in Joab's other hand, and falls victim to a fatal thrust when;

10. He smote him there with in the fifth rib . . .

The interpretation of this brief episode is that Amasa was *killed* by a *sword* (reflection) which is wielded in the *left* hand (the conscious mind). The passage, therefore, describes how Amasa became an initiate by a *reversal* of the normal procedure (Joab normally would have struck with the sword in his right hand).

An item of news featured in the national Press in December 1981 will serve to show that the emblem was employed in the Middle Ages. Art experts engaged in the renovation of Leonardo da Vinci's famous mural of the Last Supper, in Milan, were excited and puzzled by details which became visible as the grime of centuries was carefully removed. Items unseen for nearly five hundred years have gradually emerged, one of the most unusual being that Simon of Canaan was originally portrayed with a light chin stubble. The full beard familiar to modern art experts appears to be a 17th century addition, and the decision to either retain it or to show Simon in the rather strange manner that da Vinci intended has presented them with a dilemma.

The reason for the stubble, however, becomes perfectly clear when it is recalled that da Vinci's name appears on the list of Grand Masters of the Priory of Sion. The artist was a Rosicrucian. Knowing full well that the biblical Apostles were a collective personification of the conscious mind, and never real entities; that the Last Supper (final hours of meditation) indicated imminent accomplishment of the process, he decided to present the situation in his own unique way by making the disciple almost clean shaven, but not quite. Such unique application of Hermetic symbolism is evident in other da Vinci works – notably in the enigmatic smile on the *face* of the *woman* called the Mona Lisa.

I feel that these few interpretations show the beard in the Shroud to be not without its significance, and as a last word on the Shroud itself, may I point out that the actual weave of the cloth is a *three* to one twill, broken at intervals by a *forty*-thread stripe which results in a *herringbone* pattern (Pisces – the emblem of Jesus).

The Shroud is the key to present day Christianity, for it was only at its rediscovery in the Edessa Gate vault, and the subsequent revelation that it was a full length figure, did Christ begin to be represented in art work as a figure nailed to a *cross*. The earliest known example of this kind was a crucifix presented to Queen Theodolinde of Lombardy by Pope Gregory the Great, and which was deposited in the church of St. John at Monza. Gregory held the papal office from 590 to 604 A.D.

How supremely ironic it is that a symbol of the Hermetic principle – an icon of that other religion, Dualism – should be so revered and at the same time so completely misunderstood, for its true purpose is to show that the force we call God is not merely the ecclesiastical abstraction we are told it is, but a reality that can be reached by everyone, simply by the correct application of the energy already present in every human mind – meditation.

As the seventh rule of the Rosicrucians dictates;

The Rose Crux becomes – it is not made.

CHAPTER FOURTEEN

The Process

'We hide nothing from you but the process', is the maxim of the old Hermetic masters. Yet there do exist a precious few texts which dispense with the traditional allegory, to come close to expressing openly the great secret which the Adepts have sought to preserve through the ages. This is encouraging to the seeker after the truth, but I would cautiously add the following – a sentence with which the alchemist, Fulcanelli opens the last chapter of his masterly LE MYSTERE DES CATHEDRALES. He says

Nature does not open the door of her sanctuary indiscriminately to everyone.

The Hermetic secret, the basis of Dualism, is not so much a secret as a belief, for ultimate success depends largely upon the amount of faith with which the Neophyte approaches the task. I have attempted to show that while there is undeniably a secret to uncover, Man has consistently denied himself access to the key by reason of his lack of faith, even when the evidence lies in plain view.

It is with this fact in mind that we now turn to the rare texts designed to put the would-be Adept on the right path. First, let me quote the Indian relic, the Bhagavad Gita:

Thou carriest within thee a sublime Friend whom thou knowest not. For God dwells in the inner part of every man, but few know how to find him. The man who sacrifices his desires and his works to the Being from whom the principles of everything stem, and by whom the universe was formed, through this sacrifice attains perfection. For one who finds this happiness and joy within himself, and also his wisdom within himself, is one with God. And mark well, the soul which has found God is freed from rebirth and death, from old age and pain, and drinks the water of immortality.

In order to embrace this concept in the modern way, merely substitute the words 'Universal Mind' for 'God', and 'astral body' for 'soul'.

As to how this unity may be accomplished, the Bhagwat-Gita says:

262

He who thinkest constantly of me, his mind undiverted by any other object, will find me. I will at all times be easily found by a constant devotion to me.

These words are plain, speaking from the point of view of God, the universal Mind (subconscious), and call for the concentration of thought into a single direction, as symbolised by the shape of the Great Pyramid. It is now that we realise the act of prayer, as practised in a modern church, to be but a parody of the real thing, meditation.

The 'Oupnekhata', an Eastern manuscript, gives similar advice:

Breathe deep and slow and concentrate your unwavering attention into the midst of your body, into the region of your heart. The lamp in your body will then be protected against wind and motion and your whole body will become illuminated. You must withdraw your senses into yourself, like a turtle which withdraws its members within the shell. Enter your own heart and guard it, and Brahma will enter it like a fire, or a stroke of lightning. In the midst of the big fire in your heart will be a small flame, and in the centre of it will be Atma.

In this passage we must interpret 'heart' as the centre of the mind. Brahma is, of course, the Universal Mind.

An Arabian philosopher named Monoimus is cited by the 3rd century Church Father, Hippolytus as saying:

Abandon the search for God and the creation of other matters of a similar sort. Look for him by taking yourself as the starting point. Learn who it is within you that makes everything his own and says 'My God, my mind, my thought, my soul, my body.' Learn the sources of sorrow, joy, love, hate. Learn how it happens that one watches without willing, rests without willing, becomes angry without willing, loves without willing. If you carefully investigate these matters you will find him in yourself.
('Refutation of all Heresies' VIII 15, 1–2)

Hercarcas, an abbot of a monastery on the Greek island of Athos, left these directions by which his monks may acquire the clairvoyant power of initiation;

Sit alone in your room after having locked the door against all intrusion, concentrate your mind on the region of your navel and try to see with that. Try and find the seat of your heart, where the centre of power lies. At first, you will meet with nothing but darkness, but if you continue for days and nights without fatigue, you will see the light and experience inexpressible things. When the spirit once recognises its own centre in the heart, it will know what it never knew before and there will be nothing hidden from its sight, whether in heaven or upon earth.

As before, the expression 'seat of your heart' refers to the centre of the mind, not the physical heart.

To understand the mechanics of the process, to give substance to something as nebulous as thought, we must refer back to the words of the philosopher, Plato, in his CRITIAS. Therein, without actually making it blatantly obvious that he is referring to the Hermetic process, he describes how the invisible power of thought contains the action which the greater percentage of mankind continues to deny. In discussing the workings of the eye, he says

> The pure fire within us . . . (the gods) caused to flow through the eyes, making the whole eyeball, and particularly the centre part, smooth and close textured so that it would filter through only this pure fire.

Here, Plato is propounding that which the modern scientist considers to be unproven, the idea that a radiation is emitted by the eye. Later in the text, he describes what happens when the eyelids are closed.

> For when the eyelids, designed by the gods to protect the sight, are shut, *they confine the activity of the fire within*, and this smoothes and diffuses the internal motions and *produces a calm*.

Ostensibly, the philosopher is describing sleep, and then he goes on to talk of dreams. But at that point, he suddenly says

> And the principles governing *reflections in mirrors* and other *smooth reflecting surfaces* are not difficult to understand.

He then proceeds to discourse on images seen through a mirror. One translator has commented that this sudden diversion seems oddly out of place at this particular point. It was meant to be! An initiate, however, would have no difficulty in recognising that Plato was referring to the Hermetic practice. The reflection and the confinement of the 'fire' within relates to the practice of meditation, whilst the term 'fire' itself simply means the *attention* which follows the eyes and ears wherever they choose to focus.

Corroboration of this interpretation may be found in a Chinese text entitled T'AI I CHIN HUA CHIH. Transmitted orally for centuries, it was first printed in China during the 18th century. By way of Peking and Germany, the text was made available to English readers under the title THE SECRETS OF THE GOLDEN

FLOWER. The modern version contains a companion text, the HUI MING CHING. Both are initiates' manuals describing how to begin the process. However, I must advise that the text be read *carefully*, and in this respect, refer to a comment by Carl Jung in his foreword to the second edition. Therein he says that many readers tried to imitate the method described in the manual, totally misunderstanding the meaning of his original commentary – a statement inferring that nothing is to be gained by reading the Chinese text as a literal description of the process.

Whilst this warning is manifestly true, I would add that it in no way nullifies the intent of the text as a guide to discovery of the hidden process. As with all alchemical manuscripts so far discussed, including those in the Bible, this text must be compared many times with its fellows, until a gradual breakdown of entrenched thought is achieved and a full understanding of *reality* floods into the mind. Everyone appreciates that Jung was one of the most noted thinkers of his time, but readers must remember that something more than mere thought is required. The need is to find a force which supercedes the act of thinking. In speaking of the *Golden Flower*, a picturesque description of the 'second body', the text says

People without the utmost capacity for absorption and tranquillity cannot keep fast hold of it.

It is this text which speaks plainly about the 'circulation of the light' (the light of the eye – attention) – the *circulation* which has been symbolised by the sorcerer's circle and by St. Peter crucified upside down. It is aptly described as the 'backward-flowing method'. The text also speaks briefly of the three stages, saying that the pupils must go through the two lower stages in order to gain the upper one.

A fairly modern version of the Hermetic process is offered by Dr. Paul Brunton in his volume, THE QUEST OF THE OVERSELF, originally published in the late 1930s. The 'Overself' described by the author is, as one can imagine, the Universal Mind, and the text is a complete explanation of the finer points of the meditative practice. In the latter part of the book, Paul Brunton gives the best possible description of the three stages as they would be experienced by the Neophyte. He does not make a point of associating the process with mediaeval alchemy, but the reader will recognise examples of the Hermetic symbolism as the practice of mental mastery is expounded. As an instance, the uncontrolled thoughts are likened to an obstinate mule – and thus we are reminded of the ancient sign of Sagittarius, the horse throwing its rider. And as with all other Hermetic writers, Paul Brunton is most emphatic regarding the faith necessary to accomplish the task;

Patience, plus indifference to repeated failures is essential to obtain final success.

Conclusion

We have travelled a long way from the remote and picturesque village of Rennes le Chateau, passing from the world of comfortable normality to the uncertain sphere of pure thought – the realm of the Rosicrucian initiate. It is quite understandable and expected that many readers will be happy to list the foregoing material as no more than a clever manipulation of coincidental facts. Quite so; but the extensive range of the material, all undeniably traceable to a single root, should at least give evidence of some extremely powerful influence at the foundation of it all. Once you have studied the allegories for yourself and have begun to glimpse the truth behind the misconceptions to which many mistakenly adhere, you may well acquire the sudden realisation experienced by Paul Brunton, and see our modern civilisation as;

an unhappy catacomb of dormant souls.

After that, it is entirely your choice to remain with the familiar, or 'climb the high mountain' in order to see more clearly.

Before leaving, I add one important note of caution with regard to the subject of meditation, the Hermetic pathway. Many pages in this work have been devoted to showing that words can possess something other than the surface meaning, and this applies no less to 'meditation' and 'contemplation'. It is fashionable today to practise meditative thought in the form of an introspective vacancy, but the Hermetic masters knew it as something quite different. Mark well the words of the initiate Ruysbroeck, who warns;

This sinking down into subjective passivity in bare vacancy is a caricature of the perpetual willed effort required in inward contemplation . . . There is a world of difference between subjective nothingness and the high activity of spiritual intelligence. God is activity, not passivity and idleness, but an eternal striving.

BIBLIOGRAPHY

Allegro, John M. *The Sacred Mushroom and the Cross* Abacus (Sphere Books) 1973

Ashe, Geoffrey *The Virgin* Routledge and Kegan Paul 1976

Bailey, Alice A. *A Treatise on Cosmic Fire* Lucis Press London 1962

Blavatsky, Madame H.P. *Isis Unveiled* Vols I & II Theosophical Publishing House (1877)

Breyer, Jacques *Solar Arcana* France, late fifties

Brunton, Paul *The Quest for the Overself* Rider & Co.

Burton, Sir Richard *Exploration of the Highlands of Brazil* London 1868 (Vol II)

Cheetham, Erika *The Prophecies of Nostradamus* Neville Spearman 1973

Fulcanelli *Fulcanelli: Master Alchemist* (Le Mystère des Cathedrales) Neville Spearman 1971

Grant, Guy & Tony Hall *Superpsyche* Methuen, Australia 1976

Graves, Robert *The Golden Ass* (Apulius) Penguin 1950

Hartmann, Franz *Paracelsus: Life and Prophecies* Steiner Publications USA 1973

Hartmann, Franz *Magic, Black and White* Newcastle Pub. Co USA 1971

Keightley *Fairy Mythology* (1850)

Lee, Desmond *Plato: Timaeus & Critias* Penguin 1971

Mather, MacGregor *The Key of Solomon the King* Routledge & Kegan Paul, 1972

Paracelsus *Archidoxes of Magic (1656)* Reprint by Askin Publishers 1975

Perrault, Charles *Histoire du Contes Temp Passe* France 1697

Piggot, Professor Stuart *The Druids* Penguin, or Thames & Hudson 1968

Sede, Gerard de *Signe Rose Croix* Paris 1977

Selincourt, Aubrey de *Herodotus* (Histories) Penguin 1954

Sherwood-Taylor, F *The Alchemists* Granada Pub. 1976

Silberer, Herbert *Hidden Symbolism of Alchemy* Dover Publication USA 1971

Smith, Professor Morton *The Secret Gospel*

Swift, Jonathan *Gulliver's Travels* Simon & Schuster USA 1972

Vellacott, Philip *Aeschylus: Prometheus Bound* Penguin 1961

Waite, A.E. *Alchemical Writings of Edward Kelly* Samuel Weiser Ltd USA 1973

Waite, A.E. *Alchemists Through the Ages* Steiner Publications, USA 1970

Waldron, George *Description of the Isle of Man* (1730 Courtesy of Douglas Library, I.o.M.

Wallis Budge, A.E. *The Egyptian Book of the Dead* Dover Publications USA 1967

Westfall, Richard *Isaac Newton (biography) Never at Rest*

267

Wilhelm, Richard *Secret of the Golden Flower* Routledge & Kegan Paul, 1975 edition
Yates, Francis *The Rosicrucian Enlightenment* Granada Pub. 1975

ALSO

The Mutus Liber: Rupellae (Paris) (symbolic pictures)
Arabian Nights' Entertainments (Traditional)
The Old and New Testaments.
The Relatorio (from micro film copy supplied by Biblioteca Nacionale, Rio de Janeiro, Brazil) Manuscript No 152.
Hannah, Walton *Darkness Visible* Augustine Press London 1952 (for the Masonic ritual and the pictures of the 1st and 2nd degree tracing boards)
Lincoln, Henry – with Michael Baigent & Richard Leigh *The Holy Blood and the Holy Grail* J. Cape 1981

APPENDIX

(Please note that this letter has been reproduced exactly as it was originally printed and therefore its italicized words do not carry the same significance as in my own text.   R. N.)

By JONATHAN SWIFT

A
LETTER
FROM THE
GRAND MISTRESS
OF THE
FEMALE FREE-MASONS
TO
Mr. *Harding* the Printer.
Ixion the Impious, Lewd Profane,
Bright *Juno* Woo'd but Woo'd in Vain.
Long had he sigh'd for th' Heavenly Dame;
'Till *Jove* at length to quench his Flame;
Some say for Fear, some say for Pity,
Sent him a Cloud like *June* Pretty,
As like as if 'twere drawn by Painters,
On which he got a Race of *Centaurs*.
A Bite quoth VENUS——

*a. b. c. Lib.*6th.

DUBLIN:
Printed by *John Harding* in *Molesworth's Court* in *Fishamble-Street*, 1724.
A

LETTER, &c.

Mr. *Harding*,
SEEING it is of Late become a Fashion in Town, in Writing to all the World, to Address to YOU, our Society of *Female Free-Masons* has also Chosen you for our *Printer*; and so without Preface, Art, or Embelishment, (for Truth and a short Paper needs none of 'em) our *Female Lodge* has the whole Mistery as well as any *Lodge* in *Europe*, with proper Instructions in Writing; and what will seem more strange to you, without the least Taint of *Perjury*. By this

Time any *Reader* who is a *Mason*, will, I know, laugh, and not without Indignation. But that matters not much, our Sex has long ow'd yours this good Turn: You refused to admit Queen *Elizabeth*, and even *Semiramis* Queen of *Babilon*, tho' each of 'em (without *Punning*) had a great Deal of *Male Flesh* upon their Bodies; but at last you will be forc'd to own we have it; and thus it was we came by it.

A Gentleman who is a great Friend to all our Members, who has since instructed and form'd us into a *Lodge*, and whom we therefore call our *Guardian*, fell in lately with a *Lodge of Free-Masons* at O—b in V——r. They press'd him hard to come into their Society, and at length prevailed. They wanted an *Old Testament* to Swear him by. The *Inn-Keeper's* Bible having both *Old* and *New* bound up together, wou'd not do: For the *Free-Masons* Oath being of much older Date than the *New Testament*, that is from the Building of *Solomon's* Temple, (for 'till then it was but a Protestation well Larded over with *Curses* and *Execrations*) they are always Sworn on the *Old Testament* only. They offer to buy the Fellow's *Bible*, he Consents; but finding they were to Cut away the *New Testament* from the *Old* concluded them at once a Pack of Profane Wretches, and very Piously Rescu'd his *Bible*. This Custom of Swearing on the *Old Testament* only, is what has given Birth to the Vulgar Error, That *Free-Masons* Renounce the *New Testament*. So they proceed on the Rest of the Ceremony, Deferring the Oath til next Morning, One of 'em having an *Old Testament* for the Purpose at his House hard by. This 'tis true was a heinous Blunder against the Canons of *Free-Masonry:* But the Gentlemen were far gone in *Punch* and *Whisky*. In short our Friend and present Guardian is made a *Free* but *Unsworn Mason*, and was Three Hours gone on his Journey next Morning before the Merry *Free-Masons* awoke to send for their *Old Testament*; and what was worse, they had taught him the Form of the Oath against he was to Swear in the Morning.

Now as to the Secret Words and Signals used among *Free-Masons*, 'tis to be observ'd that in the *Hebrew* Alphabet (as our Guardian has inform'd our *Lodge* in Writing) there are Four Pair of Letters, of which each Pair is so like, that at first View they seem to be the same, *Beth* and *Caph*, *Gimel* and *Nun*, *Cheth* and *Thau*, *Daleth* and *Resch*, and on these Depend all their Signals and Grips.

Cheth and *Thau* are shap'd like Two standing Gallowses (of Two Legs each) when Two *Masons* accost each other, one Cries *Cheth*, the other answers *Thau*, signifying that they wou'd sooner be Hang'd on the Gallows than Divulge the *Secret*.

Then again *Beth* and *Caph* are each like a Gallows lying on one of the Side-Posts, and when used as above, imply this Pious Prayer: *May all who reveal the* Secret *hang upon the Gallows till it falls down*. This is their *Master Secret*, generally call'd the *Great Word*.

Daleth and *Resch* are like Two Half Gallowses, or a Gallows cut in Two at the Cross Stick on Top, by which, when pronounced, they Intimate to each other, that they wou'd rather be half hang'd than Name either *Word* or *Signal* before any but a *Brother* so as to be understood.

When one says *Gimel*, the other answers *Nun*; then the first again joyning both Letters together repeats Three Times, *Gimel-Nun, Gimel-Nun, Gimel-Nun*, by which they mean that they are united as one in Interests, Secresy, and Affection. This Last Word has in Time been depraved in the Pronunciation from *Gimel-Nun* to *Gimelun*, and at last into *Giblun;* and sometimes *Giblin*, which Word being by some Accident discover'd, they now adays pretend its but a *Mock Word*.

Another of their Words has been maim'd in the Pronunciation by the Illiterate, that is the Letter *Lamech*, which was the *Hush-Word*, for when spoke by any *Brother* in a *Lodge* it was a Warning to the Rest to have a Care of Lisseners. 'Tis now corruptly pronounced *Lam*, but the *Masons* pretend this also is a *Mock-Word* for the same Reason as *Giblin*: This Play with the *Hebrew* Alphabet is very antiently call'd the MANABOLETH.

When one *Brother* orders another to walk like a *Mason*, he must walk Four Steps backwards; Four, because of the four Pair of Letters already mentioned, and backwards because the *Hebrew* is Writ and Read Backwards.

As to their *Misterious Grips*, they are as follows: If they be in Company where they cannot with Safety Speak the above Words, they take each other by the Hand, one Draws one of the Letters of the *Manaboleth* with his finger on the other's Hand, which he returns as in Speaking.

It is worth observing, that a certain *Lodge* in Town Publish'd sometime ago a Sheet full of *Mock-Masonry*, purely to puzzel and banter the Town, with several false Signs and Words as *Mada* or *Adam*, Write backwards, Boas, *Nimrod, Jakins, Pectoral, Guttural*, &c. But not one Word of the Real ones, as you see by what has been said of the MANABOLETH.

After King *James* the Sixth's Accession to the Throne of *England*, he reviv'd *Masonry*, of which he was *Grand-Master*. Both in *Scotland* and *England* it had been entirely suppress'd by Queen *Elizabeth*, because she cou'd not get into the Secret, all Persons of Quality after the Example of the King got themselves admitted *Free-Masons*; but they made a kind of MANABOLETH in *English*, in Imitation of the True and Ancient One; as I.O.U.H. a Gold Key, that is, *I owe you each a Gold Key*; H CCCC his Ruin. *Each foresees his Ruin.* I C.U.B. YY for me. *I see you be too wise for me.* And a great Deal more of the same foolish stuff, which took its Rise from a Silly *Pun* upon the Word *Bee*; for you must know , that ———— A *Bee* has in all Ages and Nations been the Grand *Hieroglyphick* of *Masonry*, because it excells all other living Creatures in the Contrivance and Commodiousness of its *Habitation* or *Combe*; as among many other Authors Doctor *McGregor* now Professor of Mathematicks in *Cambridge* (as our Guardian informs us) has Learnedly demonstrated; nay *Masonry* or *Building* seems to be of the very Essence or Nature of the *Bee*, for her Building not the ordinary Way of all other living Creatures, is the Generative Cause which produces the Young Ones (you know I suppose that *Bees* are of *Neither Sex*.)

For this Reason the Kings of *France* both *Pagans* and *Christians*, always Eminent *Free-Masons*, carried three *Bees* for their *Arms*, but to avoid the Imputation of the *Egyptian* Idolatry of Worshipping a *Bee*, *Clodevaus* their first Christian King call'd 'em *Lillies* or *Flower de Luces*, in which notwithstanding the small Change made for Disguise Sake, there's still the Exact Figure of a *Bee*. You have perhaps Read of a great Number of Golden Bees found in the Coffin of a *Pagan* King of *France* near *Brussels*, many Ages after CHRIST, which he had ordered should be Bury'd with him, in Token of his having been a *Mason*.

The *Egyptians*, always Excellent and Antient *Free-Masons*, paid Divine Worship to a *Bee* under the outward shape of a *Bull*, the better to conceal the

Mistery, which *Bull* they call'd *Apis*, is the *Latin* Word for a *Bee*, the *Enigma* of Representing the *Bee* by a *Bull* consists in this; that according to the Doctrine of the *Pythagorean Lodge* of *Free-Masons*, the Souls of all the *Cow-kind* transmigrate into Bees, as one *Virgil* a Poet, much in Favour with the Emperor *Augustus*, because of his profound Skill in *Masonry*, has describ'd; and Mr. *Dryden* has thus *English'd*.

Aristeus

> Four Altars raises, from His Herd he Culls
> For Slaughter, Four the fairest of his *Bulls*,
> Four Heifers from his Female Store he took,
>
> All Fair, and all unknowing to the Yolk;
> Nine Mornings thence with *Sacrifice* and *Prayers*,
> The Gods invok'd he to the Grove repairs:
> Behold a Prodigy! for from within
> The Broken Bowels and the Bloated Skin
> A buzzing Noise of *Bees* his Ears alarms,
> Straight issue thro' the Sides assembling Swarms, *etc*.

What *Modern Masons* call a *Lodge* was for the above Reasons by Antiquity call'd a HIVE of *Free-Masons*, and for the same Reasons when a Dissention happens in a *Lodge* the going off and forming another *Lodge* is to this Day call'd SWARMING.

Our Guardian is of Opinion, that the present *Masonry* is so tarnish'd by the Ignorance of the working, and some other illiterate *Masons*, that very many, even whole *Lodges* fall under the Censure of the venerable *Chinese Brachman*, whose History of the Rise, Progress, and Decay of *Free-Masonry*, writ in the *Chinese* Tongue, is lately Translated into a Certain *Europenan* Language. This *Chinese* Sage says, the greatest Part of Current *Masons* Judge of the Misteries and Use of that Sacred Art, just as a Man perfectly Illiterate judges of an Excellent Book, in which when open'd to him he finds no other Beauties than the regular Uniformity in every Page, the Exactness of the Lines in Length, and Equidistance, the Blackness of the *Ink*, and Whiteness of the *Paper*, or as the Famous *British Free Mason* MERLIN says of the Stars in the Firmament, when view'd by a *Child*, &c. But I shall not trouble you with the Length of the Quotation at present, because *Merlin* and Fryar *Bacon* on *Free-Masonry* are soon to be dress'd up in Modern *English*, and sold by our Printer Mr. *Harding*, if duly encourag'd by Subscribers; and also a Key to *Raymundus Lullius*, without whose Help our Guardian says it's impossible to came at the Quintessence of *Free Masonry*.

But some will perhaps Object, how come your unsworn Guardian by this refin'd and uncommon Knowledge in the great Art? to which I answer that,

The Branch of the *Lodge* of *Solomon's* Temple, afterwards call'd the *Lodge* of St. *John of Jerusalem* on which our Guardian fortunately hit, is as I can easily prove, the Antientest and Purest now on Earth. The famous old *Scottish Lodge* of *Killwinnin* of which all the Kings of *Scotland* have been from Time to Time Grand Masters without Interruption, down from the Days of *Fergus*, who Reign'd there more than 2000 Years ago, long before the Knights of St. *John* of *Jerusalem* or the Knights of *Maltha*, to which two *Lodges* I must nevertheless allow the Honour of having adorn'd the Antient

Jewish and *Pagan Masonry* with many Religious and Christian Rules.

Fergus being eldest Son to the chief King of *Ireland*, was carefully instructed in all the Arts and Sciences, especially in the natural Magick, and the Caballistical Philosophy (afterwards call'd the *Rosecrution*) by the *Pagan Druids* of *Ireland* and *Mona*, the only true *Cabalists* then Extant in the *Western* World. (For they had it immediately from the *Phenecians, Chaldeans*, and *Egyptians* (which tho' but a Woman can prove). The *Egyptians* probably had it immediately from *Abraham* as the Scripture Plainly hints in the Life of that Patriarch; and 'tis allow'd I am told by Men of Learning, that the *Occult* as well as *Moral* Philosophy of all the *Pagans* was well be-sprinkl'd and enrich'd from the Caballistical School of the Patriarchs, and afterwards by the *Talmudists* and other Inferior *Rabbins*, tho' the prevailing Idolatry of those Days much depraved and vitiated it.

Fergus before his Descent upon the *Picts* in *Scotland* rais'd that famous Structure, call'd to this Day *Carrick-Fergus* after his Name, the most misterious Piece of Architecture now on Earth, (not excepting the Pyramids of the *Egyptian* Masons, and their *Hierogliphicks* or *Free Masons* Signs) as any Skillful *Free-Mason* may easily perceive by examining it according to the Rules of the Art; he built it as a *Lodge* for his College of *Free Masons* in those Days call'd *Druids*, which Word our Guardian assures us signifies an *Oak* in the *Greek* Language, because *Oak* is one of the best Timber-Trees for Building, of which especially the Marine Architecture, the *Druids* were the only Masters, tho' your Modern Term of *Mason* implys no more than a Worker in Stone, erroneously enough indeed, or at least far short of the true and antient Term of *Druid*, since the Marine Architecture the most useful Branch of the Sacred Art, corresponds naturally and perfectly with the Word *Druid* or *Worker* in *Oak*, and had nothing at all to do with Stones of any Kind, 'till *Jason* a famous *Druid* or *Free-Mason* used the *Load-stone* when he went in Quest of the *Golden Fleece* as it is call'd in the Enigmaticall Terms of *Free-Masonry*, or more properly Speaking of the *Cabala*, as *Masonry* was call'd in those Days. The use of the *Load Stone* was then and long after kept as Secret as any of the other Misteries of the Art, till by the unanimous Consent of all the Great *Lodges*, the use of it was made publick for the Common Benefit of Mankind. *Jason's* artificial *Frog* had it fixt in his Mouth, and having a free Swing in an oaken Bowl half fill'd with Water, always faced the *North* Pole, which gave rise to the Poetical Fable: That *Jason's* Frog was a *Little Familiar* or *Sea Demon* presiding over the Navigation like any other Angel Guardian. For *Free-Masons* in all Ages, as well as now, have been look'd upon to deal with *Sprites* or *Demons*, and hence came that Imputation, which they have in many Nations lain under, of being *Conjurors* or *Magitians*, Witness *Merlin* and Fryar *Bacon*.

'Tis perhaps further worth Remarking, that *Jason* took one of the Two Sacred Vocal *Oaks* of the Grove of *Dodona* to make the Keel of the *Argus*, for so his Ship was call'd, misteriously Joynning together *Architecture* or *Masonry*, and the *Druidical* Priesthood or Power of Explaining the Oracle. For our Guardian wil have it so, that the *Pagan* Priesthood was always in the *Druids* or *Masons*, and that there was a perceivable Glimering of the *Jewish Rites* in it, tho' much corrupted, as I said, that the *Pagan* Worship was chiefly in Groves of *Oak* that they always lookt upon the *Oak* as Sacred to *Jupiter*, which Notion is countenanced (making Allowance for the *Paganism*) by the

Patriarchs, for you see in *Genesis*, that *Abraham* Sacrificed under the *Oaks* of *Mamre*. *Joshua* indeed took a great Stone and put it up under the *Oak*, Emblematically joyning the Two great Elements of *Masonry* to raise an Altar for the LORD.

Our Guardian also says, that *Caesar's* Description of the *Druids* of *Gaul* is as Exact a Picture of a *Lodge* of *Free Masons* as can possibly be Drawn.

His Reasons for the *Manaboleth* are the better worth discovering, that I believe there are even some *Masons* who know nothing of it, *viz*. that is has been an Antient Practice among the *Cabalistick Philosophers* to make every *Hebrew* Letter a *Heirogliphick* Misterious in its Figure above all other Letters, as being thus Shap'd and Form'd by the immediate Directions of the *Almighty*, whereas all other LETTERS are of *Humane Invention*.

Secondly, that the *Manaboleth* has a very close and unconstrain'd Analogy with *Masonry* or *Architecture*, for that every Letter of the *Hebrew* Alphabet, as also of the *Syriac, Chaldaic, Runic*, and *Irish* Alphabets, derived from it, have their Names from *Timber-Trees*, except some few who have their Names from *Stones*; and I think its pretty plain, that *Timber* and *Stone* are as much the Elements of *Masonry* as the Alphabet is of *Books*, which is a near Relation enough between *Architecture* and *Learning* of all Kinds, and naturally shews why the *Druids*, who also took their Title from a Tree, kept *Learning* and *Architecture* joyntly within themselves.

Next Week shall be Publish'd the *Free Mason's* Oath, with the Remarks upon it of a Young *Clergyman* who has Petition'd to be admitted *Chaplain* to our *Lodge*, which is to be kept at Mr. *Painter's* Female Coffee-House every *Tuesday* from Nine in the Morning to Twelve, and the Tenth Day of every Month in the Year; where all Ladies of true Hearts and sound Morals shall be admitted without Swearing.

I think it Proper to Incert the *Free-Mason's* SONG commonly Sung at their Meetings, tho' by the By, it is of as little Signification as the Rest of their Secrets. It was Writ by one *Anderson* as our Guardian informs me, just to put a Good Gloss on the Mistery, as you may See by the Words.

SONG
I.
Come let us prepare
We Brothers that are
Assembled on merry Occasion,
Let's Drink, Laugh and Sing,
Our Wine has a Springs;
Here's a Health to an accepted MASON.

II.
The World is in Pain
Our Secrets to gain,
And still let them wonder and gaze on,
They ne'er can Divine
The Word or the Sign
Of a Free and an Accepted MASON.

III.

'Tis this and 'tis that,
They cannot tell what;
Why so many Great Men of the Nation,
Shou'd Aprons put on,
To make themselves one,
With a Free and an Accepted MASON.

IV.

Great Kings, Dukes and Lords,
Have laid by their Swords,
Our Mistery to put a Good Grace on,
And ne'er been Asham'd,
To hear themselves Nam'd
With a Free and an Accepted MASON.

V.

Antiquity's Pride
We have on our Side,
And it maketh Men Just in their Station,
There's nought but what's good,
To be understood
By a Free and an Accepted MASON.

VI.

Then Joyn Hand in Hand,
To each other firm stand;
Let's be merry and put a Bright Face on,
What Mortal can boast,
So noble a Toast,
As a Free and an Accepted MASON.

POSTSCRIPT

Mr. *Harding,*
Our *Lodge* unanimously desire you'll give their Sincere Respects to your *Ingenius* DRAPIER, to whose *Pen* we, as well as the Rest of the Nation, own our selves oblig'd. If he be not already a *Free-Mason*, he shall be welcom to be our *Deputy-Guardian.*

Your Humble Servant,

Tsrif eht Lirpa Nilbud

Thalestris

In the Dublin 1762 edition of 'A Letter from the Grand Mistess' there is a footnote: '*Tsrif eht Tsugua Nilbud.*'
'*DUBLIN, *August the* first. *Those who understand* Irish, *may find some other Meaning.*'

(Extracted from 'JONATHAN SWIFT: MISCELLANEOUS AUTOBIOGRAPHICAL PIECES, FRAGMENTS AND MARGINALIA', edited by Herbert Davis. Basil Blackwell & Mott Ltd., 1962. This extract is itself a photographic fascimile of Tract No. 12, Box 171 of the Halliday Collection in the Royal Irish Academy, Dublin).

I need hardly add that the enigmatic 'Tsrif eht Lirpa Nilbud' is 'Dublin April the First' in reverse, but would draw to the reader's attention the fact that All Fool's Day has a significance that has been lost in modern times, as it was once a 'pagan' occasion linked with the Tarot Fool and the Feast of Fools.